Natural Light

A NOVEL

Natural Light

A NOVEL

Ethel Gorham

Z

ZOLAND BOOKS
Cambridge, Massachusetts

First edition published in 1991 by
Zoland Books, Inc.,
384 Huron Avenue, Cambridge, MA 02138

PUBLISHER'S NOTE:
This book is a work of fiction. Names, characters,
places, and incidents are either the product of the
author's imagination or are used fictitiously. Any
resemblance to actual events or locales or persons,
living or dead, is entirely coincidental.

Library of Congress Catalog Card Number
90- 71655

ISBN 0-944072-14-3

First edition
Printed in the United States of America
Designed by Joyce C. Weston

for David Keith

Natural Light

A NOVEL

· CHAPTER 1 ·

MOLLY'S son Tommy had been killed in Vietnam, but it took five years before she went to see the monument that bore his name in Washington. Listed dead in the sixties—dumped into a black plastic bag with a heavy drawstring, dog tags detached—Tommy was now, in the eighties, only a name on a long list cut into a black wall. As Tommy himself might say, "Big deal."

Molly was on the Mall for another reason. She had come to march with thousands of others for a woman's right to freedom of choice. Molly was old now and her muscles cramped up. Her wonderful comfort shoes, bought for the occasion, flat and rubber-soled, were not really very wonderful. Their flatness pulled at her muscles and hurt her feet.

She had dropped out of part of the march to sit on a park bench along the route, waiting for the snake of the parade to circle Pennsylvania Avenue in a loop back to where she was sitting so she could fall again into line with her own group on its way toward the Capitol.

It was a beautiful October day, warm as summertime but with the smell of fall in the air. Molly was glad to be sitting as she watched the parade heading down—young people and old, mostly women of course, as always, but some men, some boys, students. A man, whose face she knew but not his name,

· 1 ·

someone from her neighborhood in New York, called to her jubilantly, "Come on, we're almost there, swell our ranks."

His juvenile enthusiasm irked her. It was probably his first demonstration. I'm just sitting here for a minute, she thought rather irritably, no need to call attention to it.

They had assembled in midmorning and proceeded briskly, but after hours of marching, she could feel the strain. The people around her in her own contingent had suggested she sit on the sidelines until they made their way back from the White House. When she saw the park bench in front of one of the government buildings, she was glad to slide out of line and wave the others on.

She closed her eyes, stretching her legs in front of her. They had left New York at five this morning, meeting the bus over at Central Park and Sixtieth Street. It was dark as midnight when she came out of her house into the deserted streets, quiet, everything caught in a sepia light like an Atget photograph. She didn't have long to wait until the beams of the car that was picking her up turned the corner.

"How wonderful that you made it." The cheerful voice of the driver, the newlywed wife of the newly widowed doctor, was patronizing. At least so Molly thought.

"Of course I made it," she said, as she settled down in the back between other women who nodded sleepily in greeting. "I always make it."

"I think that's terrific," said the doctor's wife, her tone motherly, charitable. I've been making it since before you were born, Molly thought, but held her tongue. She was getting testy, she felt. Especially with anyone who seemed to hint that age was catching up with her. Mustn't get cranky about that, she told herself. They're just being kind. Nevertheless she thought of the doctor's wife with annoyance as a pudgy blonde Barbie

Doll who had newly discovered feminism and political action. Hardly the spirit of sisterhood, she admonished herself. She wished she had allowed enough time for coffee. But Anna Spence, sitting next to the driver, had brought a Thermos, and when some was offered to Molly, she felt her spirits rise.

The bus was crowded and most people slept through New Jersey, Pennsylvania, Maryland, and Washington. They walked from the bus to their assigned place on the Mall, Anna Spence linking her arm through Molly's, carrying it off well as a gesture of friendship rather than as support.

"I saw the show of your work at MOMA," Anna said. "Some wonderful things."

It was the second retrospective that the Museum of Modern Art had given her photographs, and Molly was both pleased and troubled. The first show had been seven years earlier, and Molly had been stirred and exhilarated by the long walls that held all those images so dear and familiar to her. They were her own, those images, she knew every nuance of light and shade, the visual impact each was supposed to make. Each was a window into her world, her camera an extension of herself. She had been happy with that show, happy with what critics said, happy that people stood and looked and moved slowly down the corridors of the exhibition space letting the images seep into their eyes, their minds.

This time she was again glad of the praise, but as she went back again and again to see the show, she had felt a gnawing uncertainty, a dissatisfaction and a floating anxiety. I'm not moving, she thought. I haven't moved. It's what it was seven years ago, terribly terribly what it was.

"Thank you," she replied to Anna's praise. "I'm glad you liked the show." She was silent for a minute, thinking, then added, in a burst of confidence, "I'm going to try something different now. Color, maybe. A wider range. I've always worked in black and white, no cropping, no distortion. Perhaps I'll change. I want to open up the view."

It was foolish to air this with Anna Spence, whom she didn't know well at all, but it had been on her mind, thrusting toward the surface. She smiled, winding up the confidence. "Oh well," she said, "live and learn."

The groups were finally assembled, and after two hours of standing, the march was on its way. She had kept up well but now it was good to be off her feet. She breathed deeply. She wondered how long it would take for the others to make the circle. Again, she closed her eyes. Then suddenly she sat up straight, electrified. A thought had flashed across her mind. "The Vietnam monument. I've never seen it." She felt that familiar tightness in her chest. Did she want to see it? Tommy's name would be there. Tears didn't come to her eyes, but again her chest pulled tight. She could feel the pressure of angina. She fumbled in her purse for the round bottle and uncorked it. She dropped a little white pill into the palm of her hand, then lifted it to her lips to tuck it under her tongue.

Tommy. She waited for the nitro to work, then when the tightness had eased, she repeated the name half aloud. Tommy. She wondered exactly where the monument was and how long it would take her to get to it. The Mall was long and she had already walked and walked. Oh well, the doctor had said she ought to walk, it was probably good for her. Let's go, she said to herself, and rising stiffly from the park bench, turned back to the long green stretch of the Mall to the left. The day that had been so benignly warm was slowly picking up its autumnal chill. She buttoned the down jacket she was wearing and slid a wool cap that was in her pocket over her hair and ears.

At one corner, near the Smithsonian, she saw a policeman on his horse. The man and beast towered above her, black, backlit against the sun. She looked up, moving a bit away from the horse, calling in a loud voice to the mounted man, "Just where is the Vietnam monument?"

He looked at her haughtily. The horse snorted, frightening her, he was so large. Then the answer came, as if from a long distance. "Just above the Washington Monument, madam," he answered and pointed to the intrusive landmark in the distance.

She wanted to ask him if it was far, but of course the answer was as plain as day, look for yourself. She mumbled her thanks and turned toward the white shaft that pierced the cold blue sky. Distances were deceptive in this clear air. There was nothing to do except put one foot in front of the other.

She found it was far enough but she stumbled on stubbornly. Once she had started, she was determined to get there, to look, then to turn back to rejoin the march.

Beyond the Washington Monument Molly rested for a moment on a bench with a marker above it that pointed to where she wanted to go, VIETNAM VETERANS MEMORIAL. Then she rose to her feet again and walked up the path following the marker. But quickly she saw, as she turned to the right, that there were hundreds of markers—people. People in a long, slow-moving line; people by ones and twos and threes; people on the path that paralleled a shining black wall; people pointing, touching, poking at tears.

How simple it all seemed. A black wall starting low, going high, then turning sharply and going low again. Sheer shining black, engraved with names, holding back the green high ground. Here and there a little American flag, like a toy on a pointed stick, and worn wreaths with cellophane ribbons twisted by the weather. Molly stopped short as she took in the people, the black wall, the tacky little flags, the weathered wreaths. Suddenly she felt choked up, apprehensive, shaken with her own tears burning behind her eyes.

· 5 ·

She felt again the same stunned overwhelming turmoil she had once felt at the World War One cemetery in France, with its endless white crosses, row on row, stretching to an unseen horizon. Then, she had burst into tears, sobbing against Joe's shoulder, "I can't stand it. I can't stand it. Let's go." But Joe had wanted to go on, he was a history buff, he knew the names of all the battles, the pyrrhic victories and the ruinous losses. When they reached an enclosure filled with the graves of German soldiers that bounded on the fields for the English dead, she had called a halt. "No more," she said flatly. "I can't bear the awfulness of this. Those poor bastards, side by side. I'll wait in the car."

She steadied herself now and bent to decipher the names on the first low panel. She was confused by their arrangement. She had expected alphabetical order, names A to Z, the beginning or the end. But no. It was somehow in the middle, inexplicable, as she walked down slowly, following the mounting stone. The names changed their order—a group from A to Z, and then farther on another group A to Z, and then another, and then another until she seemed to reach the apex of the wall, where it said 1959. The wall then veered sharply at right angles, another tall panel marked at the bottom with the numbers "1975." From then on it was a downgoing slope, the names again in alphabetical order by groups, one group after another as the wall descended to its other low point at the end of the slope.

How will I find Tommy in this mess? she thought desperately. I don't know how they've done this. People were crowding in around her. She caught fragments of conversation, others were as baffled as she. She turned to a man and woman at the end (or was it the beginning?) who were making a rubbing of a name. Apparently they had found what they were looking for.

"How does this work?" she asked. "How do you know where to look?" The woman turned from her rubbing to wave to a group of what looked like book stands on the path above. "You have to look up the name you want." Molly could feel others surrounding her, listening to the answer, pushing closer. The woman went on. "You have to look up the name of your loved one," she said, and Molly cringed at the words. "They're in alphabetical order up there. You find your name, it gives you the number of the panel and the line. Like a road map." She had a smug satisfied look on her face because she knew all the answers.

Molly looked at her blankly, half-seeing her, half-hearing her: high-cheeked face, ruddy in the wind; brassy bleached hair; strident positive voice. Everything big. A stone angel, vaguely remembered. "Why aren't they in order?" she insisted, as if that woman might know, since she seemed to know it all.

"It's pretty cockamamie," the man chimed in, sympathetic to Molly's confusion. "They're done by the day they got killed or went missing. That's how they done it."

The day Tommy was killed? She looked baffled, hesitant. What day was that? Did anyone ever tell her? Had she ever asked? She just knew he was dead. The notice was official. Like an I.R.S. notice, like death and taxes—official.

Molly stared blankly at the man, who shook his head at her and shrugged. He turned back to the wall, intent on getting on with the rubbing. He said to her over his shoulder, "Go on up there, look it up. Anyway the park department guy is up there, see him in his uniform? He'll give you a hand."

The man from the Park Service was answering questions. She had arrived in the middle of his litany. "There are fifty-eight thousand one hundred fifty-six names," he was saying, "and that includes eight combat nurses. And they're listed according to the day of death in the combat zone only. We"—

was it the editorial we?—"we don't count anyone who might have gotten hurt in combat and then taken away to a hospital, let's say, and then died there. That wouldn't count on this monument, he'd never get in."

Certainly not, thought Molly, flippant in spite of herself, if he couldn't manage to die in place, the hell with him.

"That means," the guide went on to say, "that the number I just gave you, the fifty-eight thousand one hundred fifty-six including eight combat nurses"—he repeated the magic number carefully—"that means that's not the total of casualties, that's only them that actually died or went missing in actual combat." He stressed the words "actual combat" as if he were making a legal point. But if you were dead in Vietnam, Molly thought, weren't you dead in Vietnam? On what black wall was your name written in stone if you died in agony among the cheerful medics like someone in M*A*S*H? Molly shook her head trying to hold back her scoffing thoughts. The park guide couldn't help the words. He was a nice, mild man, the same yellow color as his clean khaki uniform with the old boy scout hat. The words had been given him.

"See where it starts? In that corner where it says 1959," he went on, "that's the date of the first casualty, an advisory team leader." He swung his hand toward the far right and then around to the low point at the left. "The names go according to dates and then you go from one low point to the other, and at the end, see"—he pointed again to the apex—"it ends in 1975. You can see the date at the bottom. The last one killed, he was on his way home, killed by the helicopter come to take him."

There was a murmur of pity and sympathy from the people around her. "On his way home, the poor guy," the man next to her said, "killed going home."

When the little knot of people around him dispersed, the

park guide helped Molly go through one of the big directories, find the name Thomas Barrett Levin, the number of the panel, the line. He wrote it down for her on a slip of paper that he took from the breast pocket of his crisp clean khaki shirt.

"If you have any difficulty, ma'am, come get me and I'll show you." He turned to answer the same question from somebody else, and then again, over and over.

A young man standing next to Molly as she turned down the path to find the right panel and the right line blurted out caustically, "Just like the military—never do anything simple if you can foul it up." People around glared at the cynical young man but no one said anything. The moment was too solemn. Molly turned to walk back to the wall, looking carefully for her panel. The crowds were larger now. Young people, old people, talking in low tones, fingers tracing names. Finally she found the panel she was looking for. Tommy's name was there, high up. She had to reach to touch it. Then she too, like all the others, traced the letters with her fingers.

Tommy's full name. But no one had ever called him anything but Tommy. Not Thomas, not Tom, certainly not Thomas Barrett Levin. Just Tommy. For a moment she thought she might cry, but she stiffened as she stood there and moved on to the path, away from the wall. The sweeping sense of grief she had felt at the first sight of the black expanse was dimmed. Instead there was a surge within her of anger, as if tracing the name, feeling it directly under the cushion of her finger, had shot through her like a drug from an intravenous needle, enflaming her nerve ends. This wasn't just a monument. It was personal. It was Tommy's name up there she had felt beneath her fingertips.

But was her grief to be erased simply because his name was here, with those thousands of others? That wasn't much of a payoff, was it? Was any payoff possible? Was there any wall high enough and deep enough and long enough to wipe out the loss of those who died in a senseless, stupid, unresolvable war? Suddenly she was outraged at the whole idea of this monument. A monument to what? It didn't even have the grace to encompass all who had lived and died and suffered in Vietnam, just the fifty-eight thousand one hundred fifty-six including eight combat nurses, who had died under arbitrary circumstances.

Molly wanted to turn to go but felt fixed in place. She looked to right and left. There were no orgies of tears as told in the stories five years ago, at the monument's unveiling: had that been hype, for publicity? Molly could see sad eyes and sad faces. It was not a joyous spot. Not for her, not for anyone. But how could it be, this monument to the loss of dearly beloved human life?

A man in a wheelchair, clearly a veteran of the war by the odd pieced-together uniform he was wearing, rolled up beside her. A man in his forties. She tried to smile in a friendly fashion as she moved aside to give him a better view. "My God," she thought. "Tommy would have been in his forties too! It's all more than twenty years ago."

The thought shocked her. She had never before followed it through in her mind. Of course Tommy would not now be a boy. In his forties! So hard to think about, so hard to imagine. He was set in her mind, like an image forever emerging out of the developer and the fixing bath, as that crazy exasperating tormented beloved kid. But he hadn't been a boy then either, had he? He had been twenty years old, old enough to make choices, old enough to weigh the consequences, old enough to go marching on.

"As he died to make men holy, let us die to make men free." The words reverberated unexpectedly, unbidden through her head, filling the interstices of her mind. She had sung them so often at assembly in her grade school. What terrible words. She shuddered at them. The Battle Hymn, a boy's song, written by a woman, but a boy's song for boys like Tommy. She felt anger and a rising hostility as the tears now ran down her cheeks. Just what television reports had said happened to everyone in front of the cold black stone. A catharsis, they had called it. She brushed her tears aside impatiently, as if they had betrayed her. All she wanted to feel was, what a waste, what a sad mad waste.

The veteran in the wheelchair was speaking. "I asked you." Apparently she had not heard his earlier question.

"I'm sorry." She turned to him, still dabbing at her face. "What did you say?" She found the interruption jarring.

"That your son up there?" he asked.

She nodded.

"My brother too," he said. "Must have died the same day. Just a kid. He was following in my footsteps." He sighed. "Monkey see, monkey do."

Molly looked more closely at him—a big man, oversized for the wheelchair, his bulky arms overflowing the side rests. He had a bushy beard, dark and mottled with gray, a scraggly mustache that overhung his lips. Everything about him seemed too much. His body for his chair, the thick beard on his face, the enormous shock of hair with the tiny VFW cap afloat on the waves. Only his empty folded trousers tucked in under his buttocks were undersized, without flesh. What was the word for it, Molly wondered, two legs gone, arms still there. Was it paraplegic? Not quadriplegic—that was everything wasn't it? *Quadri,* four. Two arms, two legs.

She wanted to know. She wanted to know where his legs had gone, how had it happened, how did he manage, where did he live, what did he think, had he gone to Vietnam on his own, or had he been drafted? He didn't look like Tommy, who could have rested on a graduate school deferment had he not been carried away by his own passionate rhetoric. And this man wasn't one of the thousands of black kids who had been given no choice. He was white and hefty, and his blue eyes, bloodshot and watery, must once have been clear and in focus. What had they seen? Then and thereafter and now?

Molly stood silent before him, tongue-tied. He said, "I'm sorry about your son, ma'am. It was a tough time. A job to be done. You should be proud."

Molly couldn't bear to answer him. Anything she might say was choked up within her. What was the use? She turned away from the wall with its names and names and names. Why wasn't the date inscribed where she could read it? The date of Tommy's death. The date of the death of the brother of the man in the wheelchair. He would know. She turned to ask but he had rolled his chair back to let others push to the front. Molly felt confused, the date was on the tip of her tongue, it began with an "A," like those other names that slipped her mind now, eluding her, tantalizing her with only the first letter as clue—or was it the last letter—or was it a letter in the middle? But the memory was sharp and clear of the day the official notice had come. It was imprinted on her brain, in her heart, in the pain in her chest, with archival permanence.

· CHAPTER 2 ·

T H E telegram was addressed to Joe. Molly looked at it and wondered. No one sent telegrams these days. Except. Except. She took a long black hairpin stuck into the heavy knot at the top of her head and used it to slit the envelope open. She knew the answer to her question—the military sent telegrams. This was a military telegram. It told Joe that Tommy was dead. She looked at it for a long time, quietly.

Why tell Joe, she thought. It's for me to know, for him to find out. It was her Tommy who was dead. Tommy, her baby. Tommy her beautiful foolish headstrong young son. And he was dead. Dead in Vietnam, what a hell of a place.

She put the telegram on the table in the front hall with all the other mail and went back to her studio, where she had been when the front doorbell rang. She sat at her work table and stared straight ahead, pushing aside the contact prints she had been examining under the magnifier.

Is this where I always am? she thought. Is this what I'm always doing? This is where I was, this is what I was doing then. She could see, as she stared, the day in May when Tommy came through that door and said to her, "I'm taking a leave of absence from school, Mother. I'm going to Vietnam."

"You're doing what?" Molly had said, her mouth open, gasping at him. "You're going where?"

"Vietnam."

"Why? You have a student deferment."

"I don't want it. It's not fair."

"But why?" she had persisted.

"Because I'm an American and this is an American war." His words were deliberate. They were calculated. They were part of an old family argument, used against Molly as an old Red.

"Horseshit," Molly had exploded. "So *you're* an American? Come on. I'm the American here. I'm more of an American than you are, kid. Don't forget that. At least I go back on both sides to the Mayflower. Let me remind you, I don't have your shtetl grandparents."

"You know what I mean, Mother, so don't twist it around." Molly looked at his young earnest serious face—set in stubborn lines, his mouth, with the new reddish scraggly mustache above it, almost motionless as he mumbled—and felt the ground slipping away from her under the work table.

"This is my country and if it's in a war, I have to be in it too." He spoke softly, so she could barely hear.

"Don't mumble," she wanted to cry out to him, as if he were still ten years old. "Speak up, speak up." Instead she clutched the edge of the table and wondered what to do.

Joe, she thought, he won't be any help. He'll be proud, damn him.

Tommy stooped a bit as he stood, looking down at her. He's so long and thin, Molly thought. He's so vulnerable. He's such a fool. She shook her head slowly. "What will Emily say?" she asked him, suddenly remembering Emily on all the peace marches and the antiwar rallies.

"I've already told her," he answered his mother. "She knows."

"She knows? This will shake her up," Molly said slowly. "When did you tell her?"

"About an hour ago."

"What did she say?"

Tommy smiled, his mustache tangling along the edges of his mouth. He hadn't quite gotten used to it. "She called me a jerk," he said. "She said I was unspeakable."

He shrugged as if it didn't matter, but Molly knew how much Emily mattered to Tommy. Emily was almost five years older than Tommy and when they were little children, Tommy had followed his big sister around like the tail on the donkey.

"Maybe Emily is right," Molly snapped at him. "You are a jerk if you go ahead with this."

"Don't put me down, Mother. Emily could be wrong, you know. She's wrong about a lot of things."

Emily had not ever been wrong for Tommy about anything until this past year. Now, suddenly, they had become belligerents on everything. One night when Tommy had been home on a weekend from college and Emily had joined them for dinner, the two had gotten into a long, tangled argument over President Kennedy that had left them screaming at one another.

"Don't tell me anyone takes him seriously," Emily had sneered. "He's just a creature of his power-hungry father, all manufactured glamor. And dangerous!"

The two quarreled over Kennedy's decision on the Bay of Pigs, his standing up to Khrushchev, the dangers of a Communist Cuba. Tommy thought Kennedy was right every time, that he spoke for a new public spirit—"Ask not what your country can do for you, ask what you can do for your country"—while Emily hooted and challenged.

"Amor Patriae?" she asked scoffingly.

"Yes. Why not?" he answered her sharply. Tommy, who had always accepted Emily's enthusiasms and her hostilities, held his ground with a new quiet determination that startled Molly.

"If you'd take off your New Left blinkers, Emily, you'd find out about Kennedy. The best minds in the country are on his side. I worked in his campaign at college. I know. You could tell who was who on the faculty, the guys for Nixon against the ones for JFK."

And later they bristled with one another over Vietnam. "Have you seen the picket lines in front of the U.N.?" Emily pointed her finger at him in warning. "Watch them grow. It will be like the French students over the war in Algeria. You'll see."

"Not everyone is storming the streets, Emily, although the newspapers and the damn TV would have you think so. Not in Paris, either, I bet."

But in the end, when Emily had taken her coat and was on her way out, she came over to Tommy and kissed him on the cheek, saying, "Okay, I love you anyway." It was Tommy whose face remained strained and closed.

"Emily!" Molly exclaimed to herself now, as she thought of the telegram out on the table. She stared at her fingertips through the magnifying glass, letting the deeply etched skin, like cracked leather under the lens, imprint itself on her mind. "Poor Emily. Poor, poor Emily."

Emily had used invective and slogans to try to stop Tommy from enlisting. Peter, Emily's husband, had used invective and irony. Joe had said Tommy was a man, able to make his own decisions. Under Joe's words Molly sensed a surprised approval—was Tommy doing something at last that made him more of a man in Joe's eyes? Did Joe see that it was a moral duty, as the recently dead Kennedy had seen it, to prevent the fall of South Vietnam to communism? Kennedy had committed the country to containment. Johnson, the new President, had "vowed to see it through." Joe made feeble sounds to Tommy about waiting, finishing graduate school at least, or getting into officer's training. But there was no way to stop Tommy. He went, and in his own way. By the end of 1963 there were more than fifteen thousand men in Vietnam. And Tommy was soon one of them.

Molly felt a sickening twist in her bowels. And now, she thought, there probably isn't enough left of him to go into a match box.

She got up from the work table, pushing the magnifying glass away from her as if she never wanted to look through it again, the enlarged images too much to bear. She walked back to the hall and picked up the telegram.

I can't just leave it here for Joe to find, she said to herself. I have to do something. Then she shook her head, exploding aloud. "Let him find it. It's his fault. The bastard."

She smoothed out the thin yellow oblong of paper and carried it with her into the kitchen. "His fault?" she asked herself in a loud voice; but as she poured a mug of the hot coffee that was always ready in the electric percolator, she thought, What am I talking about? what do I mean?

She carried the mug over to the table and sat down. Involuntarily she started to wail, as if by instinct, sitting straight-backed at the table, the yellow telegram in front of her beside the hot coffee.

"Why didn't you stop him, Joe?" she demanded in a loud choked voice. "Why didn't you prevent this? He was your son, not just mine. He would have listened to you. I blame you. I blame you. I blame you."

Her own words stopped her. Just as suddenly as she had started to cry, she stopped.

Not fair, she thought. But who's fair? Who's ever fair? But

why do I blame you, Joe? Why do I blame you for everything? She cradled the hot mug in her hands, warming to her rage. But I do, I do. I blame you for all the wars, all the rages, all the betrayals. Why? What is it about you and me, Joe, after all these years, that makes us enemies? Is this true of everybody, lovers, husbands, wives? Are we all enemy friends?

She banged her fist on the table. Fair? Fair to Joe? What the hell for? You name it, Joe, I blame you. I blame you for Vietnam, for Korea, for Hitler, for the Hitler war. I blame you for Tommy. She picked up the telegram and waved it to the absent Joe. "See. I hate you, you hear?"

Her loud voice startled her. She closed her mouth tightly and put the telegram down on the table. Then she reached for the kitchen telephone. Joe's secretary, her clipped English accent very upper class over the wire, said he wasn't in and wasn't available, was there anything she could do? "No," Molly said calmly. "Just ask him to call me when you can. Important. Very. I'll be home."

Home. Home is the place where people *live*. The dead leave holes. The roof caves in. Molly got up from the kitchen table and walked back to her big pleasant studio, which overlooked their own enclosed charming little city garden.

We have it all, don't we? she thought, looking down at the ivy and the pretty fountain. I feel as if my heart would break— then winced apologetically at herself. Hearts didn't break; what an old chestnut. But hers felt as if it would, could, there was an actual ache there. She put her hand up to feel it. "A mother's heart," her mother-in-law might have said. The emotional Yiddish used by Joe's mother never needed apologies.

But what about a father's heart? Molly thought. Isn't it the same great blood-engorged muscle as mine? Doesn't it beat with the same pain? And Emily? What about Emily? Oh Emily.

She went to the telephone and dialed Emily's number. She let it ring and ring and finally hung up. She felt as if there was no one else who wanted to know about Tommy and his death. They were otherwise occupied. It wasn't on the calendar. This was 1964. The year of death and destruction and no one was in.

She dialed her answering service. "No calls," she said, "only from Mr. Levin and my daughter." She hesitated, then added, "And call Miss Dixon at the agency. Cancel the sitting for the afternoon. Tell her a personal emergency." Molly prided herself on her professionalism. It was not like her to hold up a sitting that involved a model, assistants, an account executive, and deadlines. But it was all too much, too much. She looked around the studio, with its stacks of seamless papers in all colors, the efficient clutter of tripods and stands, all the necessary artificial lights when the outside light was not enough, and pushed it out of her mind. It was all set to go. She felt as if she herself would never be again.

The weight of the empty house came down on her. She felt herself engulfed by anger. The sense of the past swept over her, with all its ambiguities, its irretrievable sweetness and despairs. She lifted her head and started to keen, like an Irish peasant at a wake. The noise she was making startled her and calmed her down. She went back to sit at her table, her head in her hands, trying to think, waiting for the telephone to ring.

This isn't a quarrel between Joe and me, she marshaled her words in her mind. Why do I make it so? Why is there always the same implicit combat? We don't have to say anything, we just know, there's the same political, personal, psychological shit. Oh Joe, you and me and our code words. For once, let us share our grief.

She was baffled. She was confused by this mixture of grief and anger, an anger not only at Joe but at Tommy too. It was not only Tommy's death that baffled and angered her. That Tommy had gone to this war at all was so incomprehensible. Why hadn't he been out there with the others, with Emily and the children of her friends, chanting and parading and wearing buttons that said END THE WAR NOW? How did he get turned around?

"You live in a cloud, Mother," he had stormed at her during their final days of argument. "Everyone isn't against the war. You only listen to what you want to hear. Millions of people believe in our government and what it does. They want to defend it, not destroy it. Don't kid yourself."

Molly had listened to him aghast. Tommy, her son. Joe's son. The son of old Reds, of new liberals, of *nice* people. Brought up to believe—what? Brought up to believe what? Molly thought of him as a bird flying wildly before the storm, his directional signals all cockeyed. Now down, dead.

Death is the end that gives shape to the beginning, Molly thought. She put her head down on her arm and tried to think about it. Nothing came through. She sat numb and dumb, letting time well up in her. Tommy had been born in the war. What war? Had there ever been a time without war? What was *the* war to one was *that* war to another not even a generation apart. Fathers and sons, older brothers and younger, each went his own way. Right now, this minute, it was still war; war and devastation, everywhere one turned. Choose your time and place, you had it.

J O E and Molly first met in the fever of the war in Spain. War was in the air that beautiful spring. War was everywhere. No one talked about anything else except of course jobs and money and love. But war was the background, the foreground, the continuum. Not very different from what it always is, except that Molly and Joe were young. This was their time and place.

Molly wasn't called Molly then. Her name was Mary Barrett and she had come to New York from Massachusetts via Vassar. The Molly came later, when Joe decided that Mary was a George M. Cohan name that sounded mismatched with Levin. Mary liked the name Molly—she had just heard of Molly Bloom—so she accepted the change, first as one of Joe's jokes, then because she felt it suited her. It did not occur to her then but did years later, in her feminist awareness, that a woman and her last name are too soon parted by a man, and in her case, she had lost both, first and last.

They met at a party near Gramercy Park. There were lots of parties then. There were parties like this one for Spain. There were parties for the newest German refugees. There were parties for the Party. The same people seemed to go to the same parties but Mary Barrett and Joe Levin had never encountered each other.

When Mary came into the room that Sunday afternoon, she noticed him at once, in the corner over by the radio. The thought flashed through her head, I'll never make that, and then an immediate sense that she wanted to. He was tall, black-haired, with enormous black eyes in a very white, long, Talmudic face. He was wearing a brown tweed jacket and a blue chambray shirt and gray flannel slacks and he didn't look like anybody else in the room. Mary thought of the boys from Williams and Amherst, but that wasn't his look either.

She walked over to the table where the cheap red wine, the standard drink at such events, was being dispensed in paper cups. The dollar at the door covered all one could eat and two cups of the wine. It was up to you to count. After that, ten cents a drink. Mary had come this afternoon with Frances Cohen, one of her teachers at the Art Students League who had become her friend.

Mary liked going to such parties with Frances. Frances

seemed to know everyone. Everyone knew her. The two had become friends over coffee at Schrafft's, across the street from the League. In one way or another, over many months Frances had let Mary know she was a Communist, if not a Party member, since no one ever said so outright, at least one with a capital "C," very, very involved. Frances, who was soft-spoken, would let her voice drop even farther down the scale as she told Mary she couldn't do this or that on Tuesday because, and then there was an added hush, she had a meeting.

Mary secretly thought her an improbable-looking Communist, with her sweet smile and her pink plump cheeks, but her work didn't look like her either. That sweetness and pinkness were in sharp contrast to her vivid, literal paintings, men and women and children with every hungry line deeply etched, every ugly beautiful curve exploited, every pubic hair showing.

Frances had studied with Thomas Hart Benton, and his wild shapes, his furious colors, influenced her for a long time. She was one of the most popular teachers at the League. Only sometimes, in selected places, here and there, did she let her political doctrines show. They had nothing to do with her painting.

Mary nudged her. "Who is that?" she said, pointing to Joe, still fiddling with the radio dial. "Do you know him?"

Frances turned to look, narrowing her china-doll blue eyes in a squint. She wore heavy glasses when she was at work. Without them, she was blind and blinking. "That? Oh. You mean Joe Levin. Isn't he a doll?" She turned to laugh at Mary. "Forget it. He's everyone's dream lay."

"I just asked." Mary's face turned red. After two years in the city, she had not yet gotten used to New York candor. "I've never seen him around before."

Frances juggled her wine cup, nodding at people as she

sipped, waving with her free hand. She took for granted that everyone was a friend, whether or not she could see them. "He's just gotten on the Writers Project. Around the corner from you, Mary. Pretty handy." Mary was on the W.P.A., the Works Projects Administration Arts Project, going to the League in the late afternoons and evenings. "He's been in Paris, just got back. He's a bright guy, very smart, egocentric." Frances squinted at Mary. "Not your style."

"What does that mean?" Mary asked.

"Try it. See." Frances laughed. "But then again, you never know."

The loud blare of the radio crossed the room. No party was complete then without its clanging voice of doom. If someone switched it off, someone else always came into the room and switched it back on. Joe had turned it on, full force. The reporter's voice, tense and ominous, with that detached cool undertow of alarm affected by the radio newsmen, rose in the room: "In the streets of Vienna today, there's a holiday atmosphere. Every house in town has at least one huge swastika flag hanging from it and in every window, in millions of windows in fact, little paper Nazi flags are pasted. On the walls of some buildings huge portraits of Herr Hitler, some of them five stories high, gaze down upon you. The weather today has been rather fickle . . ."

Mary walked away from Fran and approached the radio. Joe Levin was listening as if he were far away, part of the roar of that crowd. Suddenly he flipped the dial and the radio was silent. Mary was standing next to him.

"That's Bill Shirer," she said. "I can't believe it's really happening."

Joe looked at Mary blankly, as if he had to pull himself out of his silence to answer. "Oh, it's happening all right. Listen."

He snapped the dial back on, with a kind of sour disdain. "... Anschluss ... one people, one Reich, one Führer." Then he clicked it off again.

Mary sipped her wine, eyeing him across the rim of her cup. "April in Vienna," she said with sardonic humor. But he didn't smile back. He didn't look friendly. He didn't look unfriendly. He looked removed, isolated, distracted. Mary continued lamely. "One wonders, is there anyone in Austria with the courage to say no."

Joe's deep-set black eyes stared at Mary. His eyes were like round coals, so black no iris showed. He seemed angry with her. "Courage? What do we know about other people's courage? We've left them with nothing to say except *ja*. So that's what they're saying." His wide handsome mouth, full pale lips, snapped shut.

Mary felt rebuffed and it annoyed her. All she wanted to do was talk to him—why not about Austria? She had all sorts of questions in mind about the Socialists, the Communists, the Jews; the kind of conversation that they were all used to having with one another. He didn't have to be so hostile. Mary wasn't accustomed to male hostility.

"My trouble," she would joke, "is that all the boys want to be my friend. They want to talk to me but they take the other girls home."

This wasn't quite true but it suited Mary to say so out of some priggish need to cover up her passionate confusions. She feared her own wants, hardly knew what they were. Other girls, at Vassar and here in New York, were beginning to carry pessaries around in their handbags and knew all the abortionists around Gramercy Park. Mary clung to the ideal of having more on her mind than sex, muddling herself senselessly before she learned they were not mutually exclusive. She secretly wished she could be as free and easy as the others. Sometimes she wondered if they really were.

Mary had a certain style and she knew it. Her black hair sprang from her head like horsehair. It was wiry and tough and curled to her shoulders like an Egyptian headdress. The bangs that came to her smooth black eyebrows were cut blunt and thick. Underneath those black brows, her light gray eyes were like wide-open steady lighthouse beams. Her eyes were beautiful. And she had a way of looking straight into the eyes of anyone she talked to that was sometimes disconcerting. She hated the freckles across the bridge of her nose and on her cheeks but used no makeup to cover them. Only her lips were made up, a vivid red, following the shape of the full lips. She was a good-looking girl. Not pretty. Handsome and small and definite.

Frances Cohen came across the room and joined her as she stood next to Joe at the radio. "Hi Joe." She waved her paper cup at him. "Get another station, why don't you? This is too awful. Let's see what's happening in Madrid."

Joe nodded to her, unsmiling, rather withdrawn. "Hi Fran. Madrid? That's another stinker. Worse than Austria." He switched the radio back on, twirled the dial and walked away from them both to join Frank Morosh, who had just come into the room.

"Rude bastard," Mary said.

"Conceited," Fran laughed. "Who wouldn't be who looked like that?"

Mary shrugged. "So what? He wouldn't give me the time of day."

Fran laughed again. "You can get the time of day from your friend Frank Morosh. Look at him. The center of the stage, as usual, the minute he comes in."

Frank was the guest of honor at the afternoon's party. The festivities were being held to welcome him and Tom Feurlich back to New York after a tour of duty with the International Brigade in Spain. This was the first of a series of money-making events to raise funds for the Brigade, with Frank and Tom as the featured attractions.

Mary knew them both well. She had been at the Savoy the night Tom decided to join the Abraham Lincoln Brigade, the American contingent of the International Brigade. As for Frank, she had had a brief, uncomfortable romance with him before that. It had hardly been an affair—a month or two in an occasionally shared bed, ended by Frank when he found that Mary's comradeship wouldn't stretch into her becoming a real Party comrade. When Frank dismissed their liaison as "politically unsound," Mary was relieved, although too much of a coward to make the decision herself.

She watched him now, with everyone crowding around him. His voice, clipped and didactic—what Mary always privately called his "commissar's voice"—rose above the din. He was greeting the elect among the chosen, conferring a few pontifical words here, a few there, or a handshake, a pat on the shoulders.

"He's okay," Frances answered rather sharply, her blue eyes squinting, pushing away Mary's irony. She added, "They say wonderful things about him in the Brigade."

Mary didn't answer. She had heard rumors that Frank had been acting as a political leader of the Brigade under the title "educational director." Everyone seemed to know what that meant, even Mary. "Party rep," they said to one another, nodding sagely. It was said in muted tones, as if even this meant more than it said.

Frank's voice now rose loudly, reaching every corner of the room as he answered someone's question. "They're no better than vermin. And we have to crush them like vermin."

As he spoke, turning his head to make certain everyone heard him, he caught sight of Mary. "Hi, Mary," he called. "What are you doing over there? Come say hello."

Mary felt it was the royal nod. She waved back to him and came over, holding her drink carefully. Joe was standing next to Frank and it was apparently a question of his that had ruffled Frank and produced his vehement answer. Mary wondered who the vermin might be this time that needed to be crushed. One was not always certain. Objective conditions, as they were wont to say, kept changing.

Frank put his arm around her shoulder and leaned down, interrupting his tirade, to kiss her cheek in greeting.

"Hello, Frank. What vermin?" she asked.

Frank dropped his arm from Mary's shoulders and turned back to Joe without answering her. He made it obvious; she was not politically important, so no answer was needed. It was Joe, whose long white face had a serious, somber look, as if he were weighing each thought, who turned to answer her question.

"Frank's talking about the POUM," he said to her. "In case you don't know, it's the *Partido Obrero Unificaciòn Marxista*— easy to translate." Joe's Spanish was deliberately precise, clear-cut; yes, easy to translate. "Fellow fighters," he added.

Frank cut him off. "Anarchists!" he spat out.

Joe continued calmly, speaking directly to Mary. "I asked Frank about it. I want to know. There have been many stories."

He spoke in the same measured tone of voice that he had used earlier to Frances. Mary liked that. She was to learn it was his tone of voice whenever what you were saying interested him.

Certainly not Williams or Amherst, she thought. He's like a young man by one of the Bellinis, elegant and pale. He should be in black velvet embroidered in gold. The image was clear in her mind.

Frank again broke into Joe's explanation. "Why talk about such scum, Joe? Trotskyists!" He articulated each word carefully, as if he were making a speech. Everyone in the crowded room was listening. "There's no other way to deal with them. They are the enemy. They must be crushed."

When Frank spoke, his face darkened. He had an obsessed look. He was tall, swarthy, very personable except when he smiled, which was seldom. His usual air was haunted and stern. His smile was stern too, lips apart, his teeth were blackened and misshapen. Once, with unaccustomed humor, he had called them his working-class teeth, English working-class teeth. Frank was from Liverpool, where his family still lived, refugees of an earlier time from Poland. Here in New York he lived with an aunt in the far wilds of Coney Island and, before his travels to Spain, rode the BMT to his job as a political cartoonist on the Party newspaper.

Joe's eyes remained fixed on Frank. He was frowning, his forehead wrinkled as he listened, nodding as Frank amplified his bitter denunciations. They were surrounded by a large group, listening and nodding too. There were no more questions now, just Frank making a speech.

Suddenly, to her surprise, Mary heard her own voice, sounding rather squeaky and uncertain, as she interrupted: "I know, Frank. You were an eyewitness to it all, so you know what's going on." She felt as if she sounded like a suppliant little girl, appealing to daddy. She hated the way her voice failed her in these kinds of situations, but she persisted. "But wouldn't it be better to join forces with the various groups in Spain, all on our side, instead of fighting one another? Isn't Franco the enemy?"

Frank looked through Mary as if she were nonexistent. "Who says these renegades are on our side?" He spat this out. Then he snubbed Mary with his worst indictment. "Don't be naive, Mary. You're being politically naive."

Mary was too embarrassed to continue and she felt her voice would fail her completely. She could do nothing except gulp the bit of wine left in the paper cup. She felt like a fool, it was so easy to put her down. Why did she always pick the wrong room at the wrong time for an argument?

Joe spoke quietly, challenging Frank. "I don't know. I'm not sure it is so naive to ask about a united front, especially in the middle of the fighting. You can settle the score later. The question now is to win. To win against Franco."

"United front!" The words leaped from Frank's lips. "Look what it did in France. You ought to know. You were there. That bastard Blum."

Mary turned away. She felt as if she had had enough. She pushed out of the group and went to refill her wine cup. There, at the improvised bar, she found Tom Feurlich.

"Tom." Mary reached out to hug him. "When did you get here? I didn't see you come in."

"A few minutes ago," he mumbled as he hugged her back. "I saw you over there with the brass, but I thought, no room at the inn." He seemed uneasy, pale and irresolute. He was supposed to be the other guest of honor of the afternoon, but he had the forlorn look of a skinny stray child. Tom had been in Spain for eight months. Mary had run into his girl, Annette, a few times during that interval; Annette had reported proudly on his exploits and his wounds.

"Annette told me you were hurt in action," Mary said. "Are you okay? You look okay."

There was concern on her face as she looked at him. She had felt warm and affectionate toward Tom ever since her first meeting with him, two years earlier at a dance at Webster Hall when they found they managed all the steps together and swung to the same beat. He made her feel at home.

"You dance just like the boys in Great Barrington, at the high school gym," she had laughed at him.

"You'd knock them dead on Fordham Road," he'd parried as he swung her under his raised arm and around.

"Oh sure I'm fine," he answered her now. "Great." He didn't look great. He looked sad and done in. Tom was always a quiet one, in spite of the dancing and the drinking and the jokes; but this was more than quiet, this seemed a retreat.

"How was Spain?" Mary asked, thinking, What a foolish question. "Tell me about it."

"Spain? Oh, Spain. What's to tell?" His words hung there, in the air. Mary suddenly remembered the gala night he had decided to go. Eight or ten or twelve of them had gone up to the Savoy Ballroom in Harlem to drink to Frank's departure. They had found a table next to the dance floor. The music was ripe and rich and the dancing fantastic. They all watched and listened with rapt enthusiasm. There must have been a dozen variations of "Honeysuckle Rose" as they talked, each more fanciful than the other, with a tenor sax moaning and groaning on the melody over and over again, and the whole room jumping. Out on the floor the dancers were swinging and swooping wildly, in, out, dip, together, and the skirts were flying around tight pants, in perfect unison, back and forth. Not like Great Barrington at all. It was a kind of rule that the dance floor was not for whites, except when a white dancer was good, really good. A rarity. Mostly they all followed the dancers on the brightly lit floor with their eyes as they talked and drank in the darkness of the ringside.

One tall girl, her head held high, wore a tight print rayon dress that ended below her knees in a wide ruffle and her stockings were green with sandals to match. Her lively strident impudent image was forever fixed in Mary's mind as the Harlem that was then.

The Savoy was a good place to celebrate in, and it was a good place for drinking. Frank had brought Mary with him. Tom Feurlich was there with his girl, Annette. Annette was big-bosomed, with a large, ruddy face. From Iowa and the University of Michigan, she now worked for the *Daily Worker*, the Communist newspaper, although at Michigan she had been interested in the theater and had won an Avery Hopwood Award for her script of a play on farm women. She looked like a farm woman herself and cultivated that look: no makeup, her red hair twisted up in a tight bun, a 4-H winner. She was dogmatic, self-assured and took an enormous pride in not being New York and Jewish but out of the true American heartland. She had a way of reminding others, including Mary, of this often; while not Jewish, Mary was suspect because she came from the effete east and Vassar. Vassar especially; it always produced a snicker.

Annette felt Iowa and Michigan gave her a particular point of view. There was a new campaign stressing communism as twentieth-century Americanism and Annette felt herself the embodiment of that new slogan. In her own mind, she was a figure on an arch of triumph, symbolic. Or perhaps Marianne, somehow at the Concord bridge. A mixed metaphor!

At one point a toast was offered to Frank on his journey to Spain. Annette turned and held her glass toward Tom.

"Here's to Tom, too, whenever he gets up the courage to go." She took a swallow and looked at him and then at everyone around the table. "If I were a man, that's where I'd be. In Spain."

Spain. The war in Spain. For everyone around that table, it was their crusade. It touched their hearts. It fired their imaginations. It drew them, a terrible lodestar, the quintessential struggle between wrong and right. They knew all the place names, the landscape of battle. Barcelona, Catalonia, Almeria, Granada, Andalusia, Madrid, Toledo.

They sang "No Passeran," drinking around a table, standing on a street corner, at parties. When they went to the Metropolitan Museum of Art, they concentrated on the Spanish masterpieces. They saw the legendary cities of dreams, rising in the shadowy green mists of an El Greco painting like an apocalyptic vision, or spread out luxuriantly in the sensuous Seville landscape of Murillo, now destroyed by shells and bombs, by looting and the racketing guns. They thought Spanish, ate paella, drank Fundador. Spain.

Ardent volunteers had rushed to join the fighting, from England and France and Holland and Sweden, on the side of the Loyalists. The Abraham Lincoln Brigade was the name given the group from America, and Frank was going off with the first boatload. These were the brave, the good, the committed. They believed this without question and with passion. These were the legendary heroes.

Mary had drunk the same toasts, sung the same songs, felt the same surge of blood against her eardrums—but even as Annette taunted Tom, she looked at him and wondered why it was necessary to go off and die in Spain. Suddenly that recurrent sense she had so often of feeling like an impostor came over her. But I really don't believe in war, she thought, what am I doing here?

The answer was simple. Mary was here because nearly everyone she knew was here. But she looked around the table at the Savoy and felt uneasy. She thought of Virginia Woolf questioning the death, in Spain, of her nephew Julian Bell. "Is it necessary always to rush into battle for the sake of ideals?" she had written. Is it necessary? Must Tom die in Spain to prove something?

Frances Cohen seemed to join Annette's plea to Tom. "Men should be prepared to die for what they believe in. Otherwise they don't believe in much." When Frances spoke in this special Party way it was always in slogans, Frances who was otherwise so subtle and acute. And Guido Renzi, with his fierce black mustachios and his gentle Bleecker Street accented voice, said, "Stinking paisanos. They're machine-gunning the fishing boats. Let's kill the bastards"—although one knew that Guido would never kill anything except a deer or a pheasant out in the hunting fields of northern New Jersey that would then turn up as a delicious venison steak or country pâté at his friendly hunt dinners.

"I'd go if they'd have me," little Bob Morley panted with delight. He was known throughout the Village for his rather mysterious *Oral History of Our Times,* and he dragged out his scraps of paper to make some illegible notes, gurgling to himself as he cheeped with glee, "Oh, Tom, what will you do? Such an important decision. Let me get it all down."

"It is the only honorable thing to do," said Frank, and since it was what he was doing, it was incontrovertibly so.

Tom looked at everyone around the table and lifted his own glass to drink. "Here's to Spain," he said in a low firm voice. "I'm joining. Maybe I can go with the same group, Frank's group, next week." He poured down his drink, rye and ginger ale, and pushed his empty glass back and forth in front of him, leaving a trail of wet circles on the table. "It's the only decent thing for a man to do."

Tom was one of the few among them with an established job. He was an instructor in the philosophy department at City College and had been living with Annette for more than a year. Somewhere or other she had a husband, so they could not marry, but she and Tom seemed close and loving and attached to one another. She reached over and touched his hand. "I'm proud of you, Tom. Really proud."

Tom had managed to arrange for a leave of absence from the college and had left for Spain at the end of the following week. Now here he was, back again in New York eight months later, standing alone in the corner. There was no sound of music playing.

"Spain?" Mary repeated to him. "Spain. How was it?"

"Spain," he answered finally. "You can't talk about it without sounding like Hemingway."

Suddenly his face broke into a big welcoming smile. Joe Levin stood next to Mary, his hand outstretched to Tom.

"Hi Tom," he said, "*wie gehts?*"

"Joe Levin! For God's sake, you old son of a gun." Tom's face was crinkled with delight. "When did you get back to New York?"

"Months ago. But you were in Spain, being a bloody hero."

"Hero, my ass."

"What about Hemingway? I caught the sacred name."

"He's there now. Just went."

"Doing what?"

"Writing I guess. Spitting blood. Gory the minute he stepped off the boat. But then, Spain's gory. If you want to know, that's what Spain is, gory as hell." He paused, then his face lit up. "But I have to hand it to Hemingway. He's writing a preface to a book of Quintanilla's drawings. Marvelous drawings. Wait until you see them."

"Quintanilla?" Joe shook his head. "I'm glad about a show. What a damn shame his other work was destroyed. I read about it. All the big frescoes. And those big murals. Are they really gone?"

Tom nodded sadly. "All gone. Everything, except those drawings. There was a show in Barcelona at Christmas. I was able to get there. It's some war, this shindig in Spain. Everything goes. Frescoes, women, children, even the bloody animals."

Mary had never seen any of Quintanilla's work. "What were the drawings like?" she asked, breaking into their conversation. "Like Goya?"

"No. Not like Goya." Tom turned to her. "Except maybe they're Spanish and terrifying about war, in the same way. Hey," he looked toward Joe, "do you know Mary Barrett?"

At last, thought Mary, a formal introduction! Joe nodded, rather solemnly.

"Mary Barrett." He repeated the name as if it didn't come easily, a foreign tongue. "Mary Barrett."

"Mary, this is Joe Levin, a broken-down old friend of mine."

"Joe Levin." Mary mimicked Joe's solemnity, saying the name slowly as if it were a surprise. Then she smiled. "I know. I asked."

He smiled back, a warm smile that seemed to color his face from forehead to chin. She hadn't expected such an open, all-embracing, illuminated smile. "I asked too," he said. "Mary Barrett."

He stood about a head and a half above her and she had a sense she was scanning his height, taking him all in.

"What are you doing here, Mary Barrett?" he asked.

"Doing here? Why the same thing you are, I guess."

"Not exactly." He turned to Tom. "I'm an old Bolshevik, eh Tom?"

Tom laughed. "City College branch."

"The old school tie," he quipped to Tom as he reached over the bar behind him and poured himself a paper cup of wine. He tasted it and grimaced. "Awful stuff. It should be against the law."

"Are you at City with Tom?" Mary asked.

"Maybe neither of us is," Tom answered. "He was and I

think I still am. I have to test my leave of absence tomorrow. But we were together at one point, weren't we Joe? The same fraternity too." They smiled conspiratorially. Mary knew what they meant.

"Did you teach there?" Mary asked Joe.

"No, that's Tom. I was a student. He was one of the few Irish to forsake the Jebbies for us."

"Not Irish," Tom corrected. "And not the Jesuits. The Christian Brothers. And I'm Deutsch-Hibernian. A New York mix, or should I say mick?"

Then both together, as if on signal, began to sing in low cracked voices to the tune of some familiar school anthem,

"City College by the subway
loud we sing thy cloistered halls
as we're walking down a hundred and thirty-seventh street
where our alma mater calls."

"Oh you're kidding," Mary laughed, "you made that up."

"What do you mean, made that up," said Tom. "It's our song. Traditional. Come on, Joe, full chorus: 'Oh yoi yoi that City College—'" He stopped abruptly, his face suddenly crushed and tired. "God that seems long ago. Gone. Down the hatch."

He looked around, away from Mary and Joe, as if every detail of the room had to be memorized before it, like everything else, disappeared from his view.

It was not a large apartment, just one big room, the top floor of a brownstone. The pale afternoon sun sifted through the long windows, lighting up the fireplace wall with its huge painting by Philip Evergood above the mantel. The painting was a somber street scene, with hungry big-faced children and garbage-strewn stoops. It hung like a banner over the crowd, but nobody looked at it. It was the Depression, that painting. Their Depression, but they were almost out of it, with something else around the corner. The young eager passionate faces had no eyes for yesterday's past, only for one another. They waved their empty paper cups like semaphores as they talked, unwilling to push over to the bar for refills lest they lose their closeness. Tom's eyes searched the dense mass and the Lily cups held high. He looked as if the semaphores were saying something to him, something that frightened and chilled him.

"Hey!" Joe caught Tom's elbow. "This party's for you. Remember? What are you doing in the corner? Come on." He pushed one hand through Tom's bended arm, catching Mary's with the other. "Let's go."

But they did not move. Tom had become rigid. Joe turned to see why. Annette had just come into the room and she stared at them, as Tom stared back. There was no waving, no greeting. The three linked together watched her as she stared. They felt a shared premonition of danger. Abruptly Annette pushed through the crowd to speak to Frank, then she and Frank turned to look toward the corner. Frank's head came close to Annette's, they were whispering. Mary could feel Joe's hand on her elbow pushing her forward, but Tom did not budge, holding them back. He was watching Annette with dreadful anguish on his freckled face. There was some weird signal in the air, some whirring of wings, the beating of drums, the noiseless high pitch of sound outside the hearing range.

Suddenly Annette moved away from Frank and stood before Tom, a fiery light in her eyes.

"What are you doing here, Tom?" she asked in a low menacing voice that carried across the room, penetrating every cortex.

Tom did not answer. The buzz in the room quieted, as if switched off. The talk and the laughter, which had blended into an insistent murmur, ceased, cut short. The buzzing young crowd was like an organism with its own life, delicately balanced in its own pulsating honeycomb. It was as if all the humans there, each so separate, were part of a whole, and the whole was unlike any of its parts. It was its own indivisible hive. When it hummed, the sound was the hum of the whole. Now, stilled, it was total silence, the hive was voiceless.

Tom looked at Annette and did not answer her.

"I said, Tom why are you here?" Annette was tall and gaunt and this minute she had the look of an avenging stone angel standing against the winds of the Great Plains. "I told you this morning you had no right to come. I warned you."

Joe released his hold on the other two and reached out his hand to Annette. "What's this all about, Annette? Who are you to tell Tom not to be here? He's a guest of honor."

She shook off Joe's hand. "Guest of honor! That's a laugh. You should have heard him last night, the dirty bastard. Attacking the party and the Brigade and Spain."

"Annette." Tom reached his hand out to her, trying to touch her arm. "That's not true, Annette. I just raised some questions." He shrugged his shoulders self-mockingly as he spoke. "I guess I'm just an old hack out of Philosophy 32 and Socrates keeps tripping me up. But what's so wrong with questions? Why can't I ask them?"

"Socrates, bullshit!" Annette exploded. "We know where your kind of questions come from. Not from Socrates."

"What's the matter with questions, Annette?" Joe asked, his voice calm and reasonable. He turned to Tom. "What kind of questions, Tom? God almighty, what's this all about?"

Tom turned to him, half in anger, half in sudden determination. "Okay. Questions like why are we fighting everyone who's on our side, for God's sake, instead of Franco?" He raised his voice, he was talking to everyone. "Sure we're all for Spain, but, Christ, what does that mean? This isn't a Communist war. Some of the Loyalists are Socialists and some are Anarchists and some are just plain Spaniards." His voice took on a quiet hard passion. "And if all the Loyalists aren't Communists, neither are all the guys in the Brigade. They're kids, mostly. And some are seamen. And we're all being fed this crap that people like Nin are traitors and that all-purpose word, Trotskyists." Tom sounded angry now. His voice was louder. Some of the parts of the hive were listening, uneasily. "Do you know what it's like in Spain now? You don't know a goddamn thing."

Annette pushed Tom angrily. "Shut up," she screamed. Joe tried to quiet her. "Stay out of this, Joe," she started to say, then shook her head. "No, stay in it. We're all in this." She turned and swept the room with her eyes. "Get this everyone. Tom sent a letter to the *Times* this morning filled with this shit."

There was a gasp, a gasp that rose from them all. They shivered in unison. Annette turned back to Joe. "How do you feel about that, Joe? What do you say now?"

There was a kind of puzzled bewilderment on Joe's white face. He seemed stunned. Frank detached himself from the group and came to stand close to Annette.

"You didn't tell me, Annette." His voice was stern, his black-browed face menacing. "When did you say he wrote the letter?"

"This morning. He told me this morning."

"Why didn't you let me know right away?" he thundered at Annette.

She cringed. "It was too late. He told me he'd already mailed it. I thought I'd tell you here, when I saw you."

He turned from her in a kind of disgust and faced Tom. Frank had taken charge, the chief. He would decide what to do. He stared at Tom. But Tom looked back steadily, his frightened air gone. "Okay," he said, "I shouldn't have come here today. I don't know what the hell I'm doing here. Habit, I guess. Nowhere else to go. I thought I could speak out openly."

"Speak out openly about what?" Frank's voice was magisterial and absolute. "About betraying the Party? About denouncing the Party to the capitalist press?" He said "the Party" in capital letters.

"I didn't denounce the Party. That's a lie. I raised some questions. I'm not the only one." He looked around the room. "Doesn't anyone here want to know what's really going on?"

No one spoke until Joe said quietly, "But a letter to the *Times*, Tom? Who the hell are you kidding?"

"Renegade," Annette screamed, the usual Party invective. "Wrecker!"

Frank took Tom's arm. "You'd better get out of here before I break your neck."

Tom tried to shake off Frank's hand. He looked at Joe.

"That's right, Tom," Joe nodded, his voice low and sad. "You're not a political infant, Tom. You know what you did."

Tom loosed Frank's arm from his sleeve. "Okay. You don't have to break my neck. And don't push. I'm going. And I'm glad. Don't forget I told you so. You're helping Franco win in Spain."

He pushed his way through the crowd, which parted to let him through, and disappeared out the door. No one extended a hand. Not Joe. Not Mary. Not Annette, whose rage seemed untouched by pain in spite of the years of love between her and Tom. It was as if Tom were the hero drummed out of the corps, the pariah, the unclean. In a panic, Mary looked at the solid phalanx in the room, the crystalline netlike honeycomb, and wanted to get back in. She took Joe's arm and pushed him forward. They looked at each other with understanding; they had shared a searing experience. They rejoined the group together.

"Let's go talk to Fran Cohen." Mary tried to speak lightly, "Let's get a drink."

"I have a better idea," Joe said, once they had stood with the group and touched base, "let's get out of here and find something to eat."

· CHAPTER 3 ·

THE air was crisp and fresh as they turned the corner into Irving Place. Above the clock on the Con Ed tower, the sky was pink and gray, the beginning of dusk. The clock face was already lit up against the falling day, and the pyramid capping the square clock tower poked into a puff of white cottony clouds. The street had a sad Sunday look, lonely and vacated, and down its empty length, at the end of it, shone the blinking lights of the Fourteenth Street movie house.

They walked along side by side, untouching, silent. Mary felt shattered. The scene with Tom had unnerved her, prying open her own Pandora's box of doubts. But she was excited too, apprehensive and expectant at the same time. They passed Pete's Tavern and Joe stopped for an instant as if inviting her in. She shook her head. The bar looked noisy and crowded. She wanted to go where they could talk quietly. She wanted to talk to him about Tom. And she wanted to find out about him. She couldn't understand his shifts of thought; first his questions about Spain, then his acceptance of Tom's damnation. As if the questions had nothing to do with the answers. She was perplexed and eager.

They passed Giusti's down the block, and now it was Mary who stopped, nodding approval, but Joe wrinkled his nose at the blast of air from the exhaust fan, spewing vapors of tomato sauce, parmesan cheese, and garlic into the air. They both pulled back from the green-and-white-striped tin awning that stretched out over the door and its bit of sidewalk.

They walked south. They walked slowly, measuring each crack in the pavement, silent, together and alone on that Sunday street, like figures in a landscape. They crossed Irving Place at Seventeenth Street, stopping to look at the Washington Irving house together. They stood in front of the run-down ramshackle house, with its drooping plants on the wrought-iron balcony, the dry-cleaning shop in the basement, the "for rent" sign on the pretty door under its drapery of iron lace, staring at it as if they were seeing it for the first time, sharply aware of one another.

Across from the house was Washington Irving High School, a big flat-faced municipal barracks of a place, with Washington Irving himself in the corner, grimly immortalized in bronze.

Joe said, "I heard Joe Curran there once, after the mutiny"— Joe Curran, the man on the waterfront, the bold dauntless leader of the seamen, whose act of defiant mutiny had swept through the newspaper headlines like a rush of salt air.

"You did?" Mary answered. "I heard him too." There was as much surprise in her voice as if their ships had crossed in the blue Aegean waters and the coincidence was uncanny, prophetic, and revelatory. They walked across Seventeenth Street with a sense of wonder that their paths had intersected and they had not known. Joe took Mary's elbow as they dodged the buses over to Union Square.

The square was filled that afternoon, as it always was, with old men huddled in their heavy overcoats, sprawled over the benches, sitting on the rim of the dry fountain in the center. They were clutching the remnants of the Sunday newspapers, long abandoned by their original purchasers, peering at the crumpled scavenged sheets in the dwindling light. Joe and Mary kicked their way through the tag-ends of the tabloid pages that lay on the paths, flat over the patchy gray grass, fluttering in the light April breeze. The headlines underfoot and propped open along the benches shouted POLICE BIGGIE IN BRONX LOVE NEST and ADOLF GETS BIG JA, all in the same type size.

On the bench, the spread-out papers were in Yiddish. Joe stopped. Mary could recognize the thorny black lettering. She knew that one was the *Freiheit,* the other the *Forward,* because each said so in English at the top. Joe's lips moved as he tried to decipher the headlines and Mary could hear him spelling out the words.

"Can you really read it?" she asked.

"Of course." He shrugged. "But not easily anymore. I'm out of practice."

"Where did you learn?" she asked in admiration.

He laughed. "I didn't have to learn. It came to me with mother's milk."

"Really?"

"Yes, really." He seemed to be laughing at her. "I couldn't speak a word of English until I was four. Learned it in kindergarten."

He turned to look at the men reading the Yiddish newspapers. They looked exactly alike. Brown fedoras pulled low on their foreheads, thin gray faces, shabby tweed overcoats. Only their newspapers differed.

"What do the headlines say?" Mary asked. "Are they about Vienna too?"

Joe sniffed. "They're both about Vienna, but each one blames the other for what's happening. It's a wonder these guys can sit next to each other without cutting one another's throats."

"They might be brothers, they look so alike," Mary said.

"They probably are." As they continued their walk, Joe added, "If they aren't brothers, they probably sit every day side by side at the same cutting-room table, hating each other's guts."

"How do you know? How do you know so much about it?"

"Oh I know," he answered firmly. "The *Forward* and the *Freiheit*. They could be my father and my Uncle Ben, the Commie and the social Fascist. I'm their *landsman,* you know."

Mary stared at Joe. He didn't look like her idea of a *landsman.* He didn't look like her idea of an immigrant Jew, or a member of the Communist party, or a writer on a W.P.A. project.

"What are you staring at, Mary Barrett?" he asked. "You seem nonplussed."

She shook her head at him. "You surprise me, I guess," she admitted. She could hardly tell him how taken she was by his physical beauty or how at odds she found it with the things he was saying.

"Where was the kindergarten where you learned to speak English?" she asked.

"Borough Park, Brooklyn" he answered.

"Where?"

"Borough Park. You get there by subway and mule train. When you arrive, you're in Minsk, Pinsk, and Poltava."

"I never heard of it," she laughed, shaking her head at him.

"A good place to visit."

They had now crossed Union Square and came down the stairs on the west side of the park.

"Come sit," he said and led her to a little niche at the edge, facing the sidewalk. It was an indentation into the square that curved around an ornamental bronze group of a dancing mother and her two children. The old men were drifting out of the park by now, some clutching the sheets of Sunday tabloid, others with hands deep in pockets, lonely silhouettes shuffling along the curb. The golden day was gone and it was almost dark now. A light flared at the street's edge.

There was an empty bench in the niche and Joe sat down, waiting for her to join him. But Mary circled the statuary group, looking for some plaque to explain why it was there. She had crossed the square a hundred times and never noticed it before.

Joe called from the bench where he sat watching her. "It doesn't say anything," he called out. "It just says '1881' and where it was cast, Stuttgart I think. I always stop here to wonder about it."

Mary looked at him curiously, seeing him clearly beneath the streetlight. She was oddly touched by this irrelevant interest in an awful, sentimental, dried-up, dirty Victorian fountain. Yes, it did say "Stuttgart 1881," revealing nothing. But Mary had the feeling it revealed something of Joe.

"Getting hungry?" he called to her as she continued around the base of the fountain. "Where shall we eat?"

"Wherever."

"How about the Jai Alai?"

"Okay. Sounds good."

He left the bench and joined Mary. They stood staring at the bronze together.

"I've never noticed this before. What made you see it?" she asked.

"I notice everything." He put his arms around her shoulders and hugged her playfully. "I noticed you. And I have a head full of odd facts, like bits of string. History fascinates me. So do old fountains and pretty girls. You'll learn that about me."

She looked at him, raising her head against his arm, taking him in. "I know a lot about you already." She laughed. "About Paris, but not why you went there, and City College and your old fraternity. But you don't know a thing about me. Nothing. You haven't even asked."

"I'll find out."

They were silent crossing Fourteenth Street. Mary was always uneasy walking past the black fortress of the Armory, with its medieval crenellated towers and its cavernous entrance. They were on that side of the street. She reached for Joe's arm and nudged him into jaywalking across to the other side. "I hate that place," she said apologetically. "I don't know why."

He simply accepted it, nodding as they continued down Seventh Avenue toward the restaurant. There was a crowd at the bar when they came in and they both saw people they knew and greeted them. But they pushed through to the backroom and chose a table for two in the corner.

The Jai Alai was part of the Spanish fever of the times. There was a feeling of communion with the Loyalists as one ate through the paella valenciana, rich with saffron and clams and mussels and chicken. One swallowed the wafers, the blood and the body with the guava paste and the caramel custard flan in pursuit of absolution. We were here: *they* were there. The food, the tastes, the smells, the Moorish lights, the murals of Basques in black berets playing the jai alai game, were all persistent reminders that there were no lights and no games now in Spain and all suffered for it. It was all very friendly and pleasant, with its undercurrent of painful commitment.

Joe and Mary ordered the paella, and when it arrived in its great round brown earthenware pan and the waiter had gone, Joe finally spoke of what was on both their minds.

"Tom's behavior was reprehensible." His tone had turned tough, canonical. "I can hardly believe it, damn fool. How infantile to go running to the press with his grievances."

Mary was silent for an instant. She debated about arguing with him, but Joe's tone provoked it. "Tom was there. He's been in Spain for eight months. I think that gives him the right to talk about it. Maybe he saw things we don't know about."

Joe shook his head. "It doesn't matter what he saw. War isn't a class in logic. It isn't a constructed syllogism with major and minor premises. It's war, for Christ's sake."

"Perhaps it isn't logic that moves Tom," Mary said. "Perhaps it is a question of ethics."

"Whatever the question, ethics or logic or military strategy, one has no right to run to the press with an exposé. That's what is at issue here. There are appropriate times and acceptable places to ask questions and find answers." He looked furious, suddenly angry with her. "I have questions too. I know you have. I heard you. You know where to ask them."

"No I don't," she said flatly. "I'm not part of the inner circle. Maybe questions are asked and answered there. But I don't think so."

"That's not so." He spoke snappishly. Mary thought she caught the same oracular, didactic tone that she always heard in Frank. "Everything is discussed. There are no questions that can't be asked. Everything is arrived at democratically."

She was going to say, "Oh, come off it," but instead raised her eyebrows and looked at him obliquely. Then he surprised her. He smiled widely, as if to draw her into a private joke they shared.

"I know." He looked at her slyly. "You're saying to yourself that's a lot of bullshit. So what if it is? You still don't run to the newspapers with the so-called inside story."

Mary nodded. Indeed she agreed. The *Times* was the enemy press to her too. She had heard the words the "kept press" since childhood and she knew that even her mother, who was intense in her denunciation of the Stalinists, who had signed petition after petition against the purges in the Soviet Union, would have viewed Tom's action with a frown. It was a fine line her mother knew how to draw between dissident and informer. Mary lacked the same balance.

"Tom may have felt there was no other way for people to learn the truth," she said.

Joe slapped his hand sharply on the table. "What's the truth? That's bourgeois nonsense. The truth is whatever is needed to win this war."

She tried to protest mildly. "Don't you believe in plain and simple truth? Objective truth? George Orwell reported last month that there were three thousand political prisoners behind the Loyalist lines. What about that? Isn't that true?"

Joe's voice and face were sardonic, almost contemptuous. "Plain and simple truth! Surely you're too educated to accept that sophistry. True? How do I know? How do you know? It's George Orwell's word against the revolutionary front in Spain. What's more important? His word, his truth, or the people's will?"

This was the kind of double-talk that made Mary flinch; the irrational rhetoric that rolled off the tongue like a figure of speech. You couldn't take it apart. It was like a French idiom. Break down the words and it didn't make sense. You had to take it as a whole, or leave it.

"Truth can be verified." She was stubborn. "And what is the people's will you talk about? To win against Franco? Or to win control of the Loyalist side?"

They eyed one another guardedly, across the table. They understood the partisan phrases, the inner syntax. They were trying each other out. He was saying you cannot, must not, criticize the Party, whatever the evidence. She was saying the evidence proves the need to criticize. But neither was saying anything so simple and direct. She itched to move from the partisan to the personal, but for this moment Tom was apparently on Joe's mind. She felt he was more disturbed than he dared admit. Tom was his friend. What did a man do about a friend who had turned pariah?

She sighed. "It's a pity Tom went to Spain at all. I was there the night he decided to go. I don't think he wanted to. He's a sweet, good, thoughtful man. He's no warrior. He's not really full of piss and vinegar."

Joe laughed. It lightened the moment. "Where are you from? Piss and vinegar! I never heard that one before."

"Great Barrington, Massachusetts," she laughed back, "where we say it all the time."

"Why shouldn't Tom have gone? Every man worth his salt is a warrior."

"What bombast. You don't believe that, do you?"

"Sure I believe it. I almost went. I almost joined when I was in Paris, dozens of my friends there went. I may still go. It all depends."

"On what? Why?"

"Because Spain is the testing ground. The Fascists are trying out all their weapons there and their new techniques. Whatever we do to stop them may finally save the world."

"Aren't there other ways to stop them?" Mary was intense, forgetting as she spoke that she really didn't want to oppose him. She wanted him to like her. She didn't want to argue. That wasn't the game. She lowered her eyes to her paella. "When did war ever settle anything?" she asked meekly.

He looked at her impatiently. "That's nonsense. And anyway this is a civil war. Don't you believe in resistance? What are you, a mouse?"

She flushed. She felt a rush of anger toward him even as she silenced herself. "I'm confused," she said, her eyes still downcast.

He threw his head back and laughed. "You need to be clarified, comrade."

She laughed too. They both understood. She raised her eyes and looked at him directly and he at her and they laughed together now, sharing the joke.

The waiter came with the check and Joe reached to pay.

"Let me split this with you," Mary said, diving for her purse on the floor next to the chair. Joe waved her aside.

"No, let me take you, our first time together."

She liked the sound of that. If this was the first time, it indicated there would be others. She nodded in agreement.

When they strolled out into the night, Joe asked where she lived.

"Oh, it's not far, on Fourteenth Street. But you don't have to bother."

"On Fourteenth where?"

"Between Seventh and Eighth. But really it's not far."

He took her arm and headed her north. "Are you always so independent?" he asked.

"Always."

"I like that." He looked down at her. "I like you too. I like the way you look. I don't agree with you but I like you."

"I don't agree with you either but thank you anyway," she murmured. The same apprehension, the same expectancy that she had felt earlier, now frightened her. She was twenty-four years old, hardly innocent, but fearful. She had never been in love before, wildly, completely, shatteringly. She wasn't sure she wanted to be. She wondered how she was going to avoid it. And she wanted desperately to have it happen.

The beautiful spring day had turned into a soft, lovely, balmy night. The streets were filled with people, although it was past ten. An evening like this brought everyone out for the last stroll of the weekend. It was one of the things Mary loved especially about New York, these lively nighttime streets. There were some boys and girls running around Abingdon Square as they passed, playing a kind of rough touch tag. There were some on roller skates and their cries rang out clearly as they swooped around. Joe and Mary stopped as if to watch them, but stopping really to prolong the moment.

"Mary Barrett," Joe said softly, as they stood there. "Mary Barrett. I'm trying to find you underneath that name."

Two boys came clattering against them on their skates and separated them. It was good-humored and happy, and when they untangled themselves from the skaters, they continued to walk holding hands.

"What are you doing here in New York?" he asked.

"I'm at the Art Students League. I go at night. I've gotten on the Arts Project. I'm a painter, a would-be painter, an artist."

"Are you any good?"

"I haven't the faintest idea. But I want to be. What else do you want to know?"

He drew her close to his side as they turned into Fourteenth Street. "I'll think of things. Right now, this is enough."

"What about you? What were you doing in Paris?"

"Paris? What was I doing there?" For a moment he became tight and distracted, disappearing into his own mood. "I was doing a lot of things."

"Were you there long?"

"Two years."

"How tremendous. What was it like? I've never been. Is it different from here?"

He laughed and nodded. "Very different. Here everyone wants to know your connection, where you're working, are you writing or painting, what are your politics. In Paris, first they talk of him and her, me and you, who loves who, are *we* going to be *us*? It's all very personal there."

"Is that why you went? In search of the personal?"

"I went there to go to medical school," he said abruptly, as if he suddenly didn't want to speak of it.

"To medical school?" she asked, surprised. "Why Paris?"

"Didn't you know? That's where all nice Jewish boys go for medical school. Jews and Italians and other assorted creeps, not good enough for the Anglo-Saxon schools here."

He now sounded amused, not bitter; quite offhand about it, as if the joke were on someone else. "Anyway, I'm glad I did," he continued. "I learned a lot. One thing I learned is that I don't want to be a doctor. A nice Jewish doctor. Not on your life."

There was a noisy crowd across the street next to the building where Mary lived. As they came toward it, they could see the soapbox in front of the *iglesia catolica,* the Spanish-American Roman Catholic church in the middle of the block. The man on the soapbox was shouting, his rapid-fire Spanish picked up by those in the crowd who echoed him.

"*Si,*" they shouted. "*Viva Franco. Guerra sin cuartel.*"

"What the hell," Joe said. "Do you always have this going on in front of your house?"

"The local rebels," said Mary. "There are a lot of Spaniards around here and they take sides." She waved to the Spanish grocery across the street and the restaurant above it. "I think they're Loyalists over there, but it's hard to tell. I prefer to think so. I shop there. But here, the iglesia is definitely Franco."

"Naturally. I'm glad you don't shop there."

They stood balancing on the curb. Joe was curious, he wanted to listen. Mary touched his sleeve and tried to pull him away. She had seen these meetings turn nasty. Suddenly, they spotted Tom Feurlich at the soapbox trying to push the speaker off his perch. He was shouting Loyalist slogans. He looked drunk, mad, wild-eyed. A streetlight lit up the scramble as a number of men jumped on Tom, holding him back, then knocking him down.

"What the hell!" Joe said. "That's Tom Feurlich. What a horse's ass, trying to break up this meeting alone."

Tom was on the ground, then pushed himself up again, swinging and lashing out in a frenzy. But there were too many against him. Someone was battering Tom's head against the soapbox as the crowd roared, cursing Tom and applauding each time his head cracked the box. Once again Tom managed to free himself, his face bleeding, the sleeve of his jacket torn off, the shirt collar ripped open.

Mary took Joe's arm and clung to it fiercely. She stood there horrified, calling, "For God's sake, Tom, come out of there. Don't fight. Come on."

Then she realized that Joe had pulled away from her grip and left her alone at the curb. He was next to Tom, trying to tear him away from the angry Spaniards, joining in the fight. Someone punched Joe's face and he tried to punch back while pulling at Tom, lifting him to his feet. The two of them were surrounded by a swirling mass of fists and kicking feet. Mary screamed at them both, "Come out, you fools. Joe, Tom, get out of there." The sound of a police whistle stopped the fight. By the time the policeman had crossed over to the crowd, all that was left of the melee was the speaker on the stand and Tom and Joe.

"What's going on here," he said, swinging his stick. "What's the beef?"

The speaker, a young small man in an open-throated white shirt with a smooth clean face like a bank clerk, broke into incomprehensible Spanish, angry and indignant as he pointed at Tom and then Joe.

"Okay, okay," said the officer. "No capeesh. What's this all about?" He turned to the others.

"Nothing officer," said Joe. "Just a little political argument. Just talking. That's all."

The officer lifted his eyebrows as he took in the bloody faces and the torn clothes. "Politics?" He decided to accept it. "Okay. Keep moving, all of you, or I'll run you in."

The young Spaniard had gotten off the soapbox and disappeared with it into the church. Tom, Joe, and Mary were left standing.

"I live here, officer." Mary pointed to the building next to the church. "Right here. We're on our way."

"Get going. Off the street," he said and, with a lordly disdain, still swinging his club, continued his walk across Fourteenth.

They walked over to the entrance of the building in which Mary lived on the third floor. She stopped and turned to look at the two men. They were both a mess.

"Come on up. You can wash upstairs," she said, her voice tired and dejected, hating the way the evening had turned out. She reached for her key.

Tom stood there, hesitant. "No thanks, Mary. I'll get back to my place somehow." He had looked reckless and drunk under the street light when he tried to break up the meeting. Now he looked bewildered and sheepish.

"Thanks, Joe," he managed to say through swollen lips. "That was a dumb thing, trying to take them on alone."

Joe answered Tom as if he were a stupid child, needing a reprimand. "What in hell were you trying to prove, for God's sake."

Tom slumped. "Nothing. Not a goddamn thing. But thanks anyway, Joe, for sticking your neck out." He hesitated. "I'll be seeing you around."

Joe held his hand out and they shook. Tom tried to laugh. "I guess we're both a couple of premature anti-Fascists."

"The worst kind," Joe said as Tom turned and walked away toward Eighth Avenue, the torn sleeve of his jacket flapping at his side.

Mary looked at Joe as she opened the downstairs door for him. Both his eyes were bruised. His jaw was starting to swell. She took him by the hand and led him up the stairs.

What a way to begin, she thought. Piss and vinegar, Joe.

· CHAPTER 4 ·

WHEN Joe took Mary to
meet his parents, she was four months pregnant. There was a
minimal bulge up front, a slight thickening of the waist, but
no other visible sign except to the sharpest, most suspicious eye.
There was no eye sharper nor more suspicious than Hester's.
Hester was Joe's mother, and in addition to that quick eye, she
had a sharp tongue and a tough, sentimental Jewish heart.
Hester's children knew that she would give them the shirt off
her back but she would skin them alive first. Fair exchange.

When Mary first met Hester, she thought she was the one
Hester was out to get. She quickly learned it was everyone
close. Strangers and *landsmen* won good words and smiles every
time. Hester was a charmer to them. She loved feeling popular.
For Mary, for Joe, for Joe's father, Sam, and for the others in
the family, there was a more honest simplicity: she hated what
she loved. She had a fierce protectiveness of her own and a
profound anger toward them all. Were they not the cause of
all her frustrations? The despoilers? The vandals? They were
the ones, she said, who sucked her dry, made her heart hurt
with worrying, tore her to pieces like wolves. She had all sorts
of extravagant phrases for what was being done to her by her
nearest and dearest.

Hester took one look at Mary and said, her tone dulcet and

deceitful as it always was when she didn't mean what she said, "So this is your girl. A nice girl, Joe. I am very pleased to make your acquaintance, miss. Come in, come in, come sit down. Such a surprise for Joe to bring his friends. I'm so happy. Sit down. A piece of cake? Tea?" She eyed Mary vigilantly as she steered her through the narrow entrance of the apartment and into the living room.

The four rooms of the apartment were directly above the Levins' little grocery store, in which both mother and father worked. The building itself was only three stories high, a narrow yellow-brick building like its neighbors up and down the avenue in Borough Park, giving the neighborhood the look of a small-town main street. As they walked from the subway station, Mary had had the feeling of Pittsfield in Massachusetts, frowsy friendly Pittsfield.

The Levins owned the building—which was not as prosperous as it sounded, since there was a large mortgage at high interest, a constant source of worry. Some years earlier they had risen from Sam's job slaving as a baster in a clothing shop to a store of their own. Above their flat, on the third floor, they had a tenant, a man and his wife and three children, and the patter of their feet and the turmoil of their lives was an accompaniment to whatever went on below.

This first time, Sam stood waiting to greet them as Mary was ceremoniously welcomed into the living room.

"Hello, Pa." Joe put his arms around his father's narrow shoulders and hugged him. "I want you to meet a friend of mine, Mary Barrett, a good friend."

"So where's a kiss for me?" Hester interjected, in a bright high playful voice. "Him he kisses."

"Hello, son," Sam said quietly. "I'm glad to see you and your friend." He put his hand out to Mary and they shook, eyeing each other. He was not as tall as Joe and his shoulders were rounded under his dark brown sweater. He had an ingrown look, his black-brown eyes as dark as Joe's, his grizzled brown hair thick and curly and cut in a brush around his round head. Mary liked his look at once. She liked Hester's too. In the light of the living room, she could see that Hester's hair had been bleached to a golden red that gave a shrill beauty to her pink face with its bright blue eyes and dimpled chin. There were pits ingrained in the plump flesh across the broad bulge of her nose, signs of an early smallpox, now like soft hollows in a down pillow. She twinkled against Sam's sturdy brownishness.

Both Hester and Sam spoke English with a Brooklyn Jewish accent. Though Hester's command of the language was more certain than Sam's, it was also more inaccurate, more peppered with the kind of twists and turns that Jewish comedians liked to mimic. It didn't matter. Hester always managed to say what she wanted to. Once Joe admitted to Mary that his mother's massacre of the language embarrassed him and made him cringe.

"But why?" she challenged him. "Language is supposed to communicate. And that's exactly what your mother does. She comes across. Even when she wants to be devious, she is."

It was easy enough for Mary to be tolerant and generous about the fractured speech. It became easier for Joe, too; after this admission they could laugh about it together. But it surprised Mary that Joe, who seemed so self-confident and quietly staunch about himself, should be so touchy and thin-skinned about his mother's paraphrases and mispronunciations.

Hester's bright blue eyes were fixed on Mary's thickened middle as she led her to the green velour upholstered armchair with its three hand-crocheted doilies; one for the head, the other two laid carefully across each bulging arm of the chair. Behind those eyes was immediate recognition of Mary's state.

Oh hell, Mary thought. I should have worn a girdle, no

matter how sick it makes me feel. But it was too late. She flushed and was annoyed that she had come with Joe at all.

"We're going to get married," Joe had said. "We might as well get the family part over with. Don't you think?"

"Eventually." Mary had hesitated. "I suppose so."

"So why not now," Joe had pressed. "The whole thing. Let's get it over with. Marriage, family, why not?"

When Joe pressed, it was Mary who pulled back. Then he forgot and it was her turn to press while he pulled away. "Marry me, marry me," he would chant in the shower. "Throw me a clean towel and marry me."

She would laugh and ask why. But then it would be her turn. "Marry me, marry me, make me an honest woman and your bride."

"Next week, on Thursday, is two o'clock all right?"

But they never seemed to get there, to City Hall, on any Thursday. Mary had met Joe's family and Joe had come to meet hers and Emily was born before they did go down and do it legally and that only because Joe was going to war and it was necessary to have the proper papers for the allotment. They hedged it by letting everyone assume they were married, including the hospital authorities for Emily's birth certificate. It pleased them, this deception. There was no reason for it except it gave them a vague sense that they were outwitting the bourgeoisie, a little in the spirit of the dear old Monsieur and Madame Poupin in *The Princess Casamassima,* they told one another. Mary, who had a habit of literary references, would insist, "That suits me fine. Let me be yours in Madame Poupin's way, in a spiritual affectional sense."

Mary tried to evade Hester's bright eyes as she sat drinking tea and eating the delicious honey cake this Sabbath Saturday. She turned her head to look around the room, with its doilies and beaded lamps and stiffly blooming paper-flower bouquets.

How odd that Joe's elegance should spring out of such a cramped, sullen room, she thought. But Mary didn't feel out of place or on alien ground. She had seen the room's like before. Sophie, her close friend at Vassar—brilliant, cultivated, as passionate about ideas as she was about her person, decking herself out with enviable chic in contrast to the world of little pearl pins and cashmere sweaters—Sophie had invited Mary to her home one Easter holiday, and home had been a long narrow flat over her parents' bakery shop on Joseph Avenue in Rochester, New York. There, surrounded by sons and daughters almost as beautiful and dazzling as Sophie, the father and mother shared in the animated conversation around the Passover table in the same broken English as Sam and Hester.

Something that Sophie had once said about differentiations, about social levels, flashed through Mary's mind now. "My parents," Sophie had said, her eyes crinkling in amusement, "are on the lowest rung of the radical greenhorn scale, if you can believe it."

Mary scoffed at her. "What do you mean?"

"Well," she tried to explain. "They belong to the Workmen's Circle, where everybody speaks Yiddish. At the Labor Lyceum, over on St. Paul's Street, they aren't quite so backward. I remember going to the Lyceum once, it was a Socialist party rally, and being overwhelmed with shame because the little girls there—about eight or nine years old, my age—wore short-sleeved dresses and knee socks with no winter underwear showing. My long-sleeved woollen undershirt that went down to my wrists and my long underpants, folded at the ankles to fit under my stockings, made great lumps, so obvious, so uncouth, so *immigrant,* that I could have died of shame. I knew at once. They were a cut above me. Oh well." Sophie had shrugged and laughed. "I figured it out then and there. No one would ever be a cut above me again."

Had Joe figured it out too? No one would ever be a cut above him? Yet he looked at home here. Mary glanced across the room and caught his eye. He smiled, and the smile enveloped her in him and in this place. She felt her heart pump furiously. She was mad about him. Wherever he was, that was her place too. She smiled back.

"So what are you doing, son?" Sam spoke cautiously, not wanting to pry, but asking out of concern.

"I'm going to a new job, Pa. Next week. In private industry." That phrase was the current shorthand for saying the job was not on the government projects, it had nothing to do with home relief. "It's a good job, Pa. A lot of money."

Sam raised his rounded shoulders. "A lot of money is good. But better still if it's a job you want."

"So what's a lot of money, son?" Hester asked, raising her voice coyly. She liked to flirt and play little games with her voice and her eyes. "A lot of money by you could be a fortune by me."

Joe was momentarily annoyed by her direct question, then he laughed. "Listen, Ma, you never ask someone exactly what he makes, but I'll tell you."

"So why shouldn't I ask exactly? It's not so private. So how much?"

Joe smiled shyly. He knew they would be stunned and pleased. Indeed, he had himself been stunned and pleased when he had gotten the job and learned the salary.

"Seventy-five dollars," he now said, casually, his tone even.

"Seventy-five dollars?" Sam asked, his voice rising in astonishment. "Seventy-five dollars a *week*?"

"Yes, Pa. Seventy-five a week."

"It's a fortune," Hester said, leaning back against the rungs of the chair, shaking her head, rolling her blue eyes to the ceiling. "It's a real fortune. Good luck, my son. Should I be happy for you?"

Sam shook his head in wonderment. "What a salary! It's wonderful. What kind of job is it, something writing, something else?"

"It's for a newspaper syndicate, Pa."

"A newspaper syndicate?"

"That's a place where a lot of writers sell their work and we resell it to newspapers all over the country." Joe's voice was patient, the tone his tempered one, the one that was always there for his father. "I'm going to be the managing editor, that's the man in the middle, sort of."

"A newspaper syndicate?" Sam shook his head, trying to understand. "It's like wholesale, yes?"

"Exactly, Pa. Exactly."

"And you're the management editor?" asked Hester. "The boss?"

She turned to look at Mary as she said this, as if to say, see, aha, what you caught, young lady.

"No, Ma, not the boss. The managing editor." His voice, when he spoke to his mother, always had a slight edge of irritation to it, like the rust on a knife. "I work for the boss. A Mr. Walden."

"You have a boss?" There was a note of disappointment in Hester's voice.

"Yes, Ma. He's the one who hired me."

"A nice man?" Hester pressed. She wanted to emphasize every bit of Joe's luck, to underscore it for Mary, and for herself.

"Well, not really, Ma. He's really a bastard." Hester waved a protest at the word. "He's not only a bastard. I think he's a Fascist. But we'll see. We shall see."

Sam frowned at the word "Fascist." He narrowed his eyes.

The word worried him. "I hope it's a good job. Nothing wrong."

"Oh no, Pa. Nothing wrong. It's a well-known place. The Acme Press. It's just that this guy is a Fascist personally, that's what I think. That's what some people say. But what do I know? That word gets thrown around a lot. I shouldn't have used it. It doesn't always mean what it says."

Sam nodded. He loved what he called serious discussions. "Nowadays, words. Who knows about words? Last week some customers by me in the store, they said that the fellow Chamberlain, the one from London, was a Fascist. They said he made a good deal for the Fascists when he went to Munich. But who knows?" Then he added in Yiddish, smiling roguishly, "Everyone hits that word over the head, it's like beating a kettle." He waved his hand at Mary to sweep her into his little joke and Joe translated for her.

It was Joe's turn to be serious. "I don't know about Munich, Pa. I think the English and the French should have been stronger with Hitler. Chamberlain acted like an old woman. I think he should have been stronger."

Sam's voice was gentle but firm and as he grew impassioned, his English and Yiddish melding: "What do you mean, stronger? Stronger? Stronger could bring a war. Who wants a war? That Englishman, dressed up like a *shmendrik,* he's an aristocrat, he's not for me, but old woman, or Fascist? No, a Fascist he's not."

"Shmendrik?" Mary asked.

"Nincompoop, I think." Joe translated, a bit in doubt. "Some of these Yiddish words are untwistable. I know what it feels like, though. A dressed-up dope." He turned back to his father.

"But what about the Jews in Germany, Pa? Anyone that gives in to Hitler hurts the Jews."

Sam snapped back flatly. "War is never good for the ordinary

Jews. The rich make money, the poor suffer. Everybody. And the Jews the worst. I don't believe in war. How can it help the Jews in Germany? It will make that crazy Hitler even crazier."

"It's only putting off the inevitable," Joe said. "It has to come."

"They call it peace in our time. Maybe it is."

"Oh come on, Pa. Peace in our time! That's for the birds. It's for the Nazis. It's the postponement they want."

"So it's a postponement. Let them put it off. Who knows, you put it off long enough, maybe it won't happen. I'm not for war. Never."

Joe retreated. He wanted no argument. He shrugged. "Maybe you're right, Pa. Maybe you're right."

Hester took advantage of the lull to swing the conversation around to Mary. "And what do you do, miss?" she asked, purring. "What kind of job?"

"I'm on the project," Mary answered, "the Arts Project, on the W.P.A." Then, to deflect Hester's questions, she added, "This cake is wonderful," nibbling at the delicious honey-soaked piece with its slivers of almond, hoping it would stay down. She was having a good deal of trouble with nausea, had been plagued by it since the first days of pregnancy, and hoped she would have no accident here.

"Project?" Hester's voice rose in disapproval, then responded to the compliment on the cake, "Good, good, have more. The project?" Now that Joe was no longer on it, she could sniff at it. "That's nice. What do you do there?"

"I'm an artist. An illustrator. When I came to New York, I had a job on a magazine, but I lost it. That's how I got on the project."

"Mary wants to paint, Ma," Joe added slowly, in an offhand way, as if it didn't matter, shouldn't matter to Hester.

Hester looked unfriendly. The words "artist," "painter," "illustrator" disturbed her. Better if this strange, obviously pregnant girl had been a schoolteacher, like one of Joe's sisters, or a social worker, like the other. Someone more sustaining for Joe. Joe's decision to give up his medical studies had been a cruel disappointment to his parents. They had argued and cried and still hoped that he would turn around and go back. At the least they wanted a wife for Joe who could further his ambitions—or their ambitions for him. Certainly not a wife who was an artist! An illustrator! A vague nothing.

Hester's scrutiny of Mary was malevolent. The mother could see that Mary was more than casual in the life of Joe. She didn't need special antennae. Mary's burgeoning presence announced it. And Mary knew that Hester disapproved. She wasn't a "somebody" for their youngest son, their darling, the "baby."

Wait until she finds out I'm a shikse, Mary thought with a kind of mischievious inner glee, she'll explode.

The key questions did come quickly. "Your parents, they're born here?" Hester asked. "*Amerikaner?*"

Mary nodded. Hester smiled. "Not greenhorns, like us, no?" Mary nodded again. "And your grandparents? From where?" Mary mumbled that they too had been born here. Hester lifted her eyes in surprise. "German Jews?" she asked. "You're from German Jews?" Hester could not conceive of any third- or fourth-generation Americans who were not originally German Jews.

Mary was silent for an instant and then plunged in, since Joe remained aloof from explanations. "No, Mrs. Levin. I'm not from a German Jewish family." Hester looked relieved, then astounded, when Mary added, "My parents aren't Jewish. They're Congregationalists," she stumbled on, then paraphrased, "Protestants"—avoiding the word "Christian," which was easy enough for her to do since she almost never used it.

Hester looked overwhelmed, unbelieving, her blue eyes wide with wonderment. "Gentile?" she asked with a rising inflection. "You're not a Jewish girl? You're a Gentile?"

Hester looked at Joe in bewilderment, but his face revealed nothing. He felt he owed no accounting and didn't intend to give one. Hester looked at Sam and it was clear that both were distressed. For a moment Mary was angry at their insularity, their parochial obsessions, and then she smiled tentatively. "It's not so bad, Mrs. Levin, Mr. Levin." She looked at each of them solemnly. "It's not so different."

Hester shook her head, disarmed for an instant by Mary's calculated disingenuousness. But Hester was deeply affected, not lightly put off.

"Not so different! How can you say?" she spoke in surprise, in disbelief. "I never thought I'd have a Gentile in my house. I don't know *goyishe*. I never had a Gentile in my house."

Mary's earlier moment of malicious glee was gone. She put down her cake and the teacup and wondered vaguely if she should feel offended. She didn't know what to feel. This was obviously so narrow-minded and prejudiced, she told herself, that she would have to deal with it cautiously. She didn't want to get up and leave in a rage. She wanted to win Hester over. She turned to Sam. He had such a gentle face, a wide forehead, heavy jowls, a strong firm chin that gave no indication of his essential weakness of spirit, his disenchantment with the struggle, any struggle, with life. Mary was to learn that Sam loved to "discuss." His energies stopped there.

"But I know you're not religious," she said to him. "Joe tells me you don't go to synagogue or anything like that."

"Synagogue!" Sam threw out the word contemptuously. "No we don't go, that's for sure. That's for fakers. Fairy tales." He stopped, shook his head slowly, profoundly troubled. "But we're

Jews. We don't go to synagogue, but we're still Jews. For us that's enough."

"But Mr. Levin. I don't understand. If you're not religious and I'm not religious, what difference does it make?"

He seemed baffled. Hester broke in.

"We don't know goyishe. That's enough. What's to understand. It don't mix."

Sam and Hester both looked fierce and adamant. Joe looked at them quietly and then spoke, his voice laying down the law.

"Listen, Ma, Pa. Mary and I," he lied, "are married. So it doesn't matter who's a Jew and who isn't. And we're going to have a baby."

Hester nodded at this, as if to say, "Of course, see?" But she was profoundly shocked. "What would your buba have said? God in heaven, it would have killed her."

"Buba is dead, Ma. So it doesn't matter what she would have said." Joe tried to keep his voice from rising.

"She would have slammed the door in your face. You couldn't set foot in her house," Hester persisted, her voice shrill.

Sam stopped her, raising his shoulders high to make his point. "So it's a good thing, Ma, she isn't alive to know it."

"Thank God," Hester snapped, raising her reddened eyes to heaven. "*Gott tsu danken!*"

Joe tried to sound jolly, while Mary sat silent, biting her tongue, ready to lash out. "Hold it Mary," he reached over to kiss her, then turned to his parents. "Let's all have a drink to the new baby, your grandchild, Ma and Pa." He smiled at them. "Bring out a little schnapps, Pa, and let's drink to it. Okay?"

The surface tension was not quite broken. Sam and Hester didn't know what to do. They both looked as if they might cry. But marriage, a baby, these were incontrovertible realities. And that oncoming baby forged an immediate family tie. So they made the best of it. They drank the schnapps and Hester put her arm around Mary and hugged her and Sam kissed her on the cheek. They were gallant about it, gallant and uneasy.

It took many years to wipe out the unease, the wariness; it took love on everyone's part. Mary remained the family oddity, the shikse daughter-in-law, the outsider. But she was also the one to whom Hester confided her troubles, her miseries, her heartaches at the perfidy of her children and friends. She would wail to her daughter-in-law that others grew rich; if only Sam were more of a man. Her constant complaint was, if only he would listen to *her.* So many opportunities had passed them by, which she had seen, which she had pointed out, but he—he was too spineless to go where she pointed. When Mary asked her why she hadn't acted on her own business acumen, she looked astonished. "A woman? I'm only a woman," Hester responded bitterly. "A woman is good for nothing."

Mary didn't agree with Hester half the time but she listened and comforted her and Hester learned to call her "her Malke, her harz, her jewel." Even when the going between Mary and Joe became rough and bitter, Sam and Hester were Mary's family and she loved them for it. She knew that Hester took a kind of pleasure in her misery, but Mary felt she would have done so if Mary were her own daughter—it was Hester's pleasure in her misery that cemented Mary into the family.

After the schnapps and the toasts, Sam and Hester asked about Mary's parents. Where did they live? They were looking for some common ground. Was there a way to blank out the dreadful reality of intermarriage? Hester, somewhat warmed by the schnapps, finally managed to say as a general comfort, "At least, Joe, you didn't bring home an *italianishe.*"

"So your father?" Sam asked. "What does he do?"

"He's a doctor, Mr. Levin. A baby doctor. A pediatrician. He's a nice man. You'll like him."

"A doctor?" Hester's voice rose in approval. This was something she understood and could take pride in. It took some of the sting out. "A baby doctor? Now you'll be able to get it for nothing, yes?"

Sam was delighted. He smiled warmly at Mary. Joe caught the look and was grateful. He leaned over Mary in the large green velour armchair and kissed the top of her head lightly.

"She's a nice girl," Sam said. "I think you have a nice girl." It didn't sound the least bit begrudging.

"I know, Pa."

"No," said Hester, "so why not? He's a nice boy." She leaned up to kiss him as he had kissed Mary and a look of pain crossed her face as he pulled away. She was so eager to touch him, to grasp him, and yet was aware that for some reason he withdrew out of her reach. Mary had heard the standard jokes about "Jewish mothers," mothers overconcerned, overpossessive, overurgent. Not so Hester. Hester had a delicate touch with Joe, making her own courteous withdrawal from him because he pulled back from her. But sometimes she felt moved to bridge the gap, doing so spontaneously: kissing him, then retreating; touching and running; playing coy but only in word and gesture, never shoving, never clutching. Joe's physical warmth was for his father and sometimes there was a rueful look of hunger on Hester's face as Joe enveloped Sam in a hug or kiss.

As Mary and Joe took their way back to the BMT that evening, she argued with him about the lie to his parents about their marriage.

"What difference does it make?" Joe answered. "It simplifies matters. I'm always simplifying matters with them. My politics, which they loathe. They can't stand the idea that I'm a Communist; my father calls me a Stalinist, he has a bone-deep hatred of the Soviet Union. They can't understand my life. I try not to argue with them. I try not to explain. Doesn't it simplify matters to tell them that we're a fait accompli?"

Mary had to concede it did. It closed discussion. Now no one could really raise hell, or make contradictory demands about how and where and with what kind of ceremony a future marriage should take place. And having established the ploy, they used it the following weekend when they went up to Massachusetts to see Mary's father and mother with the same news.

· CHAPTER 5 ·

THEY took the train to Great Barrington, bumping along the line up through Connecticut. When they reached New Milford, with the first views of the broad and lovely Housatonic River, Mary said, "It's so like a Constable painting." As the river widened under the arched and awkward bridge, she had the recurring sense of excitement that she was nearing home. It was up the river, around the bend, over the state line, home.

"We're almost there," she said, catching his arm and pointing to the curve of the river. "Look. Isn't it beautiful? See the willows along the banks and the way the green meadow swoops down? I love this country. Next there's Canaan and then we're there."

Joe caught her hand and squeezed it in his own, quick to her rush of sentiment. "How do you feel?" he asked, leaning toward her. "Are you making it?"

"Terrible," she admitted. "I just hope I can keep it down." The constant nausea, always close to the surface, was prodded by the train's coal-smoke smell, the dust of the brown plush seats, the strong whiff of carbolic from the car's lavatory nearby. They had chosen seats carefully in case of the emergency she had learned to expect. When the train pulled into the New

Milford station, she got up and stood at the open door, breathing deeply, gulping the clean air. Joe stood with her.

"I hope you like them." Mary reached up and kissed his chin, inhaling deeply the smell of his skin, which she loved and which offset the disturbing sickening odors of the outside world. "Like them!" she commanded. "I order you."

He laughed as they went back to their seats. "Okay, ma'am. I'll like them. If they like me. That always helps."

Mary looked at him steadily and he at her. There was a tremor between them, a slight vibration of tension. Mary felt she had stretched herself for his parents. She hoped he would for hers. But she wondered why they were extending themselves at all. Why were they taking their private lives to their parents, first in Brooklyn, now in Massachusetts? Why were they moving outside their own place, their own bed, their single-minded fierceness for one another in an act of tradition they both thought they scorned? They had started living together so naturally, so inevitably, without plans and considerations, yet here they were going through formalities like a couple of dutiful children.

"We're a hell of a pair of free lovers," she murmured to him. "I might just as well be bar mitzvahed."

"Girls don't get bar mitzvahed," he said dryly. "And free love went out with the narodniki."

"So whatever you call it," she snapped back. "And remember, don't argue politics."

Joe pushed his copy of *The Sunday Worker* into the side of the train seat and grinned. "Politics? Never heard of them. I'm an innocent intellectual from the wrong side of the railroad tracks. Wait and see."

There was a crowd at the Great Barrington station but it was going the other way: the Sunday exodus after Saturday night. Tanglewood and its concerts had put Great Barrington on the map with New Yorkers. Now, even in early October, with the great wooden music shed only a memory of summer, it seemed as if all New York was there, dark-browed, rushing, tempestuous. The townspeople loved the money that came in with these crowds, hated the bearers. They even begrudged the New Yorkers the golden autumn foliage they traveled so many hours to see.

As Joe and Mary came through the hurly-burly, Mary saw her mother in front of the Dodge outside the station. She was suddenly conscious of how well turned out her mother looked; little wrist-length beige pigskin gloves, pale beige cardigan sweater, white silk blouse with its little touch of embroidery at the ends of the collar, beige wool skirt, neatly unwrinkled.

She looks like such a D.A.R. lady, Mary thought with quick dismay and wanted to cry out to Joe, "But she isn't, don't trust appearances." She felt as if she wanted to protect them both, her mother and Joe. You'll never know, Joe, until you find out, she said to herself, what steel she is, what good clean steel. They were face to face, Mary embraced her mother, kissing her forehead and dodging her lipstick.

"So nice to see you, Mary." Mrs. Barrett's voice was clipped and high-pitched. So damn educated, flashed through Mary's mind. "And this must be your friend Joe that you told me you were bringing out." She turned to shake his hand, briskly, brightly. "Welcome, Joe. How good of you to come."

All the nice little niceties. All properly said. Mary wondered how her mother would take their pronouncement later, when they had their chance to make it. She'll take it well, Mary thought. Mother will take it well. She's a tough old babe.

That was a description of her mother she had picked up from her grandfather, who had been proud of his spunky daughter. Her grandfather had been the minister in town and it had fallen to Mary's mother to carry forward the banner of his beliefs. She had been a passionate suffragette, picketing the White House for the women's vote even as a high-school senior. Then a passionate follower of Eugene Victor Debs, supporting his pacifism during the war, clamoring against his imprisonment later, campaigning for him up and down New England when he ran for President of the United States beneath a banner that showed the candidate in prison uniform behind prison bars. Mary had heard the stories many times and remembered Debs himself as a guest in the house when he came to make a speech in Pittsfield, after Warren Harding had freed him from jail. Nowadays Norman Thomas was the house guest when he came to speak, and both her mother and father were his enthusiastic supporters.

Mary turned to look at Joe in the backseat of the sedan. She smiled. "Isn't it pretty through here?" They were on a narrow little road heading toward New Marlborough.

Joe nodded. "Very pretty. I've never been back off the main roads in New England. I had no idea it was so rural, so country."

"It's really rural, small-town," Mary's mother said. "There's a place below ours, Southfield, it was once a bustling little industrial town, thousands of people, hundreds of workers at the factory. You should see it now, it's almost all gone since— well, I guess since the Civil War. They manufactured buggy whips. Imagine."

"Don't they still make buggy whips, Mother?" Mary added. "Isn't the factory there the oldest still in operation in the whole country?"

Mrs. Barrett laughed. "Oh yes, it's still going. You'll have to take your friend down sometime to show him. There's an old tannery. It's only a few miles from our house. But there's no great demand for buggy whips these days."

"No, definitely a declining market," Joe said. Mary felt herself flushing at his patronizing tone. Her own voice became quite belligerent.

"The Civil War made a lot of difference around here, Joe. Everyone thinks the disasters were only in the South. But so many young men never came back. It happened almost seventy-five years ago but this area has never recovered."

"Really?" asked Joe, now interested. History always caught his attention.

"Yes, really. Farms were deserted. Whole towns closed down. So many young men were killed. Or they went to other places."

"Or they went to seed," Mrs. Barrett added. "Swamp Yankees, gone to seed. It's the kind of aftermath of war no one ever talks about."

"But sometimes necessary," Joe said curtly. "The Civil War was certainly necessary. It had to be fought, in spite of the aftermath."

Mrs. Barrett's voice was sharp. "No war is necessary," she said flatly. "I don't accept the idea of the progressive war. That's nonsense."

That was telling him! Mary glared at Joe to shut up as the car was turned sharply into the driveway that led to the house. She wanted her mother to shut up too. Mary hoped Joe wasn't ruffled by the exchange. She wanted him to concentrate on the house. She tried to see it through his eyes and held her breath as she waited for his first response.

"What a beautiful place." He got out of the car and stood looking at the white clapboard eighteenth-century house set in its vast lawn shaded by ancient elms as old as the house. He whistled with admiration.

It was a good house of its kind. Mary had been brought up to appreciate it and admire its simple distinction: its mullioned windows, the fanlight over the door, the balanced proportions.

It was the kind of house that sea captains and traders and men of substance had built for themselves and their families generations ago. Not a rich man's house but a substantial one, built for a member of the maternal family, the captain of a ship in the rum-slave-molasses trade, who had been lost at sea when his son was two years old. That son had a son who grew up to be a Congregationalist minister and an abolitionist and Mary's great-grandfather. It was he who had added the big veranda on the side of the house, facing the long meadow that stretched down to a lovely little fast-running brook.

Some of the newcomers in the area who had more recently acquired their ancient houses with tacked-on verandas grumbled about the Victorian additions and ripped them off, restoring the earlier clean stiff purity. The Barretts loved their veranda, and some of Mary's happiest early memories were of family suppers there, at the old wicker table surrounded by its clutter of battered wicker chairs.

Joe and Mary followed Mrs. Barrett through the side door to the house from the veranda, sidestepping the wicker and the two cats to enter directly into the living room. The polished wideboard cherry floors, the simple old cherry furniture, the turkey-red cotton curtains at the window, the great comfortable old sofas in front of the fireplace with its gleaming brass that caught the light of the roaring fire—it gave Mary a start.

Oh no, she thought, as if she were seeing it for the first time. It's like a dumb photograph out of *Country Interiors*. She wondered if Joe had seen the flat in Borough Park with new eyes when he brought her there. Or was he more sure of himself, more in his own skin than she was? She murmured a silent incantation to herself, please don't let Joe be put off.

But Joe wasn't put off. He stood in the center of the room and said all the right things, greeting her father, who came forward to meet them with a kindly "You must be Joe, Mary said she was bringing you out, so glad to have you," with the same easy charm: "Thank you for having me, Dr. Barrett, it's good to be here, such a beautiful place." Well, that was over with. He was here at last, looking neither aloof nor grim. Indeed, he looked wonderful to Mary in that room and she felt physical pleasure in seeing him there. It crossed her mind that she wished they were headed directly for her old bedroom behind the backstairs to spend the rest of the afternoon in their accustomed way, but her mother and father stood smiling, sherry was being offered, small talk was being made.

"This looks like a room for one of the Founding Fathers," Joe said appreciatively, as he sipped the sherry.

Mrs. Barrett smiled at him. "Well, it was, actually. But he was a canny dealer in land, not a statesman. In fact"—she looked at him puckishly—"there is a fearful amount of fancy talk hung on the Founding Fathers. Mostly they were all shop-keepers, Yankee tradesmen, at least the ones from around here."

"Thieves," Mary said.

"Oh, I wouldn't say that, Mary, not thieves. Just pretty shrewd."

Mary turned to Joe. "The one who signed the Constitution, mother's umptieth grandfather, stole half the state, but he wasn't too smart, he lost it again." She laughed with delight. "And the one they're proudest of, the cabin boy who came over on the Mayflower, never did another thing of note except run the general store in town."

"Mary," Mrs. Barrett chided her, "we're not proudest of him. Why do you say that?"

She went over and kissed her mother again on the forehead. "I'm just joking, Mother dear," Mary said. "You yourself always say about the family heritage, that that and a nickel will get you a cup of coffee. So there."

"Well that's true," Mrs. Barrett laughed. "But Joe brought the subject up." She rose to go into the kitchen.

"He didn't know any better," Mary grinned. "He'll never do it again. Want any help?"

"Not a thing to do. Just sit."

"Here, Joe." Dr. Barrett pointed to the large wing chair. "You're tall. It's a good chair for your height."

"Thank you, sir," Joe said. Sir? Mary looked sharply at him. Where had he picked that up, like a private school boy? Was it working for Mr. Walden? It was such a bit of calculated charm. She wanted to laugh and say, "Fraud." But Dr. Barrett took the "sir" for granted as he poured more sherry and then eased his own rounded bulk onto the sofa. He patted the pillow next to him. "Come, Mary, my dear. Come sit next to me. We haven't seen you in so long."

She curled up at his side. "I know, Daddy. I'm a monster. But I've been so busy. And I've been working. And going to school too. When the weekend comes, I'm done in." She put her arm through his elbow and held him close.

Mary adored her father. She loved the way he looked. She loved the way he was. Look at him now, she thought, wanting Joe's eyes to see him as she did in his chocolate-brown Harris tweed jacket, the easy dark gray flannel slacks, the blue buttoned-down oxford shirt that matched the clear blue of his eyes. Brooks Brothers blue, she would tease him. And his smile! His warm endearing smile whose shape had been defined by a lifetime of cooing and chortling at the babies who had come into his care.

Joe knew from Mary that Dr. Roger Barrett was no simple small-town pediatrician. Dr. Barrett's book on the care and raising of infants and children would have told him so, if Mary had not. When Joe first learned of the book from her, he had gone over to the public library to look it up, then had bought a copy. The clerk at the bookshop had been affable and chatty. "That's a great book. You going to have a kid? My wife wouldn't be without it, she lives by it, it's her bible."

As he went through it Joe could see why it was the guide, the last word, all over the world, translated into a multitude of languages. It had the same sweet knowing simplicity in it that he was to come to know in the man. What he offered his readers was not only the technical guidance of the most modern medical science but the wisdom of the ages. "Don't worry, trust your intuition—up to a point. Take care, love, laugh, touch. But here are a few things I've learned from my experience that could be of help to you." It couldn't be wiser, more direct, more serviceable.

Joe started reading, taking it in with a grain of salt; but the helping and understanding spirit in its pages won him over. Even Joe's usual cynicism, which measured everything with his particular slide rule of economic determinism, approved it, for the gentle voice also asked hard questions about the politics of caring and the need for social responsibility.

"My father's a Socialist," Mary had told him, intending to warn him. "My mother and father both. You won't get along politically, you with your hard-shell dogmatism." She had laughed as she said it. "But wait until you meet him. He's irresistible."

"And your mother?" Joe had asked.

Mary was quiet for a moment, mulling it over. She loved her mother, but there had been more emotional turmoil between them than with her father. Mary never knew what her mother was really thinking, no matter what words she used. She sensed a hunger within her mother, a disappointment with her life and her achievements, many though they were. She wondered how her mother had felt about home and marriage for herself, although she knew she had accepted it as a given for her time and place. Her political activity and substitute teaching had never quite satisfied her. Once she had used the word "amateur" about her life to Mary and Mary had caught the tone of regret.

But Mary was repeatedly thrown by her mother's unexpected responses and swings of mood. "I can't count on her," Mary had raged when she was fifteen and they were locked in dispute. "I never know how she'll come across." One day her mother might be superior, cold and impatient; then there would be a full turn and there she was, openhearted and enthusiastic. How explain this to Joe? Mary felt she hadn't yet sorted it out for herself. But she was fiercely loyal to her mother, even when her deeply ingrained snobbishness showed, even when her disapproval of trivialities drove Mary wild: her mother was critical of the way she wore her hair, the friends she brought home, her juvenile enthusiasms.

She should have been the president of a college, Mary often thought, instead of the head of the local PTA. But why wasn't she? She had been superbly educated at Wellesley, there was nothing in the world she could not do, but no one expected her to do it.

And no one's to blame, Mary decided. I feel that Mother assigns blame—but to what? to whom? to fate?

Later on she was to see a parallel between Hester's gnawing dissatisfaction and her mother's inner hunger. It was easy to be impatient with both for not acting on their own needs—but wasn't that too easy, too glib? Theirs was a generation caught in an evolving time. What a pity!

"Are you still on the Arts Project?" Dr. Barrett asked, as he cuddled Mary on the sofa next to him. "Are you enjoying it?"

"Oh, it's great. We're working on an index of American design and I'm learning some things I never knew about early painters and craftsmen. It's fascinating. And no boondoggle, I can tell you!"

"Boondoggle?" her father asked.

She laughed. "Isn't that an awful word? Some congressman coined it for the Arts Project. 'All that twaddle,' he said."

Joe and her father joined her in laughter. The doctor shook his head in disbelief. "Isn't that Roosevelt a smart cookie to dream up these work projects? Anything to prop up capitalism, I guess, and take our minds off the Depression."

Joe nodded his head in agreement. "Throw them a bone," he said, "and keep them quiet."

Dr. Barrett laughed. "That Roosevelt! Sometimes I think he's a genius. Then sometimes a crafty dictator leading the country toward war. I hold both points of view about him." He smiled at himself. "Interchangeably and at the same time."

"I've read your book, Dr. Barrett," Joe said, sliding away from politics. Mary shot him a grateful look. "The bookstore clerk who sold it to me said it was the bible. I can see why. Although it's more amiable than the Old Testament, I must say. That's what I particularly liked about it. It's such an amiable book."

Dr. Barrett looked pleased. "Amiable? What a nice way to put it. And you've read it? How nice of you to tell me."

Thousands of people must have told him the same thing in praise and appreciation, yet he blushed with pleasure at Joe as if he were the first to say so. Then he returned to politics. "It's a long-term change this country needs," he said, "not props. Permanent change, permanent arts projects like the one Mary's on, permanent concern for mothers and children. I've seen so much desperation out there. All these temporary arrangements to get us out of this period are only corn plasters. Roosevelt knows that. What a politico he is! Dangerous too."

"I'm grateful for the temporary plaster," Mary intervened.

"The Arts Project makes a difference to me right now, not in some future."

Her father bent over Mary's head and kissed her lightly on the top of her hair. "Of course. As a doctor I can see the sense in a bandage. But what I'd like to see is a cure."

"Perhaps surgery is the only answer," said Joe.

Dr. Barrett thought this over. "Do you mean revolution, Joe?"

Joe held the doctor's eyes for a moment, wavered, then plunged in. "Yes, revolution. I think that's what it should come to."

Dr. Barrett shook his head slowly. "Not bloody revolution, I don't think I'd like that. Revolution at the ballot box, that's what Socialists want. I think bloody revolution only leads to bloody dictatorship." He sipped his drink slowly. "Look at France in the Terror, and afterwards. Look at the Soviets now."

Mary could see Joe pulling himself up for battle. She leaped into the breach. She rubbed the rough tweed of her father's jacket. "You feel so good. I love being here."

He pulled her close to him. "I really wish you came up more often. We miss you, your mother and I."

She kissed him lightly on the chin, rubbing her face against his. "But New York is where I am, Daddy. I live there, I work there. As for you, we're lucky to find you home, you're here and there and everywhere. I don't know how Mother keeps up with you."

He laughed. "Oh she does, never fear. But don't you complain. She thinks I'm working too hard at the Children's Hospital in Boston. But I feel great. So why not?"

Mary knew her father worked long hours, always on call, with teaching stints in Boston and New York, but he never seemed harried or driven. He exuded such joy in his work, his prestige, his family, the cut of his jacket, that it spilled over with the abundance of the cup that runneth over. Her mother's life was the cup sometimes half full, sometimes half empty, never full to the brim; Mary sighed to herself, caught between pride and regret.

Her father turned to Joe. "Are you a New Yorker, Joe? I mean originally? So many New Yorkers are from other places."

"Oh, yes. Originally, aboriginally. I was born there."

"Now that's unusual," said Dr. Barrett smiling for a moment. "What part of New York? I've done some work uptown at Columbia-Presbyterian, at 168th Street. What a teaching center that is!"

Joe waved his hand airily in an elegant careless gesture. "You probably don't know my part of town. It's not one of New York's more historic districts. Borough Park in Brooklyn."

"Oh?" The "oh" was a question, not a commentary. Dr. Barrett had apparently never heard of it. "Borough Park? Sounds lovely. Is it a big park?"

"Pure ghetto, Dr. Barrett." In those days, ghetto meant Jews. The Lower East Side. Brownsville. The Grand Concourse. Borough Park. Dr. Barrett understood at once but he couldn't quite put Joe in the picture.

If there is any such thing as looking Jewish, Joe didn't, unless you knew, and then he did, like a rich, elegant, beautiful Venetian.

"Oh really?"

Joe nodded. "Oh yes. And you need a passport to get in, a Jewish passport."

Dr. Barrett laughed convivially. "Well, some of my best friends, as they say, are Jews."

It was a joke, if you took it that way, but it could be taken two ways. Joe gulped. "So are mine, including my mother and father."

"But I mean it, Joe. That's why I said it. It may be one of

those things people say but don't mean. But I'm not afraid to say it and mean it."

There was such a frank look on his face that suddenly Joe returned his smile. It was as if both had said, "This is no problem." Their understanding was kinetic and complete.

Mrs. Barrett came out of the kitchen and sat down on the other sofa, facing the three of them, sipping her sherry delicately, her eyes taking Mary in and seeing her. Mary's mother always saw her daughter; Mary loved that in her, although she sometimes felt pinched by it. She was not the same as a pet to her mother, or a stick of furniture, or any child. She was Mary. And now as Mrs. Barrett looked, seeing Mary, she knew enough to fix her attention on Joe.

"Are you an artist too, Joe?" she asked.

"No, I work for a newspaper syndicate, Mrs. Barrett. The Acme Press. I've been there a very short time, just started."

"Oh, the Acme Press?" Dr. Barrett's voice rose in question. "Isn't that run by a fellow named Walden?"

Joe looked at him in surprise. "Yes. Do you know him?"

Dr. Barrett grunted, then patted Mary's hand as he spoke, perhaps to assure her that he was friendly to Joe in spite of his words. "No. I don't know him, not personally. But he's rather a bad guy, isn't he? Very reactionary. Some of his people did a nasty column on Norman Thomas recently."

Joe looked carefully at his sherry before he answered. "Yes, I guess so." He hesitated, then went on slowly. "But Thomas has been tied up with some funny people lately, hasn't he?"

For a moment Mary thought Joe was going to add his newly acquired "sir" to take the sting out of the contention. Contradictory Joe. Even if he wanted to please, he would be stubborn about making himself clear.

"Whom do you mean, 'funny people'?" Mrs. Barrett's voice was light, so sociable.

"Well." Joe hesitated. "Hasn't Mr. Thomas been involved with the America First Committee and some of its leaders?"

Mrs. Barrett's voice continued light and sociable; she could have been talking about the county fair. "But of course he has, Joe. The America First Committee is against our getting into a war in Europe. And so is Mr. Thomas. And so am I. Aren't you?"

Joe was not used to being attacked in such a ladylike way. The gentle irony in her mother's voice irritated Mary. And she was unhappy that they had fallen into a political discussion so early on in the afternoon, even before the sherry had been drunk. She hoped Joe would do here what he had done in Brooklyn, simplify by evasion. But he didn't.

Joe's voice was friendly but firm. "If we must get into a war in Europe to stop Hitler, I think the sooner the better."

Dr. Barrett waved his hand in pleasant disagreement. "But isn't it better to try and stop Hitler in other ways? There *are* other ways, Joe."

A copy of *Time* magazine lay on the magazine rack. On its cover was an airbrush caricature of Neville Chamberlain, looking ludicrously distinguished and dried up, leaning on his umbrella. He had just returned from his meeting in Munich where he agreed to the dismemberment of Czechoslovakia. Joe pointed to it, his voice rising. "Peace in our time! What a travesty."

Mrs. Barrett met his explosion quietly. "Yes, peace in our time. I welcome the idea of living in *our* time in peace."

"But this is appeasement. It just puts off the inevitable."

"If you think war is inevitable, it will inevitably happen." Her voice was calm but it had bite. "And what does appeasement mean? It's based on the word 'peace'—pax, pacis, peace. It's not a dirty word, you know."

Her mother's adversarial tone made Mary feel ill and apprehensive. Her father reached over and touched Mary lightly on the chin with his fist, like a boxer. "Want to fight, kid?" he asked. "Heads I win, tails you lose." It was an old way they had of closing an argument. Mary smiled weakly and looked over at her mother. Her mother nodded to her, a kind of okay. Now if only Joe would shut up.

Joe's usually white face seemed even whiter and his eyes were fiercely black. Mary's mother might have been an audience of thousands. "You don't understand, Mrs. Barrett. Hitler is a threat to the whole world. Appeasement just makes him greedier, more ferocious. How can we appease that?"

Mrs. Barrett remained undaunted by his vehemence or his speechmaking but she had been quieted by the look in Mary's eyes. All she needed was a last word for her own satisfaction. "Hitler could have been stopped on a dozen occasions if we had wanted to do so," she said firmly, with no rise in her voice. "But let's hope this stops him now."

Joe's face was set and stubborn against her reasonable tone. Mary was annoyed with him. She wished he would drop the subject, talk about the big fat cat that now sat on his knee, or the radiant autumn that shone so gloriously outside the window.

Dr. Barrett lifted his glass to Joe. "Let's drink to whatever, Joe. To harmony, if nothing else." But even in his wish to smooth the waters, the good doctor was no pussycat. "It seems to me," he added, "that the greatest danger lies not in the visit of Chamberlain to Munich but the trip to Berlin of the Russian generals. That will throw a lot of people from one side to the other, enough to overturn the boat."

Joe's eyes narrowed; he looked as if he had been struck. He started up from his chair, tumbling the cat off his lap. "Oh, I'm sorry," he said vaguely to the cat. It was a distraction. He sat back and was able to say, "Impossible. All the Soviets want is collective security. That's their only aim."

Mrs. Barrett sighed, a gentle deadly sigh. "How difficult it must be for the Stalinists. There is so much double-talk to defend."

Mary looked at her mother, hating her this moment. How precise and pretty she was. Her hair, silvery blond, was brushed back smoothly from her forehead, casting a pale glow around her thin long face. She wore no makeup except a bright red lipstick—not even powder. But there was color in her cheeks and the texture of her ivory skin was firm, in spite of the wrinkles around her mouth and eyes. She had a quiet assured style, fixing her gray eyes on anyone to whom she spoke in a way that demanded attention; it was the same look Mary had. Mrs. Barrett was looking at Joe now in that loaded way of hers. What in hell is she up to, Mary wondered and was furious. She hadn't called Joe a Stalinist. She was careful not to make it a personal attack, but an attack it was. Damn her, Mary thought. What is she up to?

Mary had known in advance that there might be a clash between Joe's politics and those of her parents. Oh, the morass of left polemics, Socialists against Communists, to the death, damn it!

Dr. Barrett intervened gently. "But everyone has a right to a point of view," he said. "How about another sherry?" Joe nodded and Dr. Barrett got up to refill the little glass. When he sat down again, he couldn't resist saying, "But the Acme Press must offer you some confusion, yes? About point of view, I mean."

Joe flushed. Dr. Barrett had touched a sore spot. Joe had already confessed to Mary that he thought Walden and some of the columnists were "a bunch of Fascists." Yet here he was defending some of the editorial policy of the place. Both Mary and Joe felt the situation was as clear as mud, but they were knee deep in it.

"A job is a job," Mary managed to say defensively. "It sometimes makes for confusion."

Joe's face flushed. "I'm not confused," he said stiffly.

Mary felt she had used the wrong words. She hurried to change the subject.

"Mother, we're famished. Can I help with lunch?"

Mrs. Barrett smiled at her daughter, her tone mocking. "Don't worry, darling. We're not going to eat Joe, nor he us. I'm all set for lunch, it's a simple meal. I just thought we could take our time and have a drink before that, and talk a bit. But if that worries you, we can eat immediately. What about it, Joe?"

She had a wonderful way of acting as if these disagreements were a civilized discussion between intelligent people instead of dangerous quicksand.

Joe looked at her steadily and then he burst into laughter. "I can talk." He took his cue from her. "I can eat too. I'd like it either way, Mrs. Barrett. And I can do both at the same time."

Mrs. Barrett put down her sherry glass on the butler's-tray table, polished until it shone, its hinges dark bronze against the shining wood, and looked at Joe slyly. "Why don't you call me Mary then? I expect you'll be calling me something for a long time."

"Mary!" Dr. Barrett cautioned his wife softly.

"Well, it's true. It's plain as day."

"What's plain as day, Mother?" Mary protested.

"It's plain, isn't it, that you're going to have a baby and that Joe isn't here by accident. And so I think he should call me Mary, even if it confuses me with you as it always has done, and then give us the details, so we'll know."

Joe laughed again, as easily as she. "Okay, Mary. Anyway,

I'm calling your daughter Molly from now on because it goes better with Levin, which she is now, because we're married."

There, it was over within one gulp.

"Well," said the father.

"When?" asked the mother.

"Five months ago," Joe lied. "In April. City Hall." Mary quickly counted back mentally. How clever of Joe. It came out right.

Dr. Barrett reached over and kissed her and for an instant he looked sad. "Why didn't you let us know? There was no need for secrecy. We would have had a bang-up wedding."

Her mother rose and came to sit next to her on the sofa, kissing her too, tenderly on the forehead. Mary could feel her tenderness, but the look in her eyes was not pure delight. Mary knew that her mother was not keen about early marriage and children. She had often said that she looked on marriage and children as part of a woman's life but not the whole of it, and something to be postponed until way out there in the future. But this wasn't really an early marriage for Mary. She was twenty-four—and pregnant. So that was that. She returned her mother's kiss as tenderly as it was offered and with her own hesitations.

Mrs. Barrett disappeared into the kitchen again and then called them to join her. They settled down around the burnished-pine trestle table that faced the window overlooking the long meadow, now dusted with goldenrod and blue chicory. The cat leaped up to join them, landing in the center of the table next to the copper bowl filled with oranges and lemons, but Dr. Barrett smacked her down good-naturedly. "Worse than children," he said. "You have to tame them before you can live with them."

"That's not the advice he gives young mothers." Mrs. Barrett said, now good-natured too. "It's *you* who has to be tamed so *you* can live with your children."

"Everything works both ways." He nodded to his daughter and to Joe. "It's all give and take."

The dishes were old white ironstone, the glaze cracked here and there against the raised acanthus leaf pattern. The mats and napkins were red-checked heavy woven cotton. There was apple cider, and Mrs. Barrett reached for the salad bowl, tossing the conversation as lightly as she did the salad.

"So you're going to call her Molly?" she asked, holding back a frown as she raised the big wooden spoon and fork through the green leaves. She lifted them over and over as the oil and vinegar ran through and they all watched, glad to fix on the lifted tendrils of lettuce, without talking. With a final swoop of the greens, she offered the salad bowl to her daughter and said, "How about it Mary? How do you like being rechristened?"

Mary laughed. "It's more like being Jewished, wouldn't you say, mother?"

Her mother laughed too, somewhat uneasily. "I guess it is," she answered. "I guess so. I like the name Molly," she added. "It suits you."

"You could almost say it has a nice sturdy New England ring, doesn't it?" Mary joked back, looking at Joe, urging him to find something lighthearted to say, something, anything.

For a moment Dr. Barrett, too, looked distressed, but he reached over and patted Mary's hand, then reached for Joe's. "This is a celebration. But you've gone and done us out of a party." He suddenly smiled warmly, happily. "But you know what? I've gone to about fifty bar mitzvahs in my time, in Hartford, Boston, New York. They're wonderful, you eat and drink like feasting Romans. Why don't we have one for you, my new little Molly? A bat mitzvah I think you'd call it, they're doing it now for girls. Since you've done us out of a wedding, let's drink to a bat mitzvah, what do you say?"

Dr. Barrett laughed at his own invention and then warmed up to his subject. "Of course if the baby's a boy, we could have a wingding for the circumcision. You can eat and drink like crazy then, too."

Mary stopped him sharply. "That would hardly be necessary, Daddy. We're not religious, neither Joe nor I."

"Oh it needn't have anything to do with religion. Let me tell you about my grandmother, Joe." Mary was grateful to her father for trying to pull Joe out of his silence. "My grandmother, she was born Hannah Milton, there's a daguerrotype of her upstairs, she looks like a battle ax, but I remember her softly." He used the unexpected adverb so slyly, so precisely. "Anyway, when I was a little boy on a visit to my grandparents in Vermont, the whole family on the porch, rocking and talking after supper—I remember watching the flow of the Connecticut River down below—somehow the conversation got on to circumcision.

"'Circumcision?' my grandmother asked. 'What's that?'

"My grandfather, a bit embarrassed, tried to explain. 'Well you know, Hannah, it's when the skin at the head of a man's you-know-what is cut off.'

"'Cut off? Why cut off?' She didn't understand. Why should anyone cut it off? 'Never heard of any such thing.'

"'Well,' my grandfather told her patiently, 'I'm cut off, they did it when I was out with the Massachusetts Volunteers in the War.'" The Civil War, Dr. Barrett explained in an aside to Joe. "'And I had it done to Will here,' my grandfather said pointing to my father. 'And young Roger too.' He meant me. 'We're all circumcised.'

"My grandmother was flabbergasted. She had never seen an

uncircumcised penis, I guess. And no one had ever explained. I remember she left the porch abruptly, unable to face the idea of all this barbaric mutilation."

Please smile Joe, Mary thought, smile for God's sake. Daddy is joking. Mother is quiet. What is there to scowl at? She and Joe had appeared with their blank announcement, their hostile political opinions, take it or leave it. Her mother had to be forgiven her surprise, her shock; and there was rudeness on both sides. Mary of course forgave her because she was her mother. And Joe finally did too. He never knew what to make of her. Later he was to call her a hopeless bourgeoise. Then a reactionary social democrat. Finally, smart as a whip and my old girl.

Through the dessert and coffee and the rest of the afternoon, they all managed to skate their way over the thin ice, staying off such hazards as the war, peace, life, death, Munich, the Acme Press, Franklin Delano Roosevelt, the word "Communist," the word "Socialist." Even her father's charm couldn't close the gap. The air rang with the unspoken clashes, with turmoil and anxiety, until it was time for the late-afternoon train.

Mary's father held her close as he kissed her good-bye, suddenly with tears in his eyes. He had given her the name of a colleague obstetrician. "Just for a checkup," he urged her, "I know the clinic at St. Vincent's is great but it wouldn't hurt to see him. I'll call Steve and tell him you're coming." She reached out and hugged him back. Then he turned to Joe and swept him into his arms. "Joe, my boy, take care of Molly. She's important to me." Joe unexpectedly reached his arms around the doctor's shoulders and embraced him in return. Her mother drove them to the station almost in silence.

Joe and Mary rode home in that same silence, with barely a word until they were past 125th Street.

"I thought your father was great," Joe said as he fumbled to put the books and papers they had carried with them back into their knapsack.

"And Mother?" Mary couldn't help asking, although she knew it was treacherous ground. She wanted him to say something, even if it was the wrong thing.

"Well," he hesitated. "I think she didn't like me." He looked at Mary slyly. "I guess she's a Wasp. Pretty waspish, anyway."

"Pretty funny, ha ha." She pulled at his elbow. "Postpone your judgments, my friend, and your puns. Mother can change like that." Then she sighed, shrugged. "Well, I may be the shikse to your mother. You're the Stalinist to mine. That makes us even, both outsiders."

As they walked up the aisle at Grand Central, Joe, behind her, leaned down and said, "You know what?" in her ear. She looked up at him defiantly.

"No? What?"

"Shit," he said.

Mary smiled at him. "So?"

And so they were married, in every way except by law.

· CHAPTER 6 ·

IT was August 1939. New York dog days. The city was a steam bath, with its own special smell of fetid rotten melon. The heat hung over the city like a heavy wet curtain; heat oozed up from the cracks in the sidewalk to meet the heat that hung down. Molly was working in a small art department in a small newspaper in a small, cramped, narrow old iron-fronted building on Lafayette Street. The art director would sniff the air coming in through the open windows off the hot street and say, "Ah New York—smell it! Like one big open armpit."

There were three drawing boards in the crowded dirty room and four people jostled one another in it, Molly at the paste-up table in the corner. The fan on the floor turned from one side to the other, blowing its breeze on each in turn, rustling the tissue and throwing the overlays out of line, stirring the heavy heat lazily, round and round. Molly left work earlier each afternoon than the others—one of the conditions of her employment—and every time she gathered up her handbag and book and the groceries she had managed to shop for on her lunch hour, the chorus was "Half day, Molly? Lucky dame."

The four of them never varied their comings or goings, their greetings or their partings, their jokes or wisecracks. They had a limited range linguistically. *Libertà* was an Italian-language newspaper and there were few English words in common among members of the staff. Molly had found the job after Emily was born; it seemed a good way to learn about layout and type, and it was available. The newspaper had been set up in opposition to *Il Progresso* by a friend of Carlo Tresca, and they used to sing *"Bandiera Rossa"* together and curse Mussolini and the Fascists as they worked. It was a friendly place and Molly learned a lot about the mechanics of her job as well as a thing or two about Italian politics. The printers and linotype men were Anarchists; the art staff, indeterminate Socialist. Molly was the kid, the *bambina*. Sometimes, in the midst of the politics, Molly would find her bottom being pinched. She would slap the offending hand without even stopping to note who went with it. It was all very spirited and good-humored.

Today when she got down to the street, she felt the heat close in like a vise. It was definitely too hot to walk all the way home, but it was also too hot for the subway station at Astor Place and the change at Union Square. She walked up to Fourteenth Street and took the westbound crosstown bus to Eighth Avenue, peering up to the windows of the apartment as the bus passed beyond Seventh Avenue, to see if she could see Emily. Once she had spotted her in her high chair at the open window and had screamed at the bus driver to let her off, her child was in danger, had dashed off the bus and up the stairs in a frenzy, only to find Emily spitting happily over the precipice. After that Molly made a strict rule: no closer to the window than three feet, and when she went past the house on the bus, or on foot, she always looked up to check.

As she opened the door this late August afternoon, the light slanted through the dirt-stained windows and reached all the way to the back of the beautiful high-ceilinged room, making every corner plain.

"Roberta," she called. "I'm home."

"Yes, ma'am. I heard you." Roberta came through the door of the little hall bedroom off to the side. She was big and black and wore a print housedress that hung like a sack. Her feet were bare in straw scuffs that hardly covered her toes, leaving her fat pink heels vulnerable and naked-looking at the bottom of her fat black legs. When she walked, slowly pushing herself forward, the scuffs flapped up and down in a clickety rhythm. The sound drove Joe crazy, but fortunately he was rarely at home when Roberta was there. She came in the morning after his departure, while Molly was getting herself and Emily ready for the day, and she left when Molly returned.

"How's everything, Roberta? How's the baby?" Molly made a turn into the tiny windowless kitchenette to unload the packages.

Roberta mumbled but Molly paid no attention. It was a ritual. They really cared very little for one another. Roberta made it clear. She was black. Molly was white. She had been with them only a few weeks when the D.A.R. refused Marian Anderson permission to sing a concert in Washington, in their Constitution Hall. Molly had greeted Roberta with the news that morning, seething with indignation. Roberta hadn't quite known what Molly was talking about. Molly's indignation had left her cold.

"Who Marian Anderson?" she mumbled. "Never heard tell."

Molly protested. "She's a great artist, a great Negro singer. I think it's monstrous that they won't let her sing. And in Washington, of all places! The capital of the country!" Molly waved the morning *Times* as she raged.

Roberta looked back blankly. Her exhausted face showed no interest. Her own workday in Harlem had begun hours earlier, before she appeared for the day's work downtown. What was Marion Anderson to her, or she to Anderson, that she should weep for her?

Molly tried to inflame her further. "My mother's resigning from the D.A.R. So is Mrs. Roosevelt."

Roberta's face remained expressionless. The D.A.R.? Molly wondered if she should spell it out, Daughters of the American Revolution. Instead she was left sputtering. Clearly she and Roberta shared nothing, not even indignation. When Marian Anderson did sing that Easter Sunday at the Lincoln Memorial, Molly didn't mention it. Nor did Roberta.

Roberta's main job was wheeling Emily around the corner of Fourteenth Street for the obligatory whiff of air. Sometimes she dusted the place, sometimes she didn't. She was good with Emily and Molly was grateful for that, although sometimes Molly grumbled that all Roberta did was a "lick and a promise," and Molly had to clean and wash. Roberta herself never complained but never moved faster than she had to. Her salary was low, but so was Molly's. They both accepted the way it was.

Roberta liked to be paid on Mondays, the beginning of the week. Molly took the twelve dollars out of her purse quickly, so Roberta would know she had it, and handed it to her. Roberta took the money and folded it over and over into a tiny wad, which she tucked into the bulge of her enormous pink cotton brassiere that showed above the throat of the printed dress and under the armholes.

"The baby spit a lot today," she said, her face impassive, not a smile nor a friendly look. Molly made no attempt to force good nature on her. Roberta still had a long hot ride up to 145th Street ahead of her, and what she had up there was her own set of problems: five children, a sick mother to watch over them, and a missing husband. She reached for her large coco straw hat which hung on a hook over the sink. "I see you tomorrow."

Molly watched Roberta disappear through the door, her eyes glued as always to the delicate plush pink of her heels. Not until Roberta was gone did Molly give herself the pleasure of turning into the little hall bedroom where Emily lay waiting in her crib.

If the beautiful room that was the main one of the apartment lay under dust, not so the baby's. It was spotless. And Emily had been bathed and changed and coddled and now looked up gurgling and smiling, waiting to be embraced. Molly leaned over the high sides of the crib and picked her up, tossing her over her shoulder.

"My darling, my delicious," Molly loved to croon to her. "How good you smell, not like New York at all—like a river, like a meadow, like a bubble of soap." She tossed her up. "Did you have a fine day, did you? Did you my darling love?" She poked the baby's moist lips open. "You spit a lot, did you? Teething are you?" She rubbed her finger over her gums and found the little sharp edges. "Next thing you know you'll be old enough to vote." She lifted her high. "Old enough to vote for Roosevelt for his eighth term." She held the baby, laughing delightedly, above her head, then put her back in the crib. "Be good, Emily darling. I have to get supper. I'll be back soon."

Molly turned back to wave at Emily when she left the bedroom. Her grandmother Hester always called Emily good as gold. "A happy hooligan," her grandfather Sam called her. Molly called her that now and the baby waved her arms and legs in answer. When she was born, Joe said, "You pick a name." Molly said, "Emily," and he raised his eyebrows for explanation. "For Emily Dickinson," she said and he shrugged. But it was secretly Emily Dickinson for her mother; she didn't want to let Joe know the hidden recesses of her soul. When Molly had given her mother a collection of Dickinson's poems issued for a centennial edition of her birth some years earlier, Mrs. Barrett had hugged Molly with a kind of desperation and said, "Oh, Mary," then quoted, " 'Mine by the royal seal.' " Now

Molly would dangle Emily in the air and call, at the top of her lungs, " 'Mine by the royal seal,' " while Emily laughed her happy hooligan laugh. If Joe knew the "Emily" was for Molly's mother, he didn't let on. Molly's mother knew, but didn't let on.

Joe was bringing Frank Morosh home for supper, and Molly slipped into the kitchen to get her apron and tie it around her waist while she surveyed the main room. Even under the dust it was splendid. The floor was elegant, the brown and beige and black bits of various woods inlaid to create geometric forms were as decorative as marquetry in the most luxurious cabinet-work. "You know what a floor like this would cost nowadays to make, a real parquet floor?" Sam had said in awe, pronouncing it *parkeet,* whistling in and out the first time he saw it. "A fortune, a real fortune, even wholesale."

Even more splendid than the floor was the marble mantelpiece. Ornately carved with fruit and flora and fauna, it had a hawk in flight with a rabbit in his beak on the right column, while on the left a fox leaped toward giant clusters of dangling grapes. The ceiling was bordered with rococo plasterwork, and in the center was an elaborately carved circle of acanthus leaves from which a chandelier had once hung. It was a magnificent room which had once been the dining room of a great brownstone, when Fourteenth Street had been, in the mid-19th century, the fashionable thoroughfare of New York. Molly and Joe, with nothing to go on except a penchant for romantic history, suggested it had been the Astor mansion. "How can you know?" their friends asked. "It's about right," was the answer.

Molly looked at the room now with pleasure and dismay. This place needs cleaning. Maybe I can do it right now. She went into the kitchen looking for a broom and mop and then turned back to look again. Too hot. It looks fine.

In addition to this main room of their place—they never called it their apartment—there was Emily's bedroom, a tiny hall bedroom which had been partitioned off from the main room, a kitchen fashioned out of a converted closet and a bathroom evolved from another converted windowless cubbyhole. The only way they had of getting air into the kitchen and bathroom was to push around a pair of electric fans in an effort to suck some ventilation into the rear from the windows at the front. They were on the third floor; at street level there was a linoleum store with a perpetual sign in the front window that said GOING OUT OF BUSINESS, LAST DAYS; on the second floor was a mysterious printshop with Spaniards going in and out at all hours of the day and night; behind and above their own place were a variety of other living spaces with other tenants.

Joe and Molly were certain that the printshop was a blind for gun-running for the Franco forces in Spain. They decided that it could not be a Loyalist gathering place, certainly not with those faces, not next to the church, not without their knowing about it. Mr. Hernandez, who ran the shop, always opened and closed the door furtively, barely opening—just enough for one body at a time to slip through—then closing quietly. If Molly or Joe happened to be on the stairs at the same time that he appeared, he turned his back, fiddling with the great ring of keys that hung from a loop at the side of his leather belt. They were convinced that he was the enemy and that he regarded them in the same way. A number of times they took it upon themselves to put the place under surveillance, to see when and if shipments were being made, but they never saw anything except the comings and goings of the Spaniards.

Joe had thought of taking the matter up with some members of his unit and "flushing out the Fascists," as he said, but aside from hinting about a secret store of illegal guns, they never did anything dramatic, enjoying it all in private. When, in the spring, Madrid fell to the rebels and the Spaniards continued to come and go on the floor beneath as before, they felt that all their theories came and went with them. The war in Spain was over with. What were they up to down below? Molly and Joe never found out.

Molly loved the place; it had been hers before Joe had moved in and it became theirs afterward. It was furnished with bits and pieces of early Salvation Army and two rather good wing chairs clumsily but gaily covered in flower-spattered cretonne. The same cretonne hung lavishly at the windows. Molly's decorating ideas were simple. If you liked something, use lots and lots of it. She had bought yards of the fabric at one of the textile stores on Fourteenth near Sixth that sold seconds and irregulars, and the lavish floral display made quite a splash.

"So bourgeois," one of their friends had joked, "the best-dressed place in the Communist party." Molly had been secretly offended. Some jokes I don't like, she thought, but took private comfort in the color and warmth of the effect. Facing the great marble fireplace was a three-quarter studio bed, covered in corduroy to match the background of the cretonne. It was both their bed and the communal sofa. It was really a box spring and mattress propped on bricks and it sagged in the middle because of the weight it sometimes carried: often as many as four or five friends sprawled across it.

Against the tall windows that faced on to the street was the Knabe grand piano, which had been there since last Christmas. The saga of its arrival was symbolic to Molly of the current joy and irritation that had run through their lives, Joe's and hers, right from the beginning.

One day she had answered the downstairs bell, leaning over the stairwell in the outside hall and calling down, "Yes? What is it?"

"The piano, lady," came the stentorian call from below.

"What piano?" she bellowed back.

"Levin? Are you Levin? We have a piano for Levin."

Taken by surprise, she allowed them to haul it up—the staircase was wide enough so they didn't have to pull it up the front of the building, as in a Harold Lloyd movie—and in a daze she told them where to set it. There, where it still was, centered between the tall windows.

"Come on, play," Joe called as he came through the door that evening. "Merry Christmas."

"Merry Christmas? What is this, Joe?" Molly looked at him aghast. Surely he knew they couldn't afford a piano? "What is this all about?"

"Five dollars down, five dollars a month. It's my Christmas present. Merry Christmas." He picked her up and whirled her around, swollen though she was with child. She could smell the whiskey. She snorted indignantly and then laughed. "You've been drinking. But Merry Christmas anyway."

He laughed and whirled her around again and over to the piano bench. "Christmas! That's for goyim. This is for you. Because I love you. Come on, play."

That piano was to follow them around for almost thirty years. It never did get paid off. They were dunned for the final balance for a long time and then it was a forgotten debt, swept away with other final balances later on. But for years Molly took pleasure in playing it and Joe took delight in hearing her.

"It's a good thing you don't know anything about music," she used to say, "so you like how I play."

"I like to look at you playing," he always answered. "Maybe I like that best."

She had almost finished preparing the supper—wondering where Joe and Frank were—when the telephone rang. It was Joe's voice and she grew tense. She thought she heard in it the high ring of excitement that told her he had stopped off for one drink and then another, leaving her alone to wait hours for his arrival. Sometimes, lately, she had started leaning out the window, looking up and down Fourteenth Street, hoping to catch sight of him before his entrance at the door, thus subtracting by minutes the time of apprehension and waiting. When she finally did see him, often looking thin and tired in the heat, weaving his way along the sidewalk, she would be engulfed in waves of relief and compassion and anger, one stronger than the other.

Joe felt hampered and restricted by his job. The exuberance of the day when he came home with his first week's salary had long evaporated. What excitement they had both felt! He had managed to change his paycheck into single dollar bills. He came home that night, banging on the door, calling crazily as he opened it, "Watch out, it's raining violets," and threw the handful of seventy-five singles high into the air, scattering them across the Salvation Army braided rug.

"What's this?" she laughed at him joyously.

"What do you mean, what's this? It's money, money, money. Look." He picked up the bills and waved them in front of her nose. "Have you ever seen so much?" He grabbed a handful and danced into the little bedroom they were getting ready for the baby, the borrowed crib already set up. "See?" He drifted the money over the crib. "See, money."

"Joe." Molly had followed him laughing and scolding. "Take that filthy stuff out of the crib. It's full of germs."

He turned and grabbed her in his arms. "Of course it is. It's filthy lucre. It's capitalist gold. It's contagious. Let's hope it's catching."

But he soon found the job confining. He wanted more scope from it than was given him. He wanted to write instead of edit. He itched at the restrictions. Although he worked and wrote under another name for *The Daily Worker,* going over there Saturday afternoons, some Sundays, some evenings, he was restless and uneasy. Molly felt he was beginning to resent the domesticity too, now that he had it, and she was not able to join him rambling around town as freely as she had before Emily.

He loved to rove around. "It's like going from café to café," he would say as they went together from bar to bar, greeting friends and companions. They knew every place from Fourteenth down to Bleecker. They didn't spend much money or drink too much, but they talked and talked. It had been wonderful fun for Molly. Now there were some nights she didn't see him at all, ending her vigil by going to bed long before she could hear his stomp up the stairs, his key fumbling in the lock. Then, she felt anger rise, coupled with relief.

The anger rose in her voice now as she answered him on the telephone, before he could go on. "Joe, I'm waiting for you. Isn't Frank coming?"

He sounded strained and feverish. "Molly, listen. Frank is with me. We're together. Have you heard the news?"

The news? She felt the pain in her chest. Almost every day there was news and all of it was bad. What a year! Czechoslovakia seized by the Germans. Spain under Franco. What news? What now? "What now?" she echoed into the telephone, "and why aren't you home to tell me?" Her voice grew spiteful. "I'm waiting for you." Even with Armageddon around every corner, she wanted Joe home for supper.

"Molly, listen." Molly caught the tone of his voice. It was sober and somber. "I wanted to call you the minute I heard. The Soviet Union has just signed a nonaggression pact with the Nazis."

Molly held the receiver of the telephone close to her ear, her right hand drawing the phone itself forward so she could feel the black mouthpiece against her lips. She breathed into it.

"Do you hear me, Molly?"

"I hear you, Joe," she managed to answer. "I hear you, but I can't understand it. What does it mean? Is this a trade pact? I don't get it."

"No. This is a political pact. It's a treaty. Between the Soviets and the Germans."

"Joe. I feel dumb. I don't understand."

He sounded impatient. "What's there to understand? The Soviet Union has to protect itself. It has no alternative."

"Is that what Frank says?" Molly asked and knew it was a provocative question.

"That's what I say," he answered impatiently. Then he paused. "Frank and I have to go to Thirteenth Street right away. There will be a meeting. He came down to the office to pick me up."

Thirteenth Street meant party headquarters. It was understood. Understood also was Ninth Floor. No one needed to ask *what* Ninth Floor. Ninth Floor meant National Headquarters on Thirteenth Street. In that same building the Party newspaper was published and various district meetings were held. It was a place teeming with life and movement, and whenever anything new happened, any new development, the Party faithful came flocking to get the word.

Even as Molly clutched the telephone, she felt this would be a word that needed much explanation and would take a long time. "Why don't you and Frank come here first? Supper is ready. Then you can go." She hated to be left out. She was baffled by it all and wanted to hear more.

"Wait a minute," Joe said and she could hear him talking to Frank away from the phone. His voice came back to the mouthpiece. "Listen, Molly, Frank thinks we should go right away. We'll eat somewhere. Anywhere. I'm not hungry anyway." He sounded distressed, uncertain, agitated.

Dammit, she thought as she hung up. She was incensed at being left alone. She heard Emily in her crib and went in to see her. She changed her wet diaper sullenly. Her head was filled with questions; she sulked at being left to change diapers. Molly kicked the crib leg with her foot. Emily gurgled as the crib shook and for an instant Molly frowned, then she smiled back.

"Just us girls," she said, then laughed as the thought flashed through her head: "Men! Here we be astandin' over a hot stove all day, an' you workin' in a nice cool sewer!" Emily thought the Art Young line was funny and laughed too. Molly patted the baby's bottom after she turned her and put her face-down, her sleeping position. "Sleep, my baby," she said. "You'll know about treaties by and by."

Molly went back to the kitchen and scooped up some of the supper for herself, not bothering to set up the card table they took up and down for each meal, but balancing the plate on her knee as she sat in front of the large Philco radio. She grudgingly admitted to herself that the pilaff would keep and could be reheated for tomorrow; no need to pile petty guilt onto Joe over a wasted casserole. She suddenly felt sorry for him as she heard the radio commentator repeating the news that Joe had given her. It was true. There was a treaty between the Russians and the Nazis. Or was it a trick? Would Joe and Frank go over to Thirteenth Street and be told it was all a trick of the imperialist press? Would they learn it was another one of those Riga dispatches with no basis in fact?

I'm sure that's what it is, Molly thought, savoring her supper, talking to herself. It can't possibly be anything else. It can't possibly be. There'll be a Soviet denial at once.

She put down her plate of pilaff and went into the kitchen

to pour herself a glass of the California wine she had bought for the evening's supper. In the clatter of getting the glass and opening the bottle she almost missed the report from Tass. She approached the radio to hear it more clearly. It was an actual quotation. It was an official quotation. She could hardly breathe as she heard it. "Both parties, Germany and the U.S.S.R., desire to relieve the tension of their political relations, to eliminate the war menace and to conclude a nonaggression pact."

"No," Molly said to the four walls. "No. It isn't true."

She heard the news commentator and his voice trembled as he spoke. It was indeed a Nazi–Soviet Pact, just signed, to last ten years. There was bewilderment in the reporter's voice.

Molly's voice echoed his bewilderment. "Ten years!" But then she thought, that's ridiculous. Nothing lasts for ten minutes let alone ten years.

The idea was incredible. Molly felt her mind spinning. How will the comrades explain this one, she wondered. How will Joe? Nazis and Communists together! Molly was not a Communist, she was always firm about it, always tried to make it clear. But she had always felt that despite her reservations about some of the dogma, her unease at the purge trials, her inability to follow the twists and turns of the tortured line, some of the best people she knew were Communists, the ones she loved the most were either members of the Party or fellow travelers. But even that locution "fellow traveler" had put her back up.

"It's a straight translation from the Russian *papuchiki*," her friend Sophie had once announced with scorn. "Someone who won't belong but goes along. I have enough Russian from my parents to know that. Well they can keep it. Why can't they say it in English? Why can't they say *anything* in English? If you ask me," she had laughed, "they're mostly just toadies. And you know what that means? Do you know where the word comes from? Someone who pretends to eat toads to prove the potency of quack medicines. A medicine man's helper. How about that for swallowing a line?"

"You've just swallowed the dictionary, Sophie," Molly remembered announcing flatly. "It doesn't matter what you call Communists and their supporters, they are the ones who want to change the world for the better; they are the ones who belong to the future."

"No slogans, Mary, remember, no slogans. I'm your old friend Sophie." They were lunching at the new English Grill at Rockefeller Center—eggs benedict, Sophie was paying. They were celebrating her new job as a researcher at *Time* magazine.

"Call me Molly," Molly answered rather peevishly.

"Come on, Mary." Sophie broke into laughter that reached to the gilded Prometheus floating through his ring of fire above the skating rink in front of the restaurant. "Man escaping from marriage," Sophie called it. "You're Mary to me. I don't go along with Joe's high-handedness. You know," she added, tracing her long red fingernail across the tablecloth, "there are about eighty million people out there who wouldn't get the point. And there are millions who never heard of the Communist party or fellow travelers or the party line. I know you don't believe it. You live such a sheltered life, all of you. You think everyone is for you or against you. But I have news for you. Most people don't even know you exist."

"Not people who care," Molly answered belligerently.

"Care? Care about what? I care and I don't give a hoot for your Russian-based politics. I care about Jane Austen and T. S. Eliot and Stuart Davis's paintings, which no one else seems to care about. I care about people being hungry and I hate the idea of war. And incidentally, I care that you can't get an editorial job if you're a woman; some of those girl researchers at *Time* are a damn sight smarter than some of those guys. I know I am. But I'm not going to be locked into a goosestep, either left or right. If you must know, I'm a free-thinking, free-wheeling American. Sounds awful doesn't it? And there are more of me than there are of you."

What was Sophie thinking this very minute about this pact, Molly asked herself. Was she listening to the same news commentator, was she equally confused by the fusion of Fascists and Communists? The two poles, good and evil, now one. "How can I think, believe, act in a world in which there is no dichotomy?" she heard herself saying to Sophie.

But Molly knew her friend. Sophie would laugh at Molly's innocent polarity in the first place. Molly shook her head in bewilderment. Was Sophie right? She rushed to the phone to talk to her. She wanted to talk to someone. But she pulled back, holding the phone, uncertain. Did she have so little faith? Alas, why not her faith become, in Wordsworth's words, a passionate intuition? Whatever the answer was, Molly did not have it. The phone rang as she held it. It was her mother, and her voice at the other end sounded tired.

"Hello, dear," she said and came right to the point. "I suppose you've heard the news."

"Yes, Mother." Molly felt immediately, out of habit, on the defensive. "I just heard a report from Tass on Ed Murrow's program." Then she gave into her own feelings. "I'm stunned," she admitted. "I don't understand it."

"Yes, it's difficult to grasp," her mother agreed in her light, reasonable voice. "Your father says now they have all the pigs in one basket."

Molly stiffened. "It's all the pigs in one pen, mother. The eggs go into one basket. And I don't think that's funny."

"Oh, it's not funny. Not one bit. But whether it's in a basket or a pen, the idea is clear. The Fascists are all together now." Molly was silent. Her mother sighed. "And it's a dangerous situation."

Molly answered her starchily, regretful that she had admitted earlier to any private doubt. "I know it's fashionable to call the Russians Red Fascists but it just isn't true." Molly remembered Joe's words over the telephone. She parroted him. "There's more to this pact, Mother, than that. The Soviet Union has to protect itself. It wants to prevent war."

There was a pause. "I see. That's the line, is it?" her mother asked quietly. "I wondered what it would be. And how do you feel about the Soviet Union acting absolutely in its own interests, the devil with everyone else?"

Molly wanted to cry out to her, please explain it, then, why don't *you* explain it. Instead she replied stiffly, "It isn't a line, as you put it. There could hardly be a line yet, could there, since it just happened a few hours ago. But it makes sense. Think about it. What else could the Soviet Union do, since we won't cooperate with her? It has to find support somewhere." Molly was formulating answers as she went along, her own line, to be used until the real one came in. "After all, it made sense for the Russians and the Germans to sign a trade pact. Why not a nonaggression pact? I thought you believed in nonaggression, Mother, in nonviolence."

"I do. If it were truly nonaggression against everyone else as well as each other, I would be the first to applaud."

"Well, wait and see. Maybe that's just what it will mean."

"Do you really think so, dear? Do you?"

Instead of answering, Molly broke into tears. She hung on to the telephone and cried. She cried because Joe hadn't come home to supper. She cried because she was home alone, alone with the baby, such an inane place to be when all hell was breaking loose. And she cried because she knew that a new schism might be opening between Joe and her. She knew she could never find a way of reconciling her hatred and fear of Hitler's Germany to this pact with the Soviet Union.

"Mother," she screamed and sobbed, "for God's sake stop sounding so bland. How do I know what I think? I haven't had time to figure it out yet." Molly tried to gulp back her tears while her mother remained silent at the other end. When she quieted down, she heard her mother say, "Do you want me to hang up? Shall I call back?"

"No. I'm all right now. I don't know why I blew up. It's so hot. The day was like a wet hot shroud, it was terrible at work. I guess I'm tired. And Mother"—the magnitude of the day's news struck her with fresh vigor—"this might lead to war."

"I know. That's what makes it so awful."

"And it's a betrayal, isn't it?" Molly heard herself ask the questions and was aghast at her own rush of feelings.

Her mother paused before answering, stepping warily in order not to take sides against Joe. "It's a terrible betrayal, yes it is, but only to those who believed."

"Believed what?"

"That Russia was a reflection of their hopes." Her mother paused, weighing each word carefully. She never knew when Molly would jump against her. She almost said what she thought, bluntly, "Only the mindless can go along now"—but held her tongue. She decided on more impersonal words.

"When a country acts in its own self-interest, principle be damned, Communist or capitalist, it's the nationalist imperative. That's why I'm an internationalist." She sighed. "What a dirty word these days."

Molly could hear her hesitate and then decide against whatever further she wanted to say. "Your father sends love. So do I. Hug Emily, dear. See you soon." Her sadness and her light crisp voice lingered in the air after they had both hung up. Molly felt no gloating satisfaction in her mother's tone, although she knew that Joe would have disagreed. But Molly knew her mother. She wasn't one to be tricked into her petty partisan spitefulness. Yes, she would see this Hitler–Stalin pact as a proof of Communist hypocrisy; but it would only fill her with melancholy and fear, not with triumph.

Molly went to the window and looked out, up and down Fourteenth Street. She wasn't looking for Joe this time, she knew where he was. It was the quiet broad street, almost empty of traffic, lying exhausted in the late evening's heat, that held her. Was it her mother's gloomy alarm or her own that made the street seem suddenly desolate and forsaken? It stretched left and right between the avenues out into the dubious future, lost, all lost, nowhere to go. In the distance she could see the yellow and green crosstown bus inching its way forward. Across the street, on the stoop of the brownstone, with its rooms-for-rent sign hanging by some rusty chains across the portico, she could see an old man huddled in an overcoat sitting on the steps. What a stink he must be making, she thought, sweating in that overcoat. The sun was big and furiously red as it dipped its way into the Hudson River. Where was everybody? Why weren't they out, crying in the streets? Molly turned from leaning over the window ledge with the ringing of the telephone. It was Tom Feurlich. The gloating, missing from her mother's voice, was in his.

"They have been building up to it for months," he crowed, "the dirty bastards. But none of the comrades here knew it. Surprise!" he chuckled wickedly. "Where's Joe?"

"With Frank. They're over on Thirteenth Street."

He laughed maliciously. "Trying to get the word no doubt. How about it Molly?"

Molly was stiff. "How about what?"

"Come on, comrade. What do *you* think?"

"I'm not a comrade, Tom. As you well know."

"Or as is well known." He laughed. "Let's stick to the proper Russian idiom. Well, they're going to need a lot of phrases for this one."

"Tom!" Molly was angry. "Stop making a political game out of this. A Hitler–Stalin pact! Put your mind to it. Imagine what it means. It's the end of all our beliefs."

"The end of your beliefs maybe, Molly. Not mine." Tom's voice was no longer gloating. "The end of my beliefs, of those beliefs, came earlier. I guess each of the believers has his own personal moment for leaving the church. It depends on the paper nailed to the church door. Mine was in Spain."

Molly was silent. He continued. "I'm sorry for Joe. This is going to be rough on Joe."

Molly tried to brush this aside. "Why Joe? Why Joe especially? Why not Frank?"

"Frank's a professional. He's a priest. He's not a true believer, like Joe. A professional can always find something else to profess. Not Joe. This is the church. The only sanctified church. On this rock etcetera for Joe. You know that."

"Oh come on, Tom. He's not as rock-bound as all that. You ought to know that." What Molly meant and what Tom understood was that Joe, in spite of Tom's defection and disillusionment, had not refused Tom his friendship. Tom was part of their lives, Joe's and Molly's, perhaps sub rosa but always there. "Anyway, maybe it's all untrue. Maybe it's just a journalistic trick, dreamed up by A.P. or U.P. or the radio people, hungry for something anti-Soviet and new."

Tom laughed. "A dirty capitalist trick, dreamed up to split collective security? Is that what you mean?"

Her answer was limp. "I wouldn't put it past them."

"Okay, Molly. Dream on. Tell Joe I called. And I love you anyway."

Molly heard Emily stirring when the phone rang again, this

time Franny Cohen, urgent and disturbed. After Molly talked to her and found she knew as little as she herself did and was just as confused, she went in to pat Emily and make her comfortable. The telephone rang again and Molly flew to it. It was Mike Ernst, one of her friends from the Arts Project, and after him, it rang again, then again and again. They were all seeking one another out, bewildered, hoping that somewhere, somehow, there was an explanation, a confirmation, a denial, someone with a grain of truth. We all want it to be as easy to read as a fortune cookie, Molly thought, after the tenth call. Even Sophie, when she called, seemed shocked and unmocking, looking for a simple explanation.

They were all strung out along the telephone lines, like a gathering of villagers around the town common, hushed and expectant, waiting for the courier to bring the grim tidings. When the phone rang toward midnight and it was Joe, Molly wanted to call out along the trunk lines to all who shared them with her, "Listen, my children, and ye shall hear." But Joe flashed no signals this midnight.

"What's up, Joe? What in hell is happening?"

His voice was hushed, as if he didn't want to be overheard. "Listen, Molly. We're still here. Come on over to Thirteenth Street. I'll meet you in the lobby in thirty minutes."

"How can I come, Joe? What about Emily?"

"Emily? Won't she be okay? Isn't she asleep?"

"How can I leave her?"

He sounded impatient. "Just leave her, for God's sake, Molly. Nothing will happen. Isn't she sleeping?"

Molly decided to go. "Okay."

"Okay. Wait downstairs in the lobby. I'll be down."

She went into Emily's room and watched her asleep in her crib, her little backsides high in the air as her face snuggled into the mattress. There was no pillow to suffocate on, no blanket in the heat to get entangled in, what could happen? Molly wanted desperately to get to meet Joe, to meet the moment. She wanted to be with him, not stuck here. But did she dare leave Emily alone? She turned, blew the baby a kiss, and opened the front door.

The heat of the day had not disappeared in the night. The air remained still and heavy as Molly walked the silent street toward University Place and then down to Thirteenth. There was not a soul to be seen until she made the turn, then saw the crowd milling around on the sidewalk in front of the Party building. As she came close, she saw many she knew. People nodded to her. She nodded back. Everyone was hushed, like a crowd in front of a funeral home, talking to one another in muffled tones, no sound above a whisper. Molly saw Annette inside the lobby and pushed through to speak to her.

"Annette, hello. Any news?"

Annette looked hollow-eyed but nodded importantly. "We've just had an editorial meeting. Joe's up there yet."

"What gives?"

She looked at Molly gravely, blinking with fatigue. She waited a long moment to answer. "I don't know."

Molly returned her look. They eyed one another furtively, with disquietude. Annette was always so staunchly *regular* that Molly couldn't imagine her faltering, no matter what the Ninth Floor decisions might be.

"There's no news," Annette continued. "There's nothing to say."

Molly didn't know how to question her. Annette had never quite trusted Molly, since she was not a Party member. Joe was their go-between. Molly decided not to say any more until he came down. And it was hard to talk inside the little lobby, jammed as it was with people in front of the elevator. The bookshop that opened into the lobby was lit up, its aisles crowded; comrades had come from all over the city, all waiting for the same thing. The heat was almost unbearable, the place reeked of tobacco and sweat and fatigue.

"Will tomorrow's *Daily Worker* have a story?" Molly asked Annette.

She could barely hear the reply. "No one knows what's going on. There has been no word from Moscow." Had Annette really said it? Molly stared at her in surprise. But Molly had heard her. Could it be that the pact had been signed without telling the American Party leaders and the Party press about it beforehand? For an instant, in spite of herself, Molly felt inwardly amused, the inner amusement of the outsider.

They've been left without a line, flashed through her head. They're really up the creek. How will they manage?

Molly saw Joe get off the crowded elevator. He pushed through to her at once. "Molly, come on. Let's get a drink. I'm bushed."

Annette looked at him, saw Frank behind him, and said, "I'm coming too. I need a drink. Come on, Frank."

The four threaded a path through the crowd. Annette, Joe, and Frank were recognized as *Daily Worker* people and party notables; everyone knew that all the editorial people had been at the Ninth Floor meeting.

"What's the story, comrades?" said one. "Is it true we're on Hitler's side now?" said another. "What's the line?"

Frank shook off the retaining hands with an imperious gesture. "Listen comrades," he said, "Bittleman has been talking to us. No one is on Hitler's side. That's capitalist propaganda. Our party stands for collective security, like always. Don't worry. Read all about it in the *Daily Worker*."

"When?" someone called out.

There was no answer. Frank was able to get through the crowd and cross the street. Joe clutched Molly closer to him and rushed her across the street too. Annette followed, calling back, "don't trust the bourgeois press. And don't forget to read about it in the *Daily Worker.*"

They left a trail of uneasy murmurs behind them as the four walked over to University Place. They were headed down toward a favorite bar at the corner of Eleventh Street, Joe and Molly behind Annette and Frank.

"The crowd is going to get madder," Molly said to Joe as they walked. "They're not going to be put off with flippant double-talk."

Joe dug his fingers into her arm. "What do you mean double-talk, Molly? Flippant! No one is double-talking. Of course we haven't changed our stand. We're still for collective security. Bittleman made that clear. We're still against Hitler."

"Bittleman!" Molly snorted. He was a man she didn't know, had never laid eyes on, and knew about only as the undefined "party theoretician," although she never knew quite what that meant. Now she added, "I bet he doesn't know what's happening either."

Molly was speaking out of the vexation and confusion of the whole evening's string of telephone calls. She was not ready to accept the word of the major Thirteenth Street pundit. But she was not prepared for the bitterness of Joe's response.

"You don't know what you're talking about," he snapped at her, "so why don't you shut up." There was something rancorous in his voice. She had never heard it quite like that before. They were at the little flight of steps leading to the bar. Molly pulled away from him before they went through the door, behind the other two.

"I'm going back to Fourteenth Street," she said angrily. "It was wrong to come out in the first place, leaving Emily. I'm nervous about her. And you haven't a real clue about all this anymore than I do. Or Bittleman." She felt she was taunting him and was annoyed at herself and with him because of it.

"Then go, who's stopping you?" He put his hand on the door and went through. Molly followed him in and caught his arm. The bar was jammed. Annette and Frank were weaving through, looking for a table. Molly suddenly felt that she could not take their rehash of the day's event. She could not sit by while they sought for sustaining evasions. She might be confused, but she wasn't a fool.

"Come on home with me, Joe. Emily's alone."

"Go if you want to, I said. I need a drink." Molly looked at him in the smoky blue light of the saloon and she could see how exhausted he was, yet how keyed up. Suddenly she thought, he needs that drink, he really does.

"I'll see you later," Molly said.

She turned and ran frantically all the way home, feeling stupid and censorious and desperately apprehensive about the baby alone. She arrived in time to change Emily's diaper once again.

· CHAPTER 7 ·

FRIDAY night of that week,
they carried Emily to the subway and rode to Borough Park
for dinner with Joe's family. In spite of Sam and Hester's lack
of piety, they preserved the ritual of the Friday-night family
dinner. Except for a few deletions of protocol, the beginning of
the Sabbath was as ceremonial with them as it was in a more
religious home. Hester didn't bless the candles, electric lights
were turned on or off at will, no prayers were said. But the
feel, the flavor, the food were all very traditional. The house
always shone with a special cleanliness, what in Molly's mind
became the Friday-night look. There was the smell of freshly
baked good things, the golden-twisted challah, the butter
kuchen, the steaming carrot pudding. Hester loaded them down
with these delicacies when they left; they gave off such a
marvelous smell in their brown paper bag that, on the subway
going home, Joe and Molly would plunge into the sack again
and again (this after the enormous dinner) until there was
almost nothing left by the time they got back to Union Square.

As Molly had come to know the Friday-night look, so she
had learned the inexorable menu of the Friday-night dinner
itself. It was standard, always the same, blessed by custom in
summer or winter, in hot and humid weather or freezing cold.
Joe would sometimes say, cynically, that this was the cultural

heritage his brother glorified: that everywhere on any Friday night, in every Jewish home, from Borough Park to Burma, you could count on the gefilte fish and the chicken soup, the chicken and the challah, the sweet carrot pudding and the stewed prunes.

"Oh come on, Joe," Molly chided him. "Don't knock Nat. There's more to what he says than a menu."

"Not much," Joe answered shortly. "And if there is, I'm agin' it."

Nathan, Joe's older brother, an accountant and still unmarried, had eyed Mary with even greater disapproval and disbelief when they met than had Hester and Sam. A Zionist, a Yiddishist, he believed in the preservation and linguistic purification of the Yiddish language, in the same way the Irish believed in the mystical properties of Gaelic. He was that kind of young Jew who referred everything to his Jewishness. It was the center of his being, it was a crusade. No writer, no artist, no scientist could be mentioned without reference to whether or not he was a Jew. The jokes were Jewish, the literary links, the world outlook. Molly thought it was a drag, belligerent and intolerant, not at all like the Jewishness of Sam and Hester, who seemed to breathe it in and out with their air.

The Levin children always tried to get to their parents' home on Friday nights—except for Hannah, the social-worker sister, who couldn't come because she was married to an Orthodox Jew who refused the impurity of Hester's nonkosher kitchen. Since it was difficult to visit Hester and Sam without being offered food, Hannah and her husband were never there. It was a serious barrier and Hester would sniff about it contemptuously and mutter, "You have to come to America to hear such *bobbeh meissen*"—grandmother stories.

Tonight, there was Nat, and Sylvia the schoolteacher sister, as well as Joe and Molly and Emily. As they came up the stairs and into the flat, they could hear Hester's demanding voice from the kitchen: "So where is everyone, you could burn up here in the kitchen, it's so hot. Why don't they come?"

"They're here, Ma," Sam called out as he opened the door. "So put the supper on the table. Joe and Molly are here." He raised his arms toward Emily and took her from Joe. She leaped into her grandfather's arms and he carried her into the living room holding her high. Sylvia waved to Molly across the room and got up from the green velour chair to embrace the baby.

"Come on kid." She reached for her. "Come to your Aunt Sylvia, you nice sweet kid you." Sylvia was unmarried, tough and bitter, older than her brothers, not terribly friendly to Molly. She had gone to Hunter College and resented the very idea of Vassar. She resented Molly's possession of Joe. She resented the idea of Emily, except that she loved her. She was always quick to pick her up, fondle her, hold her close.

Sylvia spoke in what Joe caustically called "Hunter Oxford" and dressed with a gypsy bohemian flash that was amusing and attractive, reminding Molly of Sophie. Her long silver earrings tonight looked like bell pulls and swung around her face rakishly. Emily laughed at her joyously and made a lunge for her earrings.

"No Emily," Molly called, trying to grasp her fingers. "Don't do that."

Sylvia swung the baby out of Molly's reach, somewhat combatively. "She's fine. Let her play."

Hester came into the room, her arms outstretched. "So come here, my grandchild." She grabbed her from Sylvia. "Come here, mine Emily, mine jewel." She clutched the child to her forcibly. Sylvia stood for an instant, a look of outrage on her face.

"Really, Mother. No need to be so rough."

Hester laughed teasingly as she hugged Emily. "Rough? So

who's rough? If you want a baby so much," she said in the false playful way she had, "get one yourself. It's about time," she added, rubbing the words into Emily's shoulder, but everyone heard them.

Sylvia's face darkened and she turned from her mother. Joe and Molly caught each other's eye. Hester needled Sylvia ceaselessly. But if anyone had charged her with doing so, she would have denied it. Now Sam expostulated. "Listen, Mama, enough is enough."

"So what did I say, Pa?" She shrugged. "Don't make that everything I say is wrong. Come, let's go to the table." Her damage was done for the moment and her bright blue eyes looked serene and unclouded. Sylvia's face, her large black eyes rimmed with mascara, remained angry. Poor Sylvia, Molly thought. The man she loved was Italian, Catholic, married when he was eighteen to a second cousin brought over from Calabria, the father of four children. Molly and Joe had run into Sylvia with him at the Eighth Street Bar and had been introduced, but in such a frigid, distant way that they never presumed to join them at their table or ask them to theirs. Sylvia and Ben—she never called him Benito—were colleagues in the Teachers' Union, members of the organizational committee; Sylvia had given Molly the bald facts as an aside one Friday night and Molly never asked further questions. When Sylvia now glared at her mother as if she could kill her, Molly understood her rage.

The dining room was small and square. The table with its six chairs filled almost the whole space. When the chairs were pulled out on the sideboard side, they were jammed against the drawers and sometimes got tangled into the drawer handles. The family had a way of getting around the table so that those on this narrow side sat down last. There was a high chair for Emily, which was put next to Molly.

Finally they were seated, Joe and Sylvia on one side, Hester with Nat next to her on the other, Sam at the head. Hester was in constant movement. She was up and down from table to kitchen. Squeezed in as they were, no one could help her. When she was actually seated, she would lean over and pat Nat's head or his hand and urge him to take more. Nat was her favorite and she held him in an iron grip. She urged them all constantly, interrupting sentences, ignoring discussion, pushing, pressing. The night's heat weighed heavily. The quantities of food seemed mountainous. They made aimless small talk. Even Hester's urging them to eat seemed less peppery than usual.

"Will you be glad to get back to school, Syl?" Molly asked. Sylvia was one of the lucky ones, at this tag end of the Depression, with a regular appointment at Hunter High. She taught English. She tossed her earrings from side to side at the question.

"I'm glad to be back in New York, that's for sure." She had been director of a camp this summer, had just come back to town. "I wish I could do something with my summers except work like a dog."

Nat grinned. "What about the good long vacations schoolteachers get? Why are you griping?"

"It's been a lousy summer. Pay us a living wage and I'll go on vacation."

"Be happy you're not a sub," her mother said briskly, loving the use of the word "sub," it made her feel so professional. "So many girls around here, smart girls too, they're subs. At least you're a regular."

Sam felt that Hester might go back to needling Sylvia and turned the conversation abruptly. "So tell me, Joe, how do you like what they're doing to the Jews now? Your friends, I mean."

"What's that supposed to mean, Pa?"

"The Russians. With that Hitler. How do you like that?"

Joe glared at his bowl of chicken soup, sparkling with its spatter of yellow droplets of fat. He examined it as closely as if it were a pointillist painting.

Nat picked up his father's question in Joe's silence. "I see *The Daily Worker* at last got around to admitting that a Nazi–Soviet Pact even existed."

That was true. It had taken two days for the newspaper to report the news. Not until Wednesday did they do so, and another day went by until the leaders decided to call the pact a weapon for peace. There was still no firm Party stand on the question, simply an admission that a pact existed. Sam had raised a touchy point. He asked Joe the bothersome question again: "It's not so good for the Jews, huh Joe?"

They all sat quietly, stonily, waiting for Joe. It annoyed Molly. She felt as if Joe were being pinned down to a point of view he didn't make and didn't hold. But when he spoke at last, in a loud brusque voice, his words were the official ones. "The Jews can't be narrow and chauvinistic, Pa. That's the answer. It's what's good for the world that counts. What's good for peace and democracy. Jews in the Party have to think like Communists, not like Jews. This pact is the bar against another Munich."

Nat broke into spiteful laughter. "Listen, kid, save that for the soapbox. You're speaking the words of your leader, double-talk, anti-Semitic double-talk. What happened to the fight against war and fascism, my friend? Now it's peace and democracy because you're in it with the Fascists, on your way to the same war. Peace and democracy!" He tore viciously into a slab of challah. "Bullshit."

"Not at the table," said Hester. "Such words at the table." But her tone never disapproved of Nat. "Nu, children, let's talk about happier things."

Sam ignored Hester. "You know Joe, wait and see, a lot of Jews, a lot of people will leave the Communist party. Wait and see. I hear it all around me. Such a pact is no good."

Joe's white face looked strained and fierce. "Anyone who leaves the Party over this pact has no idea of the political considerations involved. They don't belong in the party. Let them join the Zionists. We want peace. We want to stay out of war. This is the way to do it."

Sam and Sylvia charged into him together. "You weren't saying this five days ago, my son," said Sam.

Sylvia shook her head, letting her earrings swing wide. "You sound like an America Firster, Joe. That's a real hundred-eighty-degree turn."

And Sam added, "So what was the matter when Norman Thomas said the same thing, only him I trust?"

Joe stared first at Sylvia and then at his father as if he had been struck. For a moment Molly thought he was going to push his chair back against the sideboard and try to crawl out and leave. But he swallowed hard and turned back to his soup, clicking the spoon against the rim of the bowl as if to emphasize his point: "All of you are always looking for something that will break up the Communist party. Instead we get stronger."

Nat laughed. "Sure, you keep getting new suckers as the old ones leave."

Sam laughed too, sourly. "A cloak-and-suiter should have such turnover. He should be so lucky."

Joe finally lost his temper, pounding his hand on the table, rattling the plates and frightening Emily. Molly leaned over to kiss her and comfort her while her father's voice rose in rage. "We get stronger because we're right. Our leaders have the courage and wisdom to pursue a policy that all of us can accept without question because it is right, dammit, it's right."

Nat again laughed mockingly. "So if you disagree, you're

wrong. Come on, Joe. Where have you left your wits? Your party is anti-Semitic, those purges were worse than pogroms. Who are the old Bolsheviks that Stalin murdered? Almost all Jews. Face it. This pact is right up Stalin's alley. It's cut to fit his cossack heart."

"Georgian," said Molly quietly, trying to be funny.

"The trouble with you, Nat," Joe answered bitterly, "is that no one in the world counts except the Jews."

"Well, no one does," Nat rapped out.

"You would see the whole world destroyed, wouldn't you, if it would benefit the Jews?"

"No one is talking about that, about destroying the world," Sam tried again to interfere.

"Yes," Nat answered Joe. "Yes I would."

"Come on Nat," Sylvia intervened. "You don't mean that. Joe is pushing you into an intolerable position."

"I do mean that," Nat said firmly. "Jews are already in concentration camps in Nazi Germany. They've been driven out of their homes everywhere the Nazis have gone in. Look at Vienna. And the racial laws in Italy. Now the Russians are with them. That's just their style too. And they won't stop there. They'll murder them out of hand, wait and see. Are we supposed to sit back and watch it happen? Better let the whole world burn then let it happen. No, Ma"—he pushed back the second helping she was offering him—"I don't want any more to eat." His quiet voice exploded at her persistence. "Enough!" she pushed back, unmoved by his rebuff.

"I think you're both crazy," Molly said. "Are there no answers except war and pogroms? Can't the world be changed without destroying it?"

"Oh, that's women's talk," said Nat impatiently, brushing her aside.

Molly flushed. "We're not in an Orthodox synagogue, Nat,"

she answered him sharply. "In my world, women are people, and women's talk is quite as good as your talk." Hester looked shocked. So did Sam. But Sylvia clapped her hands.

"Bravo, Molly. But he'll never believe you." She looked at Molly with unaccustomed approval and Molly responded to her.

"Okay, Sylvia, how do you feel about going to war to stop Hitler and killing millions of people in the process? Or burning up the world to save the Jews? Doesn't that sound like the same stuff the Liberty Leaguers are saying? Nat is saying what they are saying, but with another accent. He's turned it around."

Sylvia answered with more vigor than she had shown earlier. "But I don't like what Joe is saying either, Molly. Joe is antiwar for the moment, antiwar to suit the Soviet Union. I can't believe in a policy for last week and another one today. What about tomorrow? How about it Joe? Suppose there's another shift, what will you say then?"

Molly spoke before Joe could answer. "But what I'm saying is that it is important to be against war on principle, because you don't believe in it, because you believe in peace, because no other way is possible, no other way works."

Sam reached over and kissed Molly on the forehead. "That's my idea too. That's what I believe in. I told you already a long time, what's good for the world is good for the Jews. War is never good for the Jews."

"So why can't you accept it now, Pa?" Joe tried to sound persuasive. "That's what this pact is all about; peace, non-aggression."

"Like hell it is." Nat shook his head. "Like hell. It's temporary and it's a power play, in the Soviet interest. Like hell it means peace. Come on, Joe. You can't believe that. You know that they're ready to sacrifice the Jews in order to buy their own time."

"Damn it," Joe exploded. "Can't we ever leave the Jews out of this?"

"Leave them out of it?" said Sam. "Sure, for my part, leave them out. Who says no? But this business between Germany and Russia, it's monkey business and it means war. Wait and see."

Joe and Molly and Nat and Sylvia all leaped in, each saying something else, voices rising.

"Enough already." Hester pulled the reins sharply. "No more excitement. It's Friday night, Shabbas. It's so hot you could burn up. Look at Emily. She's going to cry, my little jewel, my little grandchild." She blew her a kiss across the table. "So quiet." She rose to clear the dishes. Sylvia and Molly rose with her to help. They accepted her ruling; they were silenced. The men got out of the cramped quarters carefully and filed into the living room, the women into the kitchen. Sylvia washed the dishes, Molly dried. Hester put things away, mumbling darkly.

"Never argue with them. It's better not to argue with them. They think they're so smart, they always have to be right." Only Sylvia and Molly were close enough to hear her.

Trust Hester, Molly thought, to have the last word.

· CHAPTER 8 ·

THE long hot week dragged on, August almost over with. Molly looked forward to the coming weekend, Labor Day, a change of season, perhaps a lessening of tension. Joe was wound up tight and so was she. He spent his days working with the Acme columns and stories on the perfidy of the Soviet Union. One of the Acme star journalists had written a biting satire on the plight of the American Communist leaders jumping from one side to the other at the crack of Moscow's whip. Joe had told Molly about it, at first angrily, but had then added, almost with a half smile of professional approval, "But it was clever. Brilliant really. That man can really write."

In the evenings, Joe was on Thirteenth Street at the newspaper, in the endless editorial meetings or writing his own bitter satires of the star journalists of his daytime life. When Molly and Joe saw each other, when they spoke, they were either testy and unable to speak freely, or tender, understanding, regretful. He would come home for a quick supper and glare at her or he would gather her in his arms and hold her wordlessly.

"Let's skip this Friday in Brooklyn," Molly said to him on Thursday. "I'll call your mother. It's too hot to move. And let's not go to Massachusetts for the long weekend. I'd rather stay home."

Joe looked at her gratefully. They were at the card table, set up in front of the window, reaching for even the smelliest breeze off the street. Joe picked up her hand and kissed it with that old-fashioned gallantry he carried off so well. "It's all too much, isn't it," he said. "I wish we could go off and get drunk."

She pulled back her hand. "That's not my idea of what to do. But let's do something. Something ordinary. Something uncomplicated. Something unemotional and untangled."

"What? Borrow Tom's old Packard, put Emily in the rumble seat, and take off for Vermont?" He was half joking, half eager. They had done exactly that on two or three occasions this long hot summer, weekends that passed in a wonderful haze of lovemaking and sunshine and multiple-choice breakfasts, and they reached across the table to hold hands at the memory. Joe shook his head. "I can't take the time."

Molly agreed. "Not on the Labor Day weekend, the traffic will be awful. Anyway, Tom will probably be using his car." She sighed. "And it's all too far. No, I mean, let's do something easy."

"I tell you what." He seemed to be weighing something carefully. "There's a guy over at Acme, I don't know if I've mentioned him to you, his name is Dick Waverly, a nice guy. I've wanted you to meet him. We have lunch together but I'd like to see him outside the office. Why don't we ask him here on Sunday or Monday, whichever day of the weekend you want. He told me he was staying in town with his brother. Maybe both of them could come. Okay?"

"Communists?" Molly asked, looking at him woefully. "I want a nice easy day."

He laughed. "Never. God, no. Much too Anglophile. Prominent old family, what Mr. Walden calls quiet money. Dick is learning the newspaper business from the cash register up. Or rather the Social Register down."

"Oh, Joe," Molly groaned. "You really love to deal in contrasts. But why not? Let's make it Sunday. Then we can sleep forever on Monday."

Friday, the next day, the first of September, brought the news of the German invasion of Poland. Molly was at work, fiddling with a pasteup, when the report came over the radio from an Italian-language station. She didn't understand it at once. It was translated with a certain amount of glee by Luigi, the Socialist. Molly's first thought was how glad she was they weren't going to dinner in Brooklyn that night to sweat that one out, nor to Massachusetts for a weekend of civilized swordplay.

Sunday came and with it, their guests. "The World's Fair?" Molly suggested, when the two young men arrived. "The Bronx Botanical Garden? The Central Park Zoo?"

Dick Waverly and his brother, John, both spoke with the private-school accent Molly remembered from certain friends and enemies at Vassar: "weerk" for "work," broad "a" for short—minor deviations, but important. Dick was tall, red-headed, freckle-faced, and amusing. He had an easy laugh that rippled at the end of his sentences, even when he wasn't being funny. The laugh just poured out in a cascade of bubbly foam. His brother, John, whom Joe had never met before, was stuffy and pompous and you could feel that he wondered what he was doing here. But here he was. Molly and Joe were quickly informed that the brothers were in town over the long weekend by accident; their parents were leaving for Europe the next day and the "boys" were staying in the hot plebeian city to see them off. From them wafted emanations of what their weekend might otherwise have been, with tennis and dancing and bridge.

Their white ducks and dirty white sneakers had a careless upper-class class that was unmistakable.

Tom Feurlich arrived in his old Packard, the noise echoing from the street below, and announced his arrival with a blast that rang through the room three stories up. He burst through the door looking like the old Packard down below—put together with spit, rumpled and second-hand. John Waverly's eyebrows went up and up. But it didn't matter. Dick was spontaneous, Joe was pleased with all his friends; everyone shook hands all around in a good mood.

They vetoed the World's Fair. They had all been there more than once since its opening earlier in the year, and the trylon and perisphere, stuck on the wet marshes of Flushing, were no longer the catchy symbols of the world of the future, good for a laugh.

"Oh, there are some good places to eat at the Fair," John drawled, "but it has really gotten awfully worn out." He sounded as if he meant "common."

They vetoed the Central Park Zoo too; too crowded, too hot. They decided to go up to the Bronx Botanical Garden. Dick and John had come in their car, an enormous hearse of an old-fashioned wooden station wagon, big enough for them all, parked out on Fourteenth Street. Molly packed a big picnic basket with tunafish sandwiches, a great hunk of yellow cheddar cheese, some tawny late-summer peaches, pretzels, Coke and beer, and a Thermos of milk for Emily. They seemed happy and lighthearted as they filed down the stairs, John Waverly holding the basket, Tom Feurlich a large brown bag of beer bottles, Dick the folding carriage for Emily, Joe with Emily on his shoulders, and Molly bringing up the rear with her Brownie camera.

Molly took some wonderful pictures that day. In the photographs Dick and Tom were clowning around with Emily in front of the great glass conservatory of the Botanical Garden. It rose like a shimmering mirage in the background.

The heat of the sun still penetrates the old photographs as it pierced the glass that day, turning the whole conformation into an iridescent fantasy, enclosing plants and people in its magic.

"I can't believe this is real," Dick said at his first look at the conservatory, staring in amazement at its elegant splendor. "I've never seen it before. A Crystal Palace in the Bronx, a pleasure dome."

"That's what's so miraculous about it," Molly agreed. "It's a figment of the imagination, a palace floating in air, near the IRT subway, not far from Mosholu Parkway, right off Southern Boulevard. Xanadu with a local delicatessen nearby."

"It reminds me of Kew," said John rather snappishly, as if he meant to say, "What is it doing *here?*"

"Yes, it's like the great palm house at Kew," agreed Joe, taking John down and reminding Molly again, as he spoke, that he had had another life, a European past they never talked about. She glanced at him. He was wearing his ceremonial air, his quiet assumption of poise, what she sometimes secretly thought of as his part-time patrician look. The Waverly brothers were products of St. Mark's and Yale. Joe matched them for a certain cut, a certain style. He matched them for a certain snobbery too. Such an odd mix, that Joe, she sometimes thought. I love it. I hate it.

The group wandered through the pavilion and into the surrounding gardens. They stopped to read the botanical signs, laughing at the Latin names, saying them aloud, quoting from their high-school Virgil and Ovid. Tom took the folding carriage in which Emily rode in state and raced down the path with it while she screeched with glee. They found a place to sit on the ground in a cool pine grove and ate chunks of the smelly cheese and the sandwiches and drank the warm beer out of their picnic basket, talking about Nietzsche and Edmund Wilson and the newly published Steinbeck. They felt easy together, even John Waverly, although Molly had a sense of how transient they were. Why are we so happy together, at this moment? she thought. Such a bunch of oddballs?

They had begun by sniffing at one another, but now, jolly with beer, they were in an ungrudging mood. Dick Waverly, his rippling laugh pouring out like a cascade of flute notes, put his arms around Tom's shoulders at one point when they were arguing about Yeats and said, "I like your brand of Irish. You're my kind of mick." Tom clipped Dick's chin playfully with his fist. "And you're my kind of stuffed shirt. All old money and no new ideas, but amiable." He jabbed him again. "Amiable as hell."

As they sauntered out of the park toward the car, Joe suggested a drink. "There's a bar over there." He pointed to Southern Boulevard. "Come on. Let's have a cold beer before heading back."

They all trooped along after him, Dick pushing Emily this time, Molly trailing with Tom.

"How do you like Joe's new friends?" Molly asked him. Tom and she had an easy camaraderie. In an unvoiced way, he was in love with her and she with him, if the word "love" is defined as caring. She never got over it; he remained in her life always. Her son, Tommy, was named for him, and she mourned him for a long time after his death on Omaha Beach. She always thought of him as her good friend, Tom Feurlich, warm and learned and intense. They were alike in their doubts and indecisions. Once she said to him, "The way we both think is through a glass, darkly."

"That's why I love you," he answered. "It's all Greek to us both."

So when Molly asked him about Dick and John Waverly, he knew they shared the same questions. He answered her half mockingly. "It's an interesting idea, crossing the tracks."

"What tracks?"

"The well-known tracks, Molly. Don't pretend innocence. John Waverly obviously feels superior to all of us New York intellectuals, by which we all know he means kikes, only he's too well-bred to say so."

"Who's a kike?" Molly stuck her chin up.

"You. Me. Anyone who doesn't have white ducks and the right grubby white sneakers to wear to a picnic. Anyone who hasn't gone to their schools or been related to their relations. People like John and Dick Waverly are related to everyone important. When they go to Washington, D.C., or to the White House or to London or Paris, it's cousin this and cousin that, Teddy you know who, and Alice so-and-so. Their uncles and their aunts have houses to loan them and give them introductions to the people as inbred as the ones they already know."

"So why," Molly asked, pulling at his elbow irritably, "are they slumming with us?"

"Put it down to Joe's charm." Tom was half mocking again.

Molly was slightly offended. "You make it sound so calculated. He likes Dick. He works with him. Isn't that enough?"

They had crossed Southern Boulevard. Ahead of them was the bar, Kearney's Tavern, with its neon lights all lit up in the bright afternoon sun, and they followed the others, who were headed toward it. Tom held her back for an instant.

"Look, Molly, I didn't mean anything disparaging. Those guys are fine. They were fun at our picnic. And Joe is eclectic. That's the essence of Joe. He refuses to be held by any tyranny, not even the tyranny of the minority he belongs to. I'm a case in point. I'm an outcast from his minority, as you know. And by their rules, he shouldn't be seeing me. Yet he does. He's my friend and I know it. And he'll see Dick Waverly as long as it suits him. Maybe as long as it's useful. So what?"

"Eclectic?" Molly asked. "Is that another way of saying fake?"

"Don't be so touchy. Inconsistent if you like. Ambiguous. Explorative. What's wrong with all that?" Tom asked flatly as they entered the darkened bar, blinded by the sudden change of light. Molly had no time to answer as they joined the others.

Joe had taken Emily out of her stroller and she was standing on a chair next to him, his arm around her waist. The electric fan on the counter blew its breeze toward her, ruffling her curly black hair as she reached out her arms for it, talking her own talk with delight.

"Fan. Fan. Look look fan fan." Her baby fingers stretched toward the whirling blades.

"She's saying 'fan,' listen to her, she's really talking," Molly exclaimed as Dick pulled a chair over for her.

"Oh, Molly," Joe teased. "She's hardly able to stand up. She's not talking. She's just making sense."

They all smiled convivially. They were still buoyant. They called to the bartender to bring them some beer and turn on the radio. The bartender quit swabbing down the dark wood of the bar and lined up the glass mugs beneath the spigots. As he drew the brown foamy brew, he called out, "Five beers coming up, coming right up," in an Irish brogue as thick as the malt.

"And don't forget the radio, my man," said John, his imitation English accent only part playful.

"One radio coming up, please to try, sir." The bartender pulled on his forelock, clowning back at John. Again they laughed as the radio resounded through the saloon: ". . . the declaration of war by Britain and France was received here in Washington with . . ."

War! The declaration of war! While they had been laughing and walking and eating and drinking out in the beautiful sunlight, under that fairy-tale dome, war was being declared. Emily kept reaching for the fan, her fingers outstretched; it was her new game. Molly reached over and put her on her lap. She clung to her. Dick and Joe leaped up to get closer to the radio that sat on the bar, but it could be heard clearly enough across the room. There was no need to move. It could be heard. Tom sat rigid, his face pink from the sun of the day, the wide smile gone. Only John Waverly seemed relieved and jubilant.

"Well." He seemed to be rejoicing. "At last! At last they're standing up like men to those Nazi–Soviet pigs."

Joe turned from the radio angrily. "It isn't the Red Army that has gone into Poland," he said sharply. "It's the Germans."

John sneered. "But they will, Joe. Wait and see. They will." The bartender had placed the beers on the table. John lifted his mug to drink. "But then, good enough. We'll have all the pigs in one sty, the easier to stick them." At last, thought Molly irrelevantly, I have the words right. All the pigs in one sty. I'll have to set mother straight.

Dick came back to the table and lifted his own mug to drink. "I drink to England," he said dramatically. He and John lifted their glasses to one another. He looked at Molly. "How about it, Molly? To England."

"Down the hatch," said John.

Molly shook her head. "I'm sorry, Dick. I can't."

"Why not," John demanded. "Are you going to drink to the Germans, for God's sake?"

Molly looked at John; he seemed like an idiot character out of an old English movie. She could not understand his joy at this thought of war. "I won't drink to any side in a war," she said. "But if I did, why not the Germans? They're human beings too."

"You can't mean that," Dick answered angrily. "There wouldn't be a war if the Germans were human. They've been the main cause of all war in our times; they're a criminal warlike people. Maybe they can be stopped now, once and for all." Up went his mug again. He and John gulped in unison.

"Death to the Germans," said Dick. No one answered him. Joe was glued to the radio; he had not returned to the table for his beer. Tom was silent.

"Get rid of the Germans," cried Dick, "and we'll never have war again."

His Boy Scout enthusiasm annoyed Molly; what he was saying seemed preposterous. "That's not even historically true," she said sharply. "You can't mean to tell me that you believe all modern war has been caused by Germans?"

Dick waved her argument aside. "There's something in the German people that's ferocious and beastly. Look at that monster Hitler."

Molly nodded. "I agree about that. The Nazis are horrible. But not all Germans are Nazis. You can't make generalities. Germans are no better or worse than any others. Come on, Dick. Think of England, bloody England and the 'arf of creation she owns."

John drew himself up straight, glaring at Molly as if she were beneath him, a lower caste. "I could not live"—his voice was loud and resonant as he intoned—"no, I could not live in a world in which there were no England."

Molly looked at him unbelievingly. He seemed totally absurd to her. She mocked his solemnity with her own. "And I cannot live in a world in which the only answer is war." She was still holding Emily, talking to John with her chin above the baby's damp warm curls.

Joe was back at the table, the radio now blaring out a comedy program, a Sunday-afternoon treat for the whole family. He picked up his beer and took a long swallow. He sat silent and stiff.

"I just hope," Molly continued, "that we're not fool enough to go chasing after England."

"You're mad and shortsighted," said Dick. "I hope Roosevelt has sense enough to declare war at once. Teach those bastards a lesson before it's too late for us all."

Joe looked at him, at all of them, for a long moment before he said, "I think it would be mad for America to go to war to save England. Americans don't want war. We ought to sit this one out."

Dick and John jumped on Joe at once, protesting, their voices loud. Then Tom, who had been quiet, said slowly, "That's a pretty loaded opinion, Joe. You've switched sides on us again, haven't you?" Tom didn't sound contemptuous or contentious. Just sad.

"No." Joe shook his head. "It just hit me. I think this country should stay out of war." His face remained white and impassive.

"Excuse me. The stench of the Nazi–Soviet Pact I smell here turns my stomach. I'm going home." Tom pushed his chair back from the table, his pink face now red with rage. "I'll wait until the Reds change their line again." He threw a quarter on the table for his share of the beer. "Thanks, Molly, for the picnic. I can't say it hasn't been grand." He waved to John and Dick. "As for you two, you sound like a couple of characters out of *A Son at the Front*." His literary reference went unanswered; poor Edith Wharton, out in the cold. He was through the door before anyone could speak.

Dick shrugged. "Takes himself seriously, doesn't he?" He turned to Joe. "Hey, you're not supporting the Commies are you?"

"Hell, no," Joe answered calmly. "I just believe this country is fundamentally, basically isolationist and I wouldn't like to see it tear off on someone else's wild goose chase."

"I didn't know you were such a reactionary," said Dick, almost relieved. The Liberty League isolationist position was one he could understand. "For a minute I thought you were a Commie."

Joe smiled into his beer, waving his mug at Dick. The comedy show on the radio ended and another news report was on.

"Come on, let's get out of here," said John impatiently. "I want to call Harry in Washington to get the right dope."

Dick watched his brother as he got up, never taking his eyes off him, weighing something carefully. Then he rose too. "Ask Harry about volunteering," he said. "We won't want to lose any time."

"Right. Maybe one of the guard regiments." Molly realized they meant in England. It was an epic game, one they didn't want to miss.

Joe and Molly rose with them, gathering up the folding stroller. Joe took Emily in his arms and they made their way to the parking lot for the return home, remaining silent in the roar of the old station wagon that rattled and banged its way downtown.

T H E shades in the living room had been drawn before going out and now it seemed cool and comfortable as they opened the door. The parting downstairs with Dick and John had been friendly enough, but Molly was glad to leave them and eager to be home, as if it were a refuge. It was still bright outside, still early as they returned, hauling Emily in her stroller through the door.

Molly washed the baby, fed her, put her to bed. There was

a heavy quiet between Joe and Molly and neither of them could even fake small talk. Emily was finally in her crib and Molly was at last in the living room with Joe. He sat in the wing chair, his head down, his hand covering his eyes.

"What about supper?" she asked. "Are you hungry?"

He looked up, desolate, his eyes intense, like hot coals. "Supper?" He seemed astonished at her question. "I wish we could go out. This place drives me crazy."

Molly looked at him, quickly angered, and snapped, "Well, we can't. Anyway we've been out. All day. Remember?"

She sat watching him. She could feel his restlessness, his impatience. Suddenly he got up and walked to the radio, switching it on. There were no news programs at the moment as he flipped the dial from station to station.

"This fucking world," he said, "it's going up in flames but there's only shit in the air."

Molly tried to speak calmly. "It's almost seven o'clock. There'll be news, then."

"Damn it, why isn't there news every single minute, this is idiocy." He seemed angry with her. She shook her head.

"Joe, don't snap at me. The whole world's in a state of chaos without your snapping at me." She glared at him.

Joe came over and kissed her forehead. "I'm sorry, Molly. I'm out of my head. War!" He walked away to the window, back to her, then away again, back and forth.

"Didn't you expect it?" she said in a low voice. "You said it was inevitable. Remember?"

He turned as if struck. "I said it, I know I said it, but I never felt it. And now it's happened, I don't know where I stand. I don't know how I feel. I don't know what I think." He looked desperate, walking back and forth.

"I thought you had all the answers, Joe." Molly couldn't help digging into him. "Today you said you hoped this country would stay out. I agreed with you. For once we agreed. A meeting of the minds."

"Christ, Molly, don't quote me on what I said, today or yesterday or tomorrow. Of course I want this country to stay out. It has to stay out. I don't want to see it involved in a bloody European war. That's what all the immigrants came to America to get away from, Europe's bloody wars."

"So? Do I hear a reluctant note in your voice? Is what you're saying only temporary and conditional?" Molly tried to hold her tongue from lashing him too severely but she could not resist adding, "You're not really against war, are you? You're just against our fighting against the Russians. That's what made Tom mad. It makes me mad too."

He stared at her. "That's right," he answered her slowly, cold with rage. "You're absolutely right. I don't want us to fight against the Soviet Union." He was silent, staring at the parquet floor as if memorizing the pattern. Then he added, "But I'll throw you a real curve, Molly. I'm with Dick too. And I'm with John. I'm against Hitler. And I couldn't live in a world in which there was no England."

Molly looked at him steadily, her gray eyes unblinking. "You sound like John Waverly. Don't tell me you're one of *them*."

"I understood what John was saying, although he sounded like a clown. I'm not one of them, as you put it, whatever that means. But think, try to think, a world without England! And what about France? What a world without France!"

"You're confused, comrade," Molly said sarcastically. "You are really confused."

They glared at each other across the room. He broke the silence. "I'm going out for a drink. I want to talk to Tom. I'm going to his place. Coming?"

"No. I can't. I don't want to leave Emily."

"Do you mind if I do?"

"Yes. Yes I do."

He came toward her and kissed her forehead again. "I'm sorry, Molly, I can't sit still here. I'm going out. I feel in the middle of a cosmic joke. Not really funny, just a one-line gag."

"No, Joe. It's just the first call of the bugle. Let's face it. It's irresistible."

He didn't answer as he unlocked the door and went down the stairs. The radio program had now changed and was sputtering the news. British aircraft were headed over Poland. Molly could see them in her mind's eye, like silver sparrows, little deadly birds, small and shining. She could hear them as they flew across the horizon, coming closer. She went to the window and looked out. She saw Joe walking toward Seventh Avenue. Then he disappeared. How light it was. Still daylight. The farmers up in Massachusetts grumbled about the newfangled daylight saving.

"It turns everything around," they said. "Maybe it's all right in the city. Go tell it to the cows."

Go tell it to the cows, she thought. Tell it to Jerusalem. Tell it not in Gath. Call it through the streets of Rome. War. War at last. War again. What everyone was waiting for. War.

· CHAPTER 9 ·

THE years of the war went by quickly even as it seemed they would never end. Later on it was called "our" war, the "good war." The good war! It changed the face of Europe and Africa and China and India and Indochina and the city of New York. It brought gas chambers and genocide and Hiroshima and the Holocaust. Dick Waverly returned to a splashy career as a newspaper columnist, but his brother, John, never did. He died in Salerno; Tom Feurlich, on Omaha Beach; Nat, Joe's brother, late in the war, in the Battle of the Bulge.

Molly worked hard during those war years. Joe was in England throughout most of them—almost three years of unbroken separation. Tommy was two and a half years old before his father laid eyes on him, and Emily was dangly and long-legged, no longer a baby, when he returned. And Molly?

"Why don't you come over to *Newscast?*" Sophie had said to her one day. Sophie had switched jobs early on in the war, leaving *Time* as a researcher to go over to *Newscast* as a reporter. "One of the blessings of the shortage of men," she said maliciously, "it's opened the usually closed doors." Sophie chortled. "Imagine—a writing job. For a woman. It would never have happened before. I feel like Rosie the Riveter up in the editorial room, doing my bit."

"Till the boys come home?" asked Molly, laughing too, rather grimly.

"Not on your life," Sophie snapped. "if they want to go off to play with their machine guns, let them. I intend to learn this job and keep it." She poked angrily at her salad and her long earrings swung wildly, side to side.

Molly had come to love Sophie, to value her directness, her sharp acute mind, her willingness to say the unsayable, and her indomitable drive. Molly treasured the fact that they went back together a long way, to the "antebellum days," as they called the time at Vassar. They had grown very close. "Better than sisters," they would say to one another, "friends." Molly would join Sophie on her periodic trips to her family in Rochester, in spite of the long train ride and the discomfort of carting Tommy and Emily with bottles and baskets and blankets. On arrival, all of them were overwhelmed with love and kisses. And "Come again, come again, come again," the voices would follow them long after the train had left the station for the return home.

The trips to Great Barrington were easier and more frequent, if less tumultuous. Her father was not only rhapsodic about the children, but helpful. He cooed but he also counseled in his gentle ironic specific way.

"I read your book all the time, Daddy," Molly told him. "I never knew before what a smartie you were."

He hugged her. "I want no faint praise from you." Then he said regretfully, "I wish you all lived around the corner so I could see you and the children all the time. And," he added, "I'd like to talk to you sometime at length about the dilemma of being alone and holding a job and caring for the children, all at the same time. There must be problems never thought of before."

Molly embraced him. "Thank you, Daddy, for even thinking about it. There *are* problems. There is such prejudice out there about where a mother's place is and what she should do about it. It sometimes seems as if the whole world was set on making you feel guilty."

He nodded in agreement. "There'll be more and more in the same boat as time goes on, Molly. We have to give it thought. There has to be room for working and loving and bringing up children. They all have to go together."

One time he said to her, "Why don't you come up here to stay with us for the duration? We'd love to have you. It would ease the burden."

She hesitated. "No, thank you. I've thought about it, don't think I haven't. But it's not what I want."

He put his arm around her shoulder. "I understand," he said, and never mentioned it again.

How abundant his love is, Molly thought. And how sustaining. She felt enormously grateful to him for it. But her mother troubled her, especially when Sophie came along to visit her family. Don't find fault, don't find fault, she chided herself. She's the way she is.

The way she was was a kind, precise, and pleasant grandmother. She would bend over the children and kiss them on the top of their heads and with a detached air give them the expensive little gifts she always had ready. But when Sophie was there, she was unable to absorb Sophie's jangly makeup and raucous clothes.

"That's rather snappy," she had once said of one of Sophie's more bizarre getups. Sophie and Molly laughed about it all the way home in the train. "Rather snappy" became a key phrase between them for anything outrageous.

"Let's face it," Sophie had added, "she means Jewish, doesn't she?"

Molly shook her head. "No, I don't think so. You don't understand my mother. I think she means New York."

"Think so?" Sophie had asked, her plucked eyebrows rising. "Same thing," she shrugged.

Sophie had even gone with her a few times to those Friday-night dinners in Borough Park, but while she could be good-humored about Molly's mother up in Massachusetts, she was impatient and irritated by her evenings with Joe's family. "I know them too well," she said enigmatically.

It was Nat who disturbed her, Nat who put her back up. Until he was drafted, he was always there when they arrived. "I can't stand his endless Zionism," Sophie complained. "It galls me the way everything is brought back to the Jewish question."

Hester angered her too. "Everything ends up meaning one thing," Sophie complained to Molly about Hester's questions. "When are you going to get married? Why aren't you married? It's time you got married."

"At least she's not trying to fix you up with Nat," Molly said. "A nice Jewish girl like you."

"God," Sophie shuddered. "No one would be good enough for her darling, least of all me."

Sophie was one of the young women who carried a pessary in her handbag, and Molly envied her her sexual openness. Molly felt that Sophie was more honest about it all than she was. Some nights she could hardly stand being without Joe to make love to her, and wished she had the courage to take advantage of the various advances that came her way. How had she continued so inhibited, so prudish, why so afraid? She admitted to herself, with a kind of self-scorn, that in spite of her contempt for the legalities of marriage, she was still tied to the idea of monogamy. Not so Sophie. When Sophie opened her handbag for whatever reason, Molly could see the little gray box, ready and waiting for all the limitless possibilities of wartime New York. Sometimes Molly's own life, with the two children and the job and the food coupons and the v-mail, seemed to her plodding and dull.

"You've been taking some interesting photographs," Sophie had continued at lunch that day, "and the magazine is going to need a replacement now that Al's been drafted, poor slob."

"But I'm not good enough to do professional work, Sophie. I just do it for fun, and because I don't seem to have time for painting these days."

"You'll learn the pro stuff, Molly. On the job. But your photographs have the essentials in them already. I've seen them. I'm not talking through my hat. You see people and places with a sharp eye. And you have the artist's sense of direct response. You're an artist after all. This is just another medium."

Molly protested. "It's all so accidental, my photography. Joe left his Zeiss Ikon behind and I started using it. I don't figure things out. They just happen."

"But that's it. I'm convinced the essence of good photography is the accidental. Being there at the right moment, the moment that counts. Knowing by instinct when that is and then letting it just happen."

"I know," Molly answered. "I know what you're saying, but there's more to it than that. Light, shade, contrast. What reproduces. What doesn't. I haven't a clue." Even as Molly protested, she felt herself fired up, challenged.

"You could learn." Sophie sounded positive, as if the matter were settled. "And there's a nice old guy on staff who would give you a hand. Lew Taylor. He's been at it since his first Brownie. Even before that, he used to do the illustrations for the news stories on the *Trib,* before they used cameras. He'll show you the ropes."

So it was settled. Molly wrote Joe about it and his little v-letter came back: "What about the kids? Isn't your part-time arrangement on *Libertà* a better deal? At least it gets you home before Emily comes back from school."

A better deal? Yes, it was, if being home when Emily returned from school was the governing factor. But Molly was tired of doing pasteups and layouts and occasional illustrations. She now had hired a pleasant Negro housekeeper, Katy Baxter, much more flexible than sullen Roberta, who took care of Tommy until three o'clock and who would be willing to stay until six to take care of Emily too. "I've sounded her out," she wrote Joe, "and she's agreed. She'll charge just a few dollars more and besides I'll be making more money." She didn't add, "and I want to do it. I'm going to do it. It's a challenge and I'll never have another chance."

She was taken to a gala lunch at the Grotto Azzurro on Mulberry Street by her three companions from the art department on her last day at the paper. When one of them, Tony Ciano, pinched her bottom especially hard, she did what she had wanted to do for a long time, she pinched him back. They laughed and drank red wine with their pasta carbonara, and she joined them singing *"Bandiera Rossa"*—all of the voices loud and clear, ringing out the final *trionphera* with a flourish.

It was fun at *Newscast*. Molly loved the feel of the place, a far cry from the cramped office downtown. It was sharp and new, a whole floor in Rockefeller Center. Everyone seemed smart and up-to-date and no one brought sandwiches to work. The restaurants on Forty-ninth and Fiftieth streets and around the corner on shabby Sixth Avenue were cozy and intimate and endlessly friendly. The bar at Henry's had its regulars who never seemed to leave, although Molly knew they did, ducking into the elevators that zoomed up and down in the various buildings that lined the Center, doing whatever stint of work was theirs, and then down again to finish the afternoon with another drink and then another.

Sophie would shake her head at the disappearing backs, lift her eyebrows to Molly in passing, pound away at her typewriter or buzz into the telephone, in endless search for her story. When she went out during working hours, it was to cover an assignment. But the lunch hour was different. Sophie liked the lunchtime gaiety at Henry's or Ralph's or Toots Schorr's, and Mollie, when she wasn't on assignment, joined her with all the others in the noise and the smoke and the constant laughter.

Later on when Molly would remember those days, they seemed lit with an incandescent glow. The people all seemed so worldly to her—witty and easy and bright. And although *Newcast* was a political publication—it had a bureau in Washington and a bureau in London and correspondents everywhere—and took political editorial positions, it was all a politics of surface. No one got angry or polemical or terribly intense. Most of the men were beyond draft age or were 4F, meaning happily unfit, or fathers of families or had been with the Office of War Information, the OWI, for a year or two in Washington. They thought of themselves as working for *Newcast,* not as making its politics. That was for the man at the top. It was he who was fiercely political. But not they. "I just work here," they'd say. The mastermind up there had an ax to grind, not they. They felt that they had only to supply the facts for him to twist as he would. Molly had the feeling that if any one of them was offered a job with a better salary, by a publication with an absolutely differing point of view, he would be off like a flash. Indeed the national affairs editor did just that, claiming it was "no skin off my ass."

How different, thought Molly, from the fierce rages and absolutism of the boys downtown. In some ways Molly liked it better this way. It was certainly easier, more agreeable. She sighed as she thought, at least for the time being.

Molly learned her professional role quickly. Lew Taylor helped, as Sophie had promised. He showed her how to carry three cameras, all loaded, to be on the ready without the problem of changing film. One was Joe's old Zeiss Ikon. Another, Joe's Foth Flex, until Lew replaced it with a real Rolliflex from the company stores. And then, miracle of miracles, a Leica rangefinder. With the Leica always around her neck, the Zeiss over one shoulder, the Rolli in the big bag, already weighed down with flash bulbs and additional film, she sometimes felt like a pack mule. "More like a working burro," Lew grinned at her, when she said this, "a cute little burro. But remember," he added, repeating this again and again, "you take the picture, not the camera. You're the one that counts."

It was his one great teaching point. "You carry the apparatus you need, but you're the eye, the seeing eye."

Her assignments weren't the big spectaculars. But she was careful and able and the reporters who worked with her were easy and satisfied. *Newscast* wasn't *Life* magazine; the photos played second fiddle to the written word and Molly knew she was no Margaret Bourke-White. She didn't want to be. It was Weegie on *P.M.* she wanted to be. She loved his crazy impromptu shots of the world whizzing around him. Everything got trapped by his lens. The guys on the courthouse steps. The kids playing hopscotch with bits of broken glass. Firemen in the snow, stopping traffic in front of a burning apartment house, the slippery foreground a dark murky sheen, puddles of melting ice, the big firetruck mysterious in the background. City streets by night, New York after dark, excitement bubbling up from the cracks in the pavement. That was Weegie.

Molly had absorbed the talk about Weegie. That he whirled

through the near and far corners of New York in his radio-equipped car. "And he does it all with a Speed Graphic," she marveled to Lew, "an old Speed Graphic at f4.5 and any old ash can as a tripod."

"So what did I tell you? It's the eye that counts. He's a screwball genius," Lew Taylor agreed. "You can't copy him. You have to *be* him. Anyway, Molly, he works for a daily New York newspaper, New York's his life. Your beat is different."

Molly enjoyed her beat; she was learning. She did well with her portraits of Washington notables on the move, movie stars on their way to sing for the troops, and a fashion show for Madame Chiang Kai-shek at a fashionable shop, where she purchased one hundred twenty-seven pairs of shoes to ease the difficulties of her life at the front. The shot Molly got of Madame Chiang seated in the Shoe Salon, surrounded by her shoes, never found a place in the magazine, but Molly had an enlargement of it made for her tiny office. "To remind me," she told Lew, "of this wonderful war."

Then it was June and already hot, with that torrid sweaty humid heat that gives New York its special summer feel. Intolerable, unbearable, New York in summer. Molly had a special concern in the summer's stifling heat. What to do about the children? Tommy was a year old and it didn't matter where he was—he could be rolled around and trundled to Abingdon Square as well as anywhere else, to play in the sandbox and toddle back and forth.

The children loved Katy Baxter, although Molly winced at the favoritism Katy showed to Tommy and tried to put it out of her mind with the thought that grandparents had favorites too, and so did parents, and children had to live with it. Katy was too important to her to quibble. But what about Emily? Emily was now five years old and some arrangements had to be made for the next months. There was a slide at Abingdon Square as well as the sandbox, but it hardly seemed enough for the long hot summer.

Molly called her mother, but with misgivings. Her mother was knee-deep in politics working for Roosevelt's fourth term. She would do whatever Molly asked of her but Molly was reluctant to ask. She hoped her mother would think to make her own proposals.

"Molly, my darling." Her mother's voice was light and loving. "How nice to hear from you. How are the children? Tommy must be big and wonderful? And Emily? Dear sweet Emily?"

"We're fine, Mother, all fine. And you and Dad?"

"Busy as always. Dad is on Thomas's advisory committee. And he's extended his practice since some of the younger doctors are gone."

"Mother," Molly cut in. "It's awfully hot here and Emily's kindergarten class shuts down next week. I wondered—"

Her mother's voice sounded joyous as she interrupted, "But Molly darling, that's just fine. All of you come here for the summer. Katy too, there's plenty of room."

Molly hesitated. "Mother, that's lovely of you, but well, you know I'm working. I can't take the summer off."

"Oh." Molly could hear her mother's small sigh over the wires. "Oh. Well come for the time you have off for vacation. You *do* get a vacation, don't you?"

"Not very much. I haven't been here long enough. I don't know, maybe I'll get a week."

"Oh, a week." A pause. "Well come then."

"Yes, Mother, of course. But I wondered. Would it be possible? Do you think"—Molly finally plunged in—"do you think you could take the children for the summer?"

Suddenly Molly herself saw how improbable this was, and how unfair of her to ask. It was all very well, she thought wearily, for her father to suggest, as he had earlier, that she and the children come home, but it was understood, wasn't it, that it would be her mother's responsibility to adjust to the change. Dear Daddy, his life wouldn't change an iota. But she couldn't expect her mother to turn suddenly into a plump homebody grandma, all cuddles and kisses and cookies, all ready to take over at a jump. Tommy and Emily were too young. It would be too much work, too much responsibility without Katy or Molly on hand. And Katy couldn't, wouldn't, leave New York. She had her own family in Harlem. And, flatly, Molly didn't want to leave her job. If nobody wanted to give an inch, why should Mother?

"I guess not, Mother. I can't get away. I can see it would be too much without me."

Molly could feel both her mother's relief and her regret. "Let's see, Molly," she said, "what we can work out. It would be good to have them. But—" her voice hung suspended.

"I know, Mother dear. Don't worry about it. Just a thought. We'll have a week together all of us, anyway."

There were a few more words, some questions about Joe. Molly sighed as she clicked off the phone. No, she didn't blame her mother. She wasn't angry.

When Molly was growing up, her mother had been the head of the Board of Education, a library trustee, and a member of the local board of the League of Women Voters. Molly had been torn both by pride in her mother's achievements and a sense of desolation and rejection. She had fretted about not being loved enough, not loved beyond anything in the world, feeling that somehow she played second fiddle to her mother's successes. Not until later did she learn that these successes were not enough, barely a drop in her mother's bucket. Molly now saw herself with her own ambitions, which did not cancel out her love for her children but had to be accommodated. She sighed. Family ties were confusing. They were so interwoven with legends and false expectations.

Her mother was honest about it. But, Molly thought desperately, how am I going to manage? Two little children, a job in the hot city, a husband in England in the Eighth Air Force. It was tough. She'd have to find another way of dealing with the problem. Perhaps it wasn't necessary to go away. Emily and she could do a lot together. They'd go to Central Park weekends and to Jones Beach and the Bronx Zoo, like all the other New Yorkers. Molly felt tired at the very thought.

She talked to Sophie about it. "I don't want to ask for a leave." She tried this tentatively on Sophie, who was now listed on the masthead. Sophie was a writer for the "National Affairs" department with her own byline on special pieces. She knew things about the inner workings that Molly didn't.

Sophie shook her head. "I don't think you'd get it. We're in a tight squeeze for staff as it is."

"That's what I thought." Molly fumbled for words. "I talked to mother about it, she's okay, she'd really help if she could, but it's too much to take on. Two little kids? Come on."

Sophie regarded Molly with raised eyebrows. "I guess."

"No, really. It's okay. We'll manage. I'm lucky to have Katy to help."

"What about Joe's parents?"

"In Brooklyn? It's as hot as New York. And with Joe's parents? They'd love the idea, but it wouldn't work, really. Sam isn't well—and, well, I don't think it would work."

Sophie shook her head, sat thinking, pursing her lips. "I have an idea," she said suddenly. "Why don't you send Emily up to Rochester to say with my family? My older sister, Jean, you know her, she's there now with her kid, about Emily's age, while her Bill is somewhere out there in Okinawa or wherever. Emily can have my old room. My parents can always absorb

· 156 ·

another kid around. You know them. They love children. What's another one to them?"

"But so much work!"

"Not really. And I'm not including Tommy. That would be too much. But Jean's child, Laurie, is all signed up for a day-camp program. You can sign up Emily too."

When Molly spoke with Sophie's mother on the telephone, her response was warm and generous. Sophie had already primed her. "Naturally," she said, "bring Emily here, she'll be a pleasure to have."

· CHAPTER 10 ·

THE wartime Empire State Express crept its way from Grand Central Station in a welter of soldiers, with duffel bags in the aisles, open windows blowing black dust and smoke, children wailing from discomfort in the heat. The singing rang throughout the train. The soldiers, happy to be on leave, were belting out their war songs in a deafening counterpoint of melody and laughter. It all pounded painfully against Molly's eardrums. So early in the morning!

Everyone moving, going, no attention paid to the signs posted everywhere: IS THIS TRIP NECESSARY? Molly was glad she had left Tommy at home with Katy, paying her extra for the weekend's work. She had Emily close to her, they both occupied one seat next to a fat Italian woman in a flowered print dress who overflowed beside them. They were lucky to be sitting at all; others were standing in the aisles, while some squatted on the duffel bags, lunch boxes open before the train reached Poughkeepsie.

The beautiful Hudson River was wide and swelling, stretching from the railroad tracks to the high white Palisades across the water. Joe always called it "the lordly Hudson" every time they swung down the West Side Highway and saw it open before them.

How Joe loved New York, she thought. Everything. It was

his town. He knew its history, the places deep in its heart, the feel of the streets. He loved the mix of its peoples. Dear Joe. Molly thought of him warmly as she took in the sweep of the water that followed the line of the train. Please come back, I need you. She felt tears pressing against the back of her eyes.

I'll never get over hating him for joining up, flashed through her head, but I'll never get over it if he doesn't come back.

Joe left before America's entry into the war, going to Canada in September of 1941 to train with the Royal Canadian Air Force. He would have been exempt, at least in the beginning, or he could have taken a wartime desk job: it would have been available to a married man, a father. But he'd volunteered, he had gone off early. Now he was a war hero, damn him, with uncountable combat missions, a Distinguished Service Cross, and a Purple Heart.

"Not serious," he had written her. "A flesh wound, maybe from our own gunner who doesn't know his right from his left, his ass from his elbow."

Molly's heart curdled at the thought. She hugged Emily to her side, upsetting the little box of crayons in her hand. "Oh, excuse me, darling." She hugged her again. "What picture are you making?" Emily had brought along a picture book for the trip.

"See, Mummy." She held it up to her. The Italian woman leaned over to look too. "Is nice," she said approvingly of the half-filled in picture of Dumbo the Elephant. "Very nice."

Emily smiled back in her own serious way. She looked like Joe. She had his white skin and his dark hair, but her eyes were as pale gray as mist, and beneath the dark brows and the long black lashes, they had a way of illuminating the pale solemn face.

Molly bent over her and kissed the top of her head. She was glad to feel Emily close to her, in spite of the heat. The Italian woman smiled and nodded approval. Molly smiled back. Molly felt enveloped in a sense of womanly comprehension, womanly coziness, like a cocoon, a padding against the pushing, noisy, soldierly fraternity swarming around them, hanging over the seats, calling to one another, the boys.

They were singing again. "Praise the Lord and pass the ammunition." In spite of herself, the words went through her head; she knew them all, the words of all the songs they sang. They kept at it and at it. "Roll out the Barrel" and then "Good-bye Mama, I'm off to Yokohama," and on and on. Just as she had gone on and on in rage at Joe.

When he came home that evening in August and told her he had volunteered, she screamed at him. "I knew it, I knew it. I knew you would, you big patriot, you stinker. Anything to get into the action. Anything to get away from home. My hero!"

Joe had stood there, taking it all in, not really part of her anger, her rage. It was as if he had already gone, leaving only the husk of self, armed against her blows.

"Why, Joe?" she finally managed to say.

He looked at her, then moved forward to put his arms around her, still silent. From within the ring of his arms, her head against his shoulder, still crying, she said, "But we were supposed to be against war. On principle. As a matter of belief."

He stroked her back and kissed the top of her hair. Finally he said, "Emily is half-Jewish, Molly. Remember that. If Hitler wins, what about Emily?"

She pushed him away, roughly, fiercely. "That's pure rant, Joe. It's bombast. It's the new Party line now that the Russians have been attacked."

He stiffened, angry now himself. "I refer you to the Nuremberg Laws, my dear Molly." His voice was cold and judicial.

"That's no Party line. That's being realistic. Why don't you try a little realism yourself, instead of all these hysterics?"

"Okay," she managed to say abruptly. "When do you go?"

"In ten days. I'm due to leave September eighth. There's a training program in Toronto, where I have to report."

For Molly there was the deepest sense of betrayal. But they went down to Maryland to get legally married because Joe felt it would make a difference for her allotment from the Canadians. He was insistent on that. She was indifferent, yet moved at least by this reminder of his sense of responsibility for her and Emily. They spent a frantic weekend together, passionate and unhappy. It was so colored by argument and unreality that at one point Molly even reminded Joe of their common contempt for the Socialists in France who in World War One abandoned their principles to vote war credits.

"Oh, for God's sake, Molly," he exploded. "Can't you face reality for once! Who the hell cares about *then*. This is *now*. Things are different now. We're not at a protest meeting, for Chrissakes. We're here. We're here to make love. I love you, I'll always love you, but this is something I have to do."

In the end, they made love and drove home quietly and a few days later Joe left.

W H E N the train stopped at Albany, many of the soldiers, dragging their duffels, clattering and shouting, got off the train. They were headed for Plattsburgh. It had taken almost five hours to make the run from New York to Albany, with the train huffing and puffing and then inexplicably coming to a standstill, endlessly en route. Emily was asleep against Molly's shoulder, and Molly's head leaned on Emily's. Their nice Italian neighbor had gotten off at Hudson, after sharing some of her salami sandwiches with them and nibbling tentatively at the chicken on white that Molly had offered her. When she vacated her seat, Molly and Emily had stretched out and fallen asleep together.

This was not a trip to make often during the summer, thought Molly, and if Emily was left with the Lerners, it would be until the end of August. She held the little girl close to her, lonely already for her, in spite of the relief Emily's absence would bring. She had a sense of quick guilt. She had been so irritable lately with Emily. She hated the impatience that flared up when she came home, tired and anxious, to find Emily waiting for her beseechingly, wanting to be played with, clutching at her, calling for attention. It seemed to Molly that no amount of affection she offered was ever enough. The child's need seemed to be bottomless, as deep as Molly's own fatigue.

There was so much for her to do when she returned after the long day at *Newscast*. There was the v-letter from Joe that came nearly every day—it had to be read before anything else was done, it was her lifeline to him. Then there was Tommy to be hugged and fussed over. And there was Katy, ready to leave the minute Molly came through the door, thrusting at her a scrawled list of supplies to be bought, reporting on the problems with the plumbing, and then making a complaint, always a complaint, about Emily.

Katy was rubbed the wrong way by Emily. She was so loving with Tommy, so sharp with the little girl. Emily's neediness irritated Katy. Emily made emotional demands she could not meet.

Molly would turn to Emily impatiently with a few brusque words to please Katy, as the tears rose in Emily's eyes. After Katy rushed through the door for her own hot trip up town Molly, without a minute to waste, would turn to hug Emily again, patting her shoulder, uncertain. She knew she ought to get rid of Katy for Emily's sake, but not now, not now. Molly needed her too much. Better to bark at Emily than to find another maid. She hugged Emily again, but it wasn't enough.

I'm sick and tired of all this domesticity, Molly would explode to herself. It's all too much, loaded on to everything else.

Molly knew that Emily missed Joe. She knew that the child was deeply afraid for him. She was only five years old but Molly could sense a desperate yearning in her and a terror over the separation with its undercurrent of loss. Sometimes they clung together passionately, the child wrapping her arms around Molly's neck with a fierce throttling hold. And once when the radio was tuned to "There'll be blue birds over the white cliffs of Dover," the two of them were locked in a torrent of tears, both faces wet, noses running, crying together in great heaving helpful sobs.

But mostly, with the pressures of her work prodding at her, Molly didn't want to share her grief, her anger, her fatigue. Her favorite phrase to herself was "It's all too much, it's all too much." It reverberated constantly in her head. She could hear it bouncing off one part of her brain to another. She would push Emily away, saying, "Wait until after I read this letter, wait until I get our supper, wait wait wait."

"I'm torn," Molly admitted sadly to Sophie one evening over a canned-salmon salad whipped together for supper in front of the open window. "I've learned to make choices. I like my work. I've chosen my work. But what a dilemma. I want to be a mother too, a full-time mother, full time emotionally. But no, never full time playing in the park." She shuddered at the idea. "I feel this interplay in me. Two powerful needs. Maternity, and me. And Emily, she's entangled in it. How does she feel about it? How will she feel? She seems so angry with me sometimes. Katy pushes her aside. I don't mean to, but so do I."

They both looked at Emily at the back of the room, out of

earshot, reading her picture book grimly, holding the volume upside-down to show her displeasure because Sophie was there to share the evening.

Sophie looked thoughtful. "Who knows? I think you can't count on the adult reactions of your kids. She may admire you one day for making a choice. Or she may resent it bitterly. Or she may feel both ways at the same time."

"But how do you resolve it?" pleaded Molly, seeking an answer, a lifeline.

Sophie smiled at her lovingly, reaching out to stroke her hand. "Dear Molly, you can't resolve it. Maybe you can only accept it. Anyway, how do I know? Perhaps the resolution is in the future, when more women learn to make choices. There may be change in the air."

Molly sighed. "Perhaps Emily will be as unfair to me as I am to my mother. Sometimes you can't win."

The guilt ran through Molly's veins as she held Emily in the train, nodding and sleeping with her, opening her eyes to see whether they were past Syracuse at last. The walk through the crowded aisle of the train to the dirty tiny toilet at the far end was treacherous. They stumbled over the sleeping soldiers, propped against their bags. "A midafternoon snooze," one of them said cheerfully to her as she stepped over him, "want to join me?" Molly was bleary-eyed and dirty and Emily's chocolate bar, bought at Albany, seemed permanently encrusted on the child's face. There was no water in the toilet sink to scrub the ravages of the journey away and Molly was too tired to try. She moistened her handkerchief with her own spit and poked at the chocolate that paved Emily's lips.

· CHAPTER 11 ·

SOPHIE'S mother was waiting on the platform in Rochester as the train pulled in. As she saw her, Molly's eyes glistened with tears of relief. Two soldiers helped Molly and Emily off the high steps on to the platform and into Leah's arms. They almost tottered down, they were so tired. Molly was hugged by the big woman, her breasts like enormous feather-filled pillows against her chest. Then it was Emily's turn to be crushed to her, kissed on the mouth, and hugged again.

"Do I have a surprise for you, Emily?" she promised in her high loud voice, in almost the same accent as Hester's, but the *r* different, not so New York. "Wait till you see, little girlie, a real surprise."

Emily regarded her gravely, her wide gray eyes blinking in the late-afternoon light, almost stunned by the rush of affection but not pulling away. "Thank you," she said solemnly, "I like surprises, Mrs. Lerner." Molly had coached her on the name, but Sophie's mother brushed it aside.

"Tante Leah," she prompted Emily. "Call me Tante Leah. And you'll be my little Emily, my nice little girl."

What a wonder Leah Lerner was! Ever since Molly and Sophie had been at Vassar together and she had been brought home for visits, Molly had found herself welcomed into the

· 165 ·

whole affectionate, noisy, spirited family. Like Joe's family, the Lerners were deeply Jewish, but it was a different Jewishness. The Lerners were Jewish Socialists, and being Socialists wasn't just political for them, a matter of accidental membership. It was their whole lives. The texture was tightly woven. They cared about the whole world, about everything. Joe's family had seemed cramped to Molly, but never the Lerners. Being Jewish Socialists was a daily responsibility and a source of joy.

They belonged to a group called the Workmen's Circle, and when Molly first heard the name "Workmen's Circle" she marveled at the strong symbolical simplicity of it. "It says so much. Who thought it up? I love it," she cried to Sophie.

Sophie laughed at her. "You get so excited by all this. As if you were on an archaeological dig among strange natives. Who thought it up? Working-class Jews, I guess."

"Do only Jews belong?" asked Molly.

"I don't know. For Mother and Dad it's where they belong. Some Jews—religious ones—have the synagogue. For Mother and Dad and their friends, who wouldn't be caught dead in a synagogue, the *Arbeiter Ring* is home."

"*Arbeiter Ring?*" asked Molly.

"Workmen's Circle. That's what it means."

Molly was fascinated by the name and the history. "But what is it?" she prodded Sophie. "Who belongs? Tell me."

Sophie shrugged. "I haven't the faintest notion. I can't describe it. It just is. It's a kind of mutual aid society with its roots in labor."

"But what is it?" Molly persisted.

Again Sophie shrugged. "Don't be such a romantic, kid. It started out as working class and Socialist with a whole set of passionate interests. A passionate interest in the Yiddish language, a passionate interest in social justice, a passionate interest in education. Humanist. I always thought of it as passionately interested in the common good as my mother and father defined it."

"But when? Where? I want to know." Molly's excitement made Sophie laugh.

"You're really a screwball with your crazy enthusiasms," she said. "But maybe I take it all too much for granted. It started in New York at the beginning of the century, down on the Lower East Side, and thousands joined. And I can remember, when I was young, it was the only game in town for people like my parents."

The meeting place in Rochester was a floor of an old office building a few blocks up the avenue. Leah Lerner went to three meetings a week. She headed the Ladies Auxiliary and she was proud of her functions. The group ran a Yiddish School, which they called the Sholom Aleichem Shule, as well as a library, and they held classes in socialism and world thought. One night during one of her visits with Sophie, there was a dance at the center and Molly went with the family. Three high-school kids made up the band, playing some of the current popular songs: a girl at the piano, one boy with an out-of-tune sax, another with a scratchy violin. They pumped away at "If You Knew Susie" and "I'm Looking Over a Four-leaf Clover" with a happy intensity. They were enthusiastic and everyone applauded. Some teenagers danced and some little children were guided around the floor in time to the music by uncertain parents.

Chairs were lined up around the circle set off for dancing and by the end of the evening, they were all occupied. "Dance Molly, go dance," Leah urged her, oblivious to the fact that there were no young men to dance with. "Go Sophie, dance."

Sophie whispered to Molly, out of the side of her mouth, "Don't pay any attention to her. She's just hoping some nice Jewish boy will arise out of the night to sweep me away."

Molly poked Sophie to be quiet.

"It's quite true," Sophie insisted. "Anything to save her daughter from the indignity of going to college and becoming an old maid."

This wasn't true. Not absolutely true. Leah was proud of her daughters at Cornell and Vassar and Sarah Lawrence. She didn't know they were the "best" schools; they were the schools that had given scholarships and inducements, and it was her daughters, after all, who were the best.

But her daughters were all pushing into their twenties and beyond, a time for marriage and babies. As Leah was ambiguous about this, she was ambiguous about much in her life. Devoted to the ideals of the Workmen's Circle though she was, Leah also cherished the idea of getting ahead, making money, having "a nice home," as she put it. Molly found her not unlike Joe's mother in this, but she was firmer in her convictions, not as insular, warmer.

The wonder of it for Molly was how surrounded Sophie's parents were by the comradeship of this group they belonged to: the picnics they went on together; these dances; the lectures they arranged and attended, with speakers brought from New York or Poland or Germany. They all spoke Yiddish to one another; they had a cult about the language, wanting to preserve it and purify it, refusing the name "jargon" given it by Jews who decried it.

They had all been part of the waves of immigration of the last century and the early years of the twentieth. Those waves had swept them past the shallows of the Lower East Side of New York on to the shores of this city, which offered them the kind of work they could do as tailors, cutters, and pressers in the clothing industry that flourished in Rochester. They all seemed the same age to Molly, of the same generation. And there was an old-world dignity about them that clung after all their years together here. They called one another by their last names, always prefixed with "Mrs." or "Mr." After years of intimacy it was still Mrs. Lerner and Mrs. Axelrod and Mrs. Goldman and Mrs. Schwartz. These were Leah's closest friends but the proprieties were observed. Only to the immediate family, the children, the closest relatives was there any relaxation of the rule.

As Leah drove Molly and Emily home from the railroad station in the old Dodge she bubbled over with enthusiasm and delight. At the house the surprise was waiting for Emily: little Laurie, Emily's age, was at her grandmother's for this summer too. Emily stood regarding the child in her own serious way. When Laurie reached out her hand to take Emily's, there was only the tiniest hesitation and the hands were joined.

"Come on out, Emily." Laurie pulled at her. "I have a new cat. You can share her too."

Molly felt relieved, her own ache at leaving Emily dispelled by the sight of the two children going off together, a good start.

"Don't worry, Molly dearest," Leah assured her. "And there's a Camp Kinder group they'll go to together starting on Tuesday. A wonderful summer. I promise you."

· CHAPTER 12 ·

ONE week after Emily's departure, Molly was called into the office by Lew Taylor.

"Listen," he said. "I hope you're ready for this. But we have no choice. You're all we've got."

"Thanks a lot, Lew, always there with a compliment," she joked as she wondered at his worried look. "What's up?"

"Trouble," he replied. "We're sending Bob Coffee out to Detroit. It looks like a storm is brewing there. All hell may break loose."

Bob Coffee was their one Negro reporter, a smart self-confident man who dressed in Tripler suits and liked to eat at the Ritz. He had gone to Harvard, earning money along the way as a redcap at Grand Central. He was a good reporter, passionate, who took pleasure in hobnobbing with gangsters and politicos and gaining an inside track, no matter how. Everything tough and shady was his beat. He loved to tell Harlem stories, his big white teeth flashing in his smooth brown face. "Don't call me colored," he would shout, "that's for the *schvarze.* I'm a Negro, by God. Negritude, that's me—a little late for the Harlem Renaissance but just in time for everything else."

One evening at an office party celebrating something or other, he caught Molly by the shoulders, spun her around, and kissed her full on the mouth. She was nonplussed but moved. She felt his power and her reaction left her startled and kept her awake for the night that followed.

"Possible riots in Detroit," Lew was saying and for a minute Molly thought, "My God, they're sending me with Bob Coffee to Detroit!"

The thought of going on an assignment with him was a mixed bag of alarm and anticipation.

But no such luck. It was a different story for her, but still the biggest one in her experience. Lew went on, "We have reports to watch out for Harlem. Possible riots up there too. We want you to cover it with Sophie Lerner. She'll give you pointers. Take what you can and follow her lead."

"When?"

"Right away. Talk to Sophie now."

First Molly called Katy and asked if she could do some extra time, perhaps stay overnight with Tommy. Time and a half for overtime, she added. Katy was reluctant but agreed. Then Molly walked over to Editorial to find Sophie. Molly had heard that Sophie was superb on assignment, quick and savvy and totally professional. They had never worked together and Molly was fired up by the idea.

"I'm here, Sophie. Lew Taylor's put me on Harlem with you."

Sophie grinned at her. "Lovely. Let me tell you how I plan it. Come and sit down." Molly could see why everyone wanted to work with her. There was no swagger, no apparent ego; she was cool, efficient, and friendly. Molly sensed that this was Sophie's professional friendliness, quite apart from the personal friendship they shared.

"I hope I'm good enough," Molly said nervously.

"You'll be good enough, don't worry. Just bring plenty of film and lots of flash. Use your Leica, I know you're more familiar with it. A larger format would be better but the thing that counts is that your camera doesn't get in the way."

Molly listened, nodding as Sophie went on. Sophie had worked out a plan with her editor; it was already underway. To begin with, a meeting at the First Abyssinian Church with the Reverend Adam Clayton Powell and some of the NAACP big shots. Pictures there, easy to take, backdrop. After that, wait for the night. A meeting had been called at the church to offset another one, an outdoor rally announced by what the Brothers called troublemakers. "After that," said Sophie, "we'll see. Maybe it will all evaporate."

But it didn't evaporate. Not in Harlem. Not in Detroit. Bob Coffee wrote a brilliant story, called "Rage in Detroit," that went round the world. The race riots uncovered the ulcerous wound in the American flesh. They exposed the myth that this was a time of unity. The unity was a fiction. The reality was dynamite. When the smoke in Detroit had cleared thirty-four were dead, seven hundred injured. This in Detroit alone. There were sporadic uprisings elsewhere, and in Harlem, the same seething fury, the same TNT, the same bottled-up rage deto-nated, leaving another six dead and devastation in the streets above 110th.

The photographs Molly took made her the talk of the mag-azine, then the talk of New York, and won her a Pulitzer Prize. Of course Bob Coffee won a Pulitzer too for his Detroit story. It was expected. But Molly's triumph was a bolt of lightning. Sophie grimaced good-naturedly at being left out of the honors but there was no spite, no envy toward Molly.

"It was all accident, Sophie." Molly spoke shaking her head, not knowing what to make of it. "No one says it, but it's the lucky accident that shows up on your negative that tells the story."

"Don't you believe it," Sophie answered.

And when she said the same thing to Lew, he cut her short. "Forget it, baby. It's the seeing eye that counts."

So Bob and Molly went to the prize reception together up at Columbia, a rather dreary affair held at the Faculty Club. "I'll ride you downtown," he said when they were leaving. She protested as he hailed a cab on Broadway. "Bob, it's too far out of your way. I'm quite used to getting around on my own."

"I know that, hon. But I feel knightly tonight." He slid his arm around her in the cab going down to Fourteenth Street and again kissed her full on the lips, opening them, his tongue against hers. She had had champagne and praise and was on a high. She kissed him back, let his hand run up under her skirt.

"Where can we go," he breathed in her ear.

"Go?" Suddenly Molly sat back against the seat, pushing him away, terrified. "Bob," she managed to say, "I don't want to go anywhere. I want to go home."

"Why?" His hands were all over her, demanding compliance.

"Because." Again she pushed him back. "Because, Bob." She hesitated at her simple-minded confession. "Because I'm just plain scared. This isn't my act at all."

He sat up straight, loosened his grip, looked at her. "What do you mean, not your act?"

"Just that. Please understand. I've never been unfaithful to Joe."

He threw his head back and laughed like a small boy. "Unfaithful? I'm not asking you to be unfaithful. That's such a cute word. I'm just suggesting we have a little fun together. I like the way you are. Don't you like me?"

She looked at him solemnly. "I like you a lot, Bob." She felt she was talking like a schoolgirl. "I think you're one of the most attractive men I know. But—oh, God—I'm not used to this. I've fenced myself in from this kind of thing. Otherwise I'd go mad."

"What kind of thing?" he insisted. "I don't want to come between you and Joe, honey. All I want to do is screw you."

She did the unexpected. She burst into tears. "I'm sorry. I'm sorry." She tried to wipe her face with her sleeve.

"Don't cry, baby." He wiped her tears with his big clean handkerchief that felt soft as silk and smelled of lemon cologne. "What a kid you are. A grown woman with two children and a Pulitzer and you haven't a clue on how to field a pass."

He made her smile. They were at Fourteenth Street, and he opened the door of the cab to let her out. "Don't worry about a thing, baby. Just remember what you've missed. But I'm not pushing, not on your life." He kissed her on the cheek and watched her go through the door. He told her later that the cab refused to take him back uptown.

"You're kidding, boy," the driver said to him. "Up to Harlem? You must be crazy." So he paid him off and took the subway at the corner and remained Molly's friend for the rest of the life left him.

He became a nationally known syndicated columnist, and was a force in the civil rights movement of the sixties. "Honey, I'm black now," he had told her somewhat ironically, "black as the ace of spades," when Molly had last seen him a few days before his death. He was going out to Los Angeles to cover the riots in Watts and he died along with more than thirty others in the crossfire. Molly mourned him for a long time. She missed his gaiety and his pride. And, out of the subconscious of long buried feelings, she regretted his failed seduction.

How she had tossed and turned the night of the Pulitzer dinner. What a cheap fool I made of myself, she thought then. I led him on. At least I looked available. Why did I turn him down? Afraid? Yes, afraid. Why? Would I have felt that way if he were white?

The thought tormented her. She would never have spoken

it aloud. The question was frightening. She wanted to believe that she had been washed clean of the sin of bigotry. But questions kept cropping up. How deeply ingrained were these ancient prejudices? She was glad no one could see into the depths of her mind and soul.

· CHAPTER 13 ·

EMILY came back to New York with a definite accent, tanned and happy and suddenly noisier and more sure of herself than ever. Their ride back together on the Empire State was as crowded and uncomfortable as the ride up, but their boxed lunch was better. Leah had packed enough for ten hungry hikers: tongue on rye bread, fried chicken, hard-boiled eggs, homemade strudel. They shared their spoils with the clutter of soldiers and sailors who again crowded the aisles, singing and sleeping as they had before. Molly felt as if she were part of a tidal wave moving ceaselessly across the land.

It was just a few days before Labor Day, still hot. Emily was entering the first grade in a few days and Molly had been talked into taking a scholarship for her at the Dalton School on the Upper East Side. It was Molly's mother who had had the idea and had pursued it. One of her closest friends was the head-mistress of the lower school and had furthered the arrangements.

Molly remembered her mother's distress at the idea of Emily at the Lerners' for the summer. What a clash of contradictions her mother was, Molly had thought with impatience. When she was told about the Camp Kinder, she had reddened. She seemed to find it hard to say but managed to say it to Molly anyway. "She's going to pick up some things she's not used to," she started. "And hard to eradicate."

"Like what, Mother?" Molly felt belligerent. Her mother fumbled for words. "Well, it's hard to put one's finger on it, but speech patterns, for example."

Molly became even more bellicose. "A ghetto accent, do you mean, Mother?"

But underneath her belligerence, Molly had had the same apprehension. I remain a snob, she thought. No matter what's happened to me, I'm still a snob—a Waspy New England Yankee snob. No better than Mother. Is it ever possible to wipe out our ingrained prejudices?

But aloud Molly flung at her, "I don't care how Tante Leah speaks, Mother, or the others too. They are generous warmhearted people, and I'll never be able to thank them enough for seeing me through this time."

Molly's mother had reddened again. Molly sensed her mother's embarrassment at having spoken at all. She knew that her mother was sometimes staggered by her own vestigial parochialism and would falter and fall back when she said things she immediately regretted. Molly knew this about her mother because she knew it about herself. In a way, they were both astride two worlds, really at home in neither. But Molly resented her mother's awareness; she hated her mother's look of compassion and understanding when sometimes she let down her defenses and acknowledged her loneliness, the pressures of work and children, the desperation of being torn from one place to the other. Molly knew her mother understood. But it irked her that her mother understood too much, that she was so privy to the tumult within her.

Mother can't win with me, she admitted ruefully to herself. When she saw the sympathy on her mother's face she wanted to cry out, "Not a word, don't say a word, let it be." And when her mother turned her eyes down, shadowing her look, not wanting to betray her emotion, Molly wanted to shout, "Well, say it, why don't you say it, it's all too much."

"It's not the usual elite private school," Mary now insisted over Molly's protests. "It isn't Spence or Chapin. It's a progressive school. There are all kinds of children there, and it's famous for its education. Don't be such an inverse snob, Molly. It's better for Emily."

The "better for Emily" won the day, although Molly wasn't entirely certain what that meant. It was true that the public school downtown was crowded, in a dilapidated building with almost no playground space, and a longish walk from the Fourteenth Street apartment. The Dalton children who lived in the Village were picked up by special bus, and a bus brought them back. The school agreed to make a stop for Emily. Molly didn't ask what the transportation would cost because her mother and father offered to pay for it.

"We've been accepted." Her letter to Joe was jocular. "There's a great pastry shop around the corner on Lexington Avenue, the kids look fine, just like kids, and Miss Harley, mother's friend, is a bit on the la-de-da side but okay. I don't know what the progressive means at this place, but it's a nice big building, well-heeled but not overwhelming. What do you think?"

Joe thought it was a good idea. He hadn't known much about private schools, he wrote, until he'd run into people like Dick Waverly and his brother at the Acme Press. "When I was growing up," his letter went on, "I thought private schools were for dummies and rich kids who got into trouble, but there's a whole world out there that takes another view. And maybe," he went on, "we'll think of finding another apartment up in that neighborhood when I come back. We'll need more space."

There was a dear, sweet domesticity about their v-letters.

They were filled with the details of their daily lives as if they were sitting face to face at the kitchen table. Back and forth, exchanging everyday concerns—the menu for tomorrow's dinner, the quality of the Spam in the mess, the pediatrician's report on Tommy, how they'd all gotten drunk on pass in London, Emily's school. Molly loved the snugness of the letters, in a way much more homey and intimate than their real life together had been. Joe couldn't write about what he was doing—and only later did she learn of the combat missions and the buzz-bombs and the flack—but he wrote her about his friends, the party menus contrived from the food packages they received, his stint teaching navigation in Northern Ireland; and when he secretly crossed over into forbidden Eire on an escapade, he wrote a cryptic message about going to visit another Molly, sweet Molly Malone, which took her two jealous days to decipher before she realized that he meant the city of Dublin.

Mingled with the bits and pieces of what the children were doing, the stomach flu going around the base, the stomach flu going around the office, they tried through the letters to weave their lives together, to connect, to be together on different sides of the ocean. Joe wrote of his disappointments in the political climate of England, his feeling that when the war was over, England would get rid of Churchill. He was bully as a war leader, Joe wrote, but he didn't understand the ordinary needs and concerns of England's working class. They wrote about what they were reading, what they were thinking; there were diatribes on both sides against Roosevelt and Churchill and Stalin and Chiang Kai-shek and Mrs. Chiang. But in the letters the world out there shrank into background and what loomed large was their personal closeness, their privacy. Molly felt that somehow they were more a family in the letters than they had ever been before.

With Emily at Dalton and Joe's suggestion that she look for

a place closer to school, Molly went on a house hunt. The prize had brought a raise and early in 1944 she found a house in the East Seventies that she thought could be managed. An 1890's vintage brownstone that had gone through a variety of cycles, from boarding house to tenement flats, it needed work. It had never been grand, but Molly could see that if stripped down it would emerge as a lovely Victorian, with high ceilings, oak floors, nice detail. The down payment, twenty-five hundred dollars, was something she could swing with a loan of five hundred dollars from her parents.

"A house!" Joe wrote. "No one in New York lives in a house."

"I was brought up to live in a house," she wrote back huffily. "People in Sheffield County don't rent, they own."

"Okay" was Joe's answer.

This month of May his letters had gotten shorter, more clipped, some of them obviously censored. Later on Molly knew why. The planning for the invasion of Europe was in progress and mail was being held back until the day in June when it happened. By that sixth of June Molly had already moved the children into the house and had started painting the bedrooms. She was on the ladder, the radio going, when the news came.

"Our expeditionary forces, under air support, have landed in Normandy. The churches are open this day for the prayers of all Americans for our boys on the beaches. This is the moment we have all been waiting for. There is a hush on the land as we bow our heads in mutual communion."

Molly slowly descended the ladder and snapped off the radio. She could hear church bells outside, somewhere on Lexington Avenue. She felt stilled and suspended, a great silence within her as the church bells clanged. Suddenly she was afraid. Air support meant Joe. She went into the kitchen, where Tommy sat in his high chair pushing his food around while Katy sat trying to read the *Daily News* as she watched him.

Molly leaned over Tommy and hugged him tightly. Katy smiled at them both above the headlines of the paper. She was living with them, now that there was a room in the house for her. She made the trip to Harlem only once or twice a week to be with her "other family," as she called her sister and her nephews.

"Something wrong, Miz Levin?" Katy asked. "You look put out."

Molly shook her head, but she bent over Katy and hugged her too.

"It's this war," she tried to explain, "they've opened a second front in Europe."

Katy shook her head and clicked her lips. "You got nothing to worry 'bout, Miz Levin. Your man'll come back. I just knows it."

"I hope so Katy. I hope you're right."

For Katy, worry about the war was personal. There were no issues bigger than the survival of the people she loved. And because she loved Molly and Tommy, had grown less testy and more caring of Emily, she loved Joe too, although they had not yet met. What were invasions, second fronts, expeditionary forces—what did they mean? If there was danger on the beaches of Normandy, that was no place for Joe. Her tone implied he'd better get going fast.

Molly hugged her again. There was nothing to say. One could only wait. And wait and wait. It was three weeks before Molly heard from Joe again, this time a packet of more than a dozen letters, mail that had been held back to guard against any news about the landings leaking out. Never had the war seemed closer than in the silences. Never had the fear that clamped her heart like an iron brace been more present. She could taste it, she could smell it. She went to work each day, shopped, played with the children, finished painting one room, then started another, all in a haze of omnipresent fear. She thought of Joe with longing. He was crazy and romantic and opinionated and sarcastic and perhaps (she wondered), occasionally unfaithful, causing her pain and fury; he was difficult to live with, but he was hers, he was in her life, no one else.

"Damn him, he shouldn't be putting me through this," she cried in rage at her reflection in the medicine chest mirror, after the letters had finally arrived and the tension had eased.

Joe came back in November, came back to the Upper East Side, to a brownstone house, a sleep-in maid, a Pulitzer Prize—winning wife, a child in private school and a child he had never seen who was walking and talking.

Molly had made the transition from one life to the other without thinking of how wide a swing it was. One thing had led to another and suddenly they weren't on Fourteenth Street with the bedbugs and the skulking Spaniards and the transient babysitters. The war wasn't over yet and it wasn't over for Joe, but he was home. He was still in uniform, on something called R&R, rest and recuperation, in line to be trained to fly B-29's in the war in the Pacific.

T H O S E were difficult days of reunion. Molly tried to take Joe's anger and bile with understanding, but she felt resentment too. Joe was aggressive about the good life civilians were leading: "You'd never know there was a war on." There was a venom in him toward the men who hadn't gone or those who had found safe and easy stations in the armed forces, or those in the Office of War Information, who wore what he called fake officer's uniforms and did "fuck all." He was vituperative and bitter about noncombat soldiers, men who had moved up in their civilian jobs, everyone who had "not been shot at."

Molly challenged him. "You're a classic case history of the returned soldier who despises the home front. You go back to Euripides."

"Aeschylus." Joe contradicted her mockingly. "I think you mean Aeschylus, my dear. He was so proud of being a combat soldier that he asked that his epitaph speak only of that."

"Euripides, Aeschylus," Molly snapped back, "don't be such a smart ass."

"Aeschylus the Athenian," Joe intoned, continuing to scoff. " 'Euphoreon's son is dead/ This tomb in Gela's cornfields covers him/ His glorious courage the hallowed field of Marathon could tell/ and the long-haired Medes too.' " He paused. "An approximate translation, but it tells the story. He was a soldier, Molly, and proud of it."

Joe was sometimes mean-spirited about her job and her damn Pulitzer, sometimes proud of her—she never knew which way the wind would blow. He would awaken in the night screaming and sweating and shouting, "Down, down, the dirty bastard, motherfucker, Nazi prick." She would shake him awake from his shattering dreams.

"Wake up, Joe. Wake up. You're home, you're here." He would toss the covers aside, get out of bed, light a cigarette, still shaking, still sweating, the cigarette hanging from his trembling lips.

"Coffee?" she would ask him. "Shall I make some?"

They would sit in the kitchen while she brewed the coffee, while they drank it, while he smoked cigarette after cigarette, lighting one with another and dragging the first puff of each deep into his lungs, until he stopped trembling and they went back to bed.

One night over the coffee he said, "I never knew before that I was such a coward. I was scared shitless all the time."

"Then why"—she hated herself for saying it but it was at the tip of her tongue—"why did you go in for so many combat missions? You could have opted out long ago, your war record intact."

It was a sore point with Molly, another one of her many sore points. There was a long pause before he answered her. "Just because I *am* such a coward," he said slowly. "I've been scared out of my skin every minute up there. I wanted to prove something to myself." ·

That's Joe, thought Molly. He has to prove something to *himself.* The hell with everyone else.

Once he admitted ruefully, "I'm like Paul in *All Quiet on the Western Front.* I ought never to have come home on leave. It is all too painful. The contrasts kill me."

Again Molly felt herself thinking and feeling on two levels. One part of her mind and heart opened up to Joe, feeling his suffering and his turmoil. The doctor at the Air Force Center, where Joe had to check in once each week, talked to him about combat fatigue and mission stress. He recommended that Joe go up to Pawling, where the Air Force had taken over a boys' school as a retreat for what Joe ironically called "poor wounded airmen." Molly said why not.

But the other part of her questioned and taunted Joe, never in words aloud, never openly, but a constant hidden chorus that mocked the stresses and strains, thought it all part of the same male swagger as the war stories told at the local saloon.

Sometimes Molly would meet Joe at Johnny's Bar late in the afternoon after work. Joe spent most of his days working on the house, stripping down the old watermarked wallpaper, tearing down the slum tenement partitions, returning the rooms to their original handsome size. But at dusk, in the late afternoon, he changed from his paint-splattered overalls to his uniform to join the crowd at Johnny's.

It was a small place with high leather-topped stools lining an oaken bar with the glint of polished brass along the edge. It was always packed with men in uniform standing shoulder to shoulder, a few women interlarded between them. Some of the men were waiting to be discharged. Others, like Joe, were waiting for transfers. Mingled with the noise and the smoke, the war stories and the dirty jokes—with snide apologies to the women present—was a sense of boisterous animosity toward all civilians.

We're the enemy, Molly would think. The enemy is us. But her mind would slide from its bitter level to the other, to the place in her inner being that understood Joe and felt compassion for him and all these other men. She could understand the confusion that must come from flying home in a matter of a few hours from a corner of hell to this cozy niche. She listened to them. They were dazed by the Battle of the Bulge; a few weeks earlier they had assumed the war was almost over, but now the future was clouded. What was to come? And in this place called home, they heard trivial, mean complaints about the scarcity of nylon stockings and food coupons and gasoline rations for the car.

"Shit," said one of the young men as he downed his fifth whiskey, "what this place needs is a good bombing. Rip it apart, I say. Let's see how they could take it. Let 'em have it. The whole country stinks."

He was a warrant officer in the Eighth Air Force. Molly had learned to distinguish some of the markings. "What about a bomb on the roof of *your* house?" she managed to say quietly. "How would you like that?"

Joe pushed his elbow into her ribs. She looked at him sullenly, then realized it wasn't her conversation. This was men's talk.

She was there just as background, to keep Joe company, always twenty paces behind as part of the pasha's female entourage.

She accepted the code of conduct with a shrug. What was the use?

The young warrant officer looked at her bleary-eyed but he answered. "If the bomb has the number of my house on it, that's the way it is, lady. What counts is to win this war. Nothing personal, understand?"

Molly looked at him steadily, deadpan. She couldn't understand what he was saying, it didn't make sense to her. They all liked to talk about bombs with numbers on them, a kind of fate, inescapable. But why would the war be won if the bombs came this way, instead of dropping over there? She felt how bitter these men were, how deep was their resentment against the people at home—their own wives and mothers and children. It seemed to her, she felt it in her bones, that it was a resentment against all the women behind the lines. They also made fun of the "shoe clerks" who sat behind desks and found cushy safe jobs, but the true venom, the hatred, the rancor was reserved for everything female. Women who took over men's jobs (how you gonna get them back on the farm?), women who struck out into careers, even the women who stayed home and did what they had always done—all were the butt of the men's fears, their sneers, their vindictiveness.

"Wait until the boys come home," they joked. "We'll keep them barefoot and pregnant."

Sometimes Joe and Molly would walk home from Johnny's Bar, silent and companionable, as if they understood in tandem what they had heard. They would mumble their reactions, each avoiding anything that might trigger an argument.

"That's a crazy kid, that Eddie," Joe said about the warrant officer. "But he's been through a lot."

Molly was silent, not wanting to ask about the "lot." In fact, she hadn't really been horrified at the suggestion that it would be a good idea to bomb New York. She had been bemused. Who was to do the bombing and would it be selective? East Sixty-fifth Street, let's say, but never Lexington and Seventy-sixth, with Johnny's Bar on the corner. And what kind of lesson was to be taught to the women left behind? Did the men really think that Rosie the Riveter would lay down her tools and return to the joy of her washing machine as a permanent thing?

"Do you think the constant bombing of London helped England get through?" she asked Joe once. "Was it a good thing, to prove Britain can take it?"

"Damn right." His answer was immediate. "It turned the country into one big battlefield and put them altogether on the same side."

"Hmm." She delayed her response. "But think of London now. I've seen the photographs. It's a ghastly shambles, all rubble and destruction."

Joe was impatient. He felt he was being needled. "At least the British women and children and the old men know it's their war too. And they're pretty gallant about it, sharing the danger."

"Gallant?" Molly tinged the question with irony. "Everyone uses that word for accepting the horrible senseless suffering."

"Yes, gallant!" Joe raged at her. "It takes a lot of gallantry to go on doing the best you can in the face of necessity."

"But," Molly persisted, "that's just the question. What is necessary about this war? I'd rather hear the British screaming, 'Enough, enough, let's get on with the peace.' And what about the bombing of Berlin? Does that make *them* gallant?"

This was a sore point, almost an unmentionable. Joe had persistent nightmares about the bombing of Berlin. He would tear at the bedsheets, wake up in a frenzy shivering and crying. Once, as he lit his inevitable cigarette, the bedcovers a tangle on the floor, he said, "A thousand bombers every day. We go in every day. The British go in every night. Imagine that city." He shook his head almost in disbelief. "It's uncivilized. We're the Mongol hordes." He took a long drag of the cigarette, exhaled it as if it were the breath of life. "I wouldn't wish it on my worst enemy."

Long ago, when he had been in Europe as a medical student, he had made a visit to Germany, to Berlin. He had loved the city with its wide streets, its great open cafés, the jaunty sexy music-hall music. He still cherished a confused admiration for the Germans. The settlement house in Brooklyn where he had gone to day camp as a child was run by German Jews, and he thought they were the most cultivated and elegant people in the world, a little snotty perhaps, snobbish toward the Eastern European Jews they were doing missionary settlement work for, but secretly, he had once confessed to Molly, he had envied their command of English and of Americanized manners and their air of superiority.

But when Molly asked questions about the ceaseless bombing of Berlin, Joe flew into a rage. "That's the trouble with you, Molly," he had snarled. "You're totally unrealistic. The Germans have to be smashed. Hitler has to be defeated. We can't have fascism hanging over the whole damn world."

She wanted to scream, "Don't sound like a propaganda poster—'Uncle Sam needs you.' We're the goodies, they're the baddies." She managed to quiet her tone of voice. "But what about the fascism on our side?" she said, wanting to quit the argument but looking for the last word. She felt like an oddball with her eccentric arguments—eccentric because they were removed from the center of what everyone was saying. "What about Stalin? What about Chiang? Do you think France is so gallant under the occupation? Hitler doesn't have a corner on fascism."

"I'm going back for a drink." Joe was vehement. "You sound like the Fifth Column. For God's sake, your kids are half Jewish. You know damn well that the words 'Red fascism' were dreamed up by the Nazis. You know that the Resistance in France is being led by the Communists. What the hell are you talking about?" He was yelling by this time.

In spite of herself, Molly's eyes filled with tears and she choked back the sobs. What was the matter with them that they couldn't get through these tense months of his leave without argument and fierce confrontation? Oh, how she wished they could lead their lives on a pleasant everyday level of quotidian concerns and sweet harmonies. Did other people tear at each other in this rapacious tormented way?

Yet they loved one another with mad romantic turbulence. The day after the argument, when Joe had gone back to Johnny's Bar and stayed out half the night, Molly found her office at *Newscast* flooded with flowers: long-stemmed red roses from one florist; a clump of moist violets from another; an enchanting cluster of daisies and blue iris from a third. The flowers kept coming all day, each with a little card that said, "Love you madly" or "You're my everything" or "Guess who?" like messages from a teenager gone wild. By the end of the day Molly was embarrassed by the floral avalanche and the jests it produced among her *Newscast* colleagues.

"What's he up to?" Sophie asked, as she came into Molly's tiny corner office. Her eyebrows lifted. "Another woman?"

Molly shook her head, her face flushed. "No, guess not. Hope not." Her voice dropped.

Sophie eyed her sharply. "So what?"

"I don't know, Sophie, we're fine. Everything's great. Then we get into these enraging arguments that just grow and grow. Mostly about politics. Mostly about nothing."

Again Sophie looked at her directly, quizzically. "About nothing? I doubt it. The trouble is you both like to be heard. And neither of you knows how to shut up."

Molly shrugged, was silent. She couldn't be open and honest about her feelings, not even with Sophie. She really did detest some of Joe's attitudes, but she loved him. Sophie sometimes put such a bright light on things, Molly thought, she lost the depth of focus. Couldn't she see that only with Joe was there a bone-and-blood closeness for her? There were the noisy dissensions, but there were also the long good deep silences. She thought of the strolls she and Joe would take, late at night, after dinner, the children in bed—arm in arm, not speaking, sniffing the night air as they made their way across Seventy-second Street until they reached Fifth Avenue. They would cross and face downtown, following the wide brick and cobblestone walk alongside the park. Across the street were the famous Fifth Avenue mansions, broad and elegant, robber-baron castles they called them and wondered about what went on inside.

At Fifty-ninth Street, where the shops began and the streetlights blazed in the gray-blue sky, they would cross at the Plaza and follow the opposite side down, stopping to gape at each store window, holding hands, muttering at the luxuries in a time of war. The beaux arts beauty of some of the buildings added to their pride in this city, this wondrous, fabulous, richly endowed city they felt to be theirs. They looked at the displays at Tiffany's and Bonwit's and Mark Cross, and then they were at the St. Regis, where it was time, said Joe, for a drink. The walk back up Madison, slower now, even more silent, hardly a word between them, Joe's arm around her shoulders, hers around his waist. It was physical. It was union. How to put it into words?

But sometimes she felt she was in a box, not a nice wooden Chinese chest all polished and lacquered bright red with bronze pulls on each side. That was a metaphor that couldn't contain her feeling. She put her mind to it, tried to imagine the narrow confines that encased her. Her box was brown paper, torn at the edges, a grocery-store carton that said TOILET PAPER or OATMEAL or PABLUM on the outside. An ordinary box into which she was packed, crouching, the lid held down by a frayed cord. She wanted to stay there forever, unable to face Joe and the war and the children and the East Side house and the East Side school and the need to maintain a reputation brought on too early and too suddenly by the Pulitzer. Sometimes her doubts flooded into the box, like the downspill from a broken gutter, drowning her in the soggy carton.

I can't make it, she thought. I drive Joe crazy, he drives me crazy. I couldn't live without him. I'll never match those Harlem pictures. I haven't the time to learn all the new techniques. Emily is at odds at Dalton, where all the kids seem so damn rich and I'm supposed to be an interested parent, which means they're always asking me to take photographs of this and that, their champion volunteer, while all the do-nothing mothers do nothing. And Emily hates that I'm not like them. Katy can't manage the house without more help. I should be home more. Oh, God. She felt herself crouching lower and lower into that brown box until she was only a grease spot on the bottom.

What could she say to Sophie? That she was boxed in? That she was drowning? Dear Sophie would recommend swimming—or getting out of the water. She loved Sophie, but Sophie was so sensible and Molly didn't feel sensible. She didn't know what sensible meant. She smiled at all the flowers. "They must have cost a pretty penny," she said ruefully. "I hope Joe didn't charge them."

They both laughed, quietly at first, and then uproariously. Sophie backed toward the door of the office, looking around again and saying, "At least it's not my funeral" as she left. Molly felt better. It's not mine either, she thought.

· CHAPTER 14 ·

JOE'S brother, Nat, was killed in January of 1945.

"The poor slob," Joe wept. "He allowed himself to be drafted into the infantry! He didn't have a chance—the Battle of the Bulge, the Ardennes! What a hellhole! It will destroy my mother."

But it didn't. Hester wore her sackcloth and ashes with dignity. It was Sam who collapsed, wailing and tearing his hair, unshaven through the week of ritual mourning for his firstborn and for weeks thereafter, unsparing in his grief. Later Nat's body was sent back to them in a box no bigger than a dog basket. There was a funeral with taps and an American flag, nicely folded, for Hester to take home.

The war in Europe ended in May and Joe was sent to Louisiana to be trained in B-29's for the Pacific war. He was home at the end of August, after Hiroshima and Nagasaki and the defeat of Japan, but they felt no sense of celebration. They were stunned by the atomic terror, unbelieving at first, then wild with anger. For a day or two after the first news, Joe kept denying it. He couldn't believe an Air Force plane could have been involved. His phone calls from Louisiana were frantic, agitated. But soon the cataclysmic event could not be denied. There were photographs. There were reports: Bill Laurence's story in the *Times* on August 7, then his eyewitness report two days later, when he flew on the plane to Nagasaki. A whole city demolished by a single bomb. It was confirmed. August 6 and 8 were undeniable facts.

"I can't believe it," they cried to each other over the long-distance lines. "This changes the world. This changes the future."

"That bastard Truman." Molly's voice was incredulous. "He told the newsmen that he went to sleep peacefully after giving the order. Imagine! He rains down havoc, destruction, Armageddon. He changes the future. Wipes out hundreds of thousands of people with one flip of the button—and just goes off to sleep!"

Joe was as shocked as Molly but tried to reason his way out.

"It isn't any worse than the firebombing of Tokyo," he argued. "It's just another weapon."

"No, Joe. Don't talk like one of the military experts. Are you repeating what's being said at the base? This is different," Molly insisted fiercely. "This will change the world. How will our kids grow up with this mushroom cloud hanging over them?"

Joe took a long time to reply. After all, Hiroshima would bring him home. He would be home for good, out of uniform and ready for all the joys of peacetime ahead. This is what the men at the base were saying, this would save lives, *their* lives. "I know," Joe said to her, "This is a hell of a way to end the war. But Molly, I won't be flying B-29's now. I'll be coming home. And," being Joe, he could not help adding, "better Hiroshima than Hitler."

And Molly, being Molly, could not help her bitter reply: "Who says?"

*　　*　　*

J O E went back to the Press, which had prospered during the war years but already felt the threat of change coming to print journalism. Television was in the offing, not yet the giant that would bring about the death of newspaper after newspaper across the country, but a beanstalk growing taller and more commanding every day.

Joe found himself tense about the future, uncertain about the present, questioning the past. He still lent a hand to the newspaper downtown, writing articles for it under an assumed name, sitting in on some of the editorial board meetings. But it was no longer wholehearted participation. The so-called Cold War had started, and while Joe, out of old habit, blamed the United States for creating and sustaining the tension, he was uneasy about the current Soviet attitudes and the hardening of Stalin's control.

He found what others before him had found, that it was painful to give up old allegiances. It sickened him to hear the morbid confessions and recriminations of those who disowned their alliances and their old beliefs. The breast-beating, the denunciations, the lurid revelations disgusted him. He detested the books that were written, the instant tell-all best-sellers; the interviews, the search for celebrity and temporary fame by those who had played insignificant roles as Communists and now sought the limelight as they confessed the past.

Joe felt himself one with the hundreds of former comrades who were quietly leaving the fold but not entirely forsaking the old friendships and the old commitments. The witch hunt had been going on for a long time; it had not been started by Joseph McCarthy. Early investigations in New York State had focused on teachers. There had been investigations of immigration policies. With the end of the war, the word "Communist" had been making everyone jump and look under the bed and into the corners of the closet for suspicious cobwebs. Eleven members of the Communist party were on trial for nine months in 1949 before they were found guilty of advocating violent overthrow of the government.

"The climate is not exactly benign," Joe would say as he threw the newspaper across the room. He felt outrage at the insensitivity and injustice of the accusations. The paranoia hung heavy. He himself waited to be uncovered and called to account and was firmly resolved never to be compliant. But his resolve was never tested. The investigative committees were as inept as they were malicious and thousands who had been Communists in the thirties and forties were never questioned.

Joe chuckled about this to Molly. "But of course," he said, "we never really did anything against the law. Neither did most of the others who were called to the witness stand. McCarthy is after stars to prove his showmanship. Sure, there was a lot of hocus-pocus and fake names and phony secrecy that went on in the Party, a kind of conspiratorial play-acting that added to the mystique. But it was phony. Really unnecessary. There were so many good things the Party stood for. They had a vision of social justice in a time of depression and need. Some of the best people I ever knew were there in the thirties."

Molly would challenge him. "But they didn't stay for long. Look at those who dropped out during the Moscow trials, or because of Spain, or who couldn't accept the Nazi–Soviet Pact."

"Okay," Joe agreed. "So they dropped out when they couldn't accept this or that. Doesn't that happen all the time in politics?" Joe spoke regretfully. He watched the dissolution with sadness and a sigh for lost ideas and ideals. If there had been a conspiracy, he felt he had been part of it and made no excuses to himself. He told Molly, "Playing along with a cheap politico like McCarthy is obscene. Leave the Party, I say, attack it if you will, but not for the benefit of that trio of clowns juggling with the Inquisition."

So far, Molly, too, had escaped the investigation. But one day her telephone rang and a brisk importunate high-pitched voice told her that he was coming around to see her within the hour. His tone implied that this was an order. She didn't catch his name but she knew at once where he came from.

By this time she was working at home, having left *Newscast* to set up as a fashion photographer. She had run into Frances Cohen at an art show after the war. Fran had three of her paintings in a group exhibition down on Eighth Street. She had already arrived at the bold flat naturalistic style that was to make her famous. Big portraits, the colors flamboyant, brash, ugly. Every detail minutely and microscopically delineated and then enlarged, magnified, distended. It was a completely personal style, her own. A micro-macro vision that jarred the senses and rattled them.

Franny herself had grown so plump and soft and pretty, like a matron on the Grand Concourse, it was hard to believe this was her work. Molly shook her head as she looked at the three canvases, thinking, They're wonderful, really, but it's amazing how you never know what goes on in anybody's head.

Suddenly, as Molly stood there, she was embraced by Franny, who had come up behind her. "I'm so glad to see you," she said, "What a long time."

Molly embraced her back. They quickly exchanged news, without too many questions. Neither wanted to bring up the old days, old ways.

"I love your work," Molly said. "All those warts and wrinkles and pubic hairs."

Franny laughed. "I guess that's what I see."

"Shocking, original. Terrific."

"That's great to hear from you, Molly. I'm glad." Franny seemed self-assured—pleased by Molly's praise but accepting it, taking it for granted. There were adorable dimples in her cheeks as she smiled but her blue eyes were steady and penetrating. "What about you, Molly? How's the picture taking coming along? Going to try for another sensational prize?"

Molly drew in her breath, shrugged. "I don't think you try for it in photojournalism, alas. I think it just happens."

"There's a lot that's accidental in painting too," Franny answered. "At least you don't always know where the controls are. But I guess they're there under all the fat."

They walked toward the back of the gallery to stand in a corner as they talked. "I have the feeling," Molly admitted, "I'd like to try something else. Something I can set up and dominate. I'd like to inch into the kind of thing Paul Strand does. Or Kertész."

"It's your old itch as a painter coming through." Franny squinted at Molly, in thought.

"But I also want to make money," Molly went on. "I need to make money. Joe can't swing our life all alone. It's gotten costly."

Franny lifted her brows in question.

Molly shook her head in a kind of answer. "I know. I just know what you want to say, Franny. But we've gotten into this and I'm not sure we want to get out. And it's not bad. Private house, kids in private school, full-time maid, next we're even talking about a house in the country." She sighed again. "Make no mistake. I like it. Joe likes it. But it means I can't take time off, go out West, study with Edward Weston, and take pictures for my own pleasure."

Again Franny eyed her thoughtfully. "Have you thought about fashion photography? Or commercial work for ad agencies?"

"What do I know about fashion?" Molly laughed. "Look at me. And I never look at ads."

"Well you should. Some are great. With a lot of art." Fran pursed her lips.

Molly watched her, wondering what she was getting at. "You can learn, can't you? You're a good learner, aren't you?" Franny persisted. "I remember when you were a very good learner," she added pointedly.

Molly was stopped short. Of course. She had always learned on the job, hadn't she? She had learned everything on the job. She stood quietly, looking at her friend.

"The guy I live with at the moment," Franny said, making a point of *the moment,* "is the art director at *Pictorial.* He used to be at *Vogue.* He knows everyone. Go see him. I'll talk to him tonight and you call him tomorrow. Okay?"

Molly nodded. "Okay," she agreed a bit sceptically. Then another thought struck her. "It would mean setting up a studio at home, wouldn't it?" She put her arm around Franny's chubby shoulders, and crushed her to her. "That would be wonderful. It would solve one of my major problems, being home more with the kids. Oh Franny"—again she hugged her—"you're not only a terrific painter. You're a great friend. What a marvelous idea!"

The idea worked. Molly called Fran's friend. He looked at her photographs, advised her, pulled the right strings. Molly stumbled a bit at first, did too much magazine editorial work at a low fee, had to learn to curb her impatience at the battery of hangers-on who were attached to each assignment—the makeup people and the so-called stylists, the fashion director and the assistants, and then the model or models, generally the most agreeable members of the team. She had been used to improvising at *Newscast,* finding relevance in the irrelevant and accidental, working entirely on her own to capture the right moment. Now everything was to be planned. The attitudes were different; so were the hard facts of budgets and schedules. She had to take out a loan to furnish and equip the dining room, which became the studio. The tall windows, facing north, overlooking the garden, let in a flood of cool, even light.

"Natural light," Molly said happily to Joe, "available light. Perfect."

She was to find her floods and spotlight more useful in the creation of the stylistic effects demanded, but she felt it augured well that the natural light would be there waiting for her when the time came.

She looked up at the windows and drank in that light. She wanted her eyes to take in all the possibilities it offered. Up until now, her camera had been her right arm, a hammer, a chisel, a tool with which to earn her living. It would now be refined and aided and bolstered and twisted into an instrument for constructing stage settings, decor, illustrations for the sale of various objects. It would be there to create desire and illusion and temptation. But somewhere in that natural light Molly saw another kind of photography, another use of the camera, another use of her own seeing eye.

Molly had stumbled into her career, but once in it, she had fallen in love with its infinite range. She had become a photography buff, a follower of the exhibitions that had begun to surface in the galleries around town. There weren't many. It was still a new enthusiasm on Fifty-seventh Street and around. She would go to the Museum of Modern Art and head directly for its photographic collection, bypassing the painting and the sculpture and the drawings for another look at Muybridge, or Gertrude Kasebier, or Clarence White. There were the stars like Alfred Stieglitz and Edward Weston and Steichen, but what a current of electricity charged the newer ones, from Cartier-Bresson to Paul Strand to Roman Vishniak to Walker

Evans and Berenice Abbott. This was the art pantheon now for Molly. It wasn't that painting was dead, but that photography was alive. And Molly with it, reaching for the light. Someday.

Now there was basic work to be done to make the area feasible, to create a dressing room out of the corner closet, to bring in plumbing. Joe turned out to be prodigious, helpful, and encouraging. He drew up some plans for the use of space, building and installing the shelves, working out a filing system for negatives and prints, adding to the electrical wiring to take care of the additional outlets for lights and other equipment. Molly would come in and marvel at him as he sawed and measured and hammered, rushing through a quick dinner on his return home in the evening, getting into the carpenter's apron he'd purchased at the local hardware store, laughing as the children tied the strings around his waist and tried to put their hands into the long deep pockets.

"Where did you learn to do all this?" Molly asked in amazement. "First the house, now this?"

"In junior high school," he mumbled as he continued to go through his toolbox looking for nails, showing off to her. "I took shop there. All the boys did; they called it manual training."

"What a useful education you had," Molly exclaimed. "Shop! The girls had cooking in my junior high. I wore a white cooking cap and a starched white apron. I learned how to make white sauce."

"Why not?" Joe leaned over to kiss her. "*Vive la différence!*"

"My cooking cap, I'll never forget it. I lost it once, anyway I couldn't find it and I had been warned not to show up without it. I stood in my closet and prayed, 'Dear God, find my cooking cap and I promise to believe in you always.' I looked down and there it was. What a triumph of prayer! My first religious experience. I almost decided to spend my life in a nunnery in gratitude."

"Thank God you didn't." He leaned over to kiss her again. "Think of what I would have missed."

When the studio was finished, Emily and Tommy were invited in for a party and Joe sang "The Worker's Flag Is Deepest Red" to them while they drank their apple juice and Molly wandered around wondering and worrying about how she was going to manage it all.

"I'm in business," she wailed to Joe, "I'm going to need someone to handle my books and send out bills and all that jazz."

"I'll help you with that too," Joe promised. "There's a guy who comes to the syndicate to do the books. He's an accountant and he's used to handling free-lance billing, because of our free-lance writers. I'll work with him on your accounts."

She groaned. "Oh, Joe, what would I do without you? I'm *in business*. I can hardly stand it."

But she enjoyed it. She laughed at the prodigality of shooting a hundred takes and then choosing the best—so different from the direct now-or-never of the old *Newscast* technique. She loved the mechanical perfection of the four-color engravings and the printing process that turned her photographs into luminous gems. And once she acquired some advertising clients, she loved the money she earned. The sums seemed to her enormous, totally out of line with what people *should* be paid, but since there didn't seem to be any rhyme or reason to any of it, she simply enjoyed it.

N O W she hoped she wasn't going to be jolted out of this by the ominous telephone call heralding a sinister visit. When she opened the door on the first ring of the bell, she was surprised at the look of the man who stood there. She had expected the F.B.I. caricature: a youngish man, square-jawed, in shiny blue-serge suit and brown fedora hat, very four-square. Instead the visitor was long, thin, dangling, in a wrinkled brown suit and spotted necktie and looked like a worried preacher.

"Yes," she said coldly. "May I see your identification please?" She kept him on the doorstep, the open door against her back. He fished out a worn leather wallet and flipped it open to a card folded in cellophane that identified him not as a member of the F.B.I. but as an investigator for the Senate Committee Hearings on Communist Influence in the Army, Senator Joe McCarthy's great televised hit parade. The shabby wrinkled card, the wrinkled suit, the wrinkled face of the man himself were all a bit pathetic.

What a great photograph he would make, went through her mind, as an illustration of the pomp and power of this grand republic at this particular McCarthy time. Like that inimitable photograph by Cartier-Bresson of the scrawny old woman, all rags and bones, draped in the American flag. But, she smiled to herself at the thought, she could hardly ask him to pose. Instead she asked him into the hall and stood there looking at him, waiting. He kept his hat on his head and dug down into another pocket for a notebook.

"You're Molly Levin, yes?" he finally asked.

"Yes," she agreed.

"What was your name before?" He looked up sharply from the notebook, confronting her, his high-pitched voice accusatory.

Her name before? Before what? She remembered. "Mary Barrett," she said. "Is that what you mean?"

He consulted his book again. "Yes," he said, "Mary Barrett. Hmmm. What was your purpose in changing it?"

"Purpose?" She was stumped. "That was my maiden name,"

she answered. "Your notebook probably tells you that. I didn't have any purpose."

This was foolish, she thought, but watch out. Did he want to prove deceit? Was she supposed to be under an alias?

"Mary Barrett." He chewed this over, she could see the cud going round and round. "That's not a Jewish name. Why did you change it?"

She was impatient. "I told you. When I got married. It's customary," she added, then went on. "Please tell me what you want to know. You have all this other stuff in the notebook in front of you. What more do you need?"

He tried to pull himself erect to show his authority. "I'm the one asking the questions, lady," he said and went back to reading the dossier in his hand. She watched him silently. Finally he said, "Do you know a woman allegedly called Frances Cohen?"

"Fran Cohen, the artist?" she repeated, now on her guard. "Yes, of course I know Frances Cohen. What do you mean 'allegedly called'?"

"How do you know her?" His air of suspicion was both frightening and absurd. Fran Cohen? Be careful, Molly, she warned herself, avoid saying too little, too much. Happily, she thought, there isn't much to say.

"I've known her for a long time."

"How?"

"The way people meet people in New York. Through work, play, the friends of friends."

"Through politics, maybe?" His voice was nasty.

"Politics? What politics? We met at the Art Students League. I know her as an artist. I was a student there some years ago."

"Hmm." He wrote in his notebook. "Where's the place?"

"Why don't you look it up in the phone book," she said to him sarcastically. "That's your job isn't it?"

She was surprised by the sudden mean squint of his eyes. "It's on Fifty-seventh Street," she added quickly, deciding not to anger him, but it was so easy to fall into the trap.

He waltzed around this with several repetitious questions, then asked the key one. "Is this Frances Cohen a member of the Communist party?"

Molly was glad she could answer truthfully. "I haven't the vaguest notion. You'd have to ask her yourself. Now please"—she decided now to be peremptory; she really didn't want it to go any further—"now please, can we finish with this? I have work to do."

To her surprise, he closed his notebook and that was that. As she let him out the door, she was sure he would head for the nearest bar to refresh himself after his labors. She had to restrain herself not to advise him on the best saloon in the neighborhood.

She never told anyone except Joe about this visit. If there was any fire, she didn't want to fuel it. Later on, when Fran Cohen had her big retrospective at the Whitney Museum, the catalogue mentioned the artist's early attachment to left-wing causes, but it was only a passing reference, a barometer of interest in the choice of subject matter. It was in another time, another place, almost another country. McCarthy was long dead and Fran Cohen's paintings, very much alive.

But in 1954, Molly was surprised by Joe's reaction when she told him that night of her visitor and his questions.

He seemed uneasy. "Better not see Fran for a while. It might not be smart."

"Smart? Oh, come now, Joe. Don't tell me you're intimidated by all this uproar?"

"Don't give me your fake heroics, Molly. No, I'm not intimidated but I'm wary. I wouldn't relish losing my job. Nor would you look with joy at losing your clients. That's the way things are nowadays."

"Aren't you exaggerating, Joe? Aside from the poor Hollywood guys and some others, the names that make the headlines, there's more slack than substance here. And what in the world does Fran have to do with Reds in the Army?"

Joe's face was tight with anger. "I don't know, Molly. And neither do you. I'm not suggesting you cut Fran dead. I merely say, watch it. Don't see her for a while until this blows over. It might be doing her a favor too."

His blandness made Molly furious. "Don't be so fucking careful, Joe. I find it distasteful."

"And I find your lack of rational thinking bloody juvenile. You want it both ways. To be a flaming revolutionary—"

"Non-Communist," Molly interrupted.

"—a bloody revolutionary on the one hand and a highly paid top fashion photographer on the other."

"And what about you, Joe? A top editor for a newspaper syndicate and a scared chicken in the corner. Why don't you speak up about all this? Why do you warn me to be careful, to shun Fran Cohen, to hide in a corner with you?"

His voice was cold. "Don't hide, Molly. It's your choice. Do as you like. Go to the Committee and say, 'You want me, I'm here. I can name names, point fingers, I dare you to touch me.'"

Molly's voice rose. "That's not what I want, Joe. You're distorting it. All I want is not to be threatened by that measly man who showed up here this afternoon. I want to defy him. Do you understand? I want to stand up to him and all the others who want to make criminals of people for the way they think."

"Okay. Bravo." He cut her short. "All we're having here as

usual is a quarrel. Not a reasonable discussion, I'm going up-stairs. Good night."

Molly telephoned Sophie the next morning and asked her to lunch. Molly leaned on Sophie's judgment. She felt that Sophie knew her way around what she called "the comrades" and could pierce the thicket of rhetoric in which their slogans were entangled, but she had always been in tempered opposition.

"I came by my hostility honestly," she would say, "it's in the blood." But Molly knew that the current witch hunt disgusted Sophie. She took no joy in it, as did some others on the non-Communist left.

Molly told Sophie about her quarrel with Joe without mentioning Fran. "I don't know what you were quarreling about, Molly," Sophie said bluntly. "Joe's right. It's not a good time. The Red Channels group is crawling all over the radio and TV stations. And some of their creeps go prowling through our corridors looking for Red skeletons. They all have a certain sly suspicious look, like peeping toms at the church supper hoping to spot naked little girls. Ants pretending to be killer bees. But," Sophie sighed, "this too shall pass. Stay out of their way I say. I'm sorry for those who've been trapped, but in the main, it could have been worse. As for courage to speak up, there isn't much of it around. It's an irony, isn't it, that the first one fearless enough to do so in the Senate was their only woman senator, Margaret Chase Smith. So much for male superiority."

· CHAPTER 15 ·

T H E man in the wheelchair at the Vietnam monument turned back to her and saw her crying, put out his hand to take hers. She let him. It felt companionable and warm.

"Don't cry," he said softly. "Was he your only child?"

She shook her head. "No," she managed to stammer. "There's my daughter too, his sister. But it doesn't matter. Even if I had had six other children, he was—He himself mattered."

The man nodded. "I know what you're saying, ma'am. It's the same thing with my brother. My mom still grieves for him as if he was the only one. Everyone counts in the eyes of the Lord. I'm with you there." He squeezed her hand. Molly felt her link to him even as his churchy words made her squirm. "I bet his sister is proud of him too." He let go of her hand gently, as if encouraging her to walk alone. "I'm going to roll back to my mates," he said. "There's a bus coming to take us back."

She watched as he twisted and turned his chair, maneuvering the wheels across the grass. He turned to wave and she waved back. From where she stood, the trick of the angle, she could see the white spear of the Washington Monument slashed across the dome of the Capitol, as if it were bisecting it. Overhead was the intermittent roar of planes taking off or landing at the

Washington National Airport nearby. And everywhere, along the paths, around the reflecting pool, up toward the Lincoln Monument, and over the bridge to Arlington Cemetery, were the joggers, the runners, the walkers in their fantasy shorts and knee warmers and brightly colored sweatshirts like a swarm of dragonflies.

The Mall seemed to her a giant necropolis from one end to the other with its memorial bridge, its memorial statues, its memorial pools, and its memorial black wall of names—only the joggers and the demonstrators and the Sunday strollers were among the living.

Again she shivered, wrapping her coat closer against the cold. "I should go. I'm going"—but she turned back to the graven stone and did what everyone did. She found the name again and traced it with her fingertips. Thomas Barrett Levin. She half wished that Emily were here, then was glad she was not. She was afraid of what Emily would feel and say.

Emily was so far away now. More than miles separated them. Tears came to her eyes again. She felt like keening. "Where are my children? Where have they gone?" My Tommy. My Emily. No longer hers. And no longer one for the other.

Emily had been a devoted big sister to her little brother. Tommy had adored her. Molly loved to watch them together, Emily's dark head leaning over Tommy's blond curls as she read to him. He had been a cherubic as a baby and remained so almost until high school. He had been so good it was hard to tell what went on under the goodness.

Emily laid down the law to him, taught him how to tie his shoelaces—not an easy trick, since he was left-handed—let him follow her to the private library on East Seventy-second Street to which they belonged, helped him with his school work, which gave him difficulty in spite of his articulateness and his flashing insight. Emily listened to him, loved him with a fierce constancy even as they grew older and the few years between them loomed large. It was to Emily that Tommy took the problems that began for him in high school. He had hated his tight inflexible school, where all the boys in their blue blazers and gray flannel slacks stuck out sorely against the grim tenements of the West Side street where their school was located. Emily had taken Tommy's part against the school and campaigned for a change when he wanted to go to a public high. Joe was opposed to it and Joe won the day. It seemed to Molly that Joe was opposed to anything that had to do with Tommy, increasingly as Tommy grew older.

She tried to defend Joe to herself, but it wasn't easy. She recognized the tensions in his life, new tensions brought on by his change of jobs. He had moved from the Press to the editorship of a parochial little magazine, published under the wing of the Jewish Philanthropic Committee, called *Critique,* which hewed rather narrowly to the Committee's line on questions that concerned the Committee itself. But Joe wanted to expand the role of *Critique,* to make it a force among intellectuals for a new wave of avant-garde analysis and orientation. The Committee leaders were eager for an expansion of the magazine's influence, and they promised Joe support, but all under the banner of anticommunism and Zionism. At bottom, in spite of any lofty literary pretensions Joe might have, the main goal of the publication was the affirmation and support of Israel.

He was jumpy, shaken by a crisis of confidence. Had he made a mistake in leaving Acme? Would he be able to get the writers he wanted to join him at *Critique?* This was a new arena for him. He admitted to Molly that he was running scared.

But Molly resented the fact that he allowed his tensions to bounce off the walls the minute he arrived home.

"Stop blasting that damn music all over the house," he would shout as the trumpets of a Miles Davis record roared down the stairs.

"Hang up your coat, dammit" were his first words as he came into the house. "Pick up your books," he bellowed as he kicked the school bag aside. "I've told you a thousand times."

"Tommy rubs Joe the wrong way," she confided to her father. "He can never do anything to please him. Joe never finds time to go to school functions, never takes him to ball games, never does anything."

"Does Tommy *want* to go to ball games?" her father asked a bit quizzically. They were walking down by the brook, Molly clearing the path with a long skinny branch she had picked up. She had driven to Great Barrington that morning to seek him out, to talk to him. She was troubled and unhappy. The touch of his rough tweed jacket felt good to her hand.

"Why don't *you* take him to ball games?" continued her father.

"Oh, don't be funny, Daddy. Isn't that what fathers are for?"

Her father stopped and turned to look at her soberly. "I'm not being funny, Molly my dear. If Tommy wants to go to ball games and Joe doesn't want to go with him, and *you* think it's important—well—don't you see, you do it. Fathers are for lots of things, just as mothers are, but ball games are not necessarily one of them."

Molly pulled at his sleeve in disagreement, but he went on, "And you're not going to change Joe by arguing about it. It's too late for that. Tommy is almost grown. Have you challenged Joe on this?"

"A million times. I have. But I don't want to challenge him now. He's so wrapped up in that magazine of his, he hasn't anything left over for anyone. I can't argue it when he's so touchy and unsure of himself."

"I agree. Don't put any more blame on Joe. For one thing, it won't do any good. Never do anything that won't do any good." He was silent for a minute, thinking. "You know Joe and I are friends. I like him very much. I value him." He turned her around to lead her back to the house. "But he's a thorny man. And he and Tommy may be involved in that old battle between fathers and sons. It goes deep, this ancient Jungian combat. My advice, Molly, is to stay out of it. It will work itself out."

"Will it? Will it work itself out?"

He smiled a bit sadly. "Maybe it will. With a little luck. But maybe not."

Her mother was waiting for them for lunch, and Molly had a sense of being petted and loved by them both. When her mother wanted to reach out and draw her close, she was endearing. Like Joe, Molly thought. She's uneven, like Joe. There are worse things in the world. Daddy's right. There is no formula about being a good mother or a good father. I don't want to fight with Joe about his son. It's between them, really.

After that day in Massachusetts, Molly felt better about it when Tommy would disappear into Emily's room; Molly knew he found solace there. She admitted ruefully to herself that she was glad not to overhear the things they must confide to each other about her and Joe, ripping them both asunder with no mercy, no irony and pity, chewing them apart.

Joe wanted Tommy to go to Harvard and insisted on his applying, but Tommy didn't get in. Joe was icy in his disappointment. Then, when Tommy said he wanted to go to a state university, maybe Wisconsin, Joe was furious and silent for days.

"Why?" Molly asked Tommy. "It's pretty grubby up there in Madison. A million undergraduates. You can do better than that."

Tommy answered her seriously, soberly. "It depends, Mother, on what you mean by better. Dad's idea of better is more establishment. Maybe that's your idea too. But it's not mine. And Emily agrees."

Molly retorted snappishly, "But Emily is pretty establishment herself. There's nothing hoi polloi about Radcliffe. Why does she advise something different for you?" Her annoyance with Emily showed.

Tommy's voice remained sober, contained. "Because we're not the same, Mother. For one thing, she got into Radcliffe and I didn't get into Harvard. For another, she's a good student, I'm not."

Molly protested, interrupting him with "But you're so bright and witty and warm."

He brushed her words aside. "Okay, Mother. I'm not a dolt. Let's agree on that. That's not why I want to go to another kind of school. But I look around me, at all the private school kids I've gone to school with. It's all *so*, I don't know—so limited. I don't want to stack myself up against Emily. Or against Dad."

Oh, thought Molly, that's the rub, there's the conflict, is that what it's all about? Aloud she said, "Dad wants what's best for you. You know that."

He spoke quietly. "Dad has an image of his son, of what's best for his son, not me."

"Listen, you haven't got it straight. Your father went to City College, out of the slums of Brooklyn. He's no Wasp adhering to the Wasp tradition."

"Don't you believe it, Ma." His voice remained quiet, without anger. "The world up in these parts is filled with phony Wasps, first-generation Wasps who talk Wasp, look Wasp, live Wasp. Imitation Wasps with Jewish jokes, the worst kind. It's not for me."

Molly was surprised at his coherence, his relentless logic. She fumbled for words but had none. Eventually Joe came out of his silence long enough to write a check for the year's expenses. "Thanks, Dad," Tommy said coolly, as he folded the check and put it in his wallet. "I thought I'd tell you. I want to teach. I don't know yet. Meanwhile I want to learn."

Emily came down from Cambridge to take Tommy to dinner at their favorite delicatessen on Sixth Avenue before Tommy took off in a beat-up car he had bought in a Village car lot, loaded with his books, his records, his hi-fi equipment, and his vision of the future. At the last moment, Joe mumbled to him, "I wish you luck," but couldn't resist adding, "I wish you were joining Emily up there."

"Thanks, Dad." Tommy replied. "I love Emily. I respect her. But Emily wants to save the world. I want to identify with it."

Wisconsin was as good a university as any other, even if it didn't suit Joe's newly acquired Ivy League prejudices. It took Tommy out of the family orbit, gave him breathing room, offered him a breeding place for the illusions of that era, the Kennedy era, when America seemed young and valiant, arrogant and all-powerful, the cop of the world, Excalibur unsheathed against the Communist hordes.

Molly listened to Tommy without argument or challenge when she visited him in Madison or he came home for his holidays. She was happy to see him so sure of himself, so full of his future, a patriotic streak in him a yard wide that she didn't agree with, but it was his after all. That Kennedy magic! thought Molly, it lights him up. The magic had even rubbed off on Emily for a while, parts of it anyway. The Peace Corps, yes. At the beginning, the "What you can do for your country," the *Ich bin ein Berliner*." For Tommy it was all the way, even the disastrous Bay of Pigs was a noble venture against the foes of freedom in spite of the failure, while the countdown with

Krushchev over the missiles in Cuba was a show of Kennedy's resolve and strength.

What a cosmic joke, went through Molly's mind, that Tommy should come around, in his own way, to all the ideas now current in Joe's head. Like father, like son, in spite of himself, Molly thought resentfully. Was it like his father's, this young man's eagerness not to miss the heroic adventure of war? Was it like his father's, that torrent of slogans about the good guys saving the world from the bad?

"Don't be bitter," she tried to tell herself, "because he doesn't listen to you. You're an old Commie to him. It's a joke. *I'm* the old Commie. Let's face it, I'm the female in the equation. The part that doesn't count."

But was there really any explanation for why Tommy had gone? If he could know about it now, in some nameless here-after, would he too wonder what his name was doing on that wall? When he enlisted, her friends had shrugged their shoulders and asked, how come? The question would make Molly so belligerent or sad or choked up that she couldn't answer. How come? If only he had been born a few years later, he might have been part of the anger in the streets, chanting, "Hey, hey, LBJ, how many kids did you kill today?" But he enlisted in the heat of the Kennedy fever, as a kind of memento mori to the martyred President. Or for whatever reason takes a young man off to war, no matter what anyone says, in his springtime, in his youth, before he knows any better.

The day the telegram came—the fateful day now binding Tommy forever to his place on the wall—Molly thrust the yellow envelope at Joe as he came through the door in response to her urgent message.

"What's up?" he asked, his face whiter than ever with apprehension, as if he knew.

Molly was silent as he held the telegram, his eyes lowered,

fixed on his name on the address as if he wanted to verify it. Then he slid out the thin small dreadful ominous and familiar oblong of paper, unable to read it, as if by not reading it somehow the message would vaporize. But he did read it at last, then looked at Molly. She felt his pain like an electric charge that coupled with her own anguish. He held open his arms to her and they both stood, not weeping, shaking against one another, holding themselves in a silent terrible shared grief.

· CHAPTER 16 ·

EMILY. Molly found the nearest park bench and lowered herself heavily. The Washington Monument spiked the darkening sky. The arrow pointing to the Vietnam wall was in front of her. I want to think about Emily, she thought. What had the man in the wheelchair said? "His sister must be proud," or something like that. Something sweet and sentimental and totally unreal. High-flown words to be set to junk music, a pop tune. Emily would hate it here. She would hate Tommy's name carved in stone. She would hate the crowds. She had been furious, outraged, scathing in her disapproval when he had enlisted. Tommy remained a bit cocky at the end, but he drew her close as he said good-bye, hurt but adamant. Emily remained reproachful even at his death, even as she wept bitterly for days, months, after the news.

I miss her so much, Molly thought. I ache with missing her.

Molly's feeling for Emily had always been so difficult to put into words. She *felt* Emily, almost as if she had never left her womb, were still attached to her by tendrils of tissue and interwoven muscle and reddened veins threaded through the flesh. Emily was an inexplicable emotion, a way of breathing in and out. "Emily is, therefore I am," she had once said to herself, striving to understand the unfathomable wonder of her daughter's presence in her life.

It wasn't, of course, entirely true. Molly was because she was. But Emily's hold on her had a transcendental power that Emily did not seek and Molly could not penetrate. It gave her joy and made her suffer. In the years that Emily was growing up, it created a warmth that enclosed them both—a physical warmth made up of hugs and kisses and constant touch. In the early sixties, when many of the young were taking the world apart, questioning the war in Vietnam, championing civil rights, and fighting to protect the environment and end the arms race, Molly felt herself one with Emily. When Emily, a student at Radcliffe, called from New London one weekend to tell her that she was on an overnight vigil protesting the atomic submarine based there, Molly wanted to rush up to join her, but refrained, thinking this is *her* vigil, her life.

But there was a future ahead never dreamed of in Molly's philosophy. A future that had its beginning in the lower school at Dalton. There Emily had become friendly with Peter and Heather Apple, attractive twins, vibrant, worldly children. Emily had gone to play with them at their house and they had been in and out of the Levin house throughout those early years. Molly had often wondered at the intimacy between this rather disdainful self-aware pair and diffident soft-spoken serious Emily.

The parents of the twins had a certain celebrity and they were incredibly rich. Emily would trot off year after year to their Christmas parties, once in a black velvet dress with lace collar that had cost a king's ransom; another time in a tucked challis princess dress that went to the ankles, bought "wholesale" out of one of Molly's fashion sittings; and another year—Molly couldn't remember, except everything was costly as befitted a guest at the Apples'.

Emily reported her impressions of the giant Christmas tree in the two-story living room that sat atop one of the notable prewar Park Avenue apartment houses. She described the ice-cream cake, twenty layers high, and the favors. She couldn't recite the guest list but somehow Molly and Joe would learn it since it was always reported in one newspaper column or another. "All the stars of stage and screen," Joe would say. "Where the elite meet to eat."

"Just jealous," said Molly.

"Of course," Joe answered.

The Apples were famous for their parties and their talents. He was a top producer of a number of television shows, she a play "angel" who made a career of investing in and supporting some of Broadway's biggest hits. But they didn't need to live off their wits. In addition to wits, they had inherited money. Jane Apple had had a fortune left her by a grandfather who had established a great mail-order business in St. Louis. And Mark Apple, the father, was richly endowed by a department store family in Cleveland.

They didn't sit on their money, Molly would say. They were part of a New York she didn't know—a splashy New York that made news for doing this or that for charity, for good works, for political prestige. In a way, Molly was jealous too. She rather envied the Apples their fifteen-room penthouse apartment, the big parties, the zest they exuded whenever she ran into them at Dalton parents' meetings. They were both so tall and good-looking and so damnably sure of themselves.

The twins, too, were tall and good-looking and sure of themselves. And so forthright! Sometimes it astonished her. Once Emily, when she was about eleven or twelve years old, asked Molly if she "ever did it?" Molly knew what she meant but she hedged. "Did what?" she asked. Emily blushed and stammered. "*You* know, Mother."

"Why do you ask?" was Molly's reply.

"Heather says her mother does it all the time. Her mother told her."

In the face of that, Molly thought, I'd better talk. And she hated her own perennial embarrassment, her own timidity, that kept her from being as open and hearty about it all as Jane Apple.

Emily and Heather remained friends through their high-school years, although they were separated as they grew up by certain differences. One day Emily came home close to tears. "Why can't I be Jewish?" she wailed.

Molly looked baffled. "Why do you want to be Jewish? Why would anyone want to be Jewish?"

"They all have so many things to do. They all go to Temple Emanu-El. They belong to the junior club there. It sounds like such fun—and I don't belong." There were tears in Emily's eyes.

Molly had no answer. She could say to Emily, go if you want to, go with Heather, I haven't any objection. But she knew that it would involve more than this. Would she and Joe have to go too? What a question! Not possible. And for that matter, why not the Congregational church around the corner? Or the Catholic church down Park? She wanted to say to Emily, choose the place where the junior club is the best and the parties the liveliest, and where your parents have no obligation to belong. Forget the religious persuasion, joining is what counts. It was all too confusing. Especially when once Emily used the work "kike" referring to the art teacher at school.

"Don't use that word." Molly spoke sharply.

"All the girls do," Emily replied. "Why can't I?"

"Certainly Heather and her friends don't use that word," Molly insisted.

Emily was astounded at Molly's ignorance. "They're just the ones."

Molly repeated this to Joe. He laughed sardonically. "That's the word the in-crowd at Emanu-El uses. It was originally coined by German Jews for the kikes from Eastern Europe. Didn't you know that?"

Molly shook her head. "Sometimes I think I don't know anything. Not a thing."

But Emily had more in her mind and heart than joining the club or going to parties. From her earliest days, she had had questions and perceptions about God and the universe that Molly did not take lightly.

"What do you believe in, Mother?" she had asked Molly when she was about ten.

"Believe in? About what?"

"I mean about God."

Molly took her time answering. "I believe in you. I believe in Tommy. In your father. In Katy. In me. Lots of things."

Emily eyed her solemnly. "But those are everyday things, Mother. It's not what I mean."

"But it's what *I* mean. I believe in everyday things, Emily. They make up my life."

"But what about out there?"

"Out where?"

Emily raised her hand to point to the heavens and then lowered it. She knew that wasn't where she meant. She made a wider gesture. "Everywhere. Where did it come from? What happens to us? Is there a God?"

Molly was silent. It was a serious question. She wanted to think about it. "I don't know, Emily. I don't really know. I wonder about it too. But what do *you* mean when you ask about God?"

Emily looked bewildered. "Some man, some big great kind man who knows it all and watches out."

"Certainly not a man. I don't think God is ever a man. If he's out there, he's something else."

"What?"

"A force, perhaps. Greater than the human mind has yet been able to imagine."

"I don't like that." Emily shook her head fiercely in denial. "I want God to be someone close, someone who tells me what to do. That's what all the other girls at school have. And it's wicked not be believe in God. Everyone says so."

Molly reached over and tried to hug her, but Emily pulled away. She wanted more than affection; she wanted truth.

Molly hesitated, then said, "Of course some people do think it's wicked not to believe in God. They think you must say you believe. But not everyone feels that way. A lot of people are like me—they don't know. They even call believing superstition."

"Superstition?" asked Emily.

"Believing in something you can't prove, like believing in witches and goblins."

"Do you think it's superstition?"

Molly hesitated again. She wanted to be more blunt. She remembered James Joyce's words—"to me it's all a mockery and beastly"—but she held back.

"Emily, my darling, I can't tell you more than this because it's all I know. I really do believe in people and living together. God doesn't tell us. We must tell ourselves."

Emily's eyes shone with tears. "I think there's a God, mother. Don't say there isn't."

"I didn't say there wasn't, dear Emily. I didn't say that at all, I said I didn't know."

"But you don't believe he's there. I know you don't. You didn't say he was." She began to cry.

Molly held her close. She wished she knew how to reassure her without lying. But the idea of a personal God was so alien to her she could not pretend. All she could do was hold the sobbing child against her breast.

Later, when Emily was older and the questions were more sophisticated, Molly tried to answer her challenge more concretely but was no more successful.

"No, I don't think it's all accidental. It seems too interwoven, too enigmatic, too complex. I wish I knew more about science going to the heart of matter, unraveling some of the mysteries. I think it must be the most fantastic thing in the world, being a scientist. But look what scientists say when asked these same questions, Emily. They ask that you think about the human mind: a miracle of coordination and complexity, but still finite. And what's out there is infinite, beyond even their comprehension or definition. They can't imagine it. I can't imagine it. I can't name it, I can't put a shape to it."

"But isn't that what religion does?" Emily asked. "Religion puts a name and a shape to it. All religion reaches beyond the finite. Perhaps it is more daring than science. It's a leap, I believe, into something beyond our knowing. We don't have to know. It's just there and we can feel it."

"Emily. I can't really argue. This is the way I think things are. You think things are something else. At least we agree on the way people should care about one another."

When the lower school sent the boys packing to other schools, since the Dalton high school was just for girls, most of the boys went to the upper-class upper-grade preparatory schools that were their natural habitats after Dalton. Peter's school was the most upper-upper-class of them all—Groton in Massachusetts.

Emily went to Radcliffe after Dalton and ran into Peter Apple at Harvard. Something had happened to him. Emily reported that he was completely changed, still arrogant and self-assured but in another way. He had taken a year off between Groton and Harvard and done the completely unexpected. He had joined a kibbutz in Israel, where he had run a tractor and worked at hard physical labor on the kibbutz farm.

"He talks about it all the time," Emily told her parents. "He's really excited."

"I never thought of him as that, *that* Jewish," Molly said. "After all, Groton isn't exactly the Lower East Side."

"Oh, Mother," Emily brushed her tone aside. "Don't be funny. Peter hated Groton. It was the first place ever in his life that he found himself stigmatized simply for being a Jew."

Later, when Emily brought Peter home to visit, Peter told them himself.

"I realized, it was so strange to me, that it had nothing to do with what I said or did or wore or thought. It simply *was*. Incredible. I even got beaten up by some of the guys, not badly, but definitely walloped. The only reason I could figure out was the Jewishness." He paused and grimaced at the memory. "But it wasn't this open hostility I minded so much as the covert kind. I felt isolated from all the camaraderie that was so palpable around me. Not until my last year was I able to make friends."

Joe was baffled. "I never thought of these preppy schools as particularly religious. I really don't know anything about Groton. It wasn't one of the first-choice schools in Brooklyn." Joe was maliciously putting himself on the other side of the tracks.

"All those schools are something," Peter answered, "something Christian, mostly Episcopal. Groton is supposed to provide an Episcopal education for Christian gentlemen. That's the motto. And there's daily chapel. All the Jewish kids who were there, about twenty of us, had to attend. But," he added in a kind of wonderment at himself, "I loved it. It was my first glimmer of religion, of God, of mystery. For one reason or another I had never felt it before."

"Not at Emanu-El?" Joe asked, half teasing him.

"No. Probably my fault. I was pretty dense then. Emanu-El seemed more get-together. But at chapel I loved the service itself; the grand sound of the King James English, the sense behind the prayers. It comforted me."

Although Peter had loved chapel and discovered a profound joy in what he called "the spirit beyond everyday life," he was never moved to conversion. "It satisfied an unrealized hunger," he tried to explain to Joe. "But there weren't the right ingredients for me. The glorious English of the King James version of the Bible wasn't enough. I just knew there was something lacking in my own life and it made me regretful."

"Was that why the year in Israel, between Groton and Harvard?"

Peter shrugged. "I suppose so. I suddenly wanted to go. I saw it as a challenging opportunity to build a good new life."

His face lit up. He was a handsome vibrant kid, Molly thought. Full of enthusiasm, eager to reach out and be liked. And Joe and Molly did like him, with few reservations. They liked his sense of joy at being alive. He had big white perfect teeth and a big laugh. Molly's father called it a "belly" laugh, a perfect description. "It starts in little babies, right down in the gut. Some gurgle with more intensity than others," her father said after his meeting with Peter, almost as if he wanted to tickle Peter and gurgle back. "It's as if right from the beginning, they're a fountainhead of delight."

Molly's mother scoffed at her husband. "Oh, come now, Roger. You see everybody back in the crib. Peter's a fine young man. I like his view of the world. He takes everything in."

Molly was content that her mother found Peter to her liking. She's not always easy to please, that one, Molly thought. Of course, the pretty notion came to her, it doesn't hurt that Peter went to Groton and his family has money. But, she scolded herself, come now, you're so ambivalent about mother you don't allow her room to be herself. In spite of her mother's liberalism, her firm engagement with consequential causes, Molly never knew when she might stumble over one or another of her mother's old snobbisms.

The approval of Peter was general. Molly and Joe drove Emily and Peter down to Brooklyn for a visit to Hester and Sam, complete with honey cake and schnapps, and after they had prodded and pushed to learn that Peter was Jewish and had been to Israel, their joy was unconfined. It occurred to Molly that the ancient snobbisms worked both ways.

Peter was indeed the star of the show. He was tall and blond and moved like a little boy in jerks and starts. Everyone was an audience for him, which he enveloped in the bounce and vitality of all his adventures.

The kibbutz had been splendid, the comrades had been splendid, Israel was splendid. There had been a lot of hard work. Peter had driven a tractor out in the hot sun. In the evening he played his guitar and joined in the singing. As he described it, everyone was caught in the amber of youth, everyone seemed eighteen years old as he was, glowing with good health and spunk—except for those elders of the kibbutz who were all old and wise. As Peter talked, films of pioneers dancing the hora in the evening light danced in Molly's head. Peter didn't make it sound like a picture postcard; no one could fault it. He gave it the authenticity of his own participation and delight.

"Did you want to stay?" asked Molly. "Why didn't you stay?"

"Well, I guess because I wanted to go to college here at

home. Maybe I'll go back, but I'm really an American; I want to be a writer here, nowhere else."

"I can understand that," Joe agreed. "It takes a certain temperament to be an expatriate."

"That's not it exactly. I don't see living in Israel as an act of expatriatism. I'm part of here. I want to go back someday, but never to live." He looked uncertain. "I can't explain. I'm crazy about the idea of Israel. I feel I belong here."

As for Emily, she was radiant with love. Her eyes followed Peter with adoring pleasure. She hung on his words, his gestures, with a fixed lambent intensity. Molly was pleased. Why not? thought Molly. He's handsome, charming, Emily has known him almost all her life, and her sober serious steadiness might be just the right counterpoint to his obviously brilliant flash.

Emily and Peter were married a few weeks before graduation in a hippie ceremony conducted by a Congregationalist minister in a red turtleneck sweater. Both read poetry to prove they were not bound by traditional strictures. Everyone came, and the little garden in the back of the house in the East Seventies was crowded with friends and relatives: the grandparents from Massachusetts, the grandparents from Brooklyn, the Apples from Park Avenue, the Lerners from Rochester, Sophie from her mews house in the Village, Bob Coffee with his newest girlfriend from Harlem, Fran Cohen with her two children the identity of whose fathers no one knew. Tommy was a beautiful best man who dropped the ring and Joe wasn't even asked to give the bride away.

Grandma Hester was shocked at the presence of the minister. Informed of the arrangements in advance, she had threatened not to come, making what Joe called a Second Avenue drama out of it. But they all knew she wouldn't have missed it for the world. She was so happy that Emily was marrying a "nice

Jewish boy," she would have put up with anything to see it through. And Joe was careful to point out to her that the minister was the newfangled kind, a friend of Peter's, who walked on picket lines and supported Israel. The last point was the telling one.

Hester and Sam had, after 1948, returned to the Orthodoxy of their ancestors and were now part of a congregation that met in a little gray-shingled synagogue in Borough Park whose members almost all came from the same little town in Byelorussia from which they had emigrated many years before. Borough Park had become a Chasidic center by this time, and Hester and Sam had to thread their way through the black-coated, black-hatted throngs on Saturday mornings to get to their own little synagogue, sniffing haughtily all the way. They were quite content to know that each side felt superior to the other, just as they had years before in their old shtetl. It made it all seem more like home.

It was 1961, and for their honeymoon Peter and Emily went down to Washington to join the Freedom Rides on their bus heading South. After graduation there was the Peace Corps in Bolivia, the return to a fierce involvement in the Civil Rights movement, and the Freedom Summer in Mississippi. They had wept with heartbreak at Tommy's death and thrown themselves even further into passionate opposition to the war. By the end of 1965 there were half a million men stationed in South Vietnam. The bombing of Hanoi had begun. Emily and Peter attended rallies, speaking and raising money, giving of themselves completely. Molly joined them on some of their marches, walking between them, holding hands, loving them desperately not only for who they were, but for what they were, too. When Peter spoke at a giant meeting in Central Park, she screamed herself hoarse with approval.

One day shone in Molly's memory with a special incandescence: a day when both her father and mother joined them for an antiwar rally in front of the United Nations building on First Avenue. Her mother was slim and elegant in her cashmere sweater and pleated skirt, wearing a button that proclaimed SANE FOR PEACE. She held her purse by its short handle straight down in her gloved hand, walking head up, back vertical, her pale hair almost white, her step quick. Still such a dear D.A.R. lady, Molly thought suddenly, overwhelmed by pride and love; she graces us all.

Her father was by now one of the leaders of the protest movement, signing petitions and letters and newspaper advertisements, quoted everywhere as head of the group "Doctors Against the War." Because his name was immediately recognized—millions of copies of his book had made it a household world—he was singled out in all the stories and reports. He was bouncy and happy this day, one arm hooked through Molly's, the other cradling her mother's, with Peter and Emily in front. He had laughed joyously, "The family that pickets together, stickets together," his smile enclosing not only them, his family, but the whole world out there, as if they were the same extended family.

Emily had shaken him playfully. "How corny can you get, grandpa?"

"Very," he acknowledged. "What's wrong with corny? It's just my style."

What style he had! What particular inclusive style!

Joe, of course, wasn't there. Hardly! Joe had his own firm point of view and it wasn't theirs. He saw the war as politically necessary, an idealistic act to save South Vietnam from the terrors of communism.

"You can't believe that," they had railed against him in turn or in one voice.

"But I do" was his response. "Shall we go over it again?"

They were a house divided, but they were all past argument. While Molly and the others were marching, Joe was watching the football game on television. He did his marching on the job in his magazine, he told them. He would even have pizzas waiting for their return, unable to resist poking fun at them, and not always with good humor, but Emily would throw her arms around him and veto any discussion.

"I won't inflict my ideas on you, Daddy," she would say cheerfully, "if you keep yours to yourself."

Later on Molly was to wonder what took Emily and Peter down the road to fundamentalist Orthodoxy. Perhaps the shocking, frightful death of Peter's parents, who crashed in their private plane and were burned to cinders in the devouring conflagration as the plane hit the earth. The rescuers saw evidence that the pilot and his two passengers had tried to claw their way out of the wreckage on the ground, but the sheet of fire locked them in. For Peter this was the worst image of all. He could absorb the idea of the sudden instant death; it was the word "clawing," used by the newspaper reports, that struck the lowest blow.

"I can't bear it," he said. "I can't get it into my head. My beautiful mother and father. I can't live with it."

When Emily and Peter returned from Bolivia, Peter had joined the staff of *The Washington Square,* a leftist weekly that was half literary, half scandal-mongering, and very "in" with a devoted following south of Fourteenth Street. He wrote articles about everything—funny, factual, lively, informed stories on rock music, civil rights, the assassinations, political power, all the storm and thunder crashing around him.

Now, some time after the death of Peter's parents, things began to change. Emily, who had been working for the American Friends Service Committee, now applied to Columbia for a grant as a graduate student in the art history department with a concentration in Judaica. And both of them started taking instruction—Molly didn't know what else to call it—in Jewish Orthodoxy. This meant, for Peter, lively conversations with an agreeable rabbi with whom he'd made friends when doing a story for his newspaper on the Jews who still remained on the Lower East Side. For Emily, it meant following Peter.

For a long time Peter had been trying to grapple with his own drift toward religion. Molly remembered his pleasure at the obligatory chapel at school, then his fascination with the details of Jewish life, questioning Hester and Sam, visiting the little synagogue in Brooklyn, and questioning his own grandfather in Cleveland about the family life in Poland. He had learned from his grandfather that his great-grandfather had been a Chasid, and now, when he saw the Chasidim on the streets of Borough Park, in their long black coats and big furry felt hats and with their dangling curls, he no longer felt them to be totally alien or weird, although he was happy not to come closer—yet.

Peter had had none of this while growing up. The brief skirmish at Temple Emanu-El had nothing to do with this. The Eastern European past of his forebears was a time out of mind, a time out of telling as he grew up. It was never talked about by his parents. Peter didn't even know it existed. Vaguely he had know that his grandparents had come from Europe, but knew nothing about the lives they had lived nor the beliefs they had held. His mother had been emotional about the Holocaust, in the way that anyone of goodwill might be. He knew of course that he was Jewish, although he was not quite certain what that might be. Groton had rubbed in the stigma; suddenly he felt himself open to the possibilities. He felt a clamoring rush of awareness, ideas, instincts, a profound stirring of ancestral brew. It fascinated him. He wanted to affirm it.

"It's almost as if I'm standing there outside, watching myself come to life," he tried to explain to Molly. "There's something here that's right for me."

He joined a *schul*—he emphasized this: certainly not a temple or even a synagogue, but an Orthodox schul, where his rabbi friend held a tiny dwindling congregation together.

When Sam, Joe's father, died, Peter took a week off from his paper and went out to Borough Park to sit in ritual mourning for him. Joe was touched and appalled, but he did not join him. He went constantly to see his mother, sat silent in the dining room across the table from her, not knowing what to say, what words to use, but he would not be one of the men in the living room sitting *shiva*.

"At least," Hester moaned and wailed, "I have a grandson, *ein shtik naches,* to say Kaddish. What sort of son are you?"

Joe couldn't or wouldn't answer. He said only, "Ma, I loved tateh," using the Yiddish word for his father he had used as a boy. "You know that. But I'm not religious. I can't make believe."

"So what's to make believe? If you loved your tateh you do what a son must do."

Joe would see Peter, unshaven, more and more haggard as the week went on, and they would wave at each other across an enormous chasm, but Joe was unable to go through the forms. He wanted only for his mother to know that he was there.

Emily came too, and Molly, but Hester could not be consoled at Joe's apostasy.

"At least you have Peter," Molly tried to comfort Hester.

"*Gott tsu danken!*" And it was on Emily's shoulder Hester cried, as if to cast out all others.

Emily began going with Peter downtown to the schul on Friday evenings and Saturdays, sitting apart upstairs in the balcony reserved for women, a scarf on her head, trying to follow what was going on down below where the few men and boys huddled in their prayer shawls when they weren't ambling up and down the aisles in haphazard fashion.

The other women in the balcony—who eyed her suspiciously, sometimes with smiles, as if they were glad she was there—were all old. She wondered about the similarity of their hairstyles, all red-gold in color, parted in the middle, with little chignons low in the back, until she learned, through her instruction, that they all wore wigs as befitted Orthodox married women.

Emily went through what she called "the whole bit" of the learning process, the trials and finally the ritual bath and the acceptance. Molly tried to find out what Emily was thinking and feeling about all this, but any questions put Emily's back up. Suddenly, dear sweet conciliatory Emily, fierce only in her sense of justice and her passionate concern for others, became intransigent and icy, locked behind a shell, a hard carapace that permitted no intrusion. Her face froze. "You'll never understand, Mother," she said flatly. "So there's no use explaining."

Molly was insistent. "You can't refuse some discussion of all this, Emily. You're a feminist, an intellectual. We've always talked. You have a responsibility to make me understand."

Molly felt it was the inconsistency and unexpectedness of Emily's new attitude that made her so thorny. How to explain the switch from the counterculture of the New Left to this embrace of a born-again orthodoxy? It was easier to be prickly on the subject than to examine the paradox.

Emily hesitated, as if conceding that she did indeed owe her mother some enlightenment. "There has been something missing for me, Mother, in the current way of looking at a woman's life. I want a family life that strengthens me as a wife and mother. I feel as a woman I'm different from Peter, a man. I welcome this difference, I look up to it. I want a life based on it, on a true Jewish traditional life."

"On the patriarchal?" Molly tried to keep dissension out of her voice. "On a society where each morning the man thanks God he is not a woman?"

"Yes." Emily's answer was slow, meditative. "What you feel is oppressive, I feel is God-given and protective of the family and the women in it." She hesitated, reluctant to argue but intent on her thought. "I feel, Mother, that you live with the illusion of independence, a false independence. I'm looking for a true free dependence based on the law."

Emily said the words with emphasis. "The law?" Molly asked.

"Yes. The law, Halachic law, a law to live by."

"I don't understand."

"How can you understand, Mother? You're too bogged down in your own orthodoxies."

But Molly wanted to understand.

"No, you don't," Joe contradicted her when she tried to talk to him. "You don't want to understand, Molly. You want to challenge."

"Well, maybe I do," she acknowledged. "But what's wrong with that? Why can't she—or even Peter—answer the challenge?"

"Because you don't challenge religion," he said flatly. "It's like sex. Or money. You can't discuss it. And this has been a century of such enormous evil, the mind can't take it in. It has to look elsewhere."

But Molly persisted. "Okay, Joe. But it's not religion I'm really questioning. It's technique. I don't question Jewishness on Peter's part or Emily's, either. And I don't question religion. It's this brand of it. Look at Freddy Green. He's a wonderful guy, rabbi of that temple on Madison where our anti-Vietnam committee meets. When you go to his services you can sit where you want to, no scuttling the women off to a corner. And Freddy talks about civil rights and love and humanity, all the things that Peter and Emily cared about. I don't understand those two with all this antediluvian nonsense they've gotten into."

Joe nodded. "I agree. But fundamentalist crap seems to be growing in this country. We've become a nation of Bible bangers. That's what's in the air. It speaks to some deeply felt need in us."

"Well, not in me. I don't feel the need." Molly shook her head. "If Peter wants to play the prodigal son come back to the faith of his fathers, why choose this particular little corner of the faith? This bias against Freddy Green, for example. 'Oh,' he sneered at me, 'your reform rabbi,' when I told him about the demonstration we're planning. Peter sometimes acts as if it was only in the shtetl in Eastern Poland that the good and positive feelings of the Jews took hold." Her voice rose in protest. "Does he ever really grasp what a shtetl was? I've seen Roman Vishniak's photographs and they're haunting, troubling. But they capture the narrowness, the restrictions, the poverty, the degradation. They break your heart because you know they're doomed! But Peter sees it all in such a romantic light, with background music out of *Fiddler on the Roof* and the colors and shapes by Chagall."

Joe listened to her with a half-mocking smile. He agreed with her. He too worried about Emily, caught up in this new wave. But he was cooler about it, more analytical. And anyway, he said, what could they do? "A ritual is the working out of the myth, it's the objectifying of it. Fundamentalism is a fad," he said. "It's a dangerous one, steeped in racism and prejudice— and I hope that it will vanish, leaving minimal bloodshed in its wake. But"—he came over and kissed her—"I think Emily is okay. She'll find her way. She's too bright, too honorable, not to."

The way was determined after June 1967. Molly never forgot the night when their friends Ken Brady and his wife came to dinner and Peter and Emily were there. The Israeli Air Force had just won its stunning victory over Egypt in the Six-Day War. Ken, an editor of one of the Luce publications, was a former Catholic, a former colonel in the American infantry, who had become a great defender of Israel.

"We need them," he would say. "We've got no one else in that part of the world. As long as they take our money and do our work, why should we complain?"

Joe and Ken and Peter were jubilant over the news of the Israeli victory, and the first drink in the garden behind the house was offered as a toast to the Israeli Air Force. The men stood up and clicked their glasses, as in a pukka officers' mess in an old war movie. The others, the women, smiled and drank too. The men reveled in the minutiae of the Israeli strategy, slapping one another on the back as they crowed over the details, offering another toast and another. It was a celebration. There was wine at dinner and more afterward, and by the end of the evening Ken and Joe were pretty drunk, Peter trailing.

Ken and Joe started singing World War Two songs and imitated the motion of dropping bombs, waving their arms, putting the "Gippos," as they called the Egyptians, to rout, laughing hilariously at the triumph. It was like a Sunday-afternoon football match on the telly, their side winning.

The women were reduced to a trio of spectators. "What are you guys so bloody sporty about?" Molly wanted to cry out. Instead she said, trying to be funny, "We might as well sit in the corner and talk about the PTA."

Ken's wife, Marion, who always held her own when it came

to liquor, said as she downed another drink, "I think it's great. I don't mind hearing them carouse over the news. I'm glad the Israelis are showing the world what for."

Molly looked at Emily, but Emily avoided her eyes, looked away.

Doesn't anyone see it? Molly thought to herself desperately, this is the worst thing that could happen to Israel. It will change everything.

Aloud she said to Marion—it was no use saying anything to the slaphappy men, crowing with delight—"It may lead Israel down the wrong road. It might lead to nuclear war, for the whole world."

Marion, whose mother had been Jewish but had converted to Christian Science long ago, held up her glass to the winner. "Let it happen. If the world can't help the Israelis, can't defend them and protect them from attack, let it all go up in nuclear smoke." She filled her glass again and waved it aloft once more. "If the Jews must go, let the world go with them."

Molly had heard this before. From Nat, long ago. From others. It chilled her, filled her with unbelieving horror. A night to remember, Molly thought as she cleaned up after the guests had gone. About six weeks later Emily called and asked if she could come down from Columbia to talk to her. Molly had a sitting at two and suggested five o'clock. "Come and stay for dinner," she said.

Emily's voice was clipped, somewhat unfriendly. "No, not dinner, Mother. I have too much to do. Let's just talk."

Molly wondered at Emily's tone. She suffered from Emily's growing alienation but tried not to speak about it for fear of enlarging it. She thought of herself as walking on the tips of her toes around Emily, trying to balance herself and avoid the booby traps here and there. It was not an easy or cozy relationship between them.

Had it ever been? Or had she just imagined the warmth, the kisses, the hugs? She had adored the way Emily looked, those clear light gray eyes, the shining hair that fell like silk to her shoulders, her slim elegant way of moving. She loved her direct intelligence too. And her learning. Sometimes Molly felt her own education had been limited. "These kids nowadays learn so much," she told Joe. Vassar had filled her in on Chaucer and Herrick and Shakespeare and Milton, but Emily talked about Heidegger and Jaspers and linguistics and Judaica. What was Judaica? How did it work into the art history Emily was involved in? Molly sometimes wondered why she still ached with maternal love for this Emily who lived behind a wall, in a world apart. I love her just the same, she thought, I love her for what she is, even if I'm not always sure what that is. She's still my dear sweet Emily, suddenly grown bristly, like a fretful porcupine, but still my own.

Emily arrived late that afternoon, looking uneasy yet belligerent, as if she had come to do battle. They embraced, but Molly felt Emily's withdrawal. They were alone. For a few minutes they exchanged polite bits and pieces of conversation, Molly asked about Peter, Emily asked about Joe. They were marking time.

Suddenly Emily put down her teacup. "Mother, Peter and I are emigrating to Israel."

Molly looked at her blankly, not quite taking it in. "You're taking a trip? For how long?"

"Not a trip, mother. We're going there to live. We've made arrangements. We're going to live in East Jerusalem for now; we've rented a place. And Peter is going to write for the *Jerusalem Post* and teach at Hebrew University. I'm going to volunteer at the Israel Museum until I can get a place teaching." She said all this quickly, as if it had been rehearsed. It was apparent, since the plans were all in place, that Peter and Emily had been arranging this for some time.

"East Jerusalem?" Molly was at a loss for questions or answers. "The part just occupied?"

"Not occupied, mother. Liberated." Emily's voice was sharp. She was establishing the guidelines for this discussion. "Yes, in Mea Shearim." She was precise. "Later on, when the plans for a settlement are complete, we'll try to be part of it. Peter knows others who are emigrating too, who want to settle on the West Bank."

"When do you go?" Molly couldn't keep her voice steady. She wanted to cry. She got up and went over to Emily sitting upright and rigid in the wing chair, and bent down to kiss her. Emily remained stiff, not reaching up to Molly, her eyes focused across the room.

"Next week," Emily replied. "We're almost all set, all packed."

Molly straightened up after the kiss, stood at the wing chair looking down at her daughter. "Then this is a last minute advisement, isn't it?" she said slowly. "It's all arranged. So quickly."

"No," Emily said quietly. "Not really quickly. Peter and I have thought about it for a long time. We think it's the place for us."

"It comes suddenly to me," Molly answered. She tried to speak calmly. Then, without planning it, in a kind of desperation, the forbidden questions she had avoided asking lest they widen the rift between them, were now spoken. "Emily, why do you push me away? I need you. I need you." She didn't mention Tommy's death. She didn't want to lean on Emily unfairly. "I want what's best for you. I'm not your enemy. There's no need for this hostility, this coldness you show."

Emily looked down at her hands, tightly clasped on her lap. "I'm sorry, mother. I love you. I don't want to hurt you," she said, "but you can't accept my religious beliefs. It's you who are hostile."

Molly tried to bite her tongue, but exploded. "Damn it. No, I'm not hostile, I don't want to be. But I don't understand this religious belief you talk about. It all seems codified to me, a ritual system of formalities. Dietary laws that may have made sense three thousand years ago in a hot climate. Emily, perhaps you can't accept my uncertitude about faith and God and the mysteries out there. Faith has always found uncertitude intolerable. You and I aren't talking about faith. It's a daily way of life I question, with its protocols and its gestures."

"There's a great moral rectitude, mother, that comes out of these gestures, as you call them. They have bound the Jewish people together for a long time. And they're important to me."

Molly was silent, uneasy, not knowing which note was the right one to strike, what to leave unsaid. "After all," she continued, "your father is quite Jewish too, Emily. These are not gestures he follows. He doesn't feel more or less Jewish because of these omissions."

"Too bad for Father. I've thought about him a lot. There must be a lot of pain in his rejection of ritual."

"I don't think so, Emily."

"I love him, Mother, but I think of him as a self-hating Jew. Even that magazine of his cares only for the power aspects of Israel. Nothing at all for the spiritual."

Molly couldn't keep a touch of anger out of her voice. "Self-hating Jew indeed! What does it mean? Someone who doesn't agree with your definitions? I've heard this epithet before."

Emily stood up. "I'm going, Mother. I have to get back uptown. There's a lot to do before we leave. And I don't want to quarrel with you. I care about you, Mother. I like the kind of woman you are, but I've always felt a sense of hollowness there at the core. A hole."

Molly tried to control her agitation. "Godless? Impious? Gentile?"

Emily looked sad. "Yes, I suppose so. Even when I was a little girl I was tormented by the fact that you couldn't or wouldn't tell me definitely about God."

She wanted to say, Emily, you are kowtowing to Peter. No, that would hurt Emily's feelings. She wanted to ask, Emily, is this a conscious choice? No, that would be taunting her. She wanted to answer Emily's charges, to defend herself. But what was there to say?

The two women stood looking at one another, hopelessly entangled, estranged. Suddenly Molly broke down, weeping, standing against the wing chair with tears coursing down her reddened face. Emily watched her uncertainly for a moment, then went over to her and held her close in her arms, letting her weep until the sobs subsided, then she released her, picked up her handbag on the side table, and left the room. Molly wanted to cry out, "Don't go, what does any of this matter, I love you, I need you," but she did nothing, just stood there sobbing helplessly again, wishing for Joe.

· CHAPTER 17 ·

MOLLY flew to Leah's funeral in Rochester. It took an hour and ten minutes from New York and Molly remembered the horrendous eleven-hour trip creeping across New York State with Emily. It was November and the plane landed in a snowstorm. From the narrow window on the strip leading to the airport all that the eye could see was flat white, held within a ribbon marked by brilliant blue lights tracing the way in. There were white lights in the near distance, at the horizon of the limited vision. The plane was at a standstill. It had arrived. She teetered down the little ladder from the plane's open door, across the snowbound field to the airport building, where Sophie waited for her behind the guard rope.

It was a cold, grim day for a funeral. Sophie had called her from Rochester that evening before to tell her of her mother's death. Leah had died in a nursing home with all her family around her except Sophie.

"I got here too late." Molly could barely hear Sophie's voice across the wire. "But it wouldn't have mattered. She hasn't known me for a long time."

It did matter. It mattered to Sophie. Molly caught the regret in the ring of Sophie's voice. For such a long time Sophie had been suffocated by the guilt and anguish she felt at the thought of her mother fighting her own mad despair at the Jewish

Home for the Aged. Five years of it. Sophie's brothers and sisters had decided to move Leah there when Sophie was in China, covering Nixon's visit. "Why did you do it!" she shouted at them on her return. "Why wasn't I asked?"

The answer was simple. "Because you weren't here. You're never here."

Later she learned that her mother had almost burned down the house, letting the gas flame rise so high it caught the box of matches at the back of the stove. It was the last in a series of mishaps and misadventures. The fall down the stairs. The terror of being stranded in the bathtub for hours, unable to climb out. Never eating.

One or the other of Sophie's two brothers, who still lived in the area, came every day, but there remained twenty-three hours each day when Leah was alone.

"Supposing she *had* burned down the house," Sophie had exploded to her brothers, "why not? At ninety-three, it's not a bad way to go. Now instead, she's in this nursing home she hates, she's lost her mind and her memory. She doesn't know who I am. I hate it. I hate it. I hate it."

"Calm down, Sophie," her older brother had told her sharply. "Mother needs care. There's no other way. Are you ready to take her home with you?"

Sophie always used to say that her mother had a pickle barrel of sweet-and-sour Jewish sayings. One of her favorites as she grew old, one she repeated to all her children with a sharp accusatory edge, was "A mother can take care of ten children, but ten children can't take care of one mother."

"Treacly, but true," Sophie told Molly. "Mother was so stubborn, she never allowed for any compromise."

"My brothers were right," Sophie admitted. "I wasn't ready to take her home with me. It made her so vicious being there, it demoralized her. She was like a caged animal. My poor mother. Where did that mean streak come from? Was it always there waiting to jump out when no holds were barred and old age gave her license?"

Once, on one of her visits, Sophie thought she had come up with a solution to the food problem. "Aha," she said as she told the story to Molly, "I had a brilliant idea. Meals on Wheels. Ever heard of it? I found the telephone number, called them, made all the arrangements, paid for a month in advance, and left my address to be billed on a continuing basis. I was blown up with pride for thinking of it. Efficient, I thought about myself, as always. Little did I know of the old lady's stubbornness. When I telephoned her a few days later to ask what she'd had for dinner, there was a long silence. Dinner? she finally asked. Yes, mother, dinner. What did they bring you? Who? The people from Meals on Wheels. I was impatient. Another long silence and finally, her voice sharper and more determined than usual, she answered, 'I told them not to come anymore.' 'Mother,' I exploded, 'you told them what?' 'Not to come anymore.' We were both silent for a long pause, then mother said with her old authority, 'Listen, daughter. Those people don't make food for my kind of people. No use their bringing it. It's a waste.' "

Molly hooted. "She's right. She's absolutely right. You know that, Sophie. Your mother isn't about to feast on creamed tuna with rice. Or chipped beef on toast. My mother, yes. But not yours."

Sophie laughed with her. "I know." But she added sadly. "I was always off-base in what I wanted to do for her. I never got it right."

Sophie and Molly threaded their way through the airport directly to the funeral home, a big Victorian house with a wide porch that had once been a proud private house on the broad avenue. Molly recognized a few of the people there, what was left of the immediate family, some of the stooped gray old men and women who had been friends long ago. A handful, really. A rabbi spoke. When he rose to take the podium, Molly looked in bewilderment at Sophie, but Sophie shrugged. "It's the new world," she whispered to Molly. "The religious revival."

"But wouldn't your mother have hated it?" Molly insisted.

"No. She would have wanted it, expected it. Israel has changed things for a lot of people. Blame it on history."

There were five cars waiting outside to take them all to the cemetery. Sophie rode up front with her brothers and sisters. Molly found a place with some Lerner cousins whose names and faces she could barely remember. It was a long time since the days when she had visited with Sophie, since Emily's wartime summer. The ride to the cemetery seemed endless. No one in the car spoke, except to say, "It's getting cold, you can smell winter—Tante Leah's better off this way, why suffer more."

The cars followed one another in slow orderly procession up the avenue, almost to the lake. Molly remembered the lake, Lake Ontario, the beach at Charlotte, and she suddenly remembered the Workmen's Circle picnics there, under the roof of the huge pavilion with its wooden benches and tables, where the women brought out the picnic baskets and the men all clustered in one corner to talk politics, while the children ran underfoot, hiding under the tables, scrambling over the benches, shouting as the women screamed at them to be quiet.

The funeral cars turned left about a mile from the lake, went down a road with a few small houses on either side; then, on the right, a cemetery. No, a series of cemeteries, spaces marked off with different names, different symbols. One with a star of David was in carved wood. Then a menorah with the name of a synagogue. The cars stopped at the one with an arched iron gate, a blazon atop it with the words WORKMEN'S CIRCLE in wrought iron.

Molly stood next to Sophie at the side of the newly dug hole beside the grave where Sophie's father lay, the plain pine box waiting for the speeches before being lowered. It was raining, a slow drizzling rain. The groups huddled under umbrellas, eager to get it over with. Molly reached out and held Sophie's hand as they listened to old Mr. Axelrod give his parting speech.

"Leah was my friend and comrade for almost seventy years." He spoke with the most enormous dignity. "In her young days she was a rebel. She worked to join the Workmen's Circle as a full-fledged member, not second class like women once joined. She was the first woman who gained her right for full membership and opened the way for many women like her to become full-fledged members. She also joined other women who organized the Workmen's Circle Ladies Auxiliary. And she did more. She organized the Women's Socialist League, Yiddish branch. Later she worked to help the Jewish workers in then Palestine and even before Israel was founded, she worked for the Pioneer Women to help working women there. She lived a full active life, mainly for a better life for mankind."

There were tears on Sophie's cheeks and on Molly's, too. "I didn't know all that," Molly whispered. How mysterious, she thought, the hidden corners in people's lives, obscured by time and ill health and the irascibilities of old age. Leah in her last years had seemed so petty and vindictive, snapping at her children, demanding and not getting the attention she desperately craved. The flaming volcanic spirit, quenched by querulousness, had turned sour and mean. The children, like Sophie, raised to be their own free spirits, had branched out into lives that took them away from Leah. Each time Sophie had come to visit during these last twenty years, she was tormented by complaints and demands. "Just my luck," her mother would say, "three daughters and not a single one home."

The sons who came each day were glossed over. She moaned and groaned over what she didn't have. Her spirit was broken by loneliness and apathy.

"I can't stand it," Sophie would cry after each visit. "I'm never going back there again."

Poor Leah. Where had the shining light gone, the free and fighting girl Mr. Axelrod talked about? Was old age always so destructive? The eulogy was almost over. By now it was in Yiddish, the language that Leah had loved so much and that few in the crowd of mourners could understand. It was the language of those grandparents from Eastern Europe, of time gone by. And Molly's rudimentary German was little help. Mr. Axelrod ended the eulogy with the Twenty-third Psalm, and the words "Peace to the one who left us, let the earth be easy for her. Let her rest in peace."

Molly watched as the pine box tilted forward, then opened, and the body in its white shroud slid into the earth. "My God, the new Orthodoxy," Sophie whispered. Afterward Molly walked through the wet cemetery with Sophie, reading the names again, weeping quietly. Waves of grief engulfed her, a sudden overpowering sweep of sadness—sadness at everything, the losses in her own life, loss everywhere, life seemed a string of losses that broke the heart and left it irremediably shattered, past cure, past mending, inconsolable. Into Molly's mind flashed the image of the cemetery in Highgate, at the northern end of London, far from the center. She and Joe had gone to pay homage at the tomb of Karl Marx and had stumbled on the graves of George Eliot and her longtime companion, George Lewes, in a tangle of vines and weeds. Eternal love, eternal togetherness, incurable loss. And all those weeping marble figures in the English cemetery in Rome—the angels leaning on pillars, the heart-breaking verses engraved on the stones, the maidens and beautiful young men, left adrift in the heavens. She had cried then for Adonais who is dead. She poked her handkerchief at her eyes. "Cemeteries! Sentiment! Raw sentiment," she tried to laugh. "I'm sorry, Sophie."

Sophie dabbed at her eyes, too. "Me too," she said. "When we were in Ireland together, remember, on the Dingle Peninsula, that old woman keening her song,

> 'Hope, youth, love, home,
> Each haunting tie that binds
> We know not how or why.'"

She reached over and held Molly close. "Dear old friend. Old songs, old friends, I feel as if I will split in two. I wish I'd been better to Mother. I wish I could do everything again."

Molly drew back. "No you don't. Not for anything in the world would I want to do it again. Nor would you, Sophie. Never. We'd better go back to the others," she said, turning Sophie around in the path. "They're ready to leave."

The two of them walked back slowly, looking again at all the names on the headstones. Goldman and Temkin and Warshaw and Lerner. "At least," Sophie said, "they're all here in the cemetery surrounding Mother and Dad. It's somehow satisfying to know that she rests among her old friends and enemies. They can debate the issues that motivated their lives for all eternity."

· CHAPTER 18 ·

T H E woman with the brassy blonde hair was still at the wall, making her rubbings. Molly could see her. She could hear her, telling the world what for. Suddenly Molly realized why the woman looked familiar. Annette, she thought, Twentieth Century Americanism. Molly smiled a small pinched smile; it was cold and she was not really amused. No, Annette would never be here. So what am I doing here? Molly asked herself again, remembering Annette.

Molly picked up Annette at Kip's Bay Plaza, swinging off the East River Drive onto First Avenue. Annette stood waiting for her at the corner of Thirty-first Street, as they had arranged. Annette had remained a big, handsome, corn-fed blonde, not really blonde any longer, but even with her hair a tumble of gray curls, the effect was big blonde.

Molly had run into her at a poetry reading at the Donnell Library some weeks earlier and they had talked during the intermission about their mutual admiration for Derek Walcott, the poet of the evening. It was safe ground, miles from their past associations. It was at the time of Molly's first retrospective at the Museum of Modern Art, across the street, and Annette, with a bit of reserve, congratulated her. She seemed both tentative and eager and a bit nasty.

Just like the old Annette, Molly thought. Always ready to fight.

"What a good show," Annette mumbled. "But I was surprised to see a one-man show at MOMA. I thought you did fashion."

Molly felt impatient, but she made her voice apologetic. "I did. Sometimes I still do for the money. But this isn't sudden. I've been showing for a long time in groups around town."

Annette shrugged. "I guess I've been out of touch with this new art photography. It was your name that brought me to the museum. I thought it was all so sudden."

"No." Molly was annoyed. "Anyway, things seem to have happened suddenly, when they surface, even if they've been going on for years. And people cross the line all the time. They do one kind of work, then another. Look at Penn, at Avedon, at Arbus."

Annette looked as if she didn't know whom Molly was talking about. Molly dragged out a name in the news. "Look at Andy Warhol. In one year he seemed to make the leap from illustrator to artist. But it was there all the time. The walls are filled with such examples."

Molly wanted to end the conversation. She didn't intend to go into it with Annette: the pursuit, the anguish, the trial and error. How talk about the joy and hard work? Hours with her camera, going everywhere, experimenting, shifting, studying, improvising. And the hours in the darkroom, radio playing country music or the opera on Saturday afternoons or the great hits of the baroque, Vivaldi, over and over again. Finally, a print might emerge and then she with it, into the air and sun of the real world, to show her photograph to Joe. Nowadays a lab did most of her darkroom work, but those long printing sessions had clarified what she was after and fixed the finished print into her line of vision.

Molly changed the subject with Annette, trying to be as warm as she could. She still felt an ancient resentment over Annette's treatment of Tom Feurlich so long ago. No affair of hers, Molly admitted to herself, but there was a lingering mistrust. Annette had had her own problems, highlighted in headlines during the fifties. She had then been married to a Hollywood writer who had defied the McCarthy committee, going down to live in Mexico City to avoid testifying. After that it had not been easy to find work except in shadowy arrangements and underpaid writing assignments under assumed names. Was Annette still the devoted wife? Molly didn't know.

"I remember the stories about you and Gil; it was rough," she said.

"Yes," Annette shook her head. "I never thanked you for the letter you sent at the time. I was grateful."

"The least one could do. Are you and Gil still together?"

"Oh, the fifties." Annette spoke lightly. "They're long ago, thank God. What a time! Those days have a special color for me—mushroom gray like a fungus poison. No, Gil and I have split. He's a big shot now at Paramount. The world turns." She shrugged. "His martyrdom. It's his big claim to fame."

"What are you doing these days?" Molly asked. "Still working?" She wanted to add, "still political?" but held back. She didn't know what that might mean "at this moment in time," as they were saying during the current Watergate hearings. And in truth, no labels applied—there was still a far left, a middle left and a near left, with the old left left behind. She was certain that wherever Annette's current enthusiasms were centered, she would be opinionated about them.

But what bounce she still had! She was working, she said, at CBS on the news side. It was okay. She was glad to be back in New York. But as they chatted, Annette suddenly said, "Look, you might be interested. Remember Max Green?"

Molly remembered him well, once the tough, determined editor of the Party's daily newspaper, a Stalinist whose fidelity to the line had been unwavering. Molly had done illustrations for some of the paper's articles in the days before August 1939, and her work had brought her within his exalted priapic radius.

"Max Green?" she repeated. "Of course I remember him. I haven't thought of him in years. He must be as ancient as we all are now. What about him?"

"He lives over in Brooklyn Heights," Annette told her. "He's interested in the new Eurocommunist movement they're talking about in France and Italy. I've gone to a few of their meetings. Want to come with me next week? You might find it interesting. Wednesday night?"

Molly didn't quite know why she agreed, but she did. Max Green departing from the Party line? She hadn't kept track but it intrigued her. She decided to go.

ANNETTE got into the car in a breeze of alcohol and Shalimar perfume and for a moment Molly regretted their rendezvous. In the light of the car panel, Annette looked blowsy. She had always drunk too much. And she used to be strident as well as opinionated. Molly turned the car left, back to the East River Drive and down toward the Battery. The lights on the river shone above and below the dark waters. To the right, before they reached the turnoff for the Brooklyn Bridge, were the fairy-tale towers of lower Manhattan, the fantastic skyline that shimmered into the night-blue sky, a chimeric fantasy. Stretched across it, suspended in air, was the bridge itself, a darkling laceworks, hung across the lighted towers like a spider's web.

"I never get over this view," Molly said, unable to contain

herself. "I know it sounds like a cliché, and it is, but this is the breathtaking moment I wait for every time I drive down here."

"It's New York, isn't it?" There was the same wonder in Annette's voice. "Everyone is down on New York these days. They say it's dirty and violent and depressing. But look at it! It's magic."

Molly nodded. Yes, it was magic. On the bridge now, with the Gothic arches rising above them, the earth below, a jumble of warehouses and old clock spires and red-brick houses and the chunky yellow square of the Watchtower building, made a splurge of color fading into the night.

"I hated Los Angeles. It's life seen from a windshield," Annette went on. "Everyone sits in their car on the freeway, reading, dictating, eating, looking at television, making love. It's home on wheels, constantly moving, if only inch by inch. That makes L.A. different from street cities. There's no body contact. It's bumper to bumper, all the way. Not like here. Sure, it's dirty and violent out on these streets, but it's also dynamic and living." Molly was suddenly glad Annette was beside her, talking her own blue streak.

"And going anywhere? Look, we're going to be in Brooklyn in ten seconds. But in L.A. no one lives close to anyone else. Everything is dispersed. You go from one end to another for a cupcake. You think nothing of an hour on the freeway for dinner, another hour to see a friend after dinner, two hours back. It's all in the evening's fun. Trees, shrubs, houses, faces, billboards, ocean, canyons—it's all the view from the windshield."

Molly made a quick turn off the bridge on the other side, Brooklyn now, and at once Caedmon Plaza.

"And the clothes," Annette continued her litany as she pointed out a place to park. "Disco clothes to go to the supermarket. All the skinny ladies in their midlife crises decked out like rock stars. Sunglasses set in enormous neon lights. 'Big shades,' you hear the girls saying, 'God, is he sexy in his big shades.' Sexy is looking like a film boy wonder. Wild curly hair, bar mitzvah eyes, pathetic passionate smile—and young. Nineteen, twenty-nine, fifty-nine—the same startled young look. Love me, love my dog."

Molly laughed as they swung the car into a space on Henry Street and followed Annette through the intricacies of the vast development. It had a decidedly middle-class air, well kept, solid lampposts with big modern globular lamps decorating the outside.

"No slum," Molly couldn't help noting to Annette.

"Oh, we're not slumming," Annette answered briskly. "These are the town burghers. Just you wait."

Up, up, up, the elevator stopped for them at the fourteenth floor. As Annette rang the bell at the second door down on the right in the hall, Molly felt an unanticipated excitement. This would be part of her past rising to greet her. When the door was opened by a young girl in a full dirndl skirt and pretty ballet slippers, Molly stood for a minute focusing on the lovely teenager and beyond the entry, into the narrow, comfortable living room with its picture window framing downtown Brooklyn.

There were about ten people sitting on the long sofa and in folding chairs around the coffee table. Molly felt as if she recognized them at once, they were of a piece, a painting holding them in time. When she tried to describe it later to Joe she said that at first it seemed like "The Night Watch." But: "No, Joe, it was weird, it was eerie, remember that movie *Sunset Boulevard*? And that scene when the young man comes in and sees the old movie stars around the table playing bridge or backgammon? All those faces, as if resurrected? Erich von Stroheim and Gloria Swanson and I forget the other names, but every face known and etched in memory, every face a relic, a vestige of another time. I had thought them all dead but there they were. That's how I felt as I stood there, seeing these people."

She paused, overwhelmed by some feeling that was inexplicable, like the sense of looking into the past and the future through a zoom lens. "There they were, caught in amber, the whole old staff of the *Worker,* transposed, transfixed, as if a genie had captured and bottled them."

Joe wanted details. "It was no genie's trick, Molly. What were they there for? I haven't heard of Max Green in years. Or Joe Black. You say you saw him too? What are they up to?"

Molly shook her head. "I don't quite know. Nothing, I think. I learned that most of them left the party in 1956, after the invasion of Hungary. They meet to discuss this new Eurocommunism. They call themselves a study group."

"That has an old familiar ring." Joe was caustic.

"And Max Green hasn't lost his pomposity. He instructed everyone there. I think the instruction was aimed at me, maybe at you, Joe, through me. Eurocommunism? It's supposed to be a new communism, free and independent of Moscow. Marxist but modern."

"That will be the day," Joe snorted.

"Come on, just listen. They quoted an Annie Kriegel in France whose book, *Un Autre Communisme,* is all the rage."

Again Joe scoffed. "I can't see those intransigent Party stalwarts up there in the nineteenth arrondissement challenging the Kremlin. There's too much going for them with the old line; it's their own *belle époque.*"

"I'm just reporting, Joe. But they say this Eurocommunism is strong in Italy, maybe in Spain."

"Well, it's strong in Brooklyn, too, I can see. They've got ten members."

Molly dismissed his sarcasm with a wave of her hand. "There's another thing, Joe, that fascinated me. They're all pro-Israel. I found that earthshaking. Old lefties, support for Israel, no questions asked."

"That's not odd, Molly. They're all Jews. That's what comes first these days. And a good thing too. Stop being so prejudiced!"

Molly looked sharply at Joe, then decided to say no more. She remembered an old argument they had once had. It didn't matter when. They had had so many.

"I feel like a fraud," she had said. "I automatically assume I'm open-minded, unprejudiced. But how many blacks do I know? Damn few in this city, which is so black. How many Arabs? Not a one. Someone said to me the other day, 'I hate Arabs,' and I asked her how many she knew. At least she was sure of herself. 'I don't have to know them to hate them.' Okay. But what kind of a world do I live in? I know so few blacks, no Arabs, no Indians, I mean the Native American kind, not a single Puerto Rican, when the streets are full of them—just clones of me, supposedly liberal, too."

Joe had his usual mocking tone. "That's cozy. You can hide all your ingrained feeling of white Gentile superiority under a mantle of well-mannered liberalism." He added magnanimously, "I don't blame you. I wish I could have the same assurance. It's where you came from."

She protested hotly, but he had touched a hidden sore, a secret place. "Well, where do you come from, smartie?" she retorted defensively. "And who do you know? I just love your bigoted ex-Communist Talmudic frame of reference. It's so open-minded."

Now she wondered what secret sore place in Joe had been

touched when she told him about Brooklyn and the old comrades in search of another god. For faith was not easily forsaken. Apostasy was a hard road. She sometimes sensed in Joe, no matter how bitterly he attacked the left, a profound regret. Max Green and the others had seemed truly tormented by the assaults on Hungary and the end of the Prague Spring. But right now, what were they studying in their study group? They continued to cling to Lenin while Jehovah thundered. And was the news she brought from Brooklyn news from home for Joe?

· CHAPTER 19 ·

MOL L Y lifted herself off the park bench, uncurling her back and stretching her neck, listening for the vertebrae to go pop. The few minutes of rest had refreshed her. She wished there was a coffee place at hand, something hot would be great. Perhaps on the other side of the black wall. She turned back to it. The sun lighting the names of the Vietnam dead was setting. Molly stopped at the stele bearing Tommy's name. She reached up again, stretching her arm in its clumsy down sleeve until her fingers followed the bite of the letters. Her finger kept spelling it out, following each indentation like Braille.

It was getting late. She had to go back to the demonstration. The name would stay there awaiting Emily's return, whenever and however or never it would be. Poor beloved Emily. Molly ached for her, recently widowed, so young, with four children. Peter's tragic death had been random, another statistic in the unending turmoil and violence in Israel. He had been a victim of a bus bombing outside Tel Aviv while en route to a lecture he was to give at the Museum of the Diaspora. On what wall, Molly wondered, would Peter Apple's name be inscribed in the Holy Land?

It was only after a long cruel silence from Emily, with the birth of Aaron, Emily's second son, that Molly and Joe had finally been asked to visit. The ice was not quite broken from that time on, but it was cracked enough to allow the water beneath it to flow. After that, they visited nearly every year and Molly and Joe were happy to be allowed that much.

"I feel it's the royal nod," Joe grumbled. "The court summons."

"Better than nothing," Molly agreed. She did not want to put into words how shattered she had been by the rejection.

Emily and Peter lived in an apartment in one of the settlements on the West Bank fifteen minutes by car from Jerusalem. The word "settlement" had always conjured up for Molly frontier living, log cabins, primitive outpost. Instead they were driven to a fascinating modern structure that rose on a gentle slope of hill above a curved driveway—a building all windows and balconies and jutting horizontals, a series of cubes stacked randomly one above the other, creating a handsome striking mass.

Most of the grown-up inhabitants of the settlement commuted to Jerusalem each day to work—Emily to the Israel Museum, Peter to the university—while the children remained behind for well-tended daycare. Theirs was an Orthodox settlement; others all along the West Bank road were not. And farther out, some were like rural communes, with gardens and vegetable patches and young women in Indian cotton dirndls. Molly was taken by the suburban feel, the suburban friendliness of the apartment building in which Emily lived. With a switch of sky and climate, it might have been a mid-luxury high-rise on the North Shore of Long Island.

Joe had cautioned Molly, on their first flight over, against political and religious discussion. "Just hugs and kisses, nothing else," he warned her. They were sitting side by side in first class for the long trip. Molly snuggled into the big armchair, sighed happily at the luxury of it. She reached over and held his hand. She felt good about the intimacy of the flight, the chance it gave them to talk without interruption, the sense of being locked out of the world, just the two of them together. It made her remember the intimacy of the v-letters they had written one another.

"Just hugs and kisses," Molly agreed. "It's what I'm looking forward to; it's what I want."

Molly cried at seeing the children for the first time, overwhelmed by her own emotion, holding the baby close to her, crooning to him, reaching avidly for Samuel, the firstborn, named for Joe's father. Samuel spoke only Hebrew. "He'll learn English later in school," Emily told her, brushing aside any of Molly's possible questions. Even under the strict rule of hugs and kisses only, Emily remained tense. She seemed ready for possible challenge, prepared to ward off the blows before they were struck. Molly could see and feel the tension.

It wasn't as grandmotherly-grandfatherly as she might have wanted, but Molly accepted what there was, grateful that the breach was bridged, if only by a roped span, rather shaky and perilous, but at least a connection over the mud-bottomed chasm.

They stayed at the American Colony Hotel in East Jerusalem, a former Turkish pasha's palace, now a charming inn with Swiss-type hotel food and a pleasant inner garden. Molly found its sophisticated Western style an anomaly, next door to Mea Shearim, the most Orthodox section of the city and a few minutes away from the Arab center near the Old City. What did the Chasidim with their sidelocks and the kaffiyeh-covered Arabs think of this elegance and charm? The movie stars who came, the guest lecturers and famous musicians, the diplomats, at home here as they might be at the Paris Ritz, did they feel alien to the neighborhood? It didn't matter. Glossy long-lined limousines whisked them away quickly enough.

Joe had introductions to some Israeli artists and writers, and with them Joe and Molly felt free to ask questions and to discuss the political tensions. Nothing was ever said to or asked of Emily and Peter about what was going on, but even without Emily or Peter around, Molly and Joe remained guarded.

"I've met some wonderful people here," Joe did say to Peter. "So hospitable. They can't do enough to make you welcome." It was all he would say. Peter, who had once been so open and eager for talk, so full of himself and touched by everyone around him, just nodded, closed the conversation, no comment.

Joe wanted to tell him about Lev, the Cultural Affairs man who was so eager to have Joe's cooperation for the International Book Fair in Jerusalem. He wanted to ask him about the director of the Israel Philharmonic, who cornered Joe to discuss a story in the magazine on the orchestra's visit to New York next year. He wanted to report how enthusiastically Rivka, the director of the Israel Museum, had praised Emily's work on the Yemen section, interspersing her compliments with requests for Joe's cooperation on a visiting exhibition from the Museum of Modern Art, "Jewish Painters of the Fifties." Molly was surprised that there was such a category; she didn't know it existed, but Rivka assured them if it didn't exist now, it would. But nothing of this was said to Peter because Joe felt he didn't want to hear.

Molly twitted Joe for being a culture czar, but he only laughed. "Sure, let's enjoy it."

Joe was impressed by the warmth and cultivation of the people he met. "Did you notice the numbers tattooed on Lev's wrist?" he asked Molly. "What a marvelous guy. He came here, a refugee, originally Viennese, when he was fourteen. He's never lost his social democratic beginnings."

"Maybe that's why you can't talk about him, or the others,

· 261 ·

to Peter." Molly said. "I have the feeling they're in different camps here. People like Lev may be an endangered species."

Joe looked at her solemnly for a moment, then shrugged. "You may be right. It's a good thing they have the Arab–Israeli conflict to sustain them, otherwise they'd tear one another apart. Worse than the Albigensian Crusade. I think we'd better limit ourselves after this when we visit."

Molly sighed. There had been some lively times this go-round. An art opening at the museum, a concert, a special poetry reading, almost like a Manhattan season. Was this, Molly wondered, the Middle East? The French restaurant served falafel as an hors d'oeuvre. Emily's display of Yemenite artifacts adjoined the gallery devoted to the Impressionists. Brief reminders, here and there, of where they were. But Joe was probably right—better to keep these visits limited.

Even after Peter's death, Emily had not wanted more than that yearly visit. There was something she feared. Some intimacy that threatened her.

Ten hours after the news reached them of Peter's death, Molly was finally able to find a flight to Israel, with a three-hour stopover in Athens. She arrived too late for Peter's funeral, which took place within the twenty-four hours permitted an Orthodox burial. On the telephone Emily had not asked Molly to come, but Molly felt her own need to be there. She wired Emily from Athens of her arrival. Emily was waiting for her, came directly into her arms, sobbing and clinging like a child. They cried together, cheek against cheek, wet with mingled tears. They stood hand in hand at the group service for the six who had died on the bus with Peter, while the prime minister made a thundering, threatening speech. TV reporters and cameras pushed in close, and Emily and Molly, with the children clustered around them, were the centerpiece of the evening's news around the world. Molly tried to shield Emily from the harrowing pressures of all the details, the friends and neighbors who came in and out of the apartment for the week of traditional mourning, comforting and caring for the children. For that week, Emily showed her need and her love and took Molly's love without question.

Then the door was again closed. Not locked. Closed. Was it because Molly had said to her, tentatively, "Would you like to come home, Emily? You know I love you."

A silence, and then the words "But I *am* home, Mother. Thank you. I love you too. I want you to know that. But this is home."

So Joe and Molly came for a week each September to see their grandchildren, four at the last, the baby, a little girl called Sarah, only two years old at the time of Peter's death. They came to hug and kiss. They brought gifts—records, books, clothes, *stuff,* as Molly called it. And they never got over the feeling of being outsiders in Emily's life, unable to jest or comment or discuss or question, lest the tight closed unsmiling look appear on Emily's face. It intimidated Molly, that look.

Once, on one of their return trips to the United States, when they felt themselves beginning to relax as they sipped the first-class champagne and nibbled at the toast with the first-class Beluga Caviar, Joe ventured to question Emily's antagonism.

"Emily has made ogres of us, Molly. I wouldn't mind turning the table. I think it's Emily who is the ogre. If she doesn't like us as parents, *tant pis*! I don't like her as a daughter."

Molly was shocked. "You don't mean that, Joe!"

"Yes, I do. She doesn't like our ideas. I don't like hers. That happens all the time between parents and children. But Emily has turned it into a venal sin. Our fault. I don't have to accept it."

Molly had tears in her eyes. "*I* have to accept it. The truth is, I need—I want—Emily more than she does me. That's also what goes on between parents and children. That's the generational gap. When children stop needing you, you begin to need them. There's nothing to do except go along with it, her way."

"No, I don't think so. I'm her father. Not her punching bag."

Molly drew a deep breath. "That's the difference between men and women."

"No, it isn't. That's the difference between you and me."

They were quiet for a long pause, then Joe reached out to touch her. "Okay, don't worry, I don't intend to drop out. Come next September I'll tag along as usual behind you. It's so boring, dammit, Molly."

"Boring!" Molly was startled. "What a thing to say. We see the children. We do touch base with Emily. Boring?"

"Yes, boring. We can't talk about anything. We can't ask about anything. Emily's become fanatically kosher—did you see, two refrigerators, one for meat, the other for dairy—and I've seen enough in Israel to know that this is a minority report."

It was Molly's turn to reach over across the armrests and touch his hand. "Don't get into an uproar, Joe. There are worse things about the religious right than *kashruth*."

He closed his hand over hers. "What upsets me is I can't quite understand our Emily. I can't understand her passion, her point of view. I don't know how she feels about what's going on around her. She used to be so aware. Alert to every political nuance. Now she seems only adamant about maintaining her purity—and the territories. I managed to get that out of her, and while she hasn't gone so far as to demand that every Arab be shipped out of the country, as some of her persuasion do, she would prefer it if they left quietly, folding their tents and silently stealing away. That's our Emily! She has a place elsewhere, a home. Why does she think she has more of a right there than people who've been there for thousands of years!"

Molly looked as if she wanted to cry. She leaned her head back and closed her eyes to control the tears. Joe reached out, his hand on her head.

"I'm sorry if what I said is hurtful." He stroked her hair, tried to be lighthearted. "You know, I think you're better-looking than you were forty years ago."

She tried to smile, her eyes still closed. "The champagne speaking."

"No, really. And that crazy hair of yours"—he kept fingering it—the result of some genetic mix-up, I bet. "Horsehair, tough and wiry, black streaked with white. The old joke, what's black and white and red all over? Molly, laugh, darling," he said shaking her.

"Ha ha. I'm laughing. You and your sixth-grade jokes." Her eyes were open now, the tears almost gone.

"I'll be glad to be home," he said, rubbing her knee. "And in bed. Laugh again."

"The old lecher rides again." Her smile was faint but there.

He kept patting her knee, trying to reassure her. "An old lecher is better than no lecher, wouldn't you say?" This time they laughed a bit together. "Guess what, Molly? I went over to the Whitney the other day. The permanent collection is superb, I never miss it when I'm in the neighborhood. Guess what they had hanging. The portrait Fran Cohen did of you. I chuckled as I looked at it. That's my Molly, I thought. That crazy raffish hair, stark naked except for some cheap red and yellow beads, sitting in a flowered Victorian chair, your snatch as tangled as your top, and bejeweled mules dangling from your toes. Where in hell did you ever get those mules? I always meant to ask you."

Molly laughed. She felt better now. Joe had carried her through. "Fran's idea. It was all Fran's idea. I was her decaying harlot. When she asked me to pose, I said in horror, '*Naked?*'

'Sure, naked,' she answered. I crawled at the idea. I'm such a prude. But the painting is all Fran—it's one of her best, isn't it? I avoid looking at it whenever they hang it, those balloon breasts and all that hair, but that's because I'm so prissy about myself."

He patted her knee again. "Good girl. Save it for the junior prom." They sipped their champagne, quiet, trying to hold on to their harmony. "Take heart," Joe finally said, "we all go through so many changes, in every way. All this with Emily may change too." Again he was quiet, then went on. "I've come up against some changes in me too, Molly."

Molly looked at him in surprise. "Like what?"

He answered slowly, somberly. "About Israel. Just coming back now, I've been thinking about it. It isn't the Holy Grail anymore."

"Was it ever?"

"Yes, it was. You've never liked the idea of it from the start. You were always anti-Zionist." Molly started to interrupt, but Joe silenced her. "But it was a real faith for me." He fidgeted, signaled the attendant for more champagne, then went on, a bitter edge to his voice. "I haven't had much luck with my Holy Grails, have I? First communism, the beginning of a better world, I thought. I should have read *The God That Failed* more carefully. And then Israel, a new cause, almost a new belief." He reached across the broad armrests to kiss her forehead. He laughed. "The one fault with first class, you're not on top of one another." Silence again, then Joe continued. "This time I say, don't laugh, Molly. Sometimes I want to laugh at myself."

"I'm not laughing, Joe. Really I'm not. I'm not even going to say I told you so. But what about the magazine and the support for Israel?"

"Oh, that's no problem. I'm all for support. I think that's

essential. It's essential to us in the United States. It's a good investment."

Molly started to protest but he pushed it away. "It's a cheap fortress."

"Cheap!" she managed to explode. "Billions of dollars every year!"

"Yes, cheap. We get a lot for our money, and it's in our interest. You see Molly, that's what I'm getting at. American interest. That's what counts."

"Your friends aren't going to like that," Molly sniffed. "The guys who pick up the tab on *Critique*."

"Don't kid yourself. As long as the money keeps coming, that's what counts to them. At the moment we're together."

"And what counts for you?"

"I've become more pragmatic than pious, you could say. That's where I'm at now." He seemed to chuckle to himself. "I've stopped being hyphenated, an American-Jew. I'm the all-American boy now, you could say. Look at me, Uncle Sammy."

Molly didn't know whether to protest or hoot. She managed to say, "Is this the new line? It's pretty cynical."

"Line? No. And why does anything that sounds patriotic offend you?"

"It doesn't, Joe. I feel patriotic, except my definition may differ from yours. Words like 'American interest' or 'American justice' make me cringe."

"Why cringe at American justice? Where in the world is it better?"

"I know—we give the rich the same right to sleep in Grand Central Station as the poor."

"Who are you quoting?" he snapped in a flash of anger, then held back. He wanted no quarrel.

"Not quoting, paraphrasing. The only words of Anatole France I remember. But Joe, I don't want to argue. I feel too

• 267 •

close to you this minute. I like the sense of your nearness. Who cares about anything else?"

Now she was the one who reached over to brush his cheek with her lips. The more things change, she thought, the more they remain the same.

· CHAPTER 20 ·

I'M engulfed by these names, I'm drowning in them, Molly thought as she turned to leave the Vietnam monument. Where did they all come from to die in Vietnam? This generation, Franklin Roosevelt had declaimed in his time, has a rendezvous with destiny. What bombast! Was every generation spawned for the same boastful destiny, doomed to die on some battlefield, far from the comforts and warmth of home, in order to give voice to some grandstand rhetoric? Some pure and simple horseshit?

Here it was twenty years after Vietnam and men were still dying everywhere: some in Beirut, in their sleep, some in the Persian Gulf, awake, some in Central America, sitting there drinking beer. Walls with names: men dead in the Civil War, their names on moss-covered monuments behind bushes; dead in World War One, their names on the bases of doughboy statues moved to make way for traffic. And the names of World War Two dead on high-school walls, or city hall walls, on walls so familiar the names seemed invisible, lost in time.

Was it better that Danny, Sophie's beloved baby, had died so young? If he had lived, on what wall would his name be carved? Was this the fate of all men ordered into battle by other men, the whole thing a man's game?

Come off it, Molly, she warned herself. Women are a bunch

of banshees too. "Attila the Hen" they called Margaret Thatcher when she ordered her war. And what about Golda Meir, who implied that there was no such thing as a Palestinian. As for Indira Gandhi, to her every Sikh was a target. No, it wasn't gender that made the difference. Was the whole damn human race born of stupidity and folly, doomed to blow itself up?

Why did she remember Danny now, dead so long ago, even before Tommy—the baby whose name would never go on any wall? Love and loss, the constant cycle of love and loss. The day Danny was born, Molly had held him in her arms, tracing the long silky strands of hair on the back of his head lovingly.

"I want to photograph him that way," she told Sophie, his mother, who lay on the hospital bed exhausted but exultant after his birth. "The wonderful vulnerable cranium of a baby with the hair licking the scalp, like a newly hatched miracle. I won't be ashamed to mimic Diane Arbus's photograph, one of her triumphs, remember?" And as she now scanned Tommy's name with her finger, she remembered sharply, with an acute gripping of her bowels, the Indian doctor tracing Danny's palm. She felt the kinetic response in her finger, the doctor's movement paralleling her own.

Molly had rushed to St. Vincent's Hospital at the telephone call from Sophie. "Come quickly, Molly, I need you." Her voice sounded urgent but in control. "I'm at the hospital with the baby. Something has happened."

"What Sophie? Of course I'll come. What is it?"

"Just come. I'm in the hall, the public phone. Twelfth Street entrance, Emergency."

Sophie looked haggard when Molly arrived, running from the taxi down the corridor to clasp Sophie to her. "Oh Sophie, love. What has happened? Where is Danny? What's the matter?" But she knew, of course. The baby had been asthmatic from birth. There had been a serious incident about three months earlier.

Sophie clung to Molly, just holding her tightly, unable to speak. Molly walked her over to one of the crowded benches lining the hallway and found room to sit down when the others moved closer to the other end. Everyone was waiting. There was the smell of fear in the air.

Molly's arm was around Sophie's shoulder, holding her close. Sophie fumbled for Kleenex, finally managed to say, "The attack came early this morning." She sobbed quietly. "I've been worried about this since the day he was born. They said as he got older it would get better. He's older, Molly. He's older now."

Molly patted her shoulder, tried to be reassuring. "He *is* older, Sophie. He's almost a year old now. He'll come through."

They sat there, close together. "When can we go in to see him?" Molly asked.

Sophie shook her head. "The sister told me to wait. She said it was better this way. They'll call us, she said."

A sister in a black dress that fell full to the floor, her young tired face encased in its white starched frame, came toward them. "Mrs. Lerner?" She spoke to Sophie. Sophie nodded, made the mechanical correction, "Miss Lerner."

"Yes." The sister acknowledged the correction with a quick nod, then took her arm and raised her from the bench. "We can go in now."

Sophie turned and held out her hand to Molly. "Come too, Molly. Please come with me."

The sister hesitated for an instant, then smiled gravely at them both. "This is only for family, but of course, come."

She led them to the end of the corridor and turned right, threading the way through cots that were lined up against the wall, some occupied, some waiting, a cluster of wheelchairs, a nurses' station with telephones ringing, which no one answered. At the end of that hall was a room to the right. The sister knocked at the door and a nursing sister opened it, her full, white stiffly laundered dress and winged wimple framed in the doorway. She stepped aside to let them in. There was a crib, oxygen machines, monitors of one kind or another, all the paraphernalia of life-saving devices. But Molly could see that life for little Danny had not been saved.

The child was dead. The young Indian doctor, a tall thin beautiful woman with a sad long oval face, picked up his hand and held it in her own, palm up. With her other hand, she reached down tenderly, her index finger tracing a line on the little palm.

"That's a long life line," she said quietly. "In our country this line means a good long strong life." She let her finger go up and down the thinly etched line on the baby's dead hand, then she took the extended arm and gently placed it back along the side of the inert body under the covers.

"A long life," Sophie repeated. "Yes, a good long life."

She didn't touch the baby. She didn't cry. She stood looking at the doctor as if she were waiting for her to change her mind, render another decision.

The doctor put her arm around Sophie's shoulders for an instant, then left. The nursing sister reached over and pulled the sheet over the baby's face.

"I want to go home," Sophie said to Molly, "please take me home."

The sister in black nodded her head to Molly. "We'll say prayers," she spoke softly. "Whatever service you want. Please call me later, ask for Sister Berenice."

Sophie was asleep when Molly arrived the day after the baby's death. Helga, an old associate from *Newscast* who had come to stay with Sophie in the house in the mews, let her in. They tiptoed through the tiny foyer to the enchanting little living room that opened on the back garden. Everything was on a small scale in the three-floor former carriage house, but it was exquisite in size and detail. It had once been part stable, part coachman's quarters. Now it was one of the jewels of Manhattan living, as fashionable as Sophie herself, with the look of old money and new chic.

"It's all a fraud," Sophie would say, "all concocted." Sophie took pleasure in her own mockery of self.

"She's finally fallen asleep," Helga said in a whisper. "Dr. Goodman left some Nembutal and it has put her out."

"That's good," Molly whispered back. "What hell."

She thought for a moment. "Has Sophie called Danny's father yet?" Molly asked Helga. "What are her plans? I called the sister at the hospital. They're waiting to hear. I haven't any idea about what one does now."

Helga nodded. "Neither do I. I don't want to do anything Sophie might not like. I know she wants the baby cremated, but that's not possible through St. Vincent's. We'll have to find another arrangement. Someone at Sophie's office is taking care of that. Sophie called them yesterday late afternoon."

"But there's still Harold to think about." Molly was uncertain about what she herself thought. Harold was married, he had another life, Sophie had accepted the givens of their relationship. Molly wondered if it was necessary to think about Harold now. She felt uneasy. It seemed unfeeling to exclude Harold from the news of his child, unwelcome as it might be to him.

Sophie awakened toward evening, while Molly was still there. She could hear Sophie moving around upstairs. "You all right?" Molly called up. "Want anything?" she waited at the foot of the stairs for an answer. After a few minutes, she mounted. Sophie was back in bed, the covers drawn up above her chin, as if she were hiding. She reached her hand out and held Molly's.

"It's God's punishment," she said. "I wanted this baby too much."

"Oh come now, Sophie," Molly stroked her hand. "God's punishment, my ass. Of course you wanted this baby. Women want babies, no matter what. And sometimes, unhappily, babies get sick and die."

Tears rolled down Sophie's cheeks. She wiped them with the edge of the bedcovers. "I know. I know the hard way. What a darling he was! Long and thin and beautiful. I couldn't stand it when he turned blue and choked and struggled for breath. And so exhausted when he came out of it, fighting to suck in the air." She began to cry again while Molly stroked her. Finally she asked, "What do I do about Harold?"

"I wondered too," Molly said. "I don't know the protocol in this."

Sophie nodded. "There isn't any protocol in anything these days. Our damnable changing mores! But," she added, "I want to do the right thing, whatever that is."

"What do you *feel* like doing?" Molly asked.

Sophie turned her head away. "That's just the problem. I don't know. What's right, what's wrong, what do I feel? Harold is a stuffed shirt but I like him. He's a good boring man and he was Danny's father."

She clung to Molly's hand, eager for an answer. "You know he's got a wife he cares about, Molly. And three teenage children. I don't think any of them ever knew about us. He offered to pay for an abortion and I said no. I was so glad to be pregnant at last. I would have gone to live on a desert isle to protect my little fetus if necessary. After all, I'm way into my forties. Right on the borderline. And when Danny was born, I let Harold know, discreetly." She managed a wan, lopsided smile. "He wasn't terribly interested. He'd had fatherhood. He was glad to be coming to the end of it, his kids almost grown. Again he offered money to help with expenses. A set sum. Something substantial. I said no. I made enough, money was no problem, Molly. I loved my baby. I was lucky, my job, my house, my baby. Oh, God." She turned her head into the pillow, not crying, unable to go on.

Molly went down to get tea and toast and to telephone Joe to tell him where she was. He had been told the evening before about the baby's death. In a low voice, speaking softly into the mouthpiece, Molly asked him what he thought about telling Harold. Joe's long simmering antipathy to Sophie surfaced. He had for a long time resented Sophie—the fact that she made more money than he did, her self-confidence, her attachment to the new women's movement. Most of all he chafed at her friendship with Molly. Having the baby without benefit of a husband was the final straw.

"It's as if men didn't count at all in Sophie's scheme of things," he had said, "they're just objects, sperm banks. Well, I tell you, men won't sit still for this, all these strident aggressive harpies."

Molly had been secretly amused at the time, considering his words so juvenile that they weren't worth answering. It amazed her to find how prickly men, even the most advanced of them, seemed to be on the subject of women and their ideas of liberation.

Now, to her question about Harold, he had an immediate answer. "Of course he has to know. He's the father, isn't he? That's still something."

She tried weakly to argue a point. "But he hasn't seen the baby in months. Danny wasn't in his life."

"Of course he was in his life!" Joe sputtered. "What are you talking about? Maybe at this point it didn't work out for him to see him often. But Danny was his son, for God's sake."

It all seemed unsatisfactory to Molly. There was no easy answer. As she prepared the tea tray, after the call to Joe, she thought it was amazing how they all muddled through somehow. Sophie would have to decide. She, Molly, was no help. Joe was no help. When Molly came into the room with the tray, Sophie was half sitting up. "I just called Harold at the university," she said, "and left a message with the operator for him to call me back. If there's any kind of little service for Danny, I want Harold to be there. At least to know about it. It's only fair."

It was Sophie's way always to cut through the fog. Harold was there with his wife when, two days later, a number of friends met at Sophie's to drink white wine and read some poetry in memorial of Daniel. Molly thought of the little gravestone up at the Pavilion at 125th Street and Riverside Drive that said TO AN AMIABLE CHILD. The words had touched her heart.

"To an amiable child," she said as she raised her glass and then burst into tears.

T H E tears washed down her face now, as she sat at the Vietnam wall. The tears were for Danny, for Tommy, for Emily too, severed from Molly's life. All the lost children. It was devastating to lose a child. No matter how young, no matter how old, it tore one apart. Children had died like flies during the Middle Ages; Molly's own great aunt had lost five children in one day to Rocky Mountain spotted fever. But these were modern times and the generations were supposed to follow their natural sequence. All children go, sooner or later. They die. They leave. A long life or a short one—*sub specie aeterni-tatas,* "in the light of eternity," said Spinoza—it is the same grief. But no, not so—the death of the young is unbearable here and now.

· CHAPTER 21 ·

MOLLY wiped her eyes as the man in the wheelchair at the Vietnam monument rolled back to her. He was still waiting for his bus. "It does the heart good to be here, doesn't it?" They were friends now. They shared the same day of grief.

What am I doing here? she thought. She walked away slowly, heavily, conscious of how her feet hurt. She wanted to say to the Vietnam vet, "I didn't come here to cry and mend my heart." Instead she said, "Good luck, take care."

The wind was cold; it was now a cruel afternoon, clouds heavy with their own weight obscured the setting sun. There was a steely edge to the October chill.

"Why did I come?" she asked herself as she walked around the corner away from the wall. "I feel like crying. I *am* crying." Her face was damp again with tears. Tommy, I'm crying for you. But I don't feel pride. I'm sorry, I don't feel pride. Her inner voice was insistent, as he stood before her inner eye, young and beautiful and determined as he had been those decades ago. All I feel, Tommy, is loss. I'm sorry, Tommy. That's all I feel, loss.

She felt the painful swelling of her heart. I need a pill. It was a warning. I need a pill, and she fumbled for her nitro. I need a pill against life and death. One nitro under the tongue isn't enough.

Love and loss, the gold-dust twins. Not one without the other. As she walked away from the wall she saw in her mind's eye the words writ up one side of the black stone wall and down the other—love and loss—blotting out the separate names, making them one.

There was a taxi at the edge of the green. She took it, glad to be out of the cold and off her feet. "Can you take me to the Capitol Building?" she asked the driver.

"That crazy demonstration is still going on, lady. Why do you want to go to the Capitol?" The driver turned to reply, taking her in, the weary look on her face, her reddened eyes, her gray-black hair blown awry by the wind.

"Because that's where I'm going," she felt like answering sharply. She wanted to snap at someone, something. It would make her feel better. "I'm in that crazy demonstration, as you call it, so get me as close as you can. Okay, driver?"

"Yes ma'am, okay, don't bite my head off. I'll take a side street up close. But," he couldn't resist adding, "you sure don't look the part, lady."

She kept her mouth closed. She'd let off a little steam, that was enough. Now she wanted to get back to her own, to be a part of something positive, something she believed in. Even if imperfect, yes. Even if ambiguous, yes. But on her side, her own kind.

The driver had to twist and turn to get there. Well, she thought, that's my style too. A zig, a zag. And when she got there, she wasn't always certain it was where she wanted to be. But close enough. At least always on her side of the street.

The speeches had already begun when Molly returned to the demonstration. It had been a long march, thousands and thousands of people, separate contingents coming into place, but the clouds heralded the need to begin in spite of the still assembling groups. Molly stood on the crowded curb looking for the group with whom she had arrived that morning and with whom she was taking the bus back to New York. She looked for their banner, the Lexington Women's Club, which Molly had joined in its beginning during the early seventies. She had never been a moving force, was content to learn and to listen to the younger members, these young women who had so many penetrating things to say about their own lives. Sometimes a word would strike her, an attitude, a phrase that sharpened her senses, brought pieces of the past to her mind, made her remember her own attitudes. She would think, "I wish I had heard some of these things long ago. It would have made a difference. I'm learning."

She had talked about this to Sophie a day or two earlier. "We're a couple of old bags, learning new ways," Sophie said to her. "But it's never too late, is it? It's terrific when every new day brings a new idea."

Sophie's long earrings jangled when she shook her head. Her hair was black streaked with gray, cropped close to her head, giving her the look of an aging eagle. She was handsomer now than ever, defined and sharply outlined, as if always silhouetted, cut against the surrounding ground. Her style had grown more personal with time, not ever simply fashionable, never moneyed, always Sophie. The marvelous cape bought in Egypt ten years ago, the mohair shawl, purple and black, picked up in France last month, the superb earrings, the theatrical jewelry, the tailored suit made for her by Norman Norell that she still wore after years and years and that she was wearing now at lunch with Molly.

Sophie had written three thoughtful books on the American reach for power since World War Two. They were what she herself called "journalistic analysis," explorations of the global strategies played out in Washington. Her fourth book had to do with women, an investigation of the meaning behind the term "women's liberation," the promises it held for everyone, men and women and children, and the manner in which the words triggered ancient resentments and perverse misinterpretations. Sophie had held up the words like a prism to the light and seen the colors and reflections they cast with a sharp eye, a biting tongue, merciless and merciful wit. The book became a best-seller, was still on the best-seller list after fourteen months.

Molly was enormously proud of her. She had told Sophie so.

"You'll have to do better than that," Sophie had said. "The real question is what do you think of the book itself? You have multiple choice, yes or no?"

Molly hugged her. "It's yes and no, Sophie. You'll get nothing straightforward out of me."

Sophie had long left her job as editor-in-chief of *The New Forum,* although she still wrote for it. A writer on *Time* magazine had called her St. Georgiana against the Dragons, a sobriquet Sophie thought was very funny. One of the Dragons she slew more than once was Joe.

"It isn't Joe," she tried to say to Molly. "It's every damn thing Joe stands for. It's everything in that reactionary, pseudointellectual magazine he edits. It's all the archconservative buddies around him who are hell bent on taking over the thought processes in the country."

"It *is* Joe," Molly said to her. "You can't stand him, Sophie. That's it."

"Nonsense. Joe isn't any different from his other cronies. They're all outrageous, all those ex-radicals who now have to prove how tough and patriotic they are. They haven't stopped crying over Watergate as if it were a defeat for the country.

They were for the war in Vietnam, more gung-ho than the Marines, although I notice not any of their sons showed up." She stopped abruptly, put her hand out to Molly. "I'm sorry. Tommy was an exception in that lot, really. How many sons of people we know ever went? I'm not being critical. I think it was right not to go. But you can't have it both ways, gung-ho at someone else's expense."

Molly didn't answer. Sophie shook her head in silence. Then she went on, quietly, "I'm sorry to remind you of Tommy, when what I wanted was to go on and on about Joe and that magazine of his. It's more than a magazine, it's an outpost of empire. All the people on it, who write for it, once wanted control and fame in the literary world. Culture power. They prided themselves on being New York intellectuals. They slyly, proudly, called themselves New York Jews. And first on their agenda was the protection and support of Israel, no matter what. Then they're for the war in Central America. Money and arms for their freedom fighters in all the odd places in Africa. Freedom fighters!" she snorted. "Anything and everything to combat the Commies, whoever they might be. Commies in every closet. Commies under every bed. It's the eighties and they're more paranoid than the witch hunters in the fifties." She shook her head fiercely. "Amazing."

Molly continued her silence. It made her uneasy to hear Sophie be so open about Joe. She had learned to temper her own doubts and opposition—even to herself. The political battles that had waged between them still flared up, but both she and Joe had learned that the code words that set off the conflagration were better left unspoken.

It sometimes amazed them that their continuing combat had not torn them apart as it had so many others. Friends and lovers, men and women passionate in their political beliefs, had been sundered by them. The thirties, the forties, the fifties, the

· 282 ·

sixties, now. The battles went on with new code words, new intransigencies.

How and why had she and Joe managed to survive together? Sometimes she thought, in self-laceration, that it was because she had been too supine, too forgiving, too hypocritical, swallowing it all. Even the infidelities. They were few. They were far between. They were painful. But from the point of view of now, after all the years together, the shared losses, the shared pleasures, what a small part they played in the sum total. She regretted only that she hadn't thought so then. Well, at least when each crisis was over, she remembered how the pain had given pleasure to Hester. Joe's mother had loved to steep herself in the embroilment, telephoning day and night to ask, with theatrical tragic concern in her voice, "Nu?"

As Molly listened to the young women around her unwilling to accept such compromises, ready to break relationships that involved years and children, she wondered if they were right, stronger than she, with more resolution, perhaps even more integrity. Did a long marriage rest on subterfuge and evasion?

All she knew was that here, in this familiar demonstration, the knowledge that Joe would be home this night when she returned, cranky as he so often was, mocking the slogans of the march, but at home, waiting for her, was a foundation on which her life was built. His presence was not always benevolent, often mean-spirited, especially when it came to the new attitudes of women, but it was secure, it was solid. And—this was the mystery, the unfathomable heart of the matter—they cared about each other deeply, bound together by a series of knots that pulled and stretched and cut the flesh but never gave.

Love, she thought, was as inexplicable as the perception of time. To see a rerun of a movie with a curly-headed child dancing with Bojangles and then a shot of the same child years later as an ambassador to an African country, all in the same seamless time frame, with no line between them, was a raw simplification of complex philosophical conceptions of the meaning and the essence of time. Yesterday, long ago, tomorrow, all on the same plane. Memories, recollections, and today's calendar, all one. Joe, young and handsome, filling her heart, making it swollen with love, standing at the window on the second floor of their house in the East Seventies, watching her as she came up the street, waving to her, waiting for her. And Joe, bitter, cynical, alien, taunting her for her demonstrations, her meetings, "her follies," as he called them with a contemptuous light laugh, making her heavy with hurt. Or Joe, desperate about his beliefs, uncertain about the inner core of his being. Time did not separate these Joes. They were one and the same. One was the other. Her mind slid between them, joined them, just as it joined one year with another, turning all the years into a broad river that flowed through her mind in an indivisible stream.

The taunts from the sidelines grew nastier as the marchers reached the speaker's stand in front of the Capitol steps. "Murderers, Commies, queers." There were children on the sidelines. One stuck out his tongue and flagged four fingers at her from the thumb perch of his nose. He was looking directly at Molly. Without thinking, she stuck out her tongue at him, then smiled. He smiled back, a look of surprise on his face. The man beside the child looked down and shook him angrily. The little boy, who was dressed in a cowboy hat and chaps and was waving a small flag, began to cry. Molly had already gone past them when she burst out laughing. The young woman walking beside her laughed too. "Talk about queers," she said. "I bet that kid dressed up like a junior Texas Ranger wouldn't know the back end of a horse if he saw one."

The jeers on the sidelines grew increasingly louder. The

words came garbled, the tested slogans of the opponents that Molly knew by heart. The young girl on Molly's left, who was carrying a banner that read MY BODY IS MY OWN, shook her head in disbelief. "They say such horrible things."

"Yes, I know," Molly sighed. "Just don't listen."

"I know they're just catchphrases," the girl said, nodding. "Just the same."

"Slogans always are," Molly replied. "Ours or theirs. It depends on your point of view."

The girl looked surprised at Molly's forbearance, as if she wanted to argue, but Molly remained silent. She wanted to save her strength for the final yards of the march. No use wasting anger or breath on the obvious. The people on the curb, catcalling and insulting, looked bedraggled and vicious to her. But what must the marchers look like to them? "Bystanders always cheer what they agree with," she managed to say.

The young woman on the right chimed in. "Sure, give them guns and flags and they love it, or girls in fancy dress twirling their sticks, and they eat it up. I know. I was a cheerleader in high school myself. We once took the schoolbus to Dallas, there were tanks and planes overhead and bands playing, and the crowd went wild."

"But," Molly agreed wearily, "show them signs that say peace or goodwill or human rights and the response is vulgar, filthy gestures, obscene words, contempt. That's the way it is."

The young girl on the left looked sad. Molly wanted to cheer her up. "Look, I come from a long line of marchers. My mother marched for a man who was in jail, he was running for President, and she used to tell me of the horrible things that were said on the sidelines. And not only words. Bystanders spit on the marchers, threw eggs and tomatoes." At home Molly had a brownish, creased photograph of young Mary Hollins, her mother, in a long dress and straw boater hat, carrying aloft a banner showing Eugene Victor Debs, who was running for President: behind bars, his prison number. "And my grandmother, too"—she turned her head from side to side to include both young marchers—"my grandmother marched in Washington, a generation before that, for the right of women to vote. You see, we win some, we lose some. I'm glad to be here marching, no matter what they say on the sidelines."

Joe had argued yesterday, his voice heavy with sarcasm and concern, "Don't you ever stop? If it wasn't the war in Vietnam, it was antinuke, or the ERA. Don't you ever learn?"

"I'm learning all the time," she snapped back at him. "It's a learning process. Continuing education."

He shrugged. "You seem to forget you're not a kid anymore. It doesn't do any good to argue. Go. I'm not stopping you. But it's a useless exercise. An exercise in futility."

"Not really," she retorted, "it may take march after march to make an impression, but I don't begrudge the time."

The wind was brisk and cold by the time their section came to the open plaza. There was much stomping of feet and flaying of arms to keep warm.

On the platform were a senator, two or three members of Congress, and a bevy of well-known women, one of whom was speaking now. Molly half listened, applauded when everyone else did, roared approval in unison. She had heard all this before too. That didn't matter. What mattered was bearing witness, taking a stand in what you believed in, making common cause. She smiled at the people around her, the new young faces, the old familiar ones with whom she had marched before.

"A great turnout," said a young woman wearing a sweatshirt that read AMNESTY INTERNATIONAL.

"My first march," said a girl wearing a T-shirt that read BRONX HIGH SCHOOL OF SCIENCE.

"You'll catch cold," said Molly to her. "You need more than a T-shirt. Here, take my scarf until we get on the bus."

I'll be glad to get seated, Molly thought, as she carefully fumbled in her purse for the little round bottle of pills. She wanted to open it unobserved and slide a pill under her tongue without being seen. It disturbed others when they saw her taking nitro, wondering if she was ill, when all she felt was a bit of chest pain, really. "Nothing to be concerned about," she wanted to say, "pay no attention." The wind was harsh. Yes, it would be good to be back on the bus.

Almost over, she thought, as she managed to lick the little pill off the palm of her hand—good, no one had noticed. She wanted to talk to Sophie about the Vietnam monument. She felt such a mix of feelings about it. She wanted to sit quietly in the bus and think of Tommy. And she had ideas about her work she wanted to sift through.

There was a lunch basket waiting for her where she had left it on her seat this morning. She hoped someone had brought coffee. She longed for some physical comfort. She hated all her little nagging aches and pains; they seemed to balloon out and spread under every inch of skin. She remembered Rubashov in *Darkness at Noon* and the toothache that took over all his senses, even as death awaited him. It was a toss-up as to whether it was mind over body or body over mind. As for the question of age, she told herself tartly, she'd been just as cold and tired when young.

At last the demonstration was over. They struggled back to where the line of buses was waiting, she and her group. Anna Spence walked with her and Molly was glad to take the arm that was offered. Finally she was there, settled back against the slope of the seat, her elbow on the window rest. It was turning dark outside, there would be no view. She felt easy now, she sighed as she relaxed, stretching her feet out under the seat in front. What a day it had been! The police would estimate it at thirty or forty thousand. Everyone knew it was closer to a hundred thousand. What did it matter? A point had been made. It was a small skirmish in a larger battle. She closed her eyes, luxuriating in the warmth. Her seat companion was a student whose T-shirt read NOW, whose leather jacket was emblazoned with a bold LOYOLA HIGH, and whose blue acid-washed jeans were carefully ripped across her knees, so the bare flesh showed. She was wearing a John Deere tractor cap backward, tufts of curly hair poking out. This year's teenage fashion.

The young woman smiled as Molly opened her eyes. "Hi. My name is Jenny. What's yours?"

She listened as Molly told her and said, "Hi, Molly," then put on her earphones to lock herself away into her own private roar of sound. They smiled companionably at each other, and Molly thought, "Good, we won't have to talk."

Jenny's earphones reminded her of her visit a few days earlier to the hospital for something called a venous test.

"A deep vein test," the doctor had explained, "to find out what's causing the ankle swelling."

The nurse at the vascular laboratory had been cute and funny. She described the process as they went along. At one point she reached for earphones to clamp around her head. "Now I'm going to be listening to what goes on. Arteries make a beat. They go click, click, click. Veins sound like waves."

Molly lay in the fetal position required, as the nurse bent over her with the earphones on, running a prod up and down her calves as she listened.

"Hmm," the nurse murmured, "listen." She held up the prod to Molly's ear. "It goes whoosh."

The nurse was right. There was a sucking, blowing sound, a kind of whirr. Like the wind, thought Molly now, her ear against the windowpane as the bus rolled down the highway. My veins are going like the wind.

It wasn't only her veins going like the wind. Her head was spinning. Her heart too. It was everything, her intestines and her liver and her pancreas and her nerve endings, all tied up in a great bloody heap so they could be ripped out and scooped up and thrown to the side the way the butcher did with the innards of the beast in front of him. That left the carcass. The good old carcass. Much good it did without those innards. Why did painters love to paint carcasses? she wondered. Soutine and De Chirico and Caravaggio. Nobody ever painted the innards, the kidney and the heart and the lungs. She wondered how they would photograph. They would just be nothing in black and white, just a blur. But in color? I'm going to switch to color, she thought, great bloody innards. It's time for a change. I've been talking about it long enough.

Molly remembered what Georgia O'Keeffe once said: "I wasn't going to spend my life doing what had already been done." Nor I, thought Molly. She remembered the change of focus she always made when she used the camera for her own explorations of shapes and light and connections. What pleasure there had been in learning to use her camera as a tool in a personal search for form and content. Better than working with pigments, better than having a pencil in hand, better than a brush, the Leica became a way of interpreting chiaroscuro and the subtleties of objects, of capturing geometric forms in the shapes of the world around her. She had become drunk on the way the exoteric, the easily accessible, flowed in a path of light into the esoteric, the mystical and the arcane. And she loved the excitement of the unexpected. No matter what was planned, so much was accident. It was what she had sensed from the first, at *Newscast*. The fortuitous, the chancy, the fluke added to the exhilarating risk.

She remembered how fascinated she had been by the lyrical vision of the early women photographers, Julia Cameron Mitchell and Gertrude Kasebier. But she had been seduced by them all, the painterly photographs of Stieglitz, the light-struck shattering work of Ansel Adams, the idiosyncratic eye of Brassaï.

At first, aside from her commissioned fashion photography, she hadn't known where to turn, inspiration was being aimed at her from all sides, like the arrows at St. Sebastian. She never felt quite sure of what she wanted to do. Slowly she had found her way. A Molly Levin photograph of an empty chair in front of a cellar window was as recognizable an image as a Molly Levin still life of a doll in a wicker rocker, melancholy and abandoned. She thought again of O'Keeffe: I don't want to spend the rest of my life doing what I've already done. I wonder how old she was when she said that. As old as I am now? No matter. I want to go on, too; I'll have to learn how.

The thought gave Molly a sense of well-being, a reach to the future. The joggling of the home-bound bus filled her head with images, with ideas. I'll have to think about David Hockney, she thought, his joined photographs go against all that I've known, but I love them. The frozen instant is no longer satisfactory for him; he calls it an exhausted vision. Do I agree? Don't I? I have so much to learn and rethink.

The young woman sitting beside her had removed her earphones. "Comfortable?" she asked Molly.

Molly turned toward her. She liked the way she looked. The fresh face, no makeup, an ivory pallor, hairline to chin, that was both childlike and knowing. "Yes, very. It's good to get off my feet. How about you?"

"Oh, I'm fine. I'm just relaxing." She hesitated for a moment. "I'm trying to figure out how to deal with my family about my being here today."

Molly looked at her questioningly. "Problems?" she asked.

"More or less. My family is Catholic."

"Oh." Molly didn't quite know what to say. "What are *you?*"

"Oh, I'm Catholic too. It's just on this question that we differ. That's true of most of my friends, too."

Molly didn't want to get into it. She could guess what the problems might be. After all, statistically, as many Catholic women practiced birth control and used abortion to end pregnancy as did the rest of the population. But how imprecisely statistics reflected the flesh and blood of living beings. How could the cold numbers reveal the guilt, the frustration, the soul searching, the painful acceptance of necessity? Molly remembered going with Frances Cohen long ago to the famous abortionist whose thriving practice flourished in a private house facing Gramercy Park. Frances was nervous, but happy to be ending an embarrassment to her lover and to herself.

It was a costly affair, this abortion, secretly arranged, dangerous only because one had to leave the doctor's office directly after. For that reason Fran had asked Molly to be with her. The procedure was efficient. Molly could see nurses and a clean surgery. It was no dark alley and there were no coat hangers. It was expensive, and one had to have the subterranean sophistication to know that it was available to all.

Fran had no guilt, no twists and turns of regrets, nothing but relief. She loved the two children she already had and looked forward to the recently awarded Guggenheim Fellowship. But what if one had neither the money nor the inside track? What if one was torn by conscience and tormented by doubt yet went ahead and did what the statistics proved was done?

Molly shook her head as she thought about it. "People do what they have to do," she said to Jenny.

Jenny nodded and leaned back against the headrest. "That's why I'm here today." She spoke softly but firmly. "I think I'm a good Catholic. I want to be. But there are God's rules and men's rules. I believe these are the rules of men. That's the truth."

Molly remained silent, listening. Jenny was so young and pretty and earnest. She felt a sudden spasm of anxiety for her and reached out to put her hand on hers. There were so many things to work out and in so little time.

"Do you have children, Molly?" Jenny asked.

Molly nodded. "Two. That is, I had two. I never know how to answer that. I feel I still have two."

"Oh." Jenny's voice was apologetic. "I'm sorry. Did one die? What happened?"

Molly lingered over her reply. "My daughter. I have a lovely daughter. She lives in Israel. My son. My son was killed in Vietnam. He was killed in the war."

"The war in Vietnam?" Jenny's voice rose in question, as if she were asking about the war in the Peloponnesus, some strange conflict out there and far away.

Jenny shook her head in wonderment. "I've seen movies about that war. Was it like the one in M*A*S*H?"

Molly reached over and put her hand again on Jenny's. "No. Not quite the same. But almost. Anyway, all wars are about the same."

"I know. Terrible. Terrifying. I'm frightened at the idea. I think war is the final pollution."

Molly laughed in agreement. "What a great way to put it. Did you think of it?"

"Just now." Jenny was thoughtful. "I'm sorry. I mean, I'm so sorry about your son. It must be devastating to lose a child. I think the worst thing."

"Yes, it is. Terrible, terrible." And almost to herself, Molly added, "You never get over it."

She had an impulse to tell Jenny about Emily and then held

back. What was the use? How could Jenny possibly understand what she herself couldn't understand?

Instead she smiled. "I know it might come as a surprise, but I still have a mother."

Jenny showed the expected surprise, her eyes opened wide in astonishment. "*You* have a mother?" Then, afraid she might be guilty of rudeness, she stumbled through the next phrase. "I mean—I wouldn't have thought it—I don't know—"

"I know, Jenny." Molly patted her hand. "It surprises me, too. It must seem improbable that I have a mother. But I do."

"She must be, I mean, she must be rather old." Jenny's face was all warmth and sympathy. She leaned lovingly toward Molly.

Molly nodded. "Oh yes, very old, ninety-six. But she's wonderful. My grandfather didn't call her a tough old babe for nothing. She's tough, all right. But she's great. In some ways I care more for her now than once upon a time."

Molly closed her eyes to see her mother more clearly, alone in that beloved house in the Berkshires, shielded by money and the good luck of having people to care for her. The woman who came in every day was the granddaughter of the one who had come in every day sixty years ago, and the handyman, who also drove the car, was Molly's age, Molly remembered him as a boy. Her mother read and wrote almost daily letters of approval or protest to the *New York Times,* the *Berkshire Eagle,* the *Boston Globe,* the *Hartford Courant,* her local congressman, her state senator, the President, and the governor on every subject from the teaching of math in the schools to the growing plight of the homeless. Her hair was white and the scalp showed pink beneath the thinning strands, but the brain within the skull kept clicking away.

It had taken Molly a lifetime to feel a profound love and accepting admiration for her, even as she was amused and somewhat nettled that the years had brought Joe and her mother into complete harmony on ideas and judgments that sometimes excluded her. Joe would drive up on the spur of the moment to take her mother to lunch, wrap her carefully in the car seat and buckle her in like a precious, fragile Battersea box; both of them, once they were at table in their favorite New Marlborough inn, would sip their sherry, vigorously lashing out at such thorns in their sides as the pro-Sandinistas or the soft-headed liberals. Her mother approved of *Critique,* read it carefully, felt Joe's neoconservatism as an evolvement of the best social democratic ideas. How they had both arrived there baffled Molly. Oh, well.

Jenny stroked Molly's hand that held hers with her free one. She wanted to comfort Molly. Molly wanted to comfort her in return. They sat silently for a moment, close and tender. Then Molly pulled back to draw her coat tightly around her and lean her head against the headrest. "I think I'll see if I can get a bit of sleep, Jenny," she said. "What about you? We both must have started at the crack of dawn."

Jenny nodded and closed her eyes. The bus was warm, comfortable. Molly felt herself drifting. "That's the truth," Jenny had said firmly. What truth? What was the truth? A formula hidden in a holy book? Or a trick clue in the Sunday's double acrostic? Something for today easily changed tomorrow? What truths could be held to be self-evident? That was the question.

Last week she had gone to a memorial service for an old acquaintance, a woman she had known for years in the odd tangential way one knew people who came in and out of one's life. The words spoken baffled her. Were they talking about the woman she had known, the rather dour, gray, kindly woman who lived around the corner and occasionally invited her for tea or a drink? Had she really been all that radiant and warm and compassionate and friendly and generous and giving? One knew that eulogies were exaggerations, and these new memorials that had replaced funerals elicited much blown-up praise, but how far from the verities was it? Molly's truth about the dear departed was not the truth of others. She emerged from the church deep in thought and confusion, even as she agreed with others that it had been a lovely service. That was one of the levels on which one lived—in a harmony not necessarily based on truth.

From the stricter, more rigorous commitments there was an inner reality, a vision that worked from the inside out, a personal truth. She felt tears behind her lids. Dear Tommy and his truth. Dear Emily and hers. Each with his own. Did they even speak the same language? One had to keep learning a changing grammar.

The bus jolted suddenly and she opened her eyes—wide open now, seeing the lights of an intersection they were lurching through, feeling the stop and start of traffic. This moment. This moment counts. This day is it. These are the only days I have—glorious, sunlit, tense, and terrible.

I'll be glad to be home, Molly thought. Joe? she saw herself calling to him up the stairs. Joe? I'm home. And Joe, she heard herself adding, forgive me. I forgive you. Suddenly she laughed to herself. I do forgive you, Joe. At least for now.